The Tone Poet

By Mark Rickert

Alpharetta, Georgia

Published in the United States by BQB Publishing
(Boutique of Quality Books Publishing Company)
www.bqbpublishing.com

Printed in the United States of America

978-1-939371-42-3 (p)
978-1-939371-51-5 (h)
978-1-939371-43-0 (e)

Library of Congress Control Number: 2014935909

Book design by Robin Krauss, www.bookformatters.com
Cover design by Dave Grauel, davidgrauel.com

Dedication

I dedicate this book to my parents, Arnold and Pamela, and my brothers, Matthew and Andrew; the roots of this book began with you guys, and so it's only fair to include you. Also, this is for my wife Cathi and our daughter Rowan. Thanks to my editor, Kim Fout, who helped me bang this thing into shape. Finally, to Stan Cooper, aka Stanager, who pried the novel from my hands and became my biggest supporter—I owe you one, Stan.

Foreword

I wanted to write horror stories at a very young age. I mostly blame my father for this. He hoarded paperback novels, and even turned the garage into a kind of library with walls packed with pulp fiction novels written by Stephen King, H.P. Lovecraft, and Peter Straub. He also hung model spaceships by fish wire from the ceiling and nailed movie posters to the wall—posters like *Alien* and *A Clockwork Orange*. I spent a lot of time in that room, sifting through floppy-eared novels before I could even read, and when I finally got the knack of it, my dad encouraged me and my brothers by bribing us—he paid us a buck for every novel we got through. Looking back, I think the first dollar I ever pocketed was earned from reading a book.

But let's face it. Most kids start off with fanciful dreams, and I think most kids eventually let them go, like a snake shedding its skin. That's probably the norm. But that's not my story. I didn't shed the skin so much as cling to it out of desperation.

When I was maybe fourteen years old, I got hooked on playing with fire. I'd take my toys outside and torch them because it made for grand special effects. Eventually, I got more creative with my experiments. Aerosol cans became flamethrowers; Dad's English Leather cologne became an agent for handheld fireballs. I'd even douse my desktop with rubbing alcohol, light it, and watch the liquid combust into seemingly harmless flames.

In retrospect, it never occurred to me that my pyro-playtime correlated with my parents' divorce, with my mother's eating disorder, or with my childhood coming to an end.

One day, I skipped school to play with fire. I conducted my experiments in the library, using a corner desk as a makeshift lab table. With rubbing alcohol and matches, I sought to unravel the secrets of fire . . . until I found myself standing there with my arm in flames. *Woosh.* I slapped at the flames with a dishrag, but then it caught fire too. I panicked. I jerked the backdoor open and threw the flaming rag outside, and then I got busy putting out my arm. Can anyone say drop and roll? In the shaky aftermath, I went to the bathroom and washed up, amazed at my luck, having escaped without burning myself to death. But in the meantime I'd forgotten all about the flaming dishrag, and by the time I returned to the library, a bigger fire had started outside, and now flames were licking up through the gaps around the backdoor. The drop ceiling tile caught fire. I tried to stop it—I went and filled a jug with water and splashed at the flames—but it was too late. The fire was spreading fast and melting plastic was falling all around me.

From that point, it was all about survival. I grabbed my dog and ran outside, and from the front lawn, I watched smoke coughing up from the rooftop. In moments there were sirens, and soon a couple of fire trucks came squeezing down our narrow street. Firemen spilled out of those trucks and squirted water all over the house until the flames went out.

The fire destroyed everything—my clothes, my books, my toys—and worse, it destroyed everything my brothers owned too. And everything my parents owned. And it gets worse. We didn't have home insurance. My dad told me this on the front lawn while the house was still smoldering. Of course, this wasn't my fault—this was my dad's responsibility—but try telling that to a fourteen-year-old kid who just burned his house down; it wouldn't matter to him, and it certainly didn't matter to me. I shouldered the blame for that too. I shouldered the blame for everything.

Obviously, my family suffered a traumatic blow. I come from a loving household, but the family quilt had come unraveled long before I set fire to that house. The fire was only an outcome of darker undercurrents; an outward expression of a dysfunctional family in the grip of eating disorders, drug addiction, and alcoholism. In the following years, I wanted to end my life. I was hurting inside, and no one thought to ask me how I was doing. Eventually I came up with a plan to rectify my screw up. I would jump off the

Briley Parkway Bridge and end it all. I already knew how to access the catwalk along the underbelly of graffiti-painted trestles. This would be a fitting and even romantic finale to my broken life.

I kicked around this idea for the next two years, all the while working up the nerve to go through with it, and by sixteen the idea was just sort of part of me. Then one day while walking to meet a friend, I was struck with a marvelous idea. What if, instead of throwing myself off a bridge, I went after my dream and committed my life to becoming a writer? The idea was so good that I had to sit down on the side of the road. I'd always known, even as a kid, that the hope of becoming a novelist was farfetched. But now what did I have to lose? I had nothing. Absolutely nothing.

So I made a pact with myself. I promised to devote my life to writing, and in return, I would get on with my life and give up this idea of doing away with myself. The parts of my fractured self shook hands, and from that moment on I had purpose, and I'm fairly certain it saved my life. At the least, it kept me going.

That was a long time ago. Even so I never forgot my agreement. I wrote short stories for the next few years but nothing much came of it. I went to college and earned a bachelor's in English. At twenty-three, I joined the Army Reserve as a photo-journalist. When I was called to duty in 2003, I started writing my first novel in Baghdad, Iraq. I wrote for two hours each day: not much, but it got me through that long year. Of course, the reality of writing proved much more difficult than the dream of writing, and it took me another nine years of rewriting and restructuring before I finished my first novel, *The Tone Poet.*

In many ways, it was this novel that got me out of that mess, and I think back to my dad's library, with all those bookshelves bending beneath the weight of paperbacks, and I can't help but wonder, would my book have a place on those shelves? I think so. In fact I'm sure of it.

–Mark Rickert
May 11, 2013

FIRST MOVEMENT
Astral Music

To his capable ears Silence was music from the holy spheres.

−John Keats, Endymion

A Symphony must be like the world. It must contain everything.

−Gustav Mahler

Overture

The Sunday morning sky rumbled with lazy thunder. Thunderheads gathered over the old chapel. Standing in the windswept lawn, Reverend Alfred Kalek uneasily watched the storm approach. Those were ominous clouds, the sort of clouds that made God-fearing men nervous, especially when they had guilty consciences. It was May 5, 1995.

The wind made the folds of paper snap in his hands. He looked down at the handwritten sheet music, at the scrawl of notes and musical symbols. The notation meant little to him; he'd had a few classes as an adolescent, nothing more. So then how could he explain that he'd written it? Surely this was a miracle. The music had simply come through him, and he'd been nothing more than a vessel.

He turned around and looked at his chapel, the Church of Harmony Hill. With its ivy-veined clapboard walls, high-pitched roof, and tall steeple, the building looked like a relic from the Old South when parishioners could show up to church barefooted and no one would think twice. Impressively, the small structure had withstood a hundred years, but now she sagged with age; her ceiling leaked and her boards creaked. In the winter, she got as cold as a meat locker, and during the summer, she became an oven. She was old, just like him, and they were both falling apart.

At the sound of tires crunching over gravel, he turned to find several cars nosing their way up the hill. He checked his watch to find only thirty minutes left on the clock. He'd been out here too long. Time to get ready. He mounted the front steps and went inside.

The dark chapel seemed hauntingly quiet. The place looked bigger on the inside, with its high vaulted ceiling and its rows of wooden pews that flanked the center aisle. Despite all his efforts to refurbish the place, the chapel still lacked a certain warmth. Its floorboards were warped and faded, and its walls were yellowed and cracked. At least he'd gotten the stained glass windows repaired after someone had shattered them with rocks.

He still remembered the first time he'd come here with Judith. She'd asked him to bring her here and waited to tell him why until they were standing on the chapel's sun-bleached lawn.

"I want us to buy it, Alfred," she'd insisted, giving one of her special smiles while the breeze fluttered her fine silver hair. "I want us to start our own church."

Holding his hand, she'd told him all about the chapel. A group of Presbyterians had built the church in 1890. Then, in the early 1940s, a group of Southern Baptists took it over, and it stayed in their possession until vandals set it on fire one night. The structure had been spared, but damaged by smoke, and the parish relocated itself to the other side of town. It would be another five years before someone came along to restore it. But the builder lost his funding and abandoned the project. After that, the city took ownership, and it was left to fall into disrepair.

"And here it's sat for ten years," she'd said, looking her husband in the eyes. "Waiting for someone like us to love it."

"We can't afford this, Judith," he'd said to her.

She'd winked at him. "Like hell we can't."

And they had. They'd somehow found the money. She'd bullied the bank and appealed to the city. In the end, she'd gotten what she wanted. But then the real work began. Squatters had used and vandalized the church. He and Judith had spent weeks cleaning up their filth: liquor bottles, needles, pornography magazines. They painted over graffiti, the random profanity, and crude images and satanic symbols. Even worse was the thick, pungent odor that permeated the chapel, and no matter how many times he'd scrubbed the floors and washed the walls, they'd been unable to exorcise the stink trapped in the wood and plaster. Nonetheless, the two of them had restored the chapel and had made it their own.

Even then Kalek had known they'd made a mistake. Someone should have torn the chapel down long ago.

Shaking the thoughts from his head, he marched down the center aisle to stand beside the organ. He waited with a copy of the Holy Bible gripped in his gnarled hands, his shoulders square and a grin fixed on his face as his guests began trickling inside.

By nine a.m., the pews were filled with smartly dressed families with crying babies and restless children. Several blue-haired elders gathered toward the front. Mostly familiar faces, but a few new ones. Kalek was happy with the overall turnout. After a year-long absence, he still had a parish. Many had come to show their support. Others, he knew, had come just to see if the rumors were true and if he really had gone crazy. Oh yes, he'd heard the rumors buzzing around town, and he'd been deeply hurt by them, but then he reminded himself that Christ received similar accusations.

Giving his tie a quick adjustment, he thudded up the steps to the stage, a powder-blue carpeted area with potted gardenias and a wooden lectern with a microphone standing toward the edge. Several rows of plastic chairs lined the back wall. A music stand with sheet music was placed before each chair.

Kalek moved around to the back of the podium and bent toward the microphone. He cleared his throat and the sound grumbled from the speakers. Everyone looked at him, their voices dropping to whispers before falling completely silent. With a smile, Kalek jerked the microphone free of its perch and huffed into it. "Praise the Lord for this turnout! God bless you all for coming this morning."

Giving a toothy grin, he shuffled over to the edge of the stage and rested his hands on his knees as he bent over and smiled at the high school students gathered in the front pew. "You all look so pretty this morning," he said. "I tell you, I sure am glad to see you here today. I really am. I know I've been gone for a long time, but I'm back with a message straight from the mouth of God."

He rose and paced the stage, taking a moment to gather his thoughts. "I want to share with you what happened to me last year. I suppose it started the morning I found Judith. Found that she'd left us . . ."

The words suddenly became lodged in his throat like chicken bones. He held his breath and fought against tears as the memory surfaced, the memory of that morning when he'd entered this very chapel and found her lying with her face to the floor. She was wearing her blue polka-dot dress, white stockings. The image held as he returned to the podium and braced himself against it.

"I, um . . ." he cleared his throat and pinched the bridge of his nose with his fingers. "The day I buried her was one of the hottest days of the summer. I was hurting inside, and I was sick with grief. And so I went home and did something . . . terrible. I tried to take my own life."

He closed his eyes and remembered. Still wearing his suit from the funeral, he'd parked his Buick in his garage. He'd left the engine running while the garage door clattered shut behind him, shutting out the sunlight. Then he'd taken the .22 mm from his glove box, shoved its barrel into his mouth, and pulled the trigger. There'd been no pain, but suddenly he'd shot upward, light as a feather, and a dreadful realization had come. *Oh Lord, what have I done?*

An agitated darkness had engulfed him with a sound, music, like the miserable wailing of a lunatic. Wanting desperately to be free of it, he'd flailed about in his spirit body, crying out for God to save him. But the music had grown louder, filling his soul with dread. He'd eventually given up the struggle, accepting that the music would consume him, and that he deserved it. *You selfish bastard. This is where you belong.*

But then a miracle had happened. His next door neighbor, Jason Miles, had heard the gunshot and rushed to help. He'd pulled Kalek from the car and resuscitated him. Even more miraculous: the bullet had somehow missed the reverend's brain. Only some nerve damage. Some hearing loss. His attempt at suicide had failed. Reverend Kalek had escaped death, but the music had stayed with him.

His thoughts returned to the church, and he cleared his throat. "In my moment of death, I experienced something remarkable. I heard music, a strange and terrifying music. Was this the voice of God? Yes, I think so. And I believe I survived so that I could share what I experienced."

His gaze swept across the multitude of upturned faces, hoping to see their eyes brighten with curiosity, but instead he found only bewildered frowns.

A few shifted in their seats. Kalek raised his Bible and waved it in the air. "Deuteronomy 31:19: 'Now therefore, write down this song for yourselves, and teach it to the children of Israel; put it in their mouths, that this song may be a witness for Me against the children of Israel.'" He slapped the podium with his hand. "Ladies and gentlemen, brothers and sisters of this church, that's exactly what I intend to do today. God gave me a second chance. He let me return so that I could share a secret with you . . . so that I could baptize you all through sound!"

He turned his eyes to the front pews where a group of students sat, their faces flushed with embarrassment. "I brought some special guests to help me deliver my message," he said into the microphone. "Please welcome to the stage the Bernie High School band."

He beckoned them with quick flaps of his hands. When the students hesitated, he said, "Don't be shy, now. Come on up here."

Slowly the students climbed onto the stage with their instruments. They hung their heads, their faces sullen, and Kalek felt like strangling every single one of them. They mulled over to the rows of plastic chairs and sat down, filling twenty-two seats. The reverend wrung his hands as he waited for them to settle down. He turned back to the audience with a grin.

"Now, I hope the students will all forgive me," he said sheepishly as he glanced over at them, "but I haven't been completely honest with them. You see, for the past few weeks, they've been practicing this particular piece, and they don't even know what it is. But if I'd told them, they wouldn't have believed me. See, I wrote a song after my . . . accident. Until then, I'd never composed a thing in my life. I still don't understand standard musical notation and don't intend to. This piece has no name. No author. And I can't claim to understand it. But I want to share it with you today. I hope you will let me."

The audience stirred. Kalek turned his back on them to face the musicians, who looked equally bewildered. The reverend gave them a moment longer to situate themselves and then raised a hand. The band waited. With a nod and a swish of his hand, the music began. First there was a reedy note wallowed from a clarinet. The violins came next, followed by the cellos, then an oboe.

One by one, the other musicians joined, until their strange, brooding music resonated across the chapel.

Swinging his hands in an attempt to keep time, Kalek coaxed the band on, even as a sick feeling overtook him. During the past few weeks as he and the high school band gathered to rehearse, Kalek had begun to question the music. It was so dark, like a horror movie backdrop. *Could this music possibly hold a mirror to God?* No, he didn't think so. And yet, he'd pushed these thoughts aside, choosing to accept that God's ways were, perhaps, beyond his understanding. For this reason, whenever the students complained about the music, he'd deceived them, saying, "You can't possibly understand this music. It was written a long time ago. This will all make sense later."

Now, in the chapel, with all these good-looking, clean people, the music just seemed somehow wicked. Everything felt wrong.

Still swinging his hands, he turned and looked at the crowd. He was met by confused expressions, gaping eyes, and slack jaws. *They hear it too*, he thought. *They hear it too!*

Just then a trumpeting fart erupted from the band.

Kalek's head whipped to the left and he snarled at the musicians, searching for the culprit who'd missed a note. His gaze fell on a boy with a crew cut in the front row, cradling a tuba in his lap. The boy's sparkling blue eyes flitted nervously at the reverend, and he hugged the instrument closer to his chest. After a moment, he pressed his lips to the mouthpiece and his cheeks swelled like fleshy balloons as he blew a low, trembling note.

Relaxing, Kalek reprised his smile and swung his hands to the beat. The band followed clumsily along. He slowed the tempo and allowed the woeful music to wash over him. *Yes, that's it. That's much better . . .*

Then the tuba erupted with a heroic, farting *Frhuuump!* The timing couldn't have been better.

Kalek, no longer keeping time, glowered at the boy. Thankfully, the band continued without his direction, even while giggles sounded from all around them. Meanwhile, the boy—his name was Joshua Hill, Kalek remembered—played dumb. He held his dented tuba up at arm's length and inspected it with a bewildered expression.

Kalek bristled. *The bastard knows exactly what he's doing!* The reverend did his best to pretend nothing had happened. The band recovered. The music continued. A few students in the back giggled behind cupped hands. Joshua Hill, now flushed with embarrassment, repositioned the tuba in his lap, placed his lips to the mouthpiece, and blew.

FFFRRHUUMMPP!

A few guffaws exploded from the audience. Several of the musicians covered their mouths, forcing back laughter, unable to keep up. The boys jammed into the chairs on either side of the tubist thought this was the funniest thing they'd ever seen and laughed until they turned red in the face.

Gnashing his teeth, Kalek hissed. "You stop that, boy. You'll ruin the whole damn sermon!"

Another blast of tuba fart.

Now the entire congregation was in an uproar. The kids on stage were having a ball with it, laughing with their heads thrown back, a few of them falling from their seats.

"You stop that!" Kalek called, trying to keep his voice lower than the music so the audience wouldn't hear. "This isn't funny!"

Joshua drew another chest-swelling breath and again blew a blast from his tuba, drawing a sound similar to the braying of a wounded animal. It reminded Kalek of a time he had, as a boy, discovered one of the neighbor's goats dying of a broken back in a creek. It had made a horrible baying sound of pain and misery—just like Joshua's tuba sounded now.

The audience laughed uproariously. It seemed everyone was in on the joke but Kalek, whose blood was at a slow boil. He swung his hands crazily, off-beat with the music.

When Joshua's eyes rolled back in his head and his cheeks swelled to unnatural proportions, Kalek's anger changed to alarm. Joshua's face had darkened to an angry shade of purple. This was no joke. It looked like the boy was choking to death. The laughter died almost immediately. The band stopped, but Joshua kept blowing.

Kalek decided to act. He reached for the tuba, clutching the rim of its wide brass bell, intending to wrench it free from Joshua's arms, but then new bellows of sound wailed from it. These were distorted and unnatural, a kind of metallic skirl that reached deep into Kalek's ears and resonated all the way down to his toes, paralyzing him with panic.

Calvin Hill, Joshua's father, shoved Kalek out of the way while several men with alarmed faces gathered around the boy. Mr. Hill tried to wrestle the tuba out of Joshua's arms, but the boy fought, wrapping his arms fiercely about the instrument's coiled pipes, holding it firmly against his chest. Mr. Hill grabbed hold of the tuba's bell, and he and another fellow gave a final jerk. This time Joshua came out of his seat and the two men went reeling back.

Joshua gave a violent blow against the mouthpiece, causing his face to swell and darken. A sound erupted, sounding like a blast from a foghorn.

Kalek's ears rang. *The boy's going to kill himself!* he thought. *He'll have an aneurysm!*

Finally, something gave. Joshua's eyes opened, fixed on Kalek, and then he tipped the bell of his tuba toward the floor of the stage. Syrupy fluid gushed from its opening. It splashed the carpet and everyone's feet, and the men all hopped back away.

Kalek clapped a hand over his mouth, mortified, and uttered, "What in the Lord's name is that?"

Panic and disgust gripped the stage. A young girl shrieked and ran from her chair. The other musicians followed, screaming and kicking through the chairs and instruments as they shoved their way off the stage. The reverend's podium fell over with a crash. Someone nearly knocked Kalek over.

It took only a few moments for the stage to clear, save for the three men who had come to Joshua's rescue. The boy had now fallen to his knees but maintained his hold on the tuba, clutching it desperately. Strings of oozing fluid hung from the tuba's bell. Mr. Hill urgently patted Joshua's back and tried to console him.

Kalek swung toward the pews. Most of the parish had now moved to the back of the chapel, where they crowded in the center aisle and tried to squeeze out the main doors. Others sat with bewildered faces. Children screamed.

The reverend licked his lips as frightened eyes looked to him for an answer. "It's all right," he called to the parish. "The boy's just sick. Perhaps somebody could call an ambulance?"

Behind him, another three blasts of sound interrupted him.

Without turning around, Kalek closed his eyes and hung his head. *That's it*, he thought. *Joshua Hill, you have ruined any chance of success for me. They will never come back now.* With a heavy sigh, he once again addressed the church. "Maybe you all should step outside."

From behind him, someone screamed. Kalek's heart skipped a beat. He turned and found a young girl—she played the clarinet—shuffling backwards, her hands clutched over her mouth. She nearly walked into the reverend, and he gripped her arms and forced her around to look at him. Her eyes were wild with fright.

Reluctantly, Kalek looked over at Joshua, who had resumed his fanatical blowing into the tuba. With the instrument's bell tipped downward, more liquid spilled from its brassy rim. Kalek could see down into the instrument's bowels. Something obstructed the bore. He leaned forward, eyes narrowed.

A fist-sized mass the purplish color of a newborn baby emerged from the instrument's bowels. The force of Joshua's breath seemed to push it along, sliding with the consistency of pudding toward the rim of the bell.

Good Lord, thought Kalek. *The boy's choked up a lung! But that's ridiculous, physically impossible.* Wringing his hands nervously, he moved closer as Joshua continued to blow feverishly into the tuba. The meaty lump slid over the rim and fell, but it never hit the floor. Instead, it hung by a fleshy rope that reached back up into the bowels of the tuba like some kind of umbilical cord.

Kalek clasped a hand over his chest and whimpered, "My Lord."

Several people moved into his way, momentarily eclipsing his view of Joshua, and someone shouted, "What in Christ's name is that?" This was followed by another series of astonished gasps.

Kalek clutched the sides of his face as his heart thudded angrily in his chest. This was wrong. All wrong.

The stage became chaotic with shouts and gagging noises. Someone started praying out loud. Kalek glanced over his shoulder and watched the people fight for the back door. He couldn't blame them. He wanted out too.

The prayer was interrupted with a sudden shout of, "Oh, my God!"

Three men charged past Kalek, jumped from the stage, and shouted at those in the aisle: "Move! Move! Move!"

Only Mr. Hill and Kalek remained on stage with Joshua, who now lay face-down, the tuba next to him on the sopping floor. Something slimy and blood-covered thrashed about in the sticky mess. The thing was alive, whatever it was, and unfinished, as if struggling to find its form.

Mr. Hill gaped at Kalek, and the reverend rasped, "What in God's name is it?"

When Hill failed to answer, Kalek moved closer and looked down at the flopping creature. Dark and glistening wet, the thing whipped its tail, coiling in on itself, using its tail to flop its way toward the pile of toppled chairs and instruments at the back of the stage.

Gripped with revulsion, Kalek charged forward and shoved the podium over on its back to smash the creature underneath. The podium crashed onto the pile.

There was no way of knowing if he'd succeeded in killing the thing.

Shoulders heaving as he gasped for breath, he backed toward the edge of the stage, where he and Mr. Hill watched quietly. A sense of dread overcame Kalek, tightening in his chest. Something moved beneath the fallen chairs, just beyond the toppled podium. He felt his knees give.

A man, naked and lean, stood slowly from the rubble. He was tall, with broad shoulders and long arms that hung at his sides. A sticky, mud-colored fluid covered his body and matted his hair to his head. But his eyes gleamed like pearls from the murk.

Screams rose behind him, accompanied by sounds of struggle as the last of the parish fought their way outside. But Kalek didn't dare take his eyes off the strange man—if he was a man at all.

A threatening silence fell as Mr. Hill, Kalek, and the stranger stared at each other. Afraid to move for fear that this stranger would strike at him, Kalek stood fixed, drawing in sharp, shallow breaths. Suddenly Mr. Hill jumped over the edge of the stage.

You son of a bitch! Kalek thought as Mr. Hill stormed down the aisle.

The naked, blood-covered man glared at Kalek. After a long moment he tilted his head and said in a deep, resonant tone, "Where am I?"

"This is my church," Kalek said in a trembling voice. "Who are you?"

The man kicked through the toppled chairs and music stands as he started toward Kalek, eyes glowing from his gory face.

"Wait a minute!" Kalek fumbled over his feet, overcome with panic, and then dropped to his knees. He threw his hands up. "Wait a minute! Don't hurt me!"

Still the stranger came, kicking through the rubble with ease.

With his heart pounding dangerously, Kalek forced himself into action. He spilled over the stage's edge, landed on numb, heavy feet, and started up the aisle. The door seemed so far away. Never had using his legs proved more difficult. Halfway up the aisle, his feet became tangled and he fell. Panicked, he threw a quick glance over his shoulder.

The stranger had followed him into the aisle and approached in a slow, easy gait, shoulders rolled back, arms swinging at his sides.

"Please!" the reverend shouted. He clutched the nearest pew and tried to pick himself up. "Stay away from me!"

But then a sharp pain exploded in his chest, sending tendrils of electricity throughout his limbs. Catching his breath, he released the pew and rolled onto his back in the aisle, his eyes fixed on the ceiling. Dark splotches filled his vision.

"Oh, God," he gasped as the pain in his chest spread hotly throughout his body. His eyes pinched shut and he whispered, "Oh, God . . . oh, God!"

Distantly, he became aware of the stranger squatting over him, his knees planted on either side of his hips. He didn't know what the stranger was doing to him, nor did he care, not even the fire that blazed in his chest mattered. But then the stranger clamped his hands over Kalek's ears. Hearing his last ragged breaths escape his lungs, Kalek gazed up at the face that hovered above him. There was nothing to be afraid of now. The worst was over; even now, the pain was subsiding, like a calming tide against the ocean shore. *Yes, just like the ocean.*

Oddly, from the hands cupping his ears, Kalek heard the ocean, the heavy crash of the water against the sand, the rush and hiss of the foam as the waves retreated. The image was calming, and he decided to let go. After all, Judith would be there, waiting for him. He would go to that ocean, where pain would not follow. No more work to be done. Only rest and dreams.

Even now, a welcoming and familiar light replaced the darkness, and faintly he heard wind chimes, an angel singing. Celestial harmony. But then the light went away.

His eyes fluttered open and he met the gaze of the stranger.

"Not yet, old man," said the man in his baritone voice. "I need you."

Somewhere far away, so deep that it seemed to come from outside the church, Kalek heard the sluggish thud of his heart. "No," he whispered. He closed his eyes again, searching for that inward light. "Let me die."

But there it was again, another beat. And another.

The stranger's teeth shined through the murk on his face. "That's it. Breathe."

Warmth flowed in waves from the stranger's hands and into Kalek's ears, then his entire body. His heart lurched triumphantly in his chest; he felt blood surge through his arteries. Shuddering, he drew a ragged breath and looked up into the stranger's face. "What are you?"

Someone called from the doorway. Then Mr. Hill marched down the aisle toward them with several men following.

"You get off of him!" Mr. Hill shouted.

The stranger rose slowly to face them.

Kalek rolled onto his side and saw the baseball bat in Mr. Hill's hand. "No, it's okay!" he called out, then added tenderly, "He spared my life."

The men approached cautiously, all except Mr. Hill, who suddenly spotted his boy lying face down onstage and rushed to help him. It was Ron Harrell, a man Kalek had known for nearly twenty years, who came and helped Kalek to his feet. The reverend wobbled on shaky knees but found his balance. He felt only the slightest pain in his chest. His shirt was drenched in sweat and blood.

"Reverend Kalek?" asked Ron, staring in white-faced horror at the blood-covered stranger standing in the aisle with them. "What's happening here?"

"A miracle," Kalek said, without looking away from the stranger. There were shouts at the chapel entrance, where several men had taken it upon themselves to bar the door and keep out those who wanted to come back inside and have a look for themselves. Kalek was grateful for this. He wanted everyone to go away and leave him alone. This was his miracle. His music had caused this to happen. And this stranger had spared his life. Onstage, Mr. Hill helped Joshua to his feet. The boy looked shaken, his eyes wide with grief, his face cast in a sickly pallor as he looked at the man to whom he'd given birth. The reverend followed his gaze and trembled with awe.

God did indeed work in mysterious ways.

Chapter 1

It was seven-fifteen p.m., March 5, 2013. Cameron Blake was already fifteen minutes late when he stepped into the Reef, a small seafood restaurant on the corner of Third and Schooner near San Diego's historic Gaslamp Quarter.

He didn't see Barbara Hughes in the dimly lit waiting area, and when he moved toward the dining area, a pretty blond hostess with a diamond stud in her left nostril stopped him with an overly friendly, "Looking for someone?"

But Cameron had already spotted Barbara, sitting alone at a corner table with a martini, trying to catch his attention by waving a hand in the air. Cameron thanked the hostess and stepped into the maze of tables, making his way to the back of the restaurant. With its dim lights and brick walls, the ambiance of an underwater cavern, it was hard to see around the Reef. Barbara's eyes glittered as he approached, but she kept her seat when he reached the table. It was an obvious show of power, as well as a typical gesture on her part, and he smiled to himself. She was a passionate businesswoman, brazen and fiercely good at her job, but she was a little ridiculous in her ways too. She couldn't take a piss without first considering a desired outcome. After working with her for the past five years, he'd become all too aware of her little flaws. She seemed oblivious that her approach was often too strong. If she wanted something from you, she'd get you in a chokehold and wouldn't let go.

"Hey, Barb, great to see you," he said with an even grin. "Sorry I'm late. Parking around here's a pain in the ass."

"No, no," Barbara retorted, shaking her head. "Honest to God, I'm glad I had a moment to myself. I've been so busy lately. And stressed. Besides, this place is cozy."

He nodded, knowing how she hated waiting and how she tracked each minute like a miser counted pennies. As he eased into the chair across from her, he couldn't help but notice that she looked a little more worn than usual. It was understandable, given that she was beyond the mid-forty age range, and smoking two packs a day wasn't helping her any. Still, she had a pretty face, and her striking green eyes still gave her a certain appeal, and she always dressed to impress. Seeing her wearing a formal jacket and skirt made Cameron wish he'd put on something a little nicer than a dinner jacket and a pair of blue jeans.

"I'm glad you came on such short notice," she said. "I really need to talk to you about something."

"So, how's life?" he said with a playful smile. It was a ruse, of course. He knew how Barbara hated small talk, but he hated jumping right to business even more. Besides, this was his turf, and if she wanted his business, she had to play his game.

With a knowing twinkle in her eye, she planted her elbows on the table and rested her chin on her entwined fingers. This was her attempt at appearing relaxed, but he noticed the tension in her muscles and the rigid angle of her back. She was trying at least.

"Oh, I'm good," she said with an uncomfortable smile. "Just busy. You know how it is."

The waitress appeared, bringing with her menus and a rundown of the evening special. Cameron thanked her and sent her away with an order of martinis—one for him and another for Barbara. He sat back and looked at her with a quiet smile.

She blushed a little and looked down, stirring the dregs of her drink with a skewered olive. "It is wonderful to see you, Cameron," she said quietly. "You look different somehow."

"Well, it's good to see you too," he said. "If I may say so, you look better than ever."

"Yes, you may say so," she said, eyes narrowing. "But I probably won't believe you. I've been up for days, and I quit smoking two weeks ago. I'm ready to strangle someone. Anyhow, I'll take the compliment." She sat back and regarded him. "Cameron, I came here on behalf of the studio to ask for a favor."

"What kind of favor are we talking about?"

"SilverReel Studios is in a heap of trouble," she said.

He opened his mouth to speak just as the waitress came back with their drinks. They waited quietly for her to leave before picking up the conversation.

"So what's the problem?" Cameron asked as he sipped his martini.

"*American Sweethearts* is our problem. Janna Cather is our problem."

His brow arched. This was record timing. She'd plunged headfirst into business, and they hadn't even ordered hors d'oeuvres. She had every reason to act this way. He knew all about the studio's recent crisis, and as an executive agent for SilverReel Studios, Barbara served as crisis control, which meant that she'd been hammered hard by the previous week's news.

"I take it Cather's arrest on Friday is making your job difficult?" he said with a little smile.

"You bet your ass it is." At the mention of Cather's arrest, all the stress and exhaustion of the situation manifested in Barbara's eyes. Her smile quivered—a smile so accustomed to her face that it had become a kind of permanent fixture there, responsible for every crease and fold around her eyes and mouth, and so it almost startled him to see it disappear. She put on another five years on the spot. "The studio is bracing itself for a deathblow to the ratings."

Janna Cather's arrest had surprised everyone. Cather had one of those innocent, made-for-Disney faces. In fact, she'd worked for Disney for the first decade of her life before landing a leading role with *Sweethearts*. So when an L.A. police officer had discovered a small vial of cocaine in Cather's glove box after pulling her over for reckless driving, the media had had a holiday. The networks relentlessly exploited Cather's arrest. Every tabloid along every grocery checkout line exhibited Cather's bewildered, mascara-streaked face. Here was the twenty-something beauty that *People* magazine had only a year earlier named America's "little princess," reduced to a befuddled, intoxicated, and sadly misguided young woman.

"I always heard that no news is the only bad news," he returned with a crooked smile.

"Don't believe everything you hear." Barbara finished her martini. She paused and dropped her gaze. "Anyhow, the studio is worried. We've put too much into the show to lose our audience, so we want to do something different—give the show a makeover and try to recapture its earlier energy. And that's where you come in. We want you to write the score." With her hands folded beneath her chin, she once again fixed him with a penetrating gaze. "I'm sure you understand the value of this opportunity. We're hoping you can give us something like you wrote before."

With an uncertain nod, Cameron sat back in his chair and looked at her. He didn't know if he could do it again. He'd started working for SilverReel in early 2007, writing the score for a similar drama entitled *The Real Me*. The studio had gambled big with that one and they'd nearly lost their standings. The show's ratings had nose-dived by the time Cameron came on board. He had written a new score that became an immediate hit, broadcast over the speakers of every elevator in North America. The show's ratings had subsequently skyrocketed, and whether Cameron's work had anything to do with the show's success became irrelevant to the studio. They'd treated him like a hero.

"Cameron, we want you to come out to L.A. and get a feel for the show. Three weeks tops." Her gaze dropped and she added, "No pressure."

He knew better than that. No pressure meant *You are our last hope*. But he'd established a strong relationship with SilverReel, and a little massaging never hurt. Neither did having friends with real Hollywood clout, even if it did mean selling his soul to the highest bidder.

But who was he kidding? He'd financed that deal a long time ago.

"You know I've quit composing, Barbara," he said in a low voice. Not very convincing. "We talked about this already."

"I know that, Cameron. I know that. But we need you. I need you. Just this one last time."

"Barbara," he said, shaking his head. "I . . ."

She stopped him with a wave of her hand. "A few weeks. That's all I'm asking. Just come out and watch. You don't have to write a thing."

With a heavy sigh, he sank back into his chair. He knew that he'd say yes—that he'd break his promise to himself. He could pull it off one last time. Besides, the studio would pay him well. "I'll think about it," he said finally. "But if I agree to do this, you'll owe me big time."

Her smile returned, and she leaned forward and touched his hand. "I knew I could count on you. I just knew it."

She went home with him after dinner. They shared drinks on the veranda overlooking the ocean. Moonlight shimmered on dark waters. Afterwards, they stumbled to the bedroom and fooled around without saying much. The sex was sufficient. Cameron felt indifferent about her, and he suspected she felt the same. They'd slept together three or four times over the past few years, and they both regretted it every time. There were never calls in between.

As they lay naked and distant from each other in the ruffled bed sheets, sharing one of her Newport menthols (apparently her idea of quitting smoking had nothing to do with smoking after sex), she asked him, "Why do you do this to yourself? You obviously don't like me. I don't know if you really like anything."

"I suppose I could ask you the same."

She hesitated and said quietly, "Why did you quit composing for SilverReel?"

He watched the drifts of smoke moving slowly over his bed through shafts of moonlight and said in a flat voice, "Because it was killing me."

She said nothing for a long while, then snuffed the cigarette into the ashtray, got out of bed, and dressed. "You know," she said, stopping at the door to look back at him. "You've changed. I feel sorry for you."

He said nothing in return, and she left.

A limousine fetched Cameron on Monday morning the following week, and by noon he was on the set of *American Sweethearts*, located within a Universal Studios back lot. He spent several hours shuffling aimlessly through the streets of a replicated West Coast suburb. Colorful bungalows, white picket fences, and rich green lawns. He felt eerily disconnected and blamed it on the fact that all these homes were fakes, cheerful facades, empty on the inside. He could relate.

Though he'd never seen *American Sweethearts*, he recognized a handful of actors. Cather was not among them. When the tapings began, he watched from the sidelines, gathering a feel for the show. He watched the actors and actresses deliver humorous, sometimes even clever, dialogue, and this proved mildly entertaining for the first day or so.

He left that evening with a melody in mind and retired to his hotel room. The studio had spared no expense. The suite was equipped with antique furniture and a fireplace, random books on the shelves, a baby grand Baldwin in the corner. He went to the bar and poured himself a glass of Glenfiddich, then walked out onto the patio and into the cool night air. He watched the headlights of cars rushing along the boulevard beneath him.

When he went inside and sat at the piano, his mind went numb. He couldn't remember the melody he'd thought of. He couldn't think of anything new. His frustration became a kind of panic. For hours he played around with various tunes until he became too tired and too drunk to go on.

In the morning he started all over with the frustrations. Every melody proved lifeless, flighty. Something was missing.

Thursday afternoon, *Sweetheart's* director Edmond Towers invited Cameron for lunch at Riso's Café, where they sat at a small table on an outside veranda facing Hollywood Boulevard. As the sun blazed and a warm breeze blew the foam from their beers, Towers yammered on about the direction he wanted Cameron to take with the score. Towers, an eccentric old man who wore a ball cap and sunglasses big enough to hide most of his face, talked frantically, never letting up for a moment. Cameron watched him with mild intrigue, nodding occasionally, not really listening at all. By twenty minutes into their conversation, Cameron felt like he'd raced a hundred-yard dash.

"So you got something in mind yet?" Towers asked with a mischievous grin. "Yeah, I bet you do."

Cameron didn't have the heart or the balls to tell him that he hadn't written a single worthwhile note. "Yeah. I'm working with a few ideas."

"Well, I know your work, Blake," Towers said. "You've done it before. This show needs something spectacular. Got it? That's what it needs. Nothing less than spectacular."

It was dark when Cameron returned to his swanky hotel room. As usual, he first poured himself a drink from the bar and finished it on the balcony. Then he once again went to the piano, an impotent lover determined to prove his manhood. With sweat gathering along his upper lip, he stared at the glossy keys.

This is the last time, he promised himself. *The last goddamn time.*

He thought about what he'd said to Barbara, likening this sort of work to slow suicide. Now, sitting at the piano, the sullen mood stole over him once more. Waves of dark despair crashed against his mind. Blood thudded in his ears.

Come on, he hissed at himself. He rubbed his temples. *Think of something for Christ's sake!*

Tower's voice came at him, thin and snakelike: *"Spectacular."*

Cameron poured another scotch, took a heavy gulp, and then ran his fingers along the keys. He played a few notes. Nothing came at first, but then he stumbled over a melody. A flash of inspiration, like something he'd dreamed. He explored the tune, teasing the idea out from his mind, allowing it to take form, note by note.

Around two in the morning, he stumbled away from the piano. He sat on the sofa and called Barbara. The phone rang a dozen times before she picked up.

"Who is this?" she said groggily.

"I think Christ said it best: 'It is finished.'"

"Cameron? Is that you?"

"I'll leave it at your office tomorrow on the way out. I'm going home." He hung up, then stared at the notepad on which he'd written his newest work. *It is shit*, he thought. *Contrived and phoned-in, but the studio will love it anyway.* So why did he feel even worse for writing the thing?

That's how you do it, he thought as he stumbled toward the bedroom, the scotch making his head spin. *That's how you give yourself away. One note at a time.*

He sprawled onto the bed, still wearing his jeans and t-shirt, and for a while he stared up at the ceiling with his arms spread out at his sides. His thoughts turned to an article written about him five years earlier in *Music Makers Magazine.* Entitled "Hollywood's Genius Tone Poet," the magazine had portrayed him as some kind of magician with a special gift for composing pitch-perfect scores for TV dramas. That same article had alluded to a far less disillusioned Cameron Blake, an artist with greater aspirations.

What the hell happened to that guy?

As the hour grew late, his thoughts darkened and festered, and he slipped into dreams.

Sunday, July 22, 1984. Cameron awoke to the hum of tires and sat up, finding himself in the backseat of the family Toyota. The sleepy blue light of a burgeoning dawn filled the windows. His dad was driving. Mom was in the passenger seat. Brent, his older brother, snored lightly in the seat next to him. Music whispered from the radio.

Rubbing his eyes, he wriggled out of his blanket, wondering how he'd gotten there. Sometime during the night, someone had carried him to the car, and now they were far from home. He looked out the window as they drove past quiet shops with dark windows, none of them familiar. Nothing stirred in the sullen light. The hour seemed somehow sacred, even to a boy of six. Blinking, too tired to ask questions, he started to drift back to sleep when a hand fell on his knee and squeezed. He opened his eyes and met his mother's gaze. She looked back at him from her seat, wearing a smile with down-turned corners.

"It's going to be okay, Cameron," she said in a soft whisper. "You just wait and see. God has something special planned for you." Tears glimmered in her eyes.

"Where are we going?" he asked.

Her brow shadowed over, and she looked at his dad, hopeful he would help her explain. It didn't take long before his father, Gar, got the hint. He spoke without taking his eyes from the road.

"You and Brent are going to Grandma Margie's for the summer," he said. Only then did his gaze break from the road to find Cameron in the rearview mirror. "You guys are going to have loads of fun. You can search for seashells on the Cape and . . . all sorts of stuff."

Cameron blinked, confused. No one had told him about this, and he felt certain it had something to do with the night before, when he'd woken to someone shouting. Worried, he had climbed out of bed and tried to wake Brent, but his big brother had only swatted him away. When sobs from the other room had grown louder, Cameron had decided to see for himself and had gone out into the hallway. At the doorway to the living room, he'd hesitated, watching his dad pace the room. His mother was there, too, curled up on the sofa with her legs folded beneath her. His parents hadn't seen him, and so he'd waited and listened.

"How could this happen, Gar?" his mother had said in a choked voice. "What about the kids? What will they do without me?"

"If it comes to that, then I'll take care of them," his father had returned. "But that's not going to happen."

"But you don't know that!"

"Gail," his father had said in a low, careful voice, "Not so loud. You'll wake the kids. I know you're upset but–"

"Upset? *Upset?* Gar, I'm scared to death."

Just then Cameron's mother had noticed him. She'd flinched, embarrassed, and tried to wipe the tears from her eyes. "Oh, hi, baby," she'd said, trying to smile. "What are you doing out of bed?"

"What's wrong?" he'd muttered just as his father had hurried over, scooped him into his arms, then carried him back to the bedroom. Tucking him beneath the covers, his father had told him, "Nothing's wrong, Cam. Now, no more getting up tonight, huh, kiddo?"

That was all he remembered. Now they were in a car, racing to Grandma Margie's house, and nothing made sense. But one thing was certain: his father had lied to him. Something was wrong. His mom had a sickly smell about her, a smell that had nothing to do with his nose. Cameron sat back in his seat and everything—the quiet buzz of the tires beneath him, the dark giving way to light, his mother's knowing expression—came into focus.

"Mom?" Cameron asked. "Are you going to die?"

A stunned silence followed. His mother dropped her eyes, as if slapped, and after a moment, she glanced at Gar, but he never took his eyes from the road. In the seat next to Cameron, Brent sat up, his blond hair a messy haystack on his head, but Cameron never took his eyes from his mother's face, and his thudding heart counted out the seconds.

Finally, his mother cleared her throat and said, "Cam, Momma's sick."

There was a lump in his throat that he couldn't swallow down. "What do you mean, 'sick'?" he asked thinly.

"Mommy's going to the hospital," his father interjected, keeping his eyes fixed on the road. "That's why you and Brent are going to stay at Grandma's house. She's going to look after you two while we get Mommy fixed."

Cameron looked at his brother, who stared back at him with dark, thoughtful eyes, and suddenly it all made sense. Brent already knew. They'd all kept it a secret from him. Somehow this only made it worse, more frightening, and bands of pressure suddenly clenched about his stomach, driving the air from his lungs.

"Mom? I don't want you to die!"

"I don't want that either, baby," she said softly and reached for him, and then the passenger window exploded in a bone-jarring collision.

Blindsided by another vehicle, the Toyota spun in circles before it tumbled off an embankment. Cameron struck the door, then the ceiling, and then the dash.

It happened so quickly, so violently, that he couldn't understand why gravity had lost hold of him. After an eternity, when the car rolled to a stop at the bottom of a ditch, he felt sick, and the world had turned upside down. Somehow, his mother hung suspended in the air above him, still belted to her seat, arms dangling at her sides, hands reaching out to him. Her eyes bulged with a look of surprise. Blood dribbled from the corners of her mouth and spattered like warm syrup on Cameron's forehead.

The shock hit him hard. He closed his eyes and became suddenly buoyant. He rose up, slowly at first, then faster, until he shot like a bullet into the darkness. Soon he saw a single star, a great blossoming light, and as he drew closer, he heard the light singing in waves of glassy whirs that somehow carried a melody. The music seemed as natural as a whale song but unlike anything he'd ever heard. If he were old enough, he would say it transcended music, especially in the way it swirled about him and spilled through him like water from a cool mountain spring.

And even more bewildering, the music was in some ways conscious. It was alive—alive and singing.

Cameron woke with a start and rolled off the bed, crashing against the hardwood floor of his hotel room. His head throbbed and a cottony film coated his tongue and the roof of his mouth. For a few moments, lying on his stomach, he drew shuddering lungfuls of air, relieved that it had only been a dream.

Just a dream. Fragments of it came back to him. He could almost hear its strange music, angelic and incomprehensible.

Hurry, he told himself. *Write it down. Quick!*

Driven by fierce determination, he crawled to the coffee table and found his leather satchel on the floor near the sofa. He turned it over and dumped out its contents, then found his journal amidst a splash of papers. Sitting with his back against a chair and his knees drawn, he opened the journal to a clean page and started to write. Already the memory was growing faint. Still, he held the tiny pencil in a death grip and scribbled frantically, allowing the content of his dream to flow through him. As always, it was like channeling a faint signal; he barely got anything down before the music began to fade.

He scratched a few more notes, then tossed the journal across the room in frustration. It was always the same. Always so close, but then gone, like a ghost.

Now his head felt like it would crack open. He buried his face in his hands and waited for it to pass. When it finally did, he stood and stumbled over to the telephone and dialed the lobby. The concierge answered and Cameron asked him to arrange for a cab.

By ten a.m., he was heading back to San Diego.

Chapter 2

It was the fourth day in May, and Cameron had spent most of his day in the cramped control room at one of SilverReel Studios' sound stages. Piles of complex-looking sound equipment were heaped near the walls, while cables snaked across the floor. Allen Filtzer, the desperately overweight sound engineer, sat at the soundboard. He was wearing his big headphones, his hands fluttering over the switches as he watched the small orchestra on the other side of the window. Despite the noise, Cameron, sitting back on his uncomfortable chair, found himself nodding off. This was his third trip to L.A. in the past month, and he'd long ago passed the Point of No Concern.

Lethargic, his eyes settled on the orchestra in the adjacent room behind the glass like fish in an aquarium, only this aquarium was dark, save for the little lights hovering over their music stands and a large movie screen that hung on the far wall showing scenes from *American Sweethearts*. Somehow the images and the music were supposed to work together. In his opinion, it looked and sounded too obvious—too heavy-handed—but what did he care? No one else seemed to.

John Bhorman, the conductor, a big man with a salt-and-pepper beard and a large pair of headphones cupped to the sides of his head, stood on a raised wooden platform at the center of the cluster of musicians. Having worked with him several times in the past, Cameron knew Bhorman was great when he wanted to be and lousy when he didn't care for the project at hand. Today was one of those latter days. Bhorman walked the orchestra through the score with almost flippant strokes of his baton, as if he despised the music as much as Cameron did.

Cameron's ear detected an imperfection. One of the musicians had fallen out of rhythm, and Bhorman heard it too. The large man suddenly threw his hands up and shouted, "No! No! No!"

Cameron rubbed his face in frustration. *Christ Jesus. This is never going to end.*

Three times now Bhorman had stopped the recording. It wasn't the musicians' fault. They were unprepared. Rushed. And each time Bhorman shouted at them, Cameron shrank into his chair, knowing that the scathing insults were in some way directed toward him.

"What the hell?" Filzer muttered to himself as he leaned his massive body back in his chair. "I wish he'd quit doing that." He flipped the lights on, causing the musicians, all of them dressed in blue jeans and t-shirts like a bunch of hipsters, to squint and squirm in their seats.

Among them, Bhorman rubbed his brow and flapped the sheet music at them. "Are we reading the same music?" After a moment, he turned and looked at Filzer through the window. "Sorry about that, Allen," he said with a shrug. "It wasn't working for me."

"Whatever you say, John," Filzer said into his microphone. "You want to break for lunch?"

"I think that'd be terrific."

"That's fine. Let's break until one." Filzer jabbed another button and turned around, facing Cameron. "I sure as hell wish he'd let me decide what sounds right or not. Fuck it. I'm ready to eat. You hungry?"

Cameron sat up and rubbed his eyes. "Not really. I think I might hang back for a while."

"Have it your way, but there's a café up the road that makes a mean hamburger."

"I'll pass."

Filzer didn't press any further as he collected his things. Moments later Bhorman stepped inside with a frustrated expression. "You guys catching lunch?"

Once again Cameron turned down the offer. "Not much of an appetite," he insisted.

Bhorman sighed heavily. "I know it's going rough today. The guys didn't get much time to rehearse."

"Yeah, I know that, John," said Cameron with an apologetic smile. He knew how the studio bullied them around and he felt partially responsible. Barbara had been in a panic ever since the day she'd called to say how much the studio liked the piece, how they wanted to go ahead and record it, and how they wanted Cameron to oversee the project. He had immediately resisted, pointing out that Bhorman hadn't had the score for more than a week and that the studio was rushing things. Barbara had sympathized, but the studio didn't care. They wanted their score, and that was that.

Cameron got out of his chair and clapped Bhorman on the arm. "You're doing a hell of a job." He looked at Filzer. "Both of you."

Bhorman shrugged, smiling crookedly. "Well, we're trying."

The two men exited the small room, leaving Cameron to himself. Alone with his thoughts, he sank into his seat, his arms folded over his chest, wondering what had gone wrong, and not just with the score, but with his whole useless life.

Twenty minutes had passed when a man wearing a black suit entered the stage room, unaware that Cameron watched him from the window of the neighboring room. Cameron started to get up but hesitated. There was something decidedly striking about the stranger. He was tall, dignified, with a strong jaw and handsome features, a face sketched with creases. His white hair formed a widow's peak above a prominent brow, and he had eyes that sparkled like chips of blue ice.

The man turned toward the window and met Cameron's gaze.

Startled, Cameron raised a hand in a half-hearted wave, hoping to mask his embarrassment. The man grinned and returned the gesture, then crossed the stage and let himself into the small control room.

"Hello," he said. "I'm looking for Cameron Blake. Do you know him?" There was a trace of a British accent underscoring the man's voice, like something buried and forgotten but nonetheless leaving an impression.

"You found him."

The man's brow arched in surprise. "Ah! Mr. Blake. I apologize for not recognizing you sooner. Do you mind if I have a moment of your time?"

Cameron didn't answer right away. He didn't want to chat. He felt tired and tangled up inside, but what choice did he have? For all he knew the guy owned SilverReel. "Yeah, that's fine." He waved to the chairs. "Have a seat."

The man took a seat, folded his legs neatly, and clasped his hands over his knee. Cameron sat on the sofa across from him.

"I'm so glad to have finally tracked you down," said the man. "Someone recently brought this to my attention. I started searching for you the moment I read the article." He held up a worn copy of *Music Makers Magazine*.

The February 2008 issue. Cameron knew it well enough. He had a whole box of them at home in his attic.

"You have a remarkable story," said the man.

"Thanks," said Cameron, still trying to figure out who he was talking to. "Do you work with SilverReel?"

"No. My name is Leonin Bloom. I'm a conductor for a chamber orchestra. Very small." The man's eyes beamed when he revealed this.

Cameron raised an eyebrow. Not what he expected. So this guy was just wasting his time. "Oh. Right on," he said, feigning interest. "Here in L.A.?"

"No. Tennessee. I'm quite sure you wouldn't know of us. We keep a low profile."

"I see."

"I wanted to talk about your music. Particularly the piece entitled 'Hear After.' It is a remarkably inspired work."

Cameron shifted in his seat. That particular work was a reminder of aspirations he'd given up on a long time ago.

"You are a truly gifted composer," Bloom went on. "But I fear you are wasting your talent with this television studio."

Cameron frowned without completely dropping his smile. For a moment, he didn't know what to say. "Wait . . . What are we talking about, again?"

Bloom's eyes narrowed. "What happened to that man I read about—the man with a passionate perspective of his music and of his art? What has become of Cameron Blake?"

"Listen. If you came just to insult me, then you succeeded. Now I think you better get out of here before I call security."

Bloom was unaffected. "First, I must know: Why have you chosen to abandon your artistic pursuits?"

"I haven't," Cameron retorted flatly.

"But you have. You are pandering your art."

"I'm not pandering," Cameron growled. "Did you see the sign out front? It says SilverReel Studios. One of the biggest television studios in the world. They pay me a shitload for my work."

"I'm sure," said the man, his grin patronizing.

Grinding his teeth, Cameron stood up and handed back the magazine. "You know what? I just remembered something. I gotta go. But it's been real nice talking to you."

Making no move to get up himself, the conductor fluttered through the pages of the magazine until he found a large black and white studio shot of Cameron. "You know, Mr. Blake, you relayed a remarkable story in this article. When I discovered that you based 'Hear After' on a near-death experience . . . well, I was extremely eager to hear it. When I had a listen, I knew you were a true artist."

"Well, I'm glad you liked it." Trembling with anger, Cameron made a move to leave, but then hesitated at the door when the man spoke again.

"You are not the only one who has heard the music from the Other Side. Did you know that? Nor are you the first to try to capture it on paper. I should know; I've spent my entire life trying to capture it."

Cameron's sneakers squeaked as he spun around. Goosebumps rippled down his arms. "Who the hell are you?"

The man turned slightly in his chair and once again smiled at him. "Please. Hear what I have to say."

Reluctantly, Cameron returned to his chair, feeling both curious and skeptical. The conductor wanted something from him, that much was obvious. Still, Bloom seemed like a man who knew things.

"Few people in this world have heard the Astral Music," the man continued. "Fewer have done so well to mimic it. Among them, you have come the closest."

As if for the first time, Cameron looked at the stranger's stern face, composed of sharp angles and hard lines. His deep-set eyes suggested a fierce intelligence.

"You have a remarkable gift, Mr. Blake. You have the ability to bring the Astral Music into physical interpretations. But I'm afraid you've squandered this talent." He looked up and made a sweeping gesture at the surrounding studio. "This is no place for an artist of your caliber. You've whored out your talents. You must know that you are capable of doing so much more. That is why I am here—to save you from yourself."

Here it comes, thought Cameron. *The catch.* "How?"

"I want to help you continue your work. Just think of what it would mean to the world if you captured the music from the Other Side and shaped it into a symphony. You came close with 'Hear After.' But I can take you further."

Cameron smiled bitterly. "This is some kind of joke, isn't it?"

"No, not a joke." Bloom reached into his coat and produced a card and handed it to Cameron. "Of course, you will need to come to Holloway and prepare to stay for a while. It will take some time to do this. I will pay you for your trouble. How does a hundred thousand dollars sound?"

Tell him no! the voice in his head shouted. *Goddamn it. Tell him no!*

Before Cameron answered, Bloom stood and brushed the wrinkles from his jacket. "Think it over. Call me when you are ready to come and visit. My contact information is on the card."

Bloom didn't wait for a response. He walked to the door and let himself out. With the control room to himself, Cameron looked at the card. In basic black and white letters were the words: *Maestro Leonin Bloom, conductor of Holloway Chamber Orchestra.* There was also an address and phone number.

Three months passed without Cameron giving another thought to the man who had managed to insult him and praise him in the same conversation.

He grew increasingly restless in the summer months. He avoided his friends and ignored Barbara's phone calls. His piano collected dust because he had no desire to play, and nothing left to write. He spent his days aimlessly perusing the Gaslamp Quarter's harbors and boutique shops, watching the tourists, drinking beers on the open terraces, engulfing himself in the smell of fried foods and the sounds of live music and snapping awnings. Some days he walked the beaches until his feet hurt and the sinking sun cued him to turn around and go home.

But then one night the dream returned—this time stronger than the last. He'd woken in the middle of the night, sobbing openly in his lonely bed with the dream music echoing in his ears. He'd gotten out his journal and scratched down what he could remember. In the morning he woke and found Bloom's card in a desk drawer next to the phone.

He didn't call the conductor.

It rained through the afternoon. After lunch he threw on a rain jacket and stepped out onto his back porch. Twenty yards out across the bleached sand, dark blue curls of the Pacific crashed into milky froth against the beach. The thrumming waves and the salty breeze calmed his nerves. He drew a deep breath and gazed out toward the horizon, where thunderheads gathered offshore like iron warships poised to attack the bungalows huddled along the coastline. Beyond them, the sun threw off ribbons of pink and orange as it sagged lazily toward the ocean. He loved the ocean, and after spending his youth with his grandmother near Oregon's Cape Lookout after his family's death, he could never get enough of the power of the sea. It was inspiring and mighty, something he liked for writing music, but it hadn't been his biggest inspiration.

He finished his drink and turned his attention to his leather-bound journal. A relic from his undergraduate years at Juilliard, the journal was brittle and yellowed at the corners. It held more than fifteen years of random entries. A musicology professor by the name of Dr. David Weis had given him the idea after pulling him aside one day after class. Cameron's grades had been in serious decline after a bout with self-doubt, and Weis wanted more out of him.

"This isn't like you, Cameron," he'd said in his thick German accent. "You are better than this."

Cameron had confessed that he hadn't been sleeping. Nightmares plagued what little rest he did get; his dreams were haunted by strange music. Dr. Weis suggested that he keep a journal. "Try to write the music. Maybe you'll learn something about yourself. Maybe the dreams will go away."

The journal had proven surprisingly effective. The nightmares did go away, but in return, he'd opened doors to deeper caverns of his consciousness, and he'd discovered a secret that his mind had tried desperately to keep: he'd heard this music as a child during a near-death experience.

He opened the journal and surveyed the pages. There were more than forty entries of musical composition. None of it made much sense when played out loud. A strange, new-agey mess. But he'd spent most of his college years obsessed with capturing this dream music—to wrench it from his mind and force it down into the journal's empty pages. The project had become like chasing his own tail, driving him crazy.

In many ways, this obsession had led to his eventual divorce. He had met Amber Novak at Juilliard during his sophomore year. A Polish virtuosa concert pianist, beautiful and hyper-sexual, she'd turned his world upside down. They'd known from the start they shared very different perspectives. Unlike him, Amber was impossibly grounded, suspicious of anything she couldn't touch or measure, and repelled by organized religion, romantic notions, and pulp fiction. Cameron, on the other hand, remained open to life's mysteries, especially when it came to love, and so he saw Amber's hardened sensibilities as something that needed to be challenged, confident their differences would only make their relationship more interesting.

But as the years passed and Cameron spent increasingly more time on his somewhat unconventional pet projects, Amber had become disenchanted with him. She hadn't trusted what he was doing, even when he'd produced a hit with "Hear After" and made them lots of money. She'd found his music alarming. It bothered her. Eventually, she'd withdrawn from him. Then, after their third year of marriage, she'd asked for a divorce. It was then, in the lonely aftermath, that Cameron had shut the door on his fantasy music. It had already taken up enough of his life. Eventually the dreams had gone.

But now they were coming back, and this worried him.

Thumbing through the pages to this last entry, Cameron studied the last piece he'd written while working in L.A. on the *American Sweethearts* project. This one looked even stranger than his previous attempts. He ran the tip of his finger along the scratchy symbols, wondering what the music would sound like. *No, I don't care.* With a sigh, he closed the journal and shoved it into the inside pocket of his rain jacket, then went barefooted down the porch steps, determined to walk a few miles before the rain came.

His feet dug into the warm sand as he trudged headlong toward the expanse of blue-gray ocean. At the tide line, he crouched down and rolled his pants up to his knees, then splashed into the foaming water as waves exploded against the shore around him. Standing there, he gazed upward at the underbelly of pastel-colored clouds. For a moment the sun pierced the overcast and doused him with its warmth. Though the sensation was fleeting, it invigorated him, like the tingling pinpricks that signaled the return of sensation to a foot that has fallen asleep.

For a while he waded into the milky foam that fizzed and roiled about his ankles, while the waves beat the sand. When he spotted a handful of seagulls cawing at each other, he made his way back onto the beach to investigate. He scared most of the birds away as he drew near. Through flapping wings he saw a severed tortoise head lying in the sand, surrounded by clumps of brown seaweed. Ropes of muscle and tendon spilled from a hole where the head once connected to its neck. Its eyes, roughly the size of boiled eggs, gaped at Cameron, who stood watching for no other reason than to satisfy a feeling of pertinence. Moments later a seagull hopped closer and plucked out one of its eyes.

He thought of his mother's eyes. She had shared a similar expression that day, long ago, after she'd slammed face-first into the dashboard. Gaping eyes. Horrifyingly empty. So empty that they'd collapsed like stars to form black holes. And they'd nearly drawn him in. And he'd almost gone.

Something caught his eye further up the coast beyond the tortoise head. Drifting toward him was a lone figure, a thin silhouette, wearing a black poncho that flailed and flapped about him like batwings.

Wiping his face with the back of his hand, Cameron turned and started back along the coastline toward his home. The wind met him head on. His jacket snapped violently about him, his hair fluttered in his eyes. When he threw a glance over his shoulder, he found the stranger following, hurrying now, waving a frantic hand at him. A muffled voice reached him across the distance.

"Something to show you!"

Cameron lowered his head into the wind and walked faster, kicking up the sand with his feet, not wanting to talk with anyone, wanting only to be alone with his thoughts. Footfalls thudded behind him.

Suddenly the man appeared before him and blocked his path. "Hey, mister! Just a moment, please!"

The man was crane-like, with long, wiry legs and torso. He had a gaunt and leathery face with a wild smile and teeth best suited for a horse. Long tangles of windblown hair spilled over his brow. Scruffy whiskers outlined his jaw and spread down his neck. Wide, crazy eyes bored into Cameron.

"Please have a look!" the stranger insisted. "I have something to show you."

He raised a fist. Something dangled from it—a stretch of netting with scraps of trash caught in it. A gust of wind curled outward from the sea and sent the netted scraps into a flurry, producing a glassy, chattering sound.

"Wind chime!" the man said proudly. A smile stretched across his face. "Make 'em myself."

Cameron shook his head. "I'm not interested."

"Oh, but you are!" the stranger insisted. "Trust me, sir. You are! Don't ya see ya'self in them strings? These are your bones, my friend. *Your* bones." He shook the wind chimes and made them chatter.

Cameron looked closer. Different lengths of fishing line hung from a dome made of driftwood. Glass beads and metal slugs formed a spiral in the strings, but there were also tiny bones; bird bones, maybe. Harbor boutique shops sold similar affairs, except those sported seashells, dried bamboo, or metal cylinders. This thing looked like it belonged hanging from the rafters of an African witchdoctor's hut. It gave Cameron an unsettling feeling, and for a long moment he couldn't tear his gaze from it.

"What'd I tell you? Something pretty to take home."

Dazed, Cameron shook his head. "I'm not–"

The man threw his head back and cackled. "I think you are, friend. I think you are. And I'll tell you what, I'll give it to you for whatever's in your pocket."

Cameron started to protest but decided against it. Again, he felt the sensation of pertinence, like he'd dreamed the whole thing, and it was worth a few bucks to get this odd man to leave. He dug his hand into his pocket and found a ten. As he held it out, the man snatched it lightning-quick, then handed him the chimes.

"Nice doing business with you," said the stranger with a knowing laugh. He pocketed the bill, gave a gratified nod, and started back down the coastline.

Cameron returned home and hung the chimes from the rafters of his veranda. When a soft wind gusted up from the shore, it stirred the thing into motion. The scraps of metal, glass, and bone made a dry chattering sound, both morbid and irresistible. He stood and stared in a kind of stupor, while something tickled the back of his mind.

Those are your bones, the man had said. *Your bones . . .*

Behind him, the rain fell again with a sudden hiss, and far away the waves roared and boomed against the sand. After a while, he went inside and dialed the number on the card that Maestro Bloom had given him.

Cameron arrived in Nashville on the third of August with only an Army-issue duffel bag packed with a few weeks' worth of clothes and a leather satchel where he kept his compositions. He didn't bother with renting a car at the airport, because he didn't know how long he would stay, and because he didn't feel like waiting in line at the checkout counter. Instead he hailed a taxi.

His first stop was a small café a mile or so from the terminal where he ordered a Reuben sandwich and washed it down with a Miller. As he scarfed down his sandwich, a big man in blue jean overalls and a Peterbilt ball cap sat down on the barstool to his left. After a moment, the guy introduced himself as Bob Fulsome. An ex-truck driver, with a face like saddle leather and thick-rimmed glasses that magnified his friendly green eyes, Bob missed the road and felt comfortable talking to strangers. Drinking a draft beer, he talked about politics and the "dumbshits" running the White House.

Cameron listened only half-heartedly while he ate. He shook his head at the appropriate moments, and Bob seemed to like that.

"So where you heading, anyway?" the man asked after finishing his beer.

"Place called Holloway," Cameron said around a mouthful of bread.

"Holloway? That's on the Cumberland Plateau. I'm passing right through there."

Cameron rose up in his chair. "Think you could give me a ride?"

The old man considered this for a moment, and then shrugged. "If you can handle riding in the back of my pickup." He turned on his stool and pointed at an old, red Ford truck sitting in the parking lot beyond the window. "I ain't alone, see. My dog Queenie's in the cab. She don't share too well." On cue, the large black Labrador poked her head out of the driver side window and sniffed the air, as if she knew they were talking about her.

Cameron laughed. "You know, I think the back of that truck would be just fine, Bob. I could use the fresh air."

Cameron paid for both their tabs and they left. For the next several hours, the old Ford rattled its way down I-24 with Cameron in the back, propped against the wall of the cab. The wind roared in his ears as he watched the world rush away from him. Wide fields of floppy-leafed tobacco and corn. Rickety barns with walls the color of driftwood. Ranch homes with front porch swings and old cars on blocks. He dozed for a while and woke with the sun falling beneath the horizon. He stretched his aching back and leaned over the truck side so he could see ahead. Twenty miles up the road, the horizon jutted sharply, forming a great mountainous swell, with the highway disappearing into its folds. They'd reached the Cumberland Plateau.

Grinning, he closed his eyes and breathed in the crisp scent of newly tilled earth and fresh greenery. Every nerve in his body hummed, and he rode that feeling for a while, dissolving into stillness as he watched with half-closed eyes the world rolling away from him. Nearly an hour later, the old man took the Holloway exit.

Chapter 3

Madison Taylor parked in the small gravel lot of the shop on the corner of Liberty and Frontier Avenues, and hesitated before she got out of her car. A sinking feeling in the pit of her gut forced her to wait. She shook her head and refused herself permission to let the usual anxious feelings crash over her.

"Not today," she whispered to herself, shoving open her door. She talked to herself more and more these days. "Only good thoughts today."

Taking a moment to lean against her car, she closed her eyes behind her glasses and took a deep breath. In her late twenties, she was tall and lean, with hazel eyes and honey-brown hair, worn back in a ponytail. She wore a loose shirt over a tank top, fitted jeans, knee-high boots, and a little straw Panama hat, just for fun. It was a cute outfit, but she felt hopelessly overdressed; considering the declining popularity of her shop, she'd be lucky if five people saw her today.

Her gaze shifted to the stylized words hanging over the front door: Beethoven's Closet. She remembered her initial excitement when she and her father had watched the carpenters erect the sign. That had been the year her mother died of cancer. Seven years ago. Back then, this had all seemed like a fine idea. She'd spotted the small two-story home, zoned for both commercial and residential prospects. Perfect for what she'd wanted to do: create a clothing shop that culled hand-tailored clothing from local and independent designers. Then she'd gone and made the mistake of telling her dad. He turned her casual interest into a passionate pursuit. He'd wanted so badly for her to have the shop. Neither of them had considered that maybe it wasn't such a good idea. Most businesses struggled here on the plateau, unless they sold hiking gear, feed, or fertilizer.

Dad, she thought with a sigh, *what the hell did we get ourselves into?*

She started down the cobble path, where she found her A-frame sign lying on its face. Frustrated, she stood it upright and brushed off the dirt. A portrait of a scowling Beethoven, caught in a rage, his wacked-out hair, his puffy jacket, even his thick brows—all deep violet to match the sign— stared back at her. She used to like the yard sign's wildish appeal in the small town of fifteen thousand. Today the portrait just seemed to express her own frustrations.

Clapping the dirt from her hands, she climbed the front steps and stopped at the door, frowning when she saw the sign in the window: "Sorry, We're Closed." She didn't like that one bit. *Carrie Belle, why didn't you open the shop? It's nearly ten-thirty for Christ's sake.*

She found her keys and unlocked the door, then shoved it open and stepped inside. The cow bell rang frantically overhead. "Hello?" she called, shutting the door behind her. "Carrie? You here?"

She's here, all right, thought Madison. *Her Beetle's parked in the driveway. This is why you don't hire friends to help run your shop.*

She stepped into the dark showroom. Six round tables, painted pink, displayed various clothes. Blouses and skirts and pieces of jewelry, all hand-tailored, every bit of it—even the clothes hanging on the racks against the walls, the older stuff that didn't sell. There were a few paintings on the walls, all of them bright and eccentric; she'd handpicked them herself. There were more upstairs. In an adjacent room, she kept a stockpile of French milled soaps, shea butter, moisturizers, those sorts of things. These products always made her shop smell nice. It was a nice contrast to the franchise stores at the nearby shopping mall.

Someone moaned from within the shop. Madison held her breath, suddenly worried. Her eyes settled on the curtain of chestnut-colored beads at the far end of the room, leading to the stockroom.

"Ungh!" There it was again—not a pained grunt, like she'd thought at first. No that was definitely not it.

"Oh, yes! Now! Now! *Now!*"

"You've got to be kidding me!" Madison said under her breath, as she charged across the room and swept back the curtain of beads with her arm. At the end of the narrow stockroom stood a skinny boy, his back to her, his jeans gathered around his ankles. A pair of cream-colored legs were wrapped about his waist.

Madison froze and clapped a hand over her mouth. Over the boy's shoulder she caught Carrie Belle's startled gaze.

"Carrie Belle!" Madison cried, as much out of surprise as disappointment. "What the hell are you doing?" Of course, she knew exactly what Carrie Belle was doing.

The contents of one shelf spilled behind Carrie Belle. Her boyfriend dropped and gathered his jeans, hiking them up his slender legs.

"Oh God, Mad! I'm sorry!" Carrie Belle cried.

Madison backed out, letting the beaded curtain fall, and braced herself against the wall, hands cupping her mouth. *Oh my God, I can't believe I just saw that!* She didn't know whether to laugh or scream.

From the other side of the curtain, Carrie Belle went on, "I'm sorry, Mad. Please don't be mad at me."

Her head rolled back against the wall, Madison stifled a nervous giggle beneath her hands.

Moments later, the beads rustled as Carrie Belle rushed out from the stockroom. She was short, round, with silky black hair that fell just below her ears. She sometimes called herself fat, but such a harsh label failed to aptly characterize her figure. Big boned, perhaps; a little plump. Either way, Madison thought Carrie Belle had a darling face and striking green eyes. But now her features were damp from aroused titillation, and her eyes were wide and desperate. "You're not mad at me, are you?"

Madison looked at her, no longer smiling. "Carrie Belle, I'm so shocked right now, I don't know what I feel. I mean, honestly. How could you do this?"

"I know! I said I was sorry!" Carrie Belle's face glowed a violent red. But a grin lurked behind her eyes.

"You think this is funny?" Madison shouted. "Absolutely not!"

Carrie Belle's boyfriend, Jon, hurried out from the stockroom, fixing his belt, grinning unabashedly. He looked sort of thuggish, with a clean-shaven head and tattoos along his forearms. "We didn't mean no harm by it, Madison," he said, his acne-scarred face burning red. "It was an accident."

Madison scoffed. "Seriously? You call that an accident?"

Carrie Belle covered her mouth with her hands to muffle a giggle.

Madison threw her hands up. "I give up, you guys. I just give up!" She went to the cashier's counter, plopped down on a stool, and buried her face in her hands. "Jon, I think you should leave."

He looked at Carrie Belle with a shrug and then left. The bell jingled over the door.

When they had the shop all to themselves, Carrie Belle walked over and leaned on the counter opposite Madison.

"The sign blew over again," Madison grumbled, avoiding eye contact with her.

"Somebody forgot their coffee this morning."

Madison glowered at her. "Don't you dare turn this around on me. I just caught you guys with your pants down. Jesus, Carrie."

Blossoms of bright scarlet colored Carrie Belle's face as she giggled. "What can I say? It was exciting. Maybe you should try it sometime."

Madison gaped. "Carrie Belle! You are pushing it. I should fire your ass."

"You can't fire me. I'm your best friend."

With a cry of frustration, Madison grabbed the mail near the counter and started sorting through bills and junk mail. Carrie Belle, leaning against the counter, watched with her chin propped in her hands. Madison ignored her.

"You gonna tell me what's wrong?" said Carrie Belle, after a long moment.

Madison shoved the mail aside, slumped over the counter, and buried her face in her hands. "I hate this place," she whispered.

"What's going on?"

"I'm tired. I'm tired of always waiting for something to happen to me."

A shadow of overwhelming concern drifted across Carrie Belle's brow, and she put an arm over Madison's shoulder. "C'mon, Mad. Don't do this. I'm sorry I upset you."

Madison sniffed and rubbed her eyes. "You're a good friend, even if you are a shitty employee."

Her friend grinned and hugged her tightly. "That's more like it."

Madison smiled wanly. "Carrie, don't you ever want more out of life?"

"No. I'm content with my life. I like it here. I like my boyfriend. I like my job."

"If you like your job so much you sure as hell don't act like it." Madison got up and walked around the counter to the big bay window overlooking Liberty Street. She pulled back the curtains and warm, refreshing sunlight spilled into the shop. "Everything just seems so . . . pointless. I don't know why I don't just pack my things and leave."

An old, heavyset man strolling along Liberty caught her attention. He wore an ill-fitted suit and moved in a lumbering gait. Sunlight gleamed against his hairless scalp. Immediately a chill raced down Madison's spine, and she folded her arms to suppress a sudden chill.

Behind her, Carrie Belle carried on about something.

"You say something?" asked Madison.

"I said, maybe you should take a vacation. You know, get away for a while."

"Yeah, right. And leave you in charge of the shop?" Madison snorted, but she was laughing on the inside. Her eyes narrowed as she tried to get a better look at the old man outside. He was one of them—from the orchestra. They were all old, and they always dressed in funeral attire. And there was something else, though she couldn't put her finger on it, a dreadful feeling whenever she spotted one of them. *Had anyone ever stopped to talk to one of them?* She didn't think so. The group had been in Holloway for ten years and to her knowledge, no one had ever said more than three words to one of them. "There's one of those creepy musicians."

Carrie Belle wormed in beside her and had a look. "Gosh," she whispered, as if afraid the old man might hear. "Those people are so creepy. I think something's wrong with them. What if they're, like, vampires or something? I mean, you never see them doing something normal, like grocery shopping or walking around the mall."

Madison let the curtains fall back into place. "Don't try to change the subject."

"You changed the subject."

Madison went to the table nearest her and began straightening blouses. "Anyhow, Carrie Belle. Seriously, this isn't a hotel. If you don't respect this place, then you'll just have to find a new place to work. Got it?"

Carrie Belle's gaze dropped, and she shoved her hands into her pockets. She nodded.

"Yeah. I got it."

"Good. Now go on and clean up the stockroom."

After Carrie slipped through the beaded curtain, Madison opened the front door and stepped out onto the porch. With the exception of a few cars, the street was empty. She folded her arms over her chest and rubbed the goosebumps from her arms. Then she flipped the sign in the door so that it read "Yes, We're Open!"

It was late in the day when the crumpled old pickup rolled into the town square and nosed in beside a parking meter. Cameron tossed his duffel bag and satchel over the side, then climbed over the tailgate.

Bob rolled down the window and gave him a warm smile. "Well, sir, I suppose this is your stop."

Cameron shook his hand. "I can't thank you enough, Bob."

Queenie barked, and the old man laughed and patted her head. "Queenie says to take care of yourself." Bob put the truck into gear and started to roll away, then added, "Hope you find what you're looking for." Then he was gone.

Cameron stretched his back as he surveyed the historic town square. The buildings lining the streets were post–Civil War structures, predominantly Colonial Revival if he had to guess, most of them standing two or three stories tall with brick walls, flat roofs, and wide cornices. Nestled at the center of the square on a large field was the stately courthouse, with columns lining its facade and a white cupola sitting on its roof like a tiny hat.

I think I just discovered the land that time forgot, Cameron thought with a grin. The place had a sleepy, old-fashioned charm about it, with American flags snapping in the breeze and awnings shading the storefronts. He didn't see a single vagrant sprawled out on the lawn, or trash in the gutters, or bars on the windows. Nor were there liquor stores or pawnshops—at least not on this side of town—to mar the small town ambiance. Holloway seemed to exist in an entirely different world than his West Coast stomping grounds.

Drawing a breath of fresh air, Cameron gathered his things and started down the sidewalk. He looked in all the shop windows, cluttered with displays of camping gear and mannequins, showcasing questionable fashion. A gaunt-faced wooden Indian stood within the inset doorway of Totem Tobacco. The scent of cinnamon and brown sugar billowed from the chimney pipes of Candy's Cookie Corner. There was also a movie rental shop (maybe the last one standing) and an old-timey café with a soda fountain and spin-top stools. Even the streets had names like Main Street and Liberty Avenue.

Setting his bags down, Cameron glanced at his reflection in a dusty used bookstore window. Staring back at him was the face he always saw, a handsome face with dark blue eyes and a strong jaw, going well with his medium build. But he'd started to show signs of his age. There was some silver in his dark hair now, a few lines around his eyes. He looked older than his thirty-six years, but it was nothing a few good night's sleep wouldn't fix.

A sound drew his attention. He looked down at his feet and found his duffel bag lying on its side. His satchel had disappeared. Frowning, he spun around and spotted a long-haired golden retriever standing in the middle of Main Street. The satchel hung by its strap, clenched between the dog's teeth.

"Hey! Hold on, now. Give that back!" He grabbed his duffel bag and charged into Main Street without looking. Tires squealed, and he jumped back onto the sidewalk. A black sedan stopped in the road. The dog growled at the car's grille, the satchel swinging from his jaws. The front flap had fallen open and sheets of paper fluttered from its opening.

Hoping to collect the windblown papers from the middle of the street, Cameron moved into the road again, this time holding his hands out at the woman driving so she would stay still. Crouching, he moved toward the animal. "It's okay, buddy. No one's going to hurt you. Just give me my bag before we both end up as roadkill."

The dog whimpered and lowered his head, preparing to relinquish his prize. Grinning, Cameron reached for his satchel when a horn blared. The dog bolted with the satchel bouncing after him, papers spilling in its wake. Cameron stood up and smiled poisonously at the driver—a pretty young girl with a nose ring. When she saw his disgust, she gave an impatient shrug.

Getting out of the road, Cameron searched for the dog. He spotted him trotting ahead with his head held high and his satchel bouncing after like "Just Married" cans tied to the rear bumper of a newlyweds' getaway car. Papers scattered in the dog's wake as he disappeared around a coffee shop. Cameron slapped his forehead. Everything he'd written in the past ten years was in that bag, including his journal.

Collecting papers as he hurried along and swearing under his breath, he followed the dog around the corner. What he'd mistaken for an alley was actually a small road called Bard Street. This narrow two-lane street ran in a steep incline as it moved away from the square. The lane was too quiet, lined with a few vacant shops with boarded windows and padlocks on the doors and several dumpsters. Only one place looked to be in business. It had a blue door and a sign that read Bard Street Tavern. Its single window was dark. A Pabst Blue Ribbon neon sign hung in the window, but it was presently unlit.

Cameron looked up the street, his gaze following along the steep hill until the road evened out again and plunged out of sight. Quiet and brooding, Bard Street seemed cut off from the lifeblood of the rest of the town, like an atrophied limb. He didn't like it, and there was no sign of the dog. He walked twenty yards and found a sheet of music in a pool of gutter water.

"Ah, goddamn it!" he moaned as he plucked it up and shook the foul water from it. His voice bounced off the tavern walls.

Up the hill a bit, he saw the dog peek from around a dumpster, the satchel swinging lazily from his mouth. The animal froze as he made eye contact with Cameron.

"Come on, boy," he said, showing his hands. "I'll buy you a burger. I just want my stuff back."

The dog dropped his bag and then disappeared up the hill.

Relieved, Cameron trotted over to the satchel and squatted down next to it. Folding back its front flap, he looked inside and found the stack of papers considerably thinner. Then he checked the outer pocket. His journal was still there. *Thank God I didn't lose that!* He sighed and sat on the dirty sidewalk. He was mad enough to chase the dog and give him a good kick. After a moment, he got up and shouldered his satchel, then started back toward the square with both of his bags. But something forced him to stop and turn around. He followed the rising hill with his eyes, wondering about the slope. Strangely compelled, he decided to see for himself. If anything, he'd have a chance at settling his score with the dog.

He walked on, and halfway up the hill, he spotted the rooftop of a massive building looming up ahead. Before he'd seen the entire structure, he knew he'd found his reason for coming to Holloway.

He knew in his gut that he'd found Maestro Bloom's concert hall.

Bard Street dead-ended in a wide plaza where a sign announced: The Calliope Auditorium. Beyond that, there was a massive post–Civil War church with soaring red-brick walls, bigger than the courthouse he'd seen earlier. The church had a steeply pitched gable roof and rows of windows with gothic arches and white hood molding. From its front portico, wide steps spilled down to the plaza.

Cameron scratched the back of his neck. The hall seemed out of place up here, hidden from the rest of the world. Not many small towns could justify the cost and upkeep of such a large auditorium. Moreover, you'd have to fund an impressive orchestra to draw a large enough group of paying visitors to keep the place running. Considering the insularity of the plateau, this didn't seem very likely.

Drawing an unsteady breath, he adjusted the duffel bag on his shoulder and set out across the plaza. Nearing the building, he became aware of a faint hum. The former church buzzed with an electric charge and the feeling grew stronger with every moment. Before reaching the steps, he passed a penny-wish water fountain. His eyes drifted to the parking lot at the right of the building, as big as a football field and empty, save for a single brown Oldsmobile. At least one person was here.

Cameron climbed the steps and found two glass entrance doors in the shade of the portico. These struck him as severely out of context, like electric windows on an antique car. Nonetheless, he went to them, cupped his hands against the glass, and peered inside, finding only a dark, empty foyer.

With a disappointed sigh, he stepped back and his gaze dropped to the brass door handles. The moment his fingers touched the cool metal, his heart quickened a beat, and a voice in his head told him to forget about it and go home. *No*, he told himself. He'd come this far. At the very least, he would hear what Bloom had to say. He gave the handle a slight tug, and just as he knew it would, the door swung open.

He padded quietly into a lofty foyer with a vaulted ceiling and clean white walls. Thick maroon carpet covered the floors. A ticket counter and a dark concession bar lined the wall to the right. Several baroque-style paintings of angels with harps and trumpets decorated the place. Two large wooden doors, serving as the central entryway into the auditorium, stood on the opposite wall. This was flanked by two staircases that led to the balcony.

"Hello?" Cameron called, as he walked farther inside. Rays of sunlight pierced the upper windows and gave him enough light to see by. When no one answered, he walked across the room, pulled the auditorium doors open, and stepped inside.

The auditorium, despite its current use, still had the look of an old, albeit massive, church. Hardwood floors, rows of oak pews, and stained-glass windows sustained the impression. A number of support columns held aloft the crescent-shaped balcony that spanned nearly as far as the stage, creating a canopy overhead. From what he could see, there were just as many pews up there. The place had a brooding atmosphere, and it smelled . . . old.

He turned his gaze to the wide stage. Lights shined down on aged boards, freshly waxed. Bright red curtains hid the back wall. Only a grand piano occupied the space in front of those curtains.

"Anyone here?" he shouted. The fine acoustics carried his voice easily across the auditorium. He could have whispered a conversation with someone standing on the opposite end of the hall. "The doors were open. I let myself in. Hope no one minds."

He waited for an answer, feeling uneasy about trespassing. Adjusting the weight of his duffel bag on his shoulder, he moved down the main aisle, passing the pews, feeling the energy of the place. His nerves jittered, the response to his fear of getting himself in trouble, but something else nagged at the back of his mind, making him feel a little sick. *I know this feeling. Like I'm walking alone in a cemetery.*

There was a flight of half-moon steps at center stage. He climbed these to the top and turned to look out at the dark seating area. Once he decided he was still alone, he made his way to the piano, a Bösendorfer concert grand. It was an elegant and regal instrument, but he still couldn't help think it looked like a coffin on display. He glided tentative fingers across its icy keys, and then the urge to sit down and play struck him. *What harm could it do?* If anything, he'd get somebody's attention, and they could lead him to Bloom. He'd been invited here, after all.

He seated himself on the small bench and played a chord to test the quality. Crisp sounds swelled from the piano's open case and drifted like streamers across the auditorium. Throwing caution to the wind, he hunkered over the keys and launched into a rhythm. He explored the piano's tones in a manner similar to someone enjoying the body of his partner for the first time. Soon, a melody revealed itself, shaping and taking form, a bluesy rhythm and soulful melody. The music came effortlessly, as if it existed somewhere outside of him, out there on its own, waiting all this time for someone to pluck it from the ether and drive it note by note into the physical realm.

But then something tickled the base of his skull, and he glanced over his left shoulder.

Toward the back curtains stood a tall black man in a navy blue worker's jumpsuit, his arms folded.

Startled, Cameron nearly leaped from the bench, but his feet got tangled. His arms flailed in an attempt to catch his balance. In seconds, he toppled backward over the bench and landed on his back, smacking his head with a dull thud.

As the lights above him became hazy stars, a dark face with bright eyes and a toothsome grin loomed over him. The face said something, but it sounded to Cameron as if someone had shoved cotton balls into his ears. The face became a shadow, and the theater darkened around him until the lights finally went out.

When Cameron woke, the face loomed over him still, only now it gave a deep, dry chuckle.

"You sure gonna feel that one in the mornin'."

Cameron, still lying on his back on the stage, reached for the back of his head and touched a lump the size of a golf ball. A rolled-up towel served as a pillow beneath his head. With a groan, he swallowed dryly and muttered, "What happened?"

"Nearly cracked your head open is what happened."

Cameron blinked again and the fuzzy apparition above him became a slender black man with a high forehead and receding hairline. There were patches of gray in his hair, and his skin was a soft brown. His eyes were calming, and wrinkles fanned out from their corners. Cameron guessed he was in his mid-fifties. A patch on his left breast pocket revealed him as the head janitor.

"You took one nasty spill over that piano bench," said the janitor in a slow, smoky voice. "Only seen that one other time before. Nineteen-seventy-six, I think it was. Man named Terence Willy. Got so drunk he fell off the stool in the middle of his act. I nearly broke a rib laughin'."

With one eye pinched shut and his head drumming, Cameron said, "Not so funny from this end."

The janitor offered his hand and helped Cameron into a sitting position.

"My name's Washington Hob—Hob to my friends." The man pointed over to a cart of cleaning supplies near the far wall. "I'm the janitor here. Now, as I recall, I'm supposed to be here. It's my job. But you, on the other hand . . . well, sir. I don't recall seein' your face around here."

"Cameron Blake." He held his hand out and Hob shook it.

"Well, Mr. Blake. You 'bout gave me a heart attack. For a second there, I thought you was a ghost."

"The feeling's mutual. Call me Cameron, by the way."

"Where'd you pick up that song, anyhow?"

Wincing against the steady thud in his head, Cameron shrugged. What had he been playing? He couldn't remember. "Don't really know, Hob. Just sort of came out." Slowly, he picked himself up. Once on his feet, he nearly lost balance.

Hob grabbed his arm. "Whoa, now. Let's get you over to that piano bench." He flipped the bench over on its feet and helped Cameron sit down. "You gonna make it?"

Bent over, arms hanging between his knees, head drooping, Cameron muttered, "Think so."

"I'm no doctor, but I know a few things about gettin' knocked upside the head. Sometimes you get a headache, sometimes a concussion, and sometimes you get a hemorrhage. Then you're in serious trouble."

Cameron gave him a crooked grin. "I think I'm okay. You didn't by chance get the tags of the truck that hit me?"

Hob chuckled. "So, Cameron Blake, what sort of business do you have with the Calliope?"

"I'm looking for a guy named Bloom."

"You mean Maestro Bloom. What d'ya want with him?"

"Not entirely sure about that. I met him a few months ago. He asked me to head this way."

"I see. Well, you missed him." Hob's gaze hardened. "He'll be back tomorrow mornin'. Anyhow, I got to get back to work, seein' as you done scuffed up my floor."

Cameron nodded. The Calliope became a massive merry-go-round, spinning in dizzying circles around him. He braced himself against the piano and waited for the nausea to pass.

"Hey, listen," said Hob, clutching his shoulder and helping him balance as he sat down. "Maybe I should give you a ride."

"Thanks, Hob. But I think I can manage."

"Like hell. You got a hotel room?"

"Not yet."

"The Cherry Tree's just off the square. Nothing fancy. But it's close."

Wincing against his throbbing head, Cameron offered a weak smile and nodded. "As long as it's got a bed, I'm sold on the idea."

Hob dropped Cameron off in front of the hotel. It was only a block or so from the square and tucked in between a number of squat brick buildings, home to attorneys' offices, bail bondsmen, and even a pawnshop. Inside the small lobby, Cameron checked in with an old woman named Darlene, who had silver curls and large glasses. She never once removed the cigarette from her mouth.

As Hob had promised, Cameron's room wasn't much, just small and drab, with a fuzzy brown carpet and dingy white walls. A queen-sized bed with a hunter green blanket sat near the wall, opposite a chintzy dresser. He stuck his head into the bathroom. Nothing special there either, besides a toilet, a single shower with water stains, and a sink. He returned to the main room and opened a window, hoping to air out the musty odor. He leaned his head outside and looked up the street. He had a good view of the neighboring rooftops all the way to the courthouse's cupola. Not the best room he'd ever stayed in, but not the worst either.

Leaving the window open, he ducked back inside, plopped down on the corner of his bed and worked off his shoes. He found the remote to the old television that hung on a wall bracket, turned it on, and flipped listlessly through the channels. Nothing but soap operas and *M*A*S*H* reruns.

Soon a sleepy fog crept over him and his eyes grew heavy. He lay back on the stiff bed and threw an arm over his eyes to shield them from the sunlight coming in through the window. Just before he drifted off, his thoughts returned to the Calliope.

Slipping gently beneath the surface of consciousness, another part of him slipped mentally into the backseat of the family Toyota. Dad was driving. Mom lying back in the passenger seat. At the other end of the backseat, his brother slept. The car's tires hummed hypnotically. His mother turned and touched his knee. *God has a purpose for you.*

Then the tires shrieked and darkness swallowed him up.

For a long while, he swam in this nothingness, until a star exploded before him, a burst of brilliant light whose fringes swayed and billowed like tufts of seaweed in a slow current. *Empyreal*, he thought. *The stuff of heaven.*

The light began to sing, a glassy, whirring sound, natural and flowing, a whale song with no discernible pattern or theme.

Wake up, he told himself. *You have to remember this. Get it down on paper.*

He woke with a start, sat on the edge of the bed, and retrieved his leather journal from his satchel. Turning on the little lamp beside his bed, he clenched a pen between his fingers and pressed its tip against the empty page.

Chapter 4

It was a pretty afternoon, with a cloudless sky and a pleasant wind that whipped and rushed about before disappearing just as suddenly. Leaving Carrie to man the shop, Madison strolled up to the Blue Cow on the square and bought a scoop of Rocky Road on a waffle cone. She had cramps and felt moody, and this was good medicine. It melted and dribbled while she walked along the shops, glancing curiously at each window.

She didn't feel like going back to the Closet. Only a few customers had come in that morning, and Carrie was incapable of shutting up. On any other day, this wouldn't matter, and on most days she liked listening to Carrie. But today, she needed quiet, she needed to think. She felt just sort of inside herself, and she didn't mind the feeling so much. It drew out the essences of things; it cast the world about her in different hues. While she finished off her ice cream, she stopped to ponder the shape of an oak tree on the corner of Cherry Tree. When she crossed the street and stepped onto the courthouse lawn, she slipped off her sandals and explored the cool grass with her toes.

Near the western side of the courthouse, she found an empty park bench in the shade of an ash tree and sat with one leg curled beneath her. The wind whispered in the leaves.

Just recently she'd started hating this place, like coming back had been the biggest mistake of her life.

Seven years had passed since she'd returned to Holloway. Before then, she'd been living in Annapolis, in a small apartment that overlooked the

Chesapeake Bay. She'd enjoyed her life there, from her work as a consultant for a small-time decorator, to her friends and favorite hangouts. Her boyfriend Ben Lewis, an officer and instructor at the Naval Academy, had seemed a promising catch at first, until things had gotten weird between them. Once they'd broken off their engagement, her life had started a downward spiral. Julie Freeland's wedding had been the final straw. A glorious white wedding on the shores of the Chesapeake Bay; everyone was so happy . . . except Madison. The wedding had merely emphasized how terribly alone she felt.

The news about her mother had come just a week later. Patty Taylor had been diagnosed with cancer. Madison had caught a flight home the next day. Returning to Holloway had awoken something in her that had long been asleep. She was scared, and sad, and maybe for those reasons she'd allowed Holloway to bewitch her with nostalgia. Comforted by its small-town charm, she had decided to stay for a while, just until this whole thing blew over.

But then her mother had died and Madison's illusions about the town had vanished. After putting her mother in the ground, she had wanted nothing to do with Holloway, but by then it was too late. Her father, Ray, needed her more than ever. He'd become an old man overnight, consumed by a smoky gray aura that you couldn't see with your eyes, but you sensed it. The moment she noticed it, she couldn't leave, even when he insisted she go.

So she'd stuck around, and she and Dad had tried their best to keep smiling, to make it through the day. It had been a particularly rainy season, as if an outward manifestation of their sadness. What broke them free of their depression was the "For Sale" sign out front of a small shop.

It had been late October, with the leaves changing, the air chilly. Madison had gone strolling to the square when she spotted the small shop. For nearly half an hour, she'd stood there on the sidewalk, gazing at the small clapboard house, imagining its possibilities. She'd always dreamed of running her own clothing store, a place where local designers contributed their creations— where clothes and art came together. Of course, she didn't have the money for something like that, and she eventually convinced herself that it was a silly idea and went on with her business.

But the thought stuck in her mind. Later that evening, as she and her dad sat at the kitchen table eating spaghetti and meatballs, she'd mentioned the shop for sale. "It's silly, of course," she'd told him, playing with her food more than eating it, "but, I don't know. It just sort of made me happy."

Her father had laid a firm hand over her own, and she'd looked up to find her father positively glowing. In moments, that all-consuming gray mist had evaporated, as if burned off by the sun. "No, it's not a silly idea, Mad. Not silly at all."

"Thanks, Dad. Still. I couldn't afford it."

"Maybe not. But I could help. Patty always insisted we max out our life insurance. I can't tell you how many times we fought over that." Smiling sadly, he'd dropped his gaze and shaken his head. "It's almost like she knew." He'd blinked, as if remembering himself, then looked at her with watery eyes. "Anyways, we could use the money—"

"No, Dad." She'd nearly jumped out of her chair. The thought of funding a silly dream with money from her mother's death had seemed somehow wrong. "I can't. I just can't."

But she could. And she had. They'd signed the note together and used the insurance claim as a down payment. Her father had done most of the work, figuring out the financial nuts and bolts. The project had given him purpose, and he'd seemed ten years younger. Never once had she told him the truth. Never had she said, *Daddy, it was just a silly thought. I didn't really want to open a shop.* Never had she said, *Daddy, I'm worried this thing might trap me in Holloway, and I don't want that to happen.*

She'd never said any of those things, and how could she? This was good for him. She couldn't take that away.

So she'd let him run with it. They'd gotten closer in those few months than they had in the past decade. The house had needed lots of work. The plumbing was old and clunky; the electrical wiring was a fire hazard. So they'd torn out walls and trimmed the floors and so on. They'd done that every day of the week except for Sunday, which Ray reserved for church and fishing with Police Chief Dunlap. After six months, they'd transformed the small shop into a little lavender dream come true. The project had been like therapy. They'd celebrated the grand opening together. Nearly the whole town had shown up, and Madison had gotten a taste of her father's joy. *Yes, she'd told herself, it just might work.*

They'd done okay at first. They'd made enough to pay the bills and keep the shelves stocked.

Then one Sunday morning she'd gone to catch her dad before church. She'd found him sitting in his favorite Lazy Boy recliner, dressed in gray sweats, his face gone the powdery gray of dried clay. Eyes like glassy marbles. Sometime the night before, probably while watching David Letterman on TV, an artery at the base of Ray Taylor's brain had ruptured, killing him instantly. No one had seen it coming, and his death, so mind-numbingly sudden, had knocked Madison for a loop. After that, the shop just sort of seemed like a concrete block chained to her ankle, dragging her beneath the surface. No matter how furiously she treaded the waters, she just kept sinking. Stuck, alone, and broke—Holloway had fooled her, reneged on its promises.

Someone strode past her bench. Snapped out of her daydream, she watched him go. He was in his mid-thirties and handsome, with dark hair and a square jaw, good build, tall enough. He was in jeans and a white t-shirt, and by the looks of the duffel bag on his back, he was either coming or going. She'd never seen him before, but she found him oddly familiar. Oddly irresistible too. As she watched him go, a sudden sadness rolled over her, momentarily ripping her from her own self-indulgence. She straightened her back and swept the hair from her eyes as she watched him disappear down Cherry Tree Avenue.

She walked back to her shop, thinking about the handsome stranger, wondering who he was and where he was heading. The moment she stepped inside, Carrie hurried past her, on her way to do something, when she stopped suddenly and turned to look at her with a mischievous grin. "Um-hum," said Carrie. "I know that smile. You met someone just now, didn't you?"

Madison looked at her in open-mouthed exasperation. Giggling, she said, "I don't know what you're talking about. I didn't meet anybody. Why are you always in my business?"

Carrie shrugged. "Well, you looked like the cat that ate the canary. Anyhow, as you're in such a good mood, I'm going to ask you for a favor: I need off early tomorrow night. I got a big date."

With a scoff of disbelief, Madison walked past her without saying anything else.

Charlie Witt shuffled out of the Piano Showcase with a grin on his face and his head swimming. He always felt like this after playing for hours on end. He felt slaked and relaxed. He even enjoyed the dull ache in his fingers and the pang at the small of his back from slumping on the stool. Seventeen and pimple-faced, he'd been habitually passed over by the girls and so he hadn't scored yet. But he'd seen enough movies to compare how he felt right now to those moments after sex: weak in the knees, satiated to the bone, sleepy, and craving a cigarette.

After school, at least twice a week, he came to the Showcase, a large shop on the end of the new Frontier Mall on Canonsburg Street. The owner, Edward Holt, gave him free rein of his floor displays, which included a dozen glossy upright, electric, and baby grand pianos. Mr. Holt told Charlie that he did this for two reasons. First, as a music lover, he enjoyed listening to Charlie practice. He also liked to challenge Charlie, who could play just about anything that Mr. Holt threw at him. Then there was the other reason—business. Mr. Holt pointed out that Charlie drew customers every time he sat at one of the models. Sometimes Charlie even agreed to demonstrate for a floundering customer. He'd helped close the deal on three different occasions.

"It's called bartering," Mr. Holt said one day, while gently polishing a piano with a piece of fine cloth. "I let you play my instruments; you help me sell them. This way we both get something out of it."

Charlie unchained his bike from a street lamp and dashed off across the open parking lot. He hopped a ditch and then cut across a busy two-lane highway. Here were more small shops and a restaurant called Toots that served beer and buffalo wings to guys who rode Harleys and drove old pickup trucks. He'd just circled around the back of the building when he noticed a dog crawling into a tipped over trash can. He skidded to a stop, jabbed two fingers between his lips, and whistled.

After a startle, a shaggy golden retriever scrambled out from the trash can and looked at him, panting.

"Sam!" Charlie shouted. "There you are you, you mangy asshole."

Sam twisted his head left and right before he recognized the boy. Then he came bounding down the alley with his tongue flapping. Charlie hopped off his bike and let it fall on its side as he dropped into a squat and ruffled Sam's neck fur.

"I thought you were gone for good." Charlie shook his head and grinned as Sam licked at his face and nearly knocked him down. When Sam's tongue slapped across his mouth, Charlie shoved him back with a disgusted laugh. "Okay, okay. Enough of that."

For a moment the boy just shook his head and gave his dog a pitying but worried look. It wasn't the first time Sam had found a way out of the fenced-in backyard and run off. Usually he hung around the neighborhood, but this time he'd stayed gone nearly a week. Charlie had just about given up looking.

Sam put a paw on Charlie's leg, and the boy nodded. "Yeah, okay. Let's get you home."

He got up, dusted the dirt from his pants, then retrieved his bike. He didn't bother riding it because Sam would probably run off. Instead, he walked alongside it.

They'd gotten to the end of the alley when something struck him hard against the back of his head, sending his glasses launching from his face. He staggered, dazed. The blow surprised him more than it hurt. He let his bike fall to the ground and spun around in time to see a football go bouncing off at odd angles until it dropped into the ditch. Further up the road three kids howled with laughter. Charlie recognized them immediately: Bobby Horton, Tim Lemone, and Jack Killen.

"Aw, shit!" Bobby shouted, clutching the bulk of his fat belly and laughing so hard he could hardly walk. "Did you see that? I nailed the faggot! Right in the fucking head!"

Blood thudded in Charlie's ears as blind rage overcame him. He should run, but the football had scared him, and all he wanted to do was hit somebody. Next to him, Sam huffed and panted. The dumb dog failed to sense any danger.

"Oh, look at 'em," Tim shouted. "I think you pissed him off."

"Leave me alone!" Charlie shouted. It was the wrong thing to say. Never in anyone's history had that command done anything but worsen the situation.

"'Leave me alone!'" Jack Kilborn echoed, pitching his voice high like a woman's, balling his hands together and tucking them beneath his chin. "Leave me alone!"

"What are you gonna do, faggot?" shouted Bobby. "You gonna take us all on?"

The adrenaline responsible for jolting Charlie's system into fight rather than flight suddenly flagged, leaving him standing alone, defenseless and afraid. As the boys moved toward him, he scooped up his bike and ran several strides before he threw a leg over the seat and started to glide. He pumped the pedals a few times as he glanced over his shoulder to make sure Sam followed. But Sam stood where he'd left him, looking confoundedly at Charlie with something like a grin on his face.

"Goddamn it, Sam!" Charlie shouted. "Come on!" He saw Jack Kilborn, a wiry kid with a blond crew cut, sneaking up with a large flat rock raised above his head. "No, don't!"

Charlie braked hard and the rear tire fishtailed, spinning the bike around so he faced the others.

But it was too late. Jack threw the rock. Sam didn't see it coming. The rock struck the dog's rear, and Sam yelped and scampered back with his tail tucked between his hind legs, whimpering.

Charlie hurried over to his dog and dropped down beside him. When he saw blood in Sam's fur, Charlie snarled at the boys. Jack looked fidgety, his face burning crimson, obviously surprised by the success of his hit. Bobby and Tim cackled with laughter.

"You goddamn assholes!" Charlie shouted. He stood up and balled his hands into fists. "I swear to God I'm gonna kill you."

Whap! Once again someone hit him with the football. This time it smashed into Charlie's face. His nose snapped, and fire flashed across his brow and cheeks as his glasses toppled off. A violent surge of pain barreled through his nervous system and he clamped his hands over his face. He dropped hard onto the ground and felt the jolt of impact race all the way up his spine, slamming into his brain. His ears rang as he felt around in the dirt for his glasses. After a moment of searching, he found them. A crack now split the left lens in two. Over the thudding and rushing of blood in his ears, he heard peals of laughter from the boys.

Sam licked at his cheek, and Charlie shoved him aside and wiped the tears from his eyes. Undaunted, Sam came back.

"Come on, Sam," he said and picked himself up.

He stood his bike upright, then threw a leg over the seat and rode off. A few yards down the road, he looked behind him. Sam hurried after him, but his back leg gave him some serious trouble. He soon fell behind by several yards. Another ten feet and the golden retriever stopped altogether.

But not Charlie. He kept going.

"Sorry, Sam," he muttered as he turned his eyes to the road ahead. He lowered his head and pumped the pedals until the tires sang beneath him. He never looked back.

If he had, he would have seen Sam just standing there, watching, whimpering.

Cameron had been in no hurry to get back to the Calliope, but somehow he'd squandered half the day. It was already two o'clock as he stood at the front steps of the old gothic church. Hands in his jeans pockets and his satchel over one shoulder, he closed his eyes and tried to convince himself to go inside.

This is what you want. Time to put this thing to rest.

Feeling small in the shadow of the Calliope, he climbed the steps and tried the front door. It opened with an easy tug on the handle. He stepped into a dark foyer and heard music echoing throughout the building. He followed the sound to the central auditorium doors. He pressed them open and stepped inside.

An intensely dramatic music—he soon recognized it as Rachmaninoff's Symphony No. 3—crashed over him as he entered the warmly lit auditorium. He glanced at the rows of pews and red velvet curtains before turning his attention to the wooden stage, where an orchestra of maybe fifty musicians had gathered. Though the pews were empty, the musicians were dressed in formal attire, as if for an evening performance, and the lights glinted off their instruments as they charged into frantic riffs. A conductor stood before them, arms swinging as the musicians followed his lead.

Clearly this was the man who had approached Cameron at SilverReel Studios. Cameron drifted down the main aisle toward the stage, but stopped when he noticed something strange about the musicians. They were all so old. Brittle creatures with sallow faces and wispy-white hair. Faces composed of paper-thin flesh pulled taut over angular bones. They weren't just old. They were ancient.

Just then a man rose from his seat in the front row. He was old, bald except for wings of white hair above his ears. Light gleamed from his black-framed glasses as he stared at Cameron. The music created a dramatic soundscape. When the old man started forward, Cameron took a backward step and considered running away. But then the music stopped in mid-phrase, and Cameron looked up to find the conductor watching him from the edge of the stage.

"Ah, there you are," said Bloom, his deep voice rolling easily across the quiet auditorium. "So good of you to come . . ." he paused for emphasis, "Mr. Blake."

Cameron opened his mouth to speak when the old man put a hand on his shoulder. Startled, he looked around into a hard, craggy face, drawing in close.

"Are you him?" asked the old man, curling his lips away from his teeth in a scowling grin. "Are you the composer?"

Already climbing down the steps of the stage, Bloom interjected. "Mr. Kalek, please refrain from making our guest feel . . . uncomfortable."

Both Kalek and Cameron turned as the conductor marched up the main aisle toward them.

When he drew near, he offered a hand to Cameron and said, "I wish I had known you were coming today. I've been awaiting your arrival since you called me."

"I didn't know myself until the last minute." Meeting the man's gaze, Cameron felt something akin to a chill. He'd forgotten the intensity of those eyes, like a dark aura.

"Anyhow," Bloom said, gesturing with one hand at the auditorium about them. "Welcome to the Calliope."

Shuffling around in a circle, Cameron took a moment to look about the expansive hall, taking in its antiquated architecture, the pews, the balcony, the red curtains that draped the walls. He froze when his eyes fell again to the stage and the old musicians, all of them watching with quiet intent, like rats hiding in the shadows.

"This place has quite a history," Bloom said behind him. "It began as a church, during the last half of the nineteenth century. In the early fifties, the Calliope became a music venue for country western singers."

"That's very interesting," Cameron said flatly.

Bloom nodded slowly. "There's more. Indeed, we have a lot to talk about. For now, why don't we talk in my office?"

"Yeah," Cameron said and cleared his throat. "Terrific."

"Excellent. Please, follow me."

To Cameron's dismay, the door to Bloom's office was somewhere at the back of the building. This meant they had to mount the steps and pass through the orchestra, beneath the scrutiny of countless rheumy eyes and shriveled faces. Nonetheless, Cameron followed Bloom and Kalek onto the stage and into the gaggle of old timers. As they marched quietly along, a smell nearly stopped him in mid-stride. *Oh geez*, he realized, *I can smell them*. A sour smell. Utterly revolting. Forcing himself to continue, he held his breath until he passed through the tall door at the back of the stage.

Here, beyond the auditorium, were long, bright corridors with white walls and polished linoleum floors. The hallways reminded him of hospitals, or morgues, and Cameron kept close to his two silent guides. After a few turns, they arrived at a large office, warmly lit, with elegant furniture, thick burgundy carpeting, and oak wall panels. The walls were lined with leather-bound books, old oil paintings of orchestras, and various portraits. The scent of cigar tobacco lingered in the air. Across the room on the eastern wall was a large picture frame window; its brocade curtains were drawn and only a sliver of light entered beneath their trim. A large mahogany desk sat in the center of the room, its surface neat and tidy. Two leather armchairs faced it.

"Please, have a seat," said Bloom. He walked to the wet bar in the far corner, where he went about fixing drinks.

Easing into one of the armchairs, Cameron put his satchel in his lap and folded his arms over it. Kalek, meanwhile, took the armchair next to him.

"You've already met my personal assistant," Bloom said from the bar. "Mr. Kalek handles most of my financial provisions and so on."

The old man nodded at him, and Cameron forced a welcoming grin. The guy made him nervous with his intense, uncertain gaze.

"You know," said Kalek, "you and I have a great deal in common. Both of us have heard the Astral Music."

"No kidding?" was all Cameron could say before Bloom placed a glass of bourbon in his hand. The ice clinked as Cameron downed half of it, then sucked at his teeth as the alcohol coursed down his throat. Feeling better already, he sank back in his chair. "Sounds like a fine orchestra you got back there," he said, hoping to break the ice before wading into stranger territory. "But, if you don't mind my asking, why are they all so, well, old?"

Bloom glided around to the back of his desk and eased into a leather wingchair. "They may be old, Mr. Blake, but those are some of the finest musicians in the world." He gazed at Cameron with half-lidded eyes, quietly measuring him. "But we will talk about them later. For now, I want to hear why you decided to come to Holloway."

Cameron looked at him blankly. "You know why I came."

"Yes. But do you?"

Cameron shrugged. "The money helps. A hundred grand is a nice incentive." It wasn't the real answer. The money didn't mean that much to him; he had plenty. But he was determined to play his cards close to his chest for now. It didn't hurt to remind Bloom of their initial agreement.

"Yes, of course," the conductor said, with a knowing grin. "I'll be sure to deposit the money into your account this very evening, just as soon as you give Mr. Kalek the proper information. You can call your bank first thing in the morning."

"Don't worry. I will." Cameron hoped his face didn't express the gut-clenching anxiety he felt. Accepting that money meant locking into an unwritten contract with something he didn't yet completely understand.

"But surely Mr. Blake didn't come to Holloway just for the money," Kalek offered, his tone somewhat mocking.

"Of course not," the maestro answered, as he leaned back in his chair. His gray eyes studied Cameron over laced fingers. "So tell us the real reason then. What really brought you here?"

"You said you could help me compose the Astral Music. So I came to see how serious you are." Cameron shot Kalek a glance. "And let's just say, when I find a hundred grand in my bank account tomorrow, I'll know you guys are serious."

The maestro spread his hands and gave a consenting smile. "Point taken."

"Now, for starters," Cameron went on, "You seem to know a lot about Astral Music. What can you tell me that I don't already know?"

Bloom gave him a knowing smile. "We will get to that. But first you must answer a few of my own questions. I want you to start at the beginning. When did you first hear the Astral Music?"

Cameron swirled his drink, rattling ice at the bottom, then finished it off. In a thin voice, he said, "I was a kid. Six years old. I was in a car accident." He swallowed. His throat was already dry as he stared blankly at the far wall, picturing the scene in his head. "Doctors say I died. Exactly four minutes—about as long as you can go before you damage the brain. That's when I first heard it."

"What did it sound like?" asked Bloom, his voice strained and eager.

Cameron met his gaze. "Well, it's hard to describe. It wasn't exactly music. I didn't hear it with my ears. It had a distant, floaty sound and a slow rhythm, something between a whale song and wind chimes. Other than that . . ." he said with a shrug, "it only makes sense in dreams."

"Fascinating," said Bloom, eyes gleaming.

"You are very fortunate to have heard this," Kalek added.

"Fortunate?" Cameron gave a derisive snort. "I lost my whole family in that wreck. Hardly what I'd call fortunate."

The old man looked embarrassed. "I only meant–"

"Thank you, Mr. Kalek," Bloom interrupted, then looked at Cameron. "Over the years you've attempted to retrieve the experience. Tell me about that."

Cameron scratched the back of his head, feeling a little embarrassed and reluctant to go on. It sounded crazy, and worse, these guys seemed to just eat it up, without any pause or hesitation. With a deep breath, he said, "I forgot the whole experience for several years. It came back to me around the time I hit puberty. And again while in college. A professor suggested I write it down. So I tried, and I kept trying for the next ten years. I guess you could say it became an obsession."

His gaze dropped to the floor as a memory surfaced of Amber standing in the doorway to their bedroom, wearing a silk nightgown, her dark hair gathered at her shoulders. She'd had a few too many drinks. Her eyes were glassy, a look of complete detachment. *"I'm leaving, Cam. I can't take this anymore. You're scaring me. All you talk about is this goddamn music. I really think you need help."* Clearing his throat, he looked down into his empty tumbler, wishing he had another drink. "I never did manage to get it down on paper."

"Most everyone who has attempted this has shared the same problem," said Bloom. "The memory of the experience has a tendency to dissolve once it reaches the light of reason."

"But the dreams inspired other works," said Cameron, "like 'Hear After,' so I suppose it wasn't a complete loss. But then when my wife left me, things just started falling apart and so I quit trying. I couldn't do it anymore. I thought that I was going crazy. So I went and found work with the television studio."

"And you did that out of spite," Bloom offered.

Cameron shrugged. "I guess I did. SilverReel wanted nothing but garbage. Melodramas with a simple melody. So that's what I gave them. It felt wrong from the beginning. But it also felt good, like I'd liberated myself. Like I was getting back at God." He scowled. "The dreams went away after that."

Bloom stood, circled around to the front of his desk, and propped himself against its edge with his arms crossed over his chest. His eyes bored into Cameron's with a kind of evangelical fervor. "Since I was a young man, I've been interested in this phenomenon. I've devoted my whole life to pursuing this music that you have trapped in your head."

"So what is it?"

"The music you heard has many names: Music universalis. Shabda. Pythagoras called it the Music of the Spheres, believing that Earth was encapsulated by a number of glass spheres that moved against each other and, as a result, created music. Later on, Johannes Kepler took a more mathematical approach by suggesting that all celestial bodies of the cosmos correlate to harmonic, and thus musical, arrangements. A wide array of theories. But these philosophers all seem to arrive at one conclusion: the Cosmos is a kind of living symphony, a musical entity whose anatomy is composed of rhythm and vibration, melody and harmony, and at times, Discord. Every particle, every life, every galaxy is but a note in a great and divine symphony. This is what the ancient philosophers called Armonia. The Harmony of the Spheres."

Cameron blinked. That this music had a name made it all the more real for him. The word "Armonia" had an eerie sound to it, and it sent chill bumps rippling down his arms. Still, he sifted through Bloom's words like a man searching for seashells on a shore of rubble: weighing, considering, and ultimately discarding the lot of them. He said thoughtfully, "I think you forgot another theory, the one that argues that the 'Astral Music' is essentially a neurological mishap caused by head trauma—a kind of temporary cross-circuiting of sensory input. Maybe even a by-product of the brain shutting down."

"Oh, I don't believe that. And neither do you." Bloom looked at him soberly for a long, quiet moment. "You see, I believe there is something much deeper going on here. I believe the Astral Music reveals much more about the nature of reality than we at first realize."

"How so?"

"I think there are times when we get a glimpse of the true nature of reality. This is usually the result of a traumatic event, say a near-death experience. The intensity of this experience can cause a temporary distortion of perceived reality. Sometimes, in this moment of cognitive collapse, the person sees the universe for what it truly is: an illusion. What's more is that the essence of this illusion is vibration—a constant flux and flow of energy, moving in endless ripples, of waves and troughs, and ultimately, providing information for the senses of its observers. In other words, reality is a vibratory illusion. So then a person like you comes along with the insight to encode those vibrations into sound. At that moment something very special happens: a complete manipulation of the illusion."

Cameron's eyes narrowed and he shifted in his seat. He'd spent years investigating the Astral Music. But the stack of books he'd read all seemed to somehow miss the mark. Bloom, however, was starting to make sense, in a strange way. He could almost see where this was going.

"Among all those who have perceived the Astral Music, no one has come so close to recording the experience," Bloom continued. "But what you did with 'Hear After' reveals a special talent. I recognized it right away. It disappointed me to learn that you only tried this once. In my mind, that experience of yours was a veritable gold mine. You could have continued to exploit it. You could have written a thousand inspired symphonies. But you stopped. Which brings us back to why you came to Holloway."

Cameron wanted to hear more. He needed it. "Go on."

"You came because you believe that I can show you how to tap Armonia again."

A quiet pause filled the moments as Bloom and Cameron stared at each other without blinking.

"Well? Can you?" Cameron asked.

Bloom smiled. "I think it is time to show you a secret."

They left the office and followed the white corridors deeper into the Calliope until they arrived at a freight elevator with a metal lattice gate pulled across its opening. Kalek hurried forward and shoved the gate back. Scuffed-up planks of wood were bolted to the inside walls and floor of the elevator cab. A naked lightbulb hung from the ceiling. After the three men had stepped inside, Kalek drew the gate noisily closed and jabbed a button on the wall. A motor whirred somewhere as the elevator jittered and lowered them down into the earth until the air smelled dank. They came to a sudden stop. The doors scraped open and Kalek stepped out. Bloom motioned to Cameron, and he followed headlong into impregnable darkness.

Even in the pitch dark, Cameron knew that the basement was enormous. Following the loud clunk of a breaker switch, a twenty-foot wide ring of sapphire lights shone from the high ceiling.

Beneath them, sprawled in a wide formation across the chamber floor, was an army of strange creatures with black chitinous exoskeletons. The creatures came in all shapes and sizes, with spindly limbs and serpentine necks. They scuttled on their bellies and lashed their tails. Their bodies writhed with a palsy, while they hissed and mewed like wild animals.

"Jesus Christ, what are they?" Cameron whispered, his heart hammering in his chest.

But it was only an illusion. Nothing really moved. He'd mistaken motion for the flow captured in their form. These were musical instruments, fashioned from a bizarre vision, an art project dreamed up by H.R. Giger. They had casings of polished black metal, some with long serpentine necks. Others bore silver wires across their spines. They were formed into sleek shapes, with long, smooth curves and twisted designs. Some stood upright like men with broad shoulders and grotesquely elongated necks. Others lay on velvet-covered display plates. As for the arrangement, the instruments formed a wide circle maybe thirty feet in diameter with a wide clearing at the center. Cameron suspected the arrangement was deliberate; the instruments would stay in this circle when an orchestra decided to play them.

Wanting a better look, Cameron moved ahead into the chamber. The floor was made of a reflective black marble. His footfalls echoed into the far reaches of the basement as he walked. Bloom followed closely. They stopped just short of the ring of instruments.

"I've never seen anything like this," said Cameron, giving a bewildered shake of his head. "What are they?"

"Musical instruments, of course," Bloom explained. "They are called the Archetypes. There are fifty of them in the collection."

The ensemble included every type of instrument. Strings and woodwinds, brass and percussions—all grouped in sections. Cameron doubted if a single one carried a clean note. How could they, when the makers had forged them from the same shiny black metal? Obviously design had taken priority over functionality. "Where did you get these?"

"It wasn't easy. They are ancient relics. They've been kept secret by different orders throughout the centuries . . . I own them now," Bloom added, as if this explained everything.

They followed along the curve of instruments, finding each shape stranger than the one before it. Some looked like spiders, some like bundles of gnarled bone. Most of the time Cameron glimpsed familiar shapes underneath, but all of them were distorted in one way or another. Some were so odd that he couldn't place them. The flute section looked like a nest of large metal spiders, with spindly legs hooking out from central shafts. The clarinets were sleek black spears with stingers, and the oboes looked like great loops of fossilized serpents. Tubas were curled up dragons, and farther along were the violins and the smaller violas and violoncellos. These had long black necks stretched from the casings like hardened taffy. Beyond were squadrons of upright basses with demon-faced scrolls.

Cameron could only scratch his head over some instruments that looked like mutated conch shells and alien insects.

"Some say the ancient Greeks made them," said Bloom. "The Pythagoreans or Orphites, perhaps. But no one knows for sure."

Another step brought them face to face with a snarling creature. Cameron jerked back and nearly tripped at the sight, but it was only a piano. It spread before him, a large concert grand. Mounted over middle-C was the misshapen skull of something long dead, with big holes for eyes, narrow slits for a nose cavity, its grin lined with pointy teeth. Rather than the typical footprint design, this piano was shaped like a giant prehistoric bat that had been steamrolled, coated in lacquer, then mounted on four legs. A knobby spinal cord began at the base of the skull and traveled down the length of the piano's large case, partitioning the lid into two parts. Thin shoots of bone, like flattened ribs, sprouted from either side of the spine and fanned toward the far edges. Looking at the thing made Cameron's skin crawl, and he kept his distance, in case it decided to chomp off his arm.

"Christ, that's one ugly piece of work there," he growled, absent-mindedly clutching his chest.

"This one has a name," said Bloom. "It is called the Dragon." He gave Cameron another few moments, then started off again.

Cameron hurried after him and quickly fell in step. "What are they for?"

"No one knows for sure," said Bloom, moving onward. "But there are theories."

"Like what?"

Bloom stopped and pivoted around to face him. "That man could use these instruments to commune with God, if he had the necessary music."

Cameron snorted. "That sounds pretty farfetched, don't you think?"

Bloom didn't answer. Instead he continued on. Cameron followed him to a narrow pass that cut through the band of instruments and led them to the middle of the formation, a round clearing formed by the wall of instruments. The black marble tile and the size and shape of the clearing reminded him of an outdoor ice-skating rink he'd once seen. A podium sat at the center of the clearing. It was black and shaped like a three-tiered wedding cake, five feet across at its base and three at its top. From here the conductor would be able to command his orchestra at 360 degrees. An overhead lamp shone a direct beam down onto it, emphasizing its importance.

"You don't believe that, do you?" Cameron asked.

Over his shoulder, Bloom said, "I believe the instruments have powers that we don't yet understand."

They cut across the clearing. When they neared the opposite wall of instruments, Cameron saw a large circular object, standing at least ten feet high, with a green tarpaulin draped over it. It gave the impression of the world's biggest framed mirror.

"What the hell is that?" Cameron whispered.

With his hands behind his back, Bloom proceeded to the draped object. He stopped and folded his arms over his chest. "That is a very special instrument. It's a sort of harp—an Aeolian wind harp, actually."

"I've seen a wind harp," said Cameron, remembering when his dorm roommate, Chris, had brought one to their room. Little more than a hollow wooden box about three feet wide and strung with harp strings, Chris had kept it in the window for a few days until someone nearly knocked it off. "Only, the one I saw wasn't so big. It plays by the wind."

"That's right. The wind blows across its strings to produce music." Bloom gazed up at the thing and said in a quiet voice, "Unfortunately, I've never taken it outside, and so I don't even know if it works. If you stay long enough, I promise to show it to you."

The thing gave Cameron the creeps. Keeping his distance from it, he stopped and scratched the back of his head. "Why exactly did you bring me down here?"

Bloom faced him. "These instruments were created for one reason: to play the Astral Music. I worked very hard to acquire them. I also have a willing orchestra. The only thing I need now is the music. And that's where you come in. I asked you to come to Holloway because I need the Astral Music. That memory of Armonia is still trapped inside of you. I can help you get it out. If you let me."

Cameron gave a wry smile. "You know how crazy all this sounds?"

Bloom gave him an amused grin as he moved closer, putting the wind harp at his back. "Maybe it is. But aren't you the least bit curious about all this?"

"I wouldn't be here if I wasn't."

"Good. Then I think it's obvious. You want to uncover the truth just as much as I do. If that's the case, then you must trust me. You must let go of your beliefs—of what you think you know of reality. Ultimately, you must be willing to explore uncharted territory."

With his hands on his hips, Cameron turned and let his gaze sweep across the circle of instruments, taking it all in as he drew in the stale air and let it out in a single exhalation. "I don't know about this, Bloom. Seems a little farfetched. Talk like this could land us both in a padded cell."

"Oh, come on, Mr. Blake," said Bloom, stepping up beside him. "Where's your sense of adventure?"

"I left it upstairs. And I'm heading back there right now." Cameron started across the clearing.

Bloom didn't try to stop him.

When he reached the band of instruments, he moved carefully, not wanting to knock one over or cut himself on a sharp edge. As he approached the elevator, Kalek shot him a curious look, then searched for Bloom, who trailed not too far behind.

"You told me that you lost your inspiration," Bloom called after him. "You told me you'd do anything to get it back. Now I'm showing you the way. Give yourself to this orchestra, and I will show you the root of inspiration."

Cameron stepped into the elevator, looked at Kalek, and said flatly, "Take me up."

Chapter 5

Cameron felt a tremendous relief as he stepped outside to face the sun-blanched plaza. His eyes were slow to adjust to the light, so he took the steps carefully. At the bottom step, he turned, looked up, glad to be done with the brooding concert hall. Bloom had nearly dragged him into a dark fantasy, a fantasy that mirrored his own, only exaggerated, drawn out to its insane conclusion. Had he wasted his time coming here? The answer was no. Meeting Bloom and seeing those dark instruments with their nightmarish casings had forced Cameron to face the facts. He'd been chasing a delusion. This was where it must end. Maybe now he could finally move on.

Amber, you were right, he thought. She had hated him for this. She hadn't believed in his pursuit of mystical music. She'd thought that it was a sign of madness. Now he knew she was right. *Why didn't I listen to you? It was crazy, and you knew it.*

He turned his back on the building and started across the plaza, passing the penny fountain on his way to the entrance of Bard Street. He felt mentally exhausted and wanted nothing more than to return to his hotel room and lie down with the AC blasting. *I'll go and sleep this off and then I'll get the hell out of town and put all this behind me.*

With the plaza behind him, he followed Bard Street's downward slope but stopped when he reached the row of dumpsters on his left. He went to the nearest one and threw its lid back, scrunching his face when he caught a whiff of its rotten odor. A noisy cloud of flies buzzed about his head.

I can end this insanity, he thought, sliding his satchel from his shoulder.

He held it over the opened dumpster, but paused. *I can start over. Today. No more of this bullshit.* Still, his fist retained a firm hold on the strap. Could he throw all this away—handfuls of original compositions, stuff he could sell to SilverReel? His music journal? Did he even have the strength to let it go?

The answer was yes.

He let the satchel drop. It struck the bottom of the bin with a heavy thud. Slamming the lid shut, he backed away from the dumpster. A voice far back in his mind shouted, *Don't do this. Don't do this!*

He walked away, telling himself that what he'd done was necessary. With his hands shoved into his pockets, he let his feet carry him down the hill, passing the dark, vacant buildings, fixing his eyes on the end of Bard Street, fifty yards down the hill, where it opened into the square—and reality.

Just then he heard the purr of an engine. He turned as a black limousine left the Calliope's plaza and glided down the road.

Shit. Cameron turned his back on the car and continued toward the square. Only a few moments passed before the car rolled up next to him on his left. A rear window lowered, and Bloom's aged but handsome face appeared, framed in darkness.

"I don't understand this," said Bloom. "You yourself confessed your passion—your need—for the Astral Music. You can't walk away from us now. This is your chance to conclude the story that began with the death of your family."

Cameron stopped, allowing the car to roll on without him for several feet before braking. With his hands in his pockets, he stood watching the car as smoke billowed from its exhaust. Bloom was right. This had to end. But it didn't have to end like this. He'd already taken that first step by throwing away his music.

The car whined as it glided back. Moments later, Bloom was looking at him from inside the open window. "Perhaps a demonstration is in order," he said.

"A demonstration?"

"How else can I convince you? The Astral Music is real. My instruments . . . they are also real. If you let me, I will show you."

Cameron didn't answer right away. Bloom, retreating from the window, took this as unspoken consent. The door opened with a click.

From within, the conductor said, "Get inside, Cameron. Trust me."

Stage lights shone down on a darkly dressed trio of musicians. Pale-faced and somber, the three men stood motionless, waiting as they cradled shiny black instruments, bizarre versions of the clarinet, flute, and oboe.

In the Calliope's auditorium, seated several rows back from the stage, Cameron folded his arms over his chest, feeling uneasy but curious. After all, he'd come all this way, and leaving without so much as a demonstration would be foolish. At least, that's what he kept telling himself.

"What music are they going to perform?" he whispered.

Beside him, Bloom said, "In addition to my unique instruments, I also have a small collection of rare compositions. Astral Music. As I said before, you are not the first to hear, or to compose. What you must understand about the Astral Music is this: no two pieces are ever alike. The experience is completely subjective, and so the artist's rendition is essentially impressionistic. That means the music is as much the artist as it is the influence."

Black instruments shimmered as music—though not in any normal sense of the word—flooded the concert hall, impossibly quiet, expanding into a resonant soundscape. Warbled and slurred, the music echoed with whale songs, howling winds, wind chimes, and ocean waves. One moment Cameron heard the strangely human touch of chanting monks, the next, the drone of machinery. Unlike anything he'd ever heard. At least, unlike anything he'd heard while awake.

Sinking back in his chair, his mouth hanging ajar, he felt himself slipping into a waking dream. Behind closed eyelids, he witnessed a cosmic lightshow, plumes of liquid light, collapsing stars, the birth of planets.

I know this sound, he thought. *This is real. This is Astral Music. Jesus Christ, what have I gotten myself into?*

Behind the Calliope, Simon, wearing a dirty black suit, hunkered over the leather satchel on the grass before him. Half an hour ago, he'd followed Maestro Bloom's guest out of the Calliope, watched him throw the satchel into the dumpster, then fetched it out when the man had gone away.

He licked his lips and fumbled with the buckle until the strap came loose. His heart quickened. Before delving further, he raised his head and sniffed the air, scanning the grassy area, making sure no one had followed him. Aside from a few AC units whirring, he had the place all to himself.

For several years, he'd come here to this narrow patch of land, a private place beyond the back parking lot, overgrown with weeds and tall grass, flanked by trees. He needed places like these. According to Maestro Bloom, Simon drew too much attention to himself. He was large and clumsy, with a hairless head, deep-set eyes, and crooked teeth. Then there was his deformity. He'd been born without ears, but not without the ability to hear.

Maestro Bloom insisted Simon keep to himself—always—so Simon came here where no one could see, and sometimes he did things. Killed animals. Played with himself. Beneath the AC units he kept a box of skin magazines, a pocketknife, and a box of matches. His private place. No one knew about it. Not even Maestro Bloom.

Satisfied that he had his privacy, he looked inside the satchel. He grunted his disappointment when he found nothing but papers. He withdrew a handful. Handwritten music. Nothing special. Then he turned the bag over and shook it until all the papers inside fell out. Nothing but garbage. No wonder Maestro's guest had thrown it out.

He paused when he noticed an outer pocket. His fingers found the zipper and snagged it open. There was something inside. A small journal with a leather cover. He drew it out and flipped it open. His eyes became narrow slits. He recognized this music, the strange and wonderful phrases. Astral Music. Maestro Bloom had a bunch of it, but Simon hadn't seen it in a long time. And he knew why. The maestro kept it hidden because it was dangerous. At least, it was if you played it with one of the Archetypes.

A sudden guffaw escaped his throat. It sounded like a loon taking flight and it echoed into the woods behind the Calliope.

Something wet and sandpaper-rough slid across his cheek. Simon threw his hands over his face. His sluggish mind had a lightning quick thought. *He came for his music! He came to kill me! Punish me for taking it!*

But it wasn't Bloom's guest. He moved his hands. It was a shaggy golden retriever. It panted, a stupid grin on its face, its fur dirty and matted with blood. Simon had seen the dog around town, sniffing the trash bins, searching for food. It hadn't found much to eat. Its ribs were showing.

Simon got onto his knees and fetched the butter biscuit from his front pocket. The thing was mostly crumbs now. He'd discovered it in the same dumpsters where he'd found the satchel. Bloom kept him plenty fed, but he liked searching the trash nonetheless.

He held the biscuit out. The dog hesitated, licked its chops, then eased forward, careful at first, and then snagged the treat from Simon's hand. The biscuit disappeared in two chomps. Simon watched. He considered snapping the animal's neck, but then the dog surprised him by licking his face.

He shoved it away, but the animal came back, licking, desperate to thank him. The need to kill or maim went away. Instead, a laugh gurgled up from Simon's chest. Slowly, he ruffled the fur beneath the dog's chin. He heard the jingling of metal and read the dog tags.

Sam.

In his hotel room, Cameron woke from a deep sleep. It took several minutes before he remembered where he was. He recalled the private performance of a trio of musicians with alien instruments—music that had worked into his brain with almost hallucinogenic influence. The rest was blurry. He lay in bed for a moment, then got up.

An hour later he stood in the dark before the Bard Street Tavern. A neon-blue Pabst Blue Ribbon sign buzzed in its window. He climbed the low steps to the door that had been painted blue a hundred years ago, now chipped and showing wood.

He went inside and found a dark, narrow barroom, with brick walls, hardwood flooring, and ventilation ducting running along the ceiling. Across the room, a group of burly men in blue jean jackets with cut-off sleeves played a game of pool. Judging from their work boots, Cameron figured most of them worked at the nearby paper mill. Johnny Cash's "Ring of Fire" droned from the jukebox as Cameron made his way to the bar.

He found a stool among a row of men drinking quietly by themselves. An older man sat hunkered over the bar, a green John Deere baseball cap shoved down on his brown hair, yellow-tinted glasses hiding his eyes. He glanced indifferently at Cameron. No one said much around the bar. Just a group of men, sitting over their beers, like the loneliest people in America. Cameron felt right at home.

The bartender came over, wiping the table before him with a dirty dishrag. He had a long face with a thin nose and scraggly hair kept tied back in a long ponytail. Several of his front teeth were missing. "Get ya something?"

"Black and tan."

When the beer came, Cameron took a sip and turned on his stool. His gaze drifted to the far end of the room, which was cloaked in shadow. Letting his eyes adjust, he noticed a stage that ran along the back wall. Someone was sitting up there in the dark, a hulking figure with beefy shoulders, perched on a stool. The tip of a cigarette burned like an evil red eye and then faded.

Behind him, the bartender said, "You want another?"

Cameron blinked. He'd finished off his beer without realizing it. He turned and waved the bartender closer, then stifled a cringe at the smell of the guy's breath. "Who's that on stage?"

The bartender placed his elbows on the bar, his leathery face crinkled into a grin that deepened the lines around his eyes. "His name's Simon. Comes in and plays every once in a while. Sometimes he plays; sometimes he jus' sits there. I don't pay him, so I don't make him do one or the other. Still, I hope he plays tonight. He puts on one hell of a show."

There was something strange in the man's tone, but before Cameron could press him further, the man named Simon climbed down from the stage. The barroom fell silent. Almost everyone made an effort to avert their eyes, except Cameron, who spun around on his stool and watched. Simon weighed close to two hundred pounds, was bald, and had a thick neck. He slouched his shoulders and lumbered like a Neanderthal, and each footstep made a heavy thud. A nearby light revealed his chalky-white face, aged and creased, with drooping cheeks and slanted eyes. He had no ears, only holes where his ears should be. He stopped at the door and looked over his shoulder.

For one shuddering moment their eyes met. Cameron felt a sudden sense of dread, a kind of psychic impression, as if he were staring into the eyes of a monster. The feeling lingered long after Simon shouldered the door open and disappeared into the dark.

"Shame he didn't play tonight," the man in the John Deere hat said evenly beside him. He kept on staring straight ahead and drinking his beer, speaking to no one in particular. "Sure would like to have seen that."

"Hey, Bent, did you hear something?" Chief Dale Dunlap asked his partner, as he slowed his police cruiser to a crawl.

He had just turned onto Bard Street, a dead-end road that no one used much. Old buildings, nearly all of them abandoned, watched the road with vacant faces, with windows like empty eyes and doorways like yawning mouths. Only Bard Street Tavern, squeezed between two vacant buildings, still managed to keep itself going. A blue neon sign blinked in its window and a weatherworn awning formed an umbrella over its rickety front porch. Music filtered out from the bar's front door, but the chief felt certain he'd heard something else entirely.

Rolling past the bar, Dunlap thrust his head out the opened window and listened as warm air rushed against his face. He heard nothing but the rumble of his engine, echoing against the brick walls. After a moment he eased back inside and shook his head. "Sounded like a . . ."

Sounded like a scream, he'd almost said, but such a thing seemed careless to blurt out. Besides, he'd been jumping at shadows all night.

Sergeant Aaron Bentley, "Bent" to all his friends, sat forward, snapped off the radio, and listened, looking like an idiot in the green glow of the dashboard lights with his mouth hanging open. Both officers listened intently.

At fifty-six years old, Dale Dunlap still considered himself in good health and strong as a mule. Standing just over six feet tall, with broad shoulders and hands the size of cement blocks, people tended to trust his authority. But just lately he'd begun to feel his age, especially in the mornings when he'd find an old, weathered face staring back at him from the bathroom mirror. Moments like these also tested his age. He'd stopped trusting himself.

After a moment, Bentley shook his head. "I don't hear nothin', Chief. Probably just somebody . . ."

Dunlap held up a hand as he heard the sound again. Bentley flinched and sat back with a sour face. Holding his breath, the chief once again poked his head outside, listening. The cruiser topped the hill and entered the plaza where the Calliope's hulking silhouette expanded across the horizon. The chief braked and put the car into park, and both officers listened.

Dunlap had once considered the Calliope just about the greatest place on earth, back in the early fifties when country music singers performed a country music much different from present-day standards. It was almost too long ago to remember. For decades, the concert hall had slowly fallen into disrepair, a dive where anyone with a guitar could sing.

A ghostly squeal broke the silence—the sound of a pig getting its throat cut. Dunlap and Bentley both bristled, their eyes bulging.

"What the fuck is that?" Dunlap whispered. He leaned over the steering wheel to get a better look at the music hall. Several lights illuminated the top landing, causing the glass front doors to shine. A dark figure was standing on the top step. It was nothing but a silhouette, standing still, but Dunlap felt eyes boring into his skull.

"You know what that is?" said Bentley. "That's a violin."

Dunlap nodded, squinting to get a better look. "You see him up there? What's he doing?"

"I think someone decided to make a little music," Bentley offered.

Dunlap looked at him. Bentley stared back, both of them sensing something out of place. It was irrational that someone would stand up there in the middle of the night and serenade an empty plaza. A warm breeze wafted through the open windows, smelling of the river only a quarter mile beyond the concert hall.

For years, Holloway's legislation had squabbled over the concert hall's fate, beginning when Hal Barrett, the previous owner, had died in his sleep. Barrett had left the building to Fairfax County as a gesture of goodwill toward his hometown. But the blessing had quickly become a curse. Right away, some big questions had arisen. On one hand, a group had petitioned to put the Calliope on the state registry for historical conservation. This meant that the county would ultimately take full responsibility for the building's maintenance and upkeep. An opposing group had argued that such a feat would only burden taxpayers with restoration fees. It was in the county's best interest, they'd pointed out, to allow investors to purchase the building and keep it running. They'd finally settled on the latter. The Calliope went on the market. A decade passed, and she'd sat on the county's property books, draining the town's budget.

Then one day Leonin Bloom showed up. He'd bought the Calliope and thrown around enough money to send heads spinning. It was another year before Dunlap had met Leonin Bloom at a fundraiser, hosted by Mayor Finny and other big players within the community. Dunlap still remembered his first impression of the man. Cultured. Handsome. Intense. Like a politician. Maybe that's why the mayor had admired him so much. Maybe that was also why Dunlap had felt an intuitive disliking toward him. The one time he had done a little background investigating, he'd gotten a call from the mayor, instructing him to "mind his own goddamn business."

After that, Dunlap stayed away. After all, the bastard wasn't doing anything illegal; at least, nothing that he could see. Over the years, Bloom and his musicians had become more and more reclusive until no one ever saw them anymore. They'd inspired spooky stories, and a myth shrouded the entire group now.

And now the place was alive again.

"You know something?" Bentley said in a cracked voice, his face looking boyish in the dash lights. "That son of a bitch is giving me the goddamn creeps."

A chill suddenly scurried down Dunlap's back. He nodded, grabbed the gear shift, and jerked it into reverse. "Yeah," he muttered, jamming his foot to the gas pedal and sending the cruiser darting backwards in a tight curve. Shifted around and peering out the back window, Dunlap swung the cruiser around so that it faced the exit. He looked over at Bentley and tried to sound calm. "How 'bout we get the fuck out of here?"

Chapter 6

Cameron woke the next morning haunted by regret. His journal. He'd spent years filling its pages with otherworldly music, glimpses of dreams and death, only to throw it away just to indulge a single irrational impulse.

What was I thinking? My journal. My work. Those pages were filled with Astral Music. Rare. Powerful. And I just threw it away.

The thought ruined his breakfast at Dooley's, a little diner on the square. Afterwards, he walked directly to Bard Street, intent on retrieving his satchel, but when he reached the dumpsters, they were already emptied. He went inside the nearest shop to inquire.

He didn't like the answer he got.

The pain of loss followed him all the way to the Calliope, but once he stepped inside, he forgot all about it.

"Just tell me one thing," said Cameron, as he stood before the maestro's desk, leaning forward with his hands braced against the edge so he could look directly into the conductor's eyes. "What happens if we actually do this?"

Bloom sat back in his chair with both elbows resting on his desktop and the fingers of each hand laced together. He regarded Cameron thoughtfully for a moment. "I can't say for sure, Cameron. But isn't doing something for the sake of curiosity enough?"

"No. Not good enough." Cameron straightened and ran a hand over his jaw, where a five o'clock shadow was forming. "All my life this thing has haunted me. I've had this feeling, like I was supposed to hear that music so I could write it down. Then you show me the Archetypes. You say you know how to make it happen. But you still haven't told me why."

Bloom's eyes burned brightly. "To be honest, I don't have a reason for you. Why does man need to know anything? Why explore the stars or question the nature of existence? We do these things because we must. You and I have everything needed to solve a very old mystery. What is the Music of the Spheres? Who knows what the answer will yield? Maybe nothing at all. Or maybe it will reveal something extraordinary—an explanation of what we are and where we come from. Maybe even the nature of God."

Sighing, Cameron all but collapsed into the armchair behind him. He leaned forward and braced himself for the commitment he was about to make. Even though he'd convinced himself earlier that day this was the right thing to do, he suddenly felt wrong about it.

"Okay. To hell with it," he said. "I'm in."

"I am glad to hear that, Mr. Blake."

"It's Cameron," he said. "When do we do this thing?"

"I admire your enthusiasm. But I must warn you. We have a long road ahead of us. One does not tap the memories of the soul without certain preparations."

"What sort of preparations?"

"Attuning. You must first achieve a state of psychological and spiritual preparedness before you can compose Armonia. Not an easy task, I assure you. I have something that will help. But this will not happen overnight."

Cameron's shoulders sagged. He hadn't intended on staying in Holloway more than a few weeks. This only gave him more time to change his mind. "Shit, Bloom. I don't have all the time in the world. I've got a life. Bills to pay. How long are we talking about?"

"That all depends on you." Bloom spread his hands. "You must respect the gravity of our endeavor. We are attempting to mimic the rhythms, impulses, and vibrations of the universe. This won't be easy. But I do believe the rewards will be beyond anything we can imagine."

Cameron considered this quietly.

"Together you and I can achieve great things. But first you have to trust me."

"So when do we start?"

Bloom leaned back with his hands on his desk. "I promised you that I would help you tap your creative potential. That is precisely what we must do first. So tomorrow evening, you will join me for your first session. Call it a training exercise. As I already mentioned, I have something that will help you."

"What is it?"

Bloom smiled and whispered, "Inspiration."

Mr. Tom Farrell, Bernie High's music director, grinned eagerly when Charlie stepped into his small, book-cluttered office. An old man in a suit was sitting in a plastic chair to his left.

"Come on inside, Charlie," said Mr. Farrell from behind his desk. His smile vanished the moment he saw the boy's bruised face. "You hurt yourself?"

"Fell off my bike," Charlie said. Same excuse all day. He didn't feel like explaining how some assholes had thrown a football at him.

Mr. Farrell looked like he wanted to say more but then dismissed it. Instead, he waved a pudgy hand at the old man. "This is Mr. Kalek. He's the administrator with the Holloway Orchestra."

Charlie swallowed the lump in his throat. Until this moment, he'd thought that maybe someone had found out what he did with his free time in the toilet stalls during lunch period. He didn't know why he'd been summoned. But at least he knew it wasn't because of that.

"Nice to meet you, sir," he said to the old man.

"Sit down, Charlie," said Mr. Farrell. He was a beefy man with a pink face, and his flabby chin shook like Jell-O when he spoke. "We want to talk to you about something."

Charlie scuffled over to the chair and sat down. He put his hands in his lap and dropped his gaze to the floor. Adults made him nervous.

"Mr. Kalek, here," said Mr. Farrell, "came today on behalf of the Holloway Chamber Orchestra. Apparently, you've got their attention."

"That's right," Kalek added with a grin. He sat with his bony knees together and his briefcase in his lap. "Mr. Bloom has taken a great deal of interest in your skills as a pianist, and he wants you to consider coming to the Calliope and auditioning for a seat in the orchestra."

Before Charlie could so much as breathe, Mr. Farrell sat forward and said, "As you know, Charlie, this is a great honor. Until now, the Holloway Orchestra has kept its doors completely shut to outside musicians."

"Mr. Bloom has a strict philosophy when it comes to his orchestra," said Kalek. "He doesn't usually allow others into the group. But he's making an exception. And he has his eye on you."

"Why me?" said Charlie, meeting his gaze. He was sure Kalek had a few wires crossed.

"Why, because, well, because . . ." Kalek looked stumped for words. He looked over at Mr. Farrell for help.

"Because you are the best pianist this school has to offer," said Mr. Farrell. "And we are all very proud of you. I stand firmly behind you on this. So does the entire music department."

"Eh, Charlie," Kalek interrupted, "perhaps I could convince you to meet with Mr. Bloom. He will explain more to you. Here is my card." He handed a crisp business card to him. "I hope you will come by and talk to him. Today after school, if possible."

"Today?" said Charlie. His voice cracked with surprise.

"Why not?" Mr. Farrell asked. "Something more pressing, Charlie?" He laughed as if in on some joke.

"No," said Charlie. "I guess not."

It was nearly sundown when the taxi nosed its way into the open front gates of Orpheum Manor. Cameron, sitting in the backseat with his face pressed against the dirty window, gazed at the mansion sprawled across the hilltop like some mossy-stoned English country house. Its gray rock walls, interspersed with beams of red timber, rose up like shelves of broken earth. Its shingled peaks broke the canopy of the surrounding oaks and ash. The place cast an inky black shadow across the lawn, and the windows scattered across its facade were all dark and curtained.

As the taxi followed the driveway, Cameron noticed several more properties on the estate beyond the manor. The first two were wooden-framed guest houses, both modest in size and nondescript. Then he saw the soaring rooftop of a third structure, this one twice the size of the front mansion.

"What in the hell is that?" Cameron muttered.

"Oh, that? That's the old Beachum Sanitarium," said the driver, who until now had been content with driving in silence.

Cameron glanced at the rearview mirror at his driver. The guy must have been in his early fifties, but there was something undeniably childish about him. He wore a boonie hat pulled down to his ears, its strap dangling beneath his chin. He had a round, friendly face, with skin the color and texture of a crumpled paper bag, probably from having worked a lifetime out in the sun. He wore a threadbare Hawaiian shirt, and Cameron guessed, Bermuda shorts to match. "I didn't catch your name," said Cameron.

The man looked over his shoulder and smiled amiably. "Name's Buzz."

"All right, Buzz. What else do you know about this place?"

The man shrugged. "Aw, heck, just about everything, I s'pose. My mom used to tell me stories about it. Some doctor and his wife—she was a nurse—built the sanitarium after the Civil War. They wanted to rehabilitate wounded soldiers. Only problem was the tuberculosis outbreak. Killed a bunch of people, and they had to shut it down after that."

The driveway swung right and Cameron got a better look at the sanitarium, about a football field away. The massive, dilapidated structure looked like something out of a nightmare, a hulking building of brick walls and narrow windows. Its roof gave way to gables and dormers, where chimneys and stovepipes sprouted like blackened weeds. A covered porch, enclosed by busted railings, ran the length of its face, partially concealed by bushes and fir trees, giving it a brooding, haunted atmosphere, almost watchful.

The driveway ended in a cul-de-sac before the mansion, and Cameron lost sight of the sanitarium. He reached over Buzz's shoulder and slapped a twenty dollar bill into the man's hand. "Will that do?"

"Oh, that's more 'n enough." Buzz smiled and tucked the twenty into his shirt pocket, then plucked a card from it and handed it to Cameron. "Here's my number in case you need us. Me and my brother Kevin own the business together. Ain't a time of day one of us can't be persuaded to give you a ride. If I can't, Kevin will do it."

Cameron promised he would, got out, and watched as Buzz sputtered away down the long driveway. An uneasy feeling came over him, as if someone was watching him from one of the windows. Just as he drew a calming breath, the front doors of the mansion swung open, and Kalek stepped outside.

"Mr. Blake, we thought something had happened," said the old man. "I sent one of our limos to your hotel to pick you up, but you were already gone."

"You know, I avoid riding in limos," said Cameron as he tromped up the steps. "They make me feel like an asshole." He smiled playfully, but Kalek didn't seem amused.

"Please come inside." The old man turned on his heels and marched inside, leaving Cameron to stare after him with a faltering grin.

Cranky old bastard, he thought as he stepped inside. He stopped just inside the foyer, mouth gaping as he turned in a circle and took in the high ceiling, tall windows, and staircases that reared up to the next floor. The mansion seemed even bigger inside. There were a number of servants drifting about, but they paid him no attention.

They moved deeper into the house, working their way along the western wing until arriving at a tall oak door. Kalek tapped on it twice and swung it open.

They entered into a dimly lit study, a large room carpeted with Persian rugs and furnished with Victorian chairs, tables, and cabinets made of black walnut, bog oak, and rosewood. Then there was the clutter: a rich array of art and collector's pieces, a suit of armor, a marble statue of a Greek goddess, oil paintings on easels, which shared the walls with bookshelves. And finally, a piano.

Among the treasures, Bloom, overdressed as usual, sat at a round table at the center of the room. He didn't bother getting up.

"Mr. Blake," he said, raising up from his chair. He smiled and motioned to an empty chair. "So good of you to come. Please have a seat."

Kalek nodded, and Cameron moved ahead, glancing about him as he took a seat at the table. His eyes fell to a polished wooden box beneath Bloom's folded hands. The box looked like a humidor. A small stack of paper and a pen lay next to the box.

"Quite a setup you have here," said Cameron.

"As you already know, I am a passionate collector."

Cameron wondered, *How the hell does he pay for all this?*

"I hope you are enjoying your stay in Holloway so far?"

"It's fine. But I'm ready to get to work."

"Yes, of course," said Bloom. "I assure you, we all are. And today is our first step in that direction. Somewhere inside of you is the memory of Armonia. All we have to do is find it and bring it to the surface."

"So how do we do it?"

"We must first exorcise the demons," said Bloom, smiling mischievously.

"Sounds painful," Cameron said, trying to keep things light. It didn't work. His gaze fell to where Bloom laid his hands over the wooden box.

"For many years, I have been searching for a Tone Poet, that is, someone like you who has touched Armonia, the vibratory center of all things, and whose astral body, as a result, resonates with those divine vibrations."

Cameron blinked. The *Music Makers* article had also referred to him as a tone poet, in an entirely different capacity, of course. He put his hands up. "Slow down. Astral body?"

"Put aside your beliefs and consider this. Every person has a soul, or astral body, which in turn resonates with its own vibratory pitch. Think of this as your own personal energy field."

"I got it. I think. So you're saying that my . . . soul . . . resonated at a certain frequency when I came into contact with . . . "

"Armonia. Yes." Bloom held up a finger. "But a problem presents itself. The astral body cannot hold that resonant vibration for long. Over time, the experience wanes, becomes buried beneath discordant impressions. This is certainly the case with you."

Cameron snorted. "That's an understatement."

"Yes. Your soul is plagued with Discord, and this creates interference.

The astral body cannot remember its resonant state at the moment it came into contact with Armonia until you have harmonic balance."

Cameron nodded. "So what do we do?"

"We compose Nocturnes."

With a cold grin, Bloom spun the wooden box around and opened its lid. Lying across a crumbled bed of midnight blue velvet was a tuning fork, seven inches long, made from a bronze-like alloy. Two delicately sculpted snakes with fine scales and rubies for eyes were curled about its two prongs.

"The Tongue," said Bloom. "A unique instrument. Most tuning forks produce tones by which a musician tunes his instrument. This fork, however, produces a tone by which the musician tunes himself. This is called Attuning."

Swallowing around a dry throat, Cameron studied Bloom's face, while alarms rang in his head. *Attuning? God, this is crazy.*

"You see," Bloom went on, "certain sounds, properly chosen, can actually heal the astral body. Each session with the fork will bring you closer to inner harmony. And once you have Attuned, you will never be the same again. You will know how to hear the universe, and when you can do that, you will hear the music of God."

Cameron chewed the inside of his cheek. The fork looked ominous in the candlelight, somehow pagan. He could almost hear it ringing, but that must have been his imagination. "How long will this take?"

"Who can say? Seven sessions at least—one session for each chakra. But it may take more than that. Ultimately, it will rely on you."

Chakras. Cameron knew a little about those. Imaginary energy points. New Age hocus-pocus. He decided not to press the subject further for now.

The maestro plucked the fork from the velvet and held it between his thumb and forefinger, allowing the light to glint off its edges. Cameron's eyes went to it.

Kalek got up from his chair and went to the windows and began drawing the curtains. One by one, the windows were draped, and the room became darker and darker, until Cameron could hardly see the man sitting across from him. Soon, Kalek returned, struck a match, and lit a candle at the center of the table.

"Gentlemen, I apologize," said the old man, looking from the maestro to

Cameron with jittery eyes, "but I must be going. I will be nearby if you need me." He crossed the room and then back-stepped through the French doors while drawing them shut. Before disappearing altogether, he said, "Good luck, Mr. Blake." Then he was gone, leaving Cameron and Bloom alone at the table.

Cameron cleared his throat. Kalek's hurried exit gave him an uneasy feeling. All about the room, the candles sputtered and danced.

"Please, take this now." Bloom handed him the fork.

The instrument was much heavier than he'd anticipated. He held it by the stem, allowing the candlelight to gleam against its intricate metalwork. The serpents coiled about its prongs seemed animate. He felt the buzz of electricity work its way down his arm. "So how does it work?"

The maestro sat back in his chair with his arms crossed over his chest. "Once you strike the fork against a solid surface, it will begin ringing. In turn, it will force your astral body to sympathize with its peculiar tone. When this happens, the Attuning process will begin." Bloom leaned forward, his eyes wide with excitement. "By its very nature, the Tongue has certain . . . consequences. As the soul begins to harmonize, it will reject Discord as something . . . abject. Once this Discord reaches the light of consciousness, it will have a sound, and it must be written down. Write it down and be free of it."

The fork emanated strong pulses down Cameron's arm. He laid his left hand flat on the stack of blank music sheets.

"So let's begin, shall we?" Bloom's brow darkened and he said, "Tap the fork." When Cameron hesitated, the man leaned forward, bared his teeth, and hissed, "Tap it!"

Swallowing the lump in his throat, Cameron closed his eyes. He ignored the rabid instinct to put the fork down. He'd come too far to turn away now. If there was any truth in all this, he'd find out soon enough. He held his breath and struck the tuning fork against the edge of the oak table.

A sudden metallic skirl, like microphone feedback, rang from the small instrument. He nearly dropped the fork as several more tones rang impossibly at once. The sound filled him with something dark and corrupt.

The buzzing of houseflies. Screams of pain and anger. Sorrowful sobs. A terrific ache thrummed in his head, causing his teeth to rattle in their sockets. Blood spilled from his ears and nose. Pressure swelled at the base of his skull, threatening to crack it open.

Cameron clenched his teeth, groaned. He dropped the fork and it clattered to the table. *Oh God, help me!* Then another thought: *This is why Kalek left in a hurry. So he wouldn't have to hear this.*

A cold darkness spilled into the room, snuffing out the candle flame, and throttling him with a bout of rabid depression. Fantasies of suicide raced through his mind. He imagined slitting his wrists with a rusted razor blade. He saw himself hanging from a rope, his feet kicking beneath him.

"Your soul wants to resonate with the fork," said a far-away voice. "Let it!"

Cameron felt his thoughts dissolve. He was only a small boy, alone and frightened, and sitting on a bench before a massive black piano. He looked down at the piano keys. He didn't know this piano, and he was too short for the stool. Catching his breath, he looked around the antiquated room. Shafts of moonlight angled in through tall windows and painted blue rectangles across a marble floor. There were paintings on the walls and bookshelves lined with dusty books. A dark fireplace yawned open like the mouth of a corpse. How had he gotten here? Where were his mom and dad? In his growing confusion, he felt the touch of eyes on the back of his neck. Oh God, he was scared. Mom and Dad and Brent—they were all gone, weren't they? They'd died and left him alone.

Wood creaked. Standing on the back of the piano was a small boy with thick blond hair. It was Brent, his older brother. He knew that without having to look. But he looked anyway. Brent wore the same shorts and t-shirt that he died in. Blood was still splashed down his front.

"Go on and play something, Cam," said Brent. He sounded mad. He had every right to be. "That's what you're supposed to do, isn't it? Well, isn't it?"

Cameron's eyes widened with a sudden flash of inspiration. Music would make the nightmare go away.

He closed his eyes and began playing. The music came easily, a sad, aching melody, somehow familiar, somehow connected to his body. Playing it was like lancing the poison from an old wound. He gave himself freely to it, and with every note, he felt the release of ancient pressures in his chest.

This is me. These are my bones. My pain is music.

Icy cold fingers touched the back of his neck. Cameron snapped his head around to find his mother standing next to him, wearing her burial dress, her head grotesquely swollen, the way she'd looked while lying in her coffin.

She whispered, "You remember the song, don't you, Cam?"

Panic gripped him. "No, I don't remember it, Mom! I can't remember!"

Brent, still standing atop the piano, spoke up, "But you have to remember."

"I didn't do it, Brent. It wasn't my fault. I didn't want you to die!"

Just then the wood cracked like thin ice beneath Brent's feet, and he dropped into a splintered hole on the back of the piano. As Cameron watched, the hole filled with blood that sloshed over the edges and ran in rivulets along the top of the piano.

Cameron sobbed—it was an old pain, one he'd kept bottled up for a long, long time. Again, a hand touched his arm, but this time it was Bloom who shook him and then pressed a pen into his hand. They were both seated at the table. He hadn't moved at all.

"That's it, Cameron," Bloom whispered urgently. "There is your inspiration. Now write, damn you. Write!"

Cameron blinked, disoriented, sluggish. His eyes raced to the piano, over by the window. But how?

"Do as I say," Bloom hissed.

Cameron looked down at the blank music sheets scattered before him. He suddenly realized that he didn't want to compose. The idea frightened him. He shook his head and stifled tears. "No. I can't. Please, don't make me."

"Do you want this nightmare to end? Then write the fucking thing down!"

It seemed wrong. Those dark feelings had no place in the real world, even if only in the form of music. Still, the sound was rattling around in Cameron's head, and he had a feeling that it would just go on and on if he didn't obey Bloom.

Finally, Cameron set the fork on the table, picked up his pen and a handful of paper, and started writing.

Gold capped the treetops as the sun plunged beneath the horizon. Thunderheads the size of blue whales rolled in, as if they'd been waiting for the sun to go down before starting any trouble. Hob could smell the coming rain in the air. It was nice.

He rocked somberly in his rocking chair on his front porch, which he'd built himself the summer before last. His Gibson guitar rested quietly in his lap. As a steady breeze rushed at him, bringing with it the smell of pine, he walked his fingers along the fretboard, playing a lick that expressed the bittersweet passage of the sun. The small Guerrilla amplifier at his side threw the rusty sounds across his yard.

In the dying light, Boots Bailey's heavy silhouette came strutting across Hob's weedy lot. Boots wore his familiar khaki pants and cotton shirt, rolled up to the elbows. He was heavy-set, with an ashy face and graying hair. He carried his guitar with one hand and a bottle of Jack Daniels in his other.

Son of a bitch remembered to bring the juice this time, thought Hob as his fingers skittered up the fretboard. Wednesday night jam sessions had become an unspoken tradition for the two since Clara had passed away in the summer of 2007. Boots would come over, and the two would play out on the front porch every Wednesday night. But both of them were getting on in their years, and recently they seemed to cancel more sessions due to health complications. Either it was Boots's hemorrhoids burning him up so he couldn't sit still or Hob's arthritis drawing up his fingers. It was a sad and sobering realization. They were getting old.

Sometimes they hardly said a word to each other and just played. Boots didn't bother with saying hello when he thudded up the creaky porch steps and settled into the chair next to Hob. Boots didn't have to ask him if he wanted a drink. That was understood. Boots splashed three fingers of Jack into the glasses that Hob had set out for them. Hob kept a bottle in the cabinet beneath the sink for the few occasions that Boots forgot his. With a glassy clatter, they made a silent toast and drank. Then Hob returned to the lick he'd been fooling with, and Boots joined in neatly with his impeccable ear. For a while, the corner of West Cheatham Street and Moonlight Drive echoed with their somber and gritty sound.

When an hour or so passed, Hob leaned his guitar against the wall behind him and gazed pensively out at the old houses across the street of the lower-end neighborhood. At one time it'd been all right, but now most of the homes had fallen into disrepair. Ronny Wood, his neighbor across the street, hadn't cleaned his yard or mowed the grass in several months. There was an old jalopy sitting on blocks in the corner of the lot, with weeds grown all around it.

But Hob wasn't thinking about the state of the neighborhood or about calling up Ronny about neglect. Instead, his mind returned to that strange fellow he'd met at the Calliope. Cameron Blake.

"Know what tomorrow is?" Hob asked in a rusty voice.

Boots shrugged. His chocolate-colored skin sank him easily into the shadows, while his thick-rimmed glasses reflected the glowing tip of Hob's cigarette. "August seven, I s'pose."

"That's right. August seven. The day Clara left this earth, God rest her soul."

Boots set his guitar down. "That so?" He shook his head and tut-tutted sympathetically.

Hob shook his head. "All these years gone by an' I still ain't got over her."

"Well, Clara was a good woman," Boots said, as if that explained it all. And in a way, it did.

Drawing from his cigarette, Hob winced as a curl of smoke burned at his eyes.

"You believe in ghosts?"

Boots' eyes widened in surprise. "Say what?"

"I was scrubbin' floors at the Calliope when I heard music from the auditorium. Wasn't nobody supposed to be in there, so I went to check it out. The closer I got, the more familiar it sounded. I thought to myself, 'No, I'm just makin' shit up.' So I stopped and listened, and you know what I heard?"

"Not a clue."

"Somebody was playin' one of Clara's songs. 'The Color Blues'—you remember the one?"

"Well, sure I do," Boots said with a nod. "Played it right here on this porch a thousand times."

Hob nodded and rubbed the goosebumps from his arms. "Clara wrote that song. Hell, we sort of wrote it together. She sang it nearly every show."

During the last ten years of Clara's life, before cancer had turned her belly into one big tumor, Clara and Hob had traveled as a small band. They played two or three shows a week, on the road from Charleston to Atlanta and sometimes all the way out to Austin. Clara had a smoky voice, and she felt every note. Hob played the guitar. Sometimes he sang too. Stephano "Biz" Wheaton played the keys.

"At first I thought it was a ghost. You know how that place can be. Then I just figured it was somebody who knows me and wanted to mess with my head some. Even thought it might be you. So I crept over to the stage door and cracked it open a bit, so I could get a better look. Well, this cat . . ." Hob shook his head, "I ain't never seen him before. A white boy. He didn't know I was there, neither. I scared him shitless. Guy jumped so hard he fell off the bench and busted the shit out of his head."

"Damn!" Boots said, cackling and slapping his knee.

"He did too," Hob went on. "Damn near cracked his skull open. Thought he was gonna have a concussion."

The two laughed at this for another moment before Hob became somber again and looked at Boots's white eyes, now seeming to float in the dusky dark. "But when I asked him where he'd learned the song, he just looked at me like I was crazy. Said he couldn't remember what he was playin'."

Far away, thunder rolled, a muffled sound, ominous, but somehow comforting. They both turned their heads, gazing out at the darkening sky. It had gone a bruised color, with yellow around the edges.

Boots sighed and shoved his glasses up the ridge of his nose with a finger.

"You know, I bet that fella heard it at one of Clara's shows. You guys got around back in the day."

Hob shook his head quietly. "Man, I don't think so." He looked at Boots. "You know what I think?"

His friend said nothing for a long moment, but his eyes were wide and alert. "Oh, I suppose you gonna say somethin' like it was her."

"You damn right. It was her, Boots." Hob gazed out at the starless sky. "She's tryin' to tell me somethin'."

Boots quietly drew from his cigarette. "You start talkin' like that and before long you gonna start believin' it. That old girl's been gone a long time."

"Don't matter. I know what I heard." Hob splashed some more whiskey into his glass and gulped it down with a grimace, then said it again, this time to himself. "I know what I heard."

"Fat whore? Fat whore?" Carrie Belle muttered to herself as she hurried down the dark sidewalk, head bent against the rain that fell in gray sheets. She stayed close to the shops; every now and then she caught a break beneath an awning, but it was too late to stay dry. The storm had come fast and hard. Puddles had already started forming on the sidewalks, reflecting the glow from the streetlamps. Caught without an umbrella, she now found herself completely soaked, with mascara running down her cheeks and her hair matted to her face.

But she didn't care. She was beyond caring about anything. At least she didn't have to hide her tears. The rain took care of that.

She said it once more, just to test and measure the sound of those two words—just to relive the sting of embarrassment. She couldn't believe that he'd called her that. He knew how sensitive she was about her weight.

I hate him, she thought. *I've never hated anyone so much in my life.* She considered going back and spitting in his face. She should have done that the first time and saved her drink.

The rain came down harder. There was nothing left to do but trudge onward and get to Karma Koffee as fast as she could. That's where she'd find her friends, people who loved her, who would never call her such awful insults.

The rain had started two hours earlier, around the time Carrie Belle and Jon had sat down for dinner at the Lemon Tree, the nicest restaurant on the square. This had been Jon's treat, a special date, and it had started out so nicely, with candlelight and soft music. But then they'd moved on to drinks—vodka martinis. These came and went quickly. Both of them got fairly sloshed after their third. She'd been comfortably buzzed when Jon leaned forward, touched her hand, and asked something he'd never asked before.

"So tell me, how many guys have you been with?"

Carrie Belle had nearly choked on her drink. She'd blushed, refused to talk about it, but after he pushed and prodded, she relented. "Eight guys," she'd said, although that wasn't exactly true. There might have been a few more. But it all sort of depended on what you what you counted as sex and what you counted as just old-fashioned fooling around.

The conversation had been fun at first, sort of sexy, too, and Jon kept pressing her, smiling all the while. He wanted to know who she'd slept with and when, about the crazier places she'd done it. She even confessed to the time she and Roger Doolittle had gotten it on behind the bleachers during a Bernie High football game. She'd never told that to anyone.

The whole time she talked, Jon had acted like it was no big deal, like it didn't bother him at all, and she'd felt sort of liberated with talking about it. She should have seen the trap he so carefully set. The more she divulged about her sex life, the redder his face got. Then came an unpleasant gleam in his eyes and an edge to his voice. Of the eight boys she'd been with, she'd only told him the names of seven. Then she'd gone and mentioned Cooter, something of which she was not very proud. The conversation soured.

"Cooter Scruggs?" Jon had nearly come out of his chair. "You let that piece of shit fuck you? Gaw-damn!"

He said that last word with such disgust that she'd felt like crying.

For a moment she just sat there, stunned, her mouth hanging open, as if he'd just slapped her in the face. She knew Cooter's reputation. He treated girls like pigs. She'd heard all sorts of stories about blowjobs in the boys' restrooms. She figured Cooter told stories about her too. But what did she care?

"I can't believe you fucked him," Jon said it loud enough for the old couple sitting at the neighboring table to hear and cast them nasty looks.

Carrie Belle reacted without thinking. Suddenly the rest of her martini went right into his face. Everyone turned around then, a hundred eyes, gaping with something between shock and amusement. She'd been so humiliated, and it must have been the embarrassment that pushed Jon over the edge, causing him to stand up, knock his chair over, and shout, "You're nothin' but a fat whore!"

Everyone in the restaurant heard him. There were gasps and even a few giggles. Carrie Belle had burst into tears and went running out of the restaurant. She'd never been so humiliated in all her life.

The sky rumbled and she wiped her face. The night had gotten even darker, and now she was wet and cold. "I guess it's over then," she sobbed. They couldn't get back together, if only as a matter of principle. When lightning flashed, she looked to her right, just beyond the coffee shop. Bard Street. She saw a neon light buzzing in a window. A drink sounded better than coffee.

She splashed over to the mouth of the narrow road, where rain spilled in rivulets from the cornices of the old buildings. Bard Street was dark, with only that single light buzzing away. She knew the place. The Bard Street Tavern. She'd never been there before, but it was obviously open.

She stomped up the rickety front steps. At the door she hesitated, but then heard music, and laughter too. She shoved the door open and went inside.

Everyone looked at her when she closed the door behind her. It was quiet and dark. Cigarette smoke gathered around the dim ceiling lights. A few men sat at the bar along the far wall. Three men stood docilely at the pool table. There weren't any women around, but this didn't bother her much as she shook off the rain and crossed the creaky wooden floor toward the bar.

She sat at a corner barstool and began rummaging through her purse until she found a crumpled pack of cigarettes. After stuffing one between her lips, she tried lighting it, but her hand shook so violently that she couldn't get the flame to its tip.

Finally, a fist reached out from the other side of the bar, and a small flame leaped from it. Carrie Belle looked up and met the bartender's watery eyes, and then leaned forward until fire glowed from the tip of her Marlboro.

"Thanks," she said thinly, exhaling a cloud of smoke. Nervously, she scanned the place. They were all still looking at her. It scared her. They seemed somehow expectant. "Can I get a Crown and Coke?" she asked quietly.

The bartender planted both hands on the bar and regarded her with a cold gaze. His face was dry and wrinkled. A rubber band kept his long greasy hair out of his face.

"Please?" she added bitterly.

He turned away. She blew a cloud of smoke and became suddenly aware of the prying eyes of several men. She threw a quick glance over her shoulder.

Someone at the pool table struck a chair with his stick and shouted, "Cocksucker!" His opponent responded with a wild cackle.

The bartender returned with her drink and slid it to her. She frowned at it: it was a shot of whiskey and not the drink she'd ordered. But before she could say anything, the man leaned forward, lips drawn into a sneer. "Drink up and get the fuck outta here."

Carrie met his cold stare. She felt suddenly vulnerable. "W–why? Did I do something wrong?"

Just then a light came on at the far end of the barroom. She spun around on the stool for a look, but her purse spilled from her lap. Bottles of makeup rolled across the floor.

"Goddamn it!" she hissed and dropped down from the stool. Squatting, she scooped up her things—lipstick, eye shadow, tissues. A tube of lip gloss had rolled beneath the bar, and she reached for it when a sharp, high-pitched squeal cut through the room's silence.

She turned and looked across the barroom where an overhead light shined down on a small stage where a man sat perched on a stool. A drab gray suit hung loosely from his meaty frame. Not a single hair sprouted from the dome of his head. He was old, but his face had a plump, almost childish look to it. Carrie Belle wondered if he had some sort of mental impairment, like Down syndrome. Even stranger was his instrument. He held it like a violin, with one end tucked beneath his flabby chin, and the opposite end pointing away from him. But she'd never seen a violin like this. The thing looked like it was sculpted from black glass, with a grotesquely stretched neck that tapered into a curlicue at its end.

Carrie Belle swallowed nervously. She wanted to leave, but something kept her from following her gut instincts. Maybe it was the alcohol;

maybe it was her fight with Jon. Whatever the reason, she climbed back onto her barstool, scooped up her shot, and downed it with one swallow. The whiskey boiled in her stomach and made her ears ring. She felt better already.

The musician played a kind of squeal that reminded her of the mood-setting music in a horror movie. The sound rose like a bottle rocket and hung there in the air, startling her and forcing her to look at him. Sitting alone like an ogre, his apish frame too big for his stool, the musician swayed as he sawed at the strings with his bow. He conjured a slow melody that reminded Carrie Belle of someone crying. She was so moved by the music, she caught herself tearing up.

He called me a fat whore, she thought. *I can't believe he called me that.*

Brushing the tears from her eyes, she looked for the bartender, hoping to ask for another drink. She found him standing at the far end of the bar, watching her. She didn't like the way he stared. Refusing to let him scare her off, she raised her empty glass and shook it. When he came over with her drink, she drank it down in one swallow.

For a moment, the world went away, and there was only Carrie Belle and the musician. She felt a sudden empathy for the man; felt sorry for him and disgusted with herself for thinking that he looked ugly. She'd failed to see his inner beauty. That was her problem—she chose the men in her life based on their looks, instead of their hearts.

I'll never make that mistake again, she thought.

The music comforted her, warmed her bones. She thought how ironic it was to find such sweet music in a such a dive.

A sob escaped her throat. She bit her lips, feeling embarrassed, fighting like hell to keep from breaking down. Not here. Not with all these men watching her. They would think she was weak. And fat. And a whore.

The bartender returned with another shot of whiskey, and she drank it without taking her eyes from the man on stage. Her head was spinning now.

"Wanna dance?" someone whispered in her ear, his breath reeking of sour beer and cigarettes. She turned and faced a tall man in his early forties with a sallow, angular face of hard ridges. He had ratty brown hair swept back from his brow, and hands that looked like slabs of rock.

"You want to dance to this?" she asked mockingly, snorting a laugh. "It's not exactly disco."

As she spoke, the music grew more sluggish, unnaturally sluggish, oozing like liquid rubber. The room tilted and she swooned on her stool. Catching herself, she shook her head and forced her eyes open.

"It'll dance," said the man.

She got a better look at him, jaundiced eyes, crooked yellow teeth. With her head swimming, the man's face came in and out of focus. He was almost handsome. With a little shrug she threw her arms up and said, "Fine then. Let's dance!"

She all but fell into the man's arms, and he scooped her up and spun her around, until both of them stumbled into the clearing before the stage. She closed her eyes as the room spun about them. Round and round they went as the strange music grew louder. The idea of dancing to this music struck her as absolutely hilarious. She threw her head back and laughed as the music slowed and slurred. In her delirium, she found herself ravishingly turned on. She bit her tongue and leaned forward to kiss her stranger.

He pressed his lips against hers, then slipped his tongue inside her mouth. "That's it, bitch," he whispered, grinning. "Let's dance."

The music lurched and then sank even lower, and Carrie imagined the music as a kind of tar, gooey, sticky. It made her giggle uncontrollably. But then her dance partner whirled her around in one direction, and then the other. They were dancing, she supposed, although it felt more like she was riding on the Tilt-A-Whirl. When her partner buried his face into her breasts, she threw her head back and moaned. Only vaguely did she realize that the others in the bar had formed a circle around them. The lights from the stage glistened on their sweaty brows. Their eyes were dark and hard and hungry.

Let them watch, she thought. She wanted them to watch, and just for fun, she jerked off her blouse and threw it over her head.

The men roared a cheer.

From miles away, she felt her partner bite into the nipple of her left breast. Then he hefted her up, and she wrapped her legs around his thighs. He held her aloft, giving her a kind of bird's eye view of the entire bar. A man standing nearby dropped his jeans around his ankles and clutched his dick in one gnarled hand. He gave it a few violent pumps as she watched. The guy next to him did the same. But then their faces melted into a collective blur as her stranger spun her around again. She could smell the men around her—not just their cheap cologne and cigarette breath, but something more, something almost animal.

The music melted into a smear of notes and the lights followed suit, becoming soft and gooey, dissolving into colored streaks. The song rose to a warbling, womanish scream, and suddenly the world tipped, and Carrie Belle found herself on her back, lying on the stage floor. Though the back of her head cracked angrily against the wooden platform, she giggled uncontrollably. Either the alcohol or the music had made her numb. She felt like she'd jammed a finger into a plug socket and tapped into a kind of electric euphoria. The buzz coursed through every limb, and each strum from the musician's violin increased the sensation.

She rolled her head back and looked up until she found the violinist sitting on his stool above her. She got a good look at his face. He didn't have any ears. Frowning, she tried to roll onto her belly, wanting a better look. But she couldn't move. Her stranger had crawled on top of her, pinning her down. He was fumbling anxiously with his belt, while spittle formed at the corners of his mouth.

Nothing seemed to make sense. Everything had taken on a strange consistency, like melted plastic. Her exposed breast flopped and jiggled, and she wondered when she had taken her shirt off. It was all a dream. It had to be. She was quite sure.

"Hey!" she shouted when she felt the man's hands reach under her skirt. Her voice sounded miles away. "What are you doing?"

She felt the fabric of her panties give as the stranger tore them free. The room kept spinning as he laid his entire weight on top of her. His breath was hot and heavy against her throat. While denied of good looks, her stranger made up for it in being immensely endowed. With a heavy grunt, he rammed his full length inside her.

She cried out. The whole thing was just a dream—it had to be a dream. Simple and reassuring music folded about her and her lover, like a fairytale song, and when she groaned, her voice wafted above her, rising above the stage where it became entangled with the music and harmonized with it.

Pleasure swept over her. Why not? It was only a dream. Splinters from the stage floor bit into her buttocks and legs, but the tiny pinpoints of pain only drove her into deeper ecstasy. She ran her hands beneath her stranger's shirt and dragged her nails down along his spine, carving trenches into his flesh. He howled and rammed harder and harder.

She closed her eyes. Her body lurched with each thrust. She bent her head close to his ear and whispered, "I feel like I'm being fucked by God." When she opened her eyes, she found his face hovering close with a rapt expression, eyes rolled back, showing only white.

Something drew her attention to the far corner of the stage where the shadows stirred. Frowning, she squinted and strained her eyes. A small figure was squatting in the shadows, crouching, naked. No, not a man at all. The thing was perched on four long, tawny legs. It had black, leathery skin and eyes that glowed like burning coals. A dog, maybe . . .

It moved closer. It had a face. No, it had her face.

She gasped. "Oh my God!"

She lifted her head. Her lover had vanished. The bar was empty, at least, from what she could tell.

Except him. The violinist was still sitting on his stool behind her, playing his strange, terrible music. She felt warm fluid between her thighs and looked down at herself. Her skirt was stained with blood, and pools of it spread out from either side of her. She screamed again, unleashing a raw and ragged sound that harmonized with the sounds of the violin. She screamed until her voice cracked and her throat sprayed small flecks of blood and spittle.

The music played on, long into the night, long after Carrie's screams had faded and the rain had moved westward.

Boots had gone home long ago, but Hob stayed on the porch with his guitar, watching the sun go down, playing melodies that made him think of Clara's thin, youthful face. The portrait shimmered in his mind like a reflection on the surface of a pond. His fingers eked out his heartache in the form of melodic riffs.

"Seems like a lifetime ago," he said with a sad grin. He took a swig from the bottle of Jack, and the whiskey stoked the fire in his chest. He set the bottle aside and then strummed a few chords from his guitar out of desperation, as if catharsis could lance the ache in his heart. His fingers walked along the fingerboard as he hummed, exploring a few melodies and chasing a few into the corner. Like a magician he wove his aching heart into a bluesy melody, shaping it with delicate and experienced fingers. He went on playing until his fingers ached and there was nothing left inside.

He set his guitar aside and turned on the small radio that he kept on the coffee table. It hissed and bellowed raw and grainy classics from the past. That's exactly where he belonged—in the past. He couldn't escape it, nor did he want to. He thought about going inside and crawling into bed, but even as he thought this, he drifted toward sleep, his head bobbing, until his chin came to rest on his chest.

Only an hour or two passed before something woke him. His neck stiff, his mouth tasting horrible, he sat up in his chair and blinked. The radio hissed like a frightened alley cat. Its tiny screen glowed a somber green. He wasn't exactly sure what had woken him. He'd been dreaming about Clara, but the contents of that dream dissipated.

Smacking his lips and trying to get the taste of battery acid out of his mouth, he started to rise from the rocking chair when the radio began changing stations all by itself. White noise became snippets of music as the dial ran through a number of stations, from old country melodies to rhythmic rock tunes. This ended when the radio alighted on a final station playing Billie Holiday's "Autumn in New York," Clara's favorite song.

Hob bolted upright, his heart pounding, his skin crawling. A soft, powdery scent suddenly pervaded the small porch, a mixture of honeysuckle and peppermint. He knew the scent well. From the night of their first kiss, Hob would bury his face in the crook of Clara's neck and draw in her scent, as if he could just breathe her into his soul. When she had told him that she didn't wear perfume—in those days she wouldn't have had the money to buy it—Hob refused to believe her. It was her natural scent, the biological product of sweat glands and pheromones and his own imagination.

Now the scent was so strong that tears rushed to his eyes. He searched the dark, feeling her presence, a kind of warm familiarity. The feeling became so strong that he stood and asked softly, "Clara, baby? Is that you?"

The moment he spoke, the radio lost its hold on the rogue airwaves and fell into static hiss. He reached over to jerk its cord from the wall when the static formed a single word.

"Hhhhob?"

He jerked his hand back from the radio and stumbled over his own feet. His eyes were wide and his heart racing dangerously.

"Hhhhob, you hear me, Hhhhob?" It was only a static whisper, but Hob knew the voice just the same, hearing it as clearly as a voice through the telephone. It was Clara.

He held his breath, his eyes gaping.

"It's time, Hob. You know what you gotta do."

Chills scurried down his spine. "Holy Jesus," he whispered, trembling. "That you, Clara?" he asked, feeling ridiculous the moment the words left his lips.

"You have to do it," said the hissing voice. *"You have to burn it down."*

Hob waited breathlessly for more, but the radio slipped comfortably into its groove of static, and after a while he lowered himself back into his chair. He waited another hour, hoping for another message from Clara. While the voice had given him a jolt, sleep eventually found its way back, and eventually he passed out in his chair.

Friday, just after six o'clock in the evening, Madison locked up the shop and put the closed sign in the window. She stood in front of the phone, debating, and after a moment, she picked it up and dialed Carrie's cell. It went immediately to voicemail. Madison hung up.

She knows it's me, thought Madison. *She didn't come in today because she's suffering from a hangover and now she's ignoring me. There's nothing to worry about.*

She slammed the phone down on the counter and walked to the window. There was some sunlight left. A kid went zooming down the road on his bike.

"Well, you better have a good story," said Madison to her absent employee. "If not, I swear to God I'll fire you this time."

But she wasn't mad. Her anger had become concern sometime after five in the evening, after she'd exhausted the different reasons why she should fire her friend. She didn't want to fire her anymore. Now she was just plain worried.

Debussy's "Claire de Lune" came through the speakers of the small radio on the counter behind her. She turned it up and let the music flood her small shop, as if it could chase away her worry with a pretty melody. It worked for a moment, but then her cat Mozart leaped onto the counter and knocked over a display of beeswax lip balm tins. She nearly screamed.

"Mozart!" she shouted and threw one of the tins at him. It barely missed. "You little shit! Don't forget who feeds you around here."

The cat hopped onto a neighboring display table and began cleaning himself. Madison sighed and began picking up lip balm. The moment she finished, the radio belched a sudden hiss and lost its station.

Frowning, she emptied her hands and went to the radio. She reached a hand toward it and the radio found its station by itself. Debussy had been replaced with another song. She recognized the smooth melody of "Hear After," a song she'd fallen in love with while on a sailboat, drifting across the Chesapeake Bay with a group of friends the day after Julie Freeland's wedding. It had been this bittersweet melody that had launched her into fits of tears. She'd cried like a baby while her friends had tried desperately to cheer her up. That song had pulled the rug from beneath her feet, and she'd made the decision then and there to return home to Holloway. She cringed. Even now it embarrassed her to think about it.

The phone rang. Madison spun around and looked at it. "Well it's about goddamn time!"

She already knew what Carrie would say. She'd piss and moan about how she was so sorry. She'd tell some story about how she'd gotten wasted the night before and how she'd slept through the day. It was always the same.

I should fire her, thought Madison. *I'll tell her not to come back. Not tomorrow. Not ever.* With a sigh, she jammed the phone against her ear. "Thanks for calling Beethoven's Closet," she said in a flat voice.

"Hello? Madison?" It wasn't Carrie's voice.

"That's me."

"This is Linda Meadows. Carrie Belle's mother."

"Oh. Hello, Mrs. Meadows." Frowning, Madison sat down on the stool behind the counter. She had a sudden sinking feeling in her gut. It was unusual that Mrs. Meadows would call the shop.

"Madison, I was wondering, have you seen Carrie Belle lately?"

"Well, no, Mrs. Meadows. Not since yesterday."

"Oh. Okay." The woman's voice sank to a sullen pitch.

"You haven't talked to her?"

"No. She didn't come home last night."

The sinking sensation grew stronger, and Madison pressed the phone closer to her ear. "Did you call Jon?"

A silent pause stretched out from the other end. "I talked to him just a while ago. Said they got into a fight and she left him at the restaurant. No one's seen her since. I'm worried sick."

Madison tried to think where Carrie Belle would have gone. It wasn't like her to just disappear. "She must have found some friends last night. I'm sure she's all right."

"But she was supposed to work today?"

Madison held her breath. She hesitated. "Yes."

"Oh, Lord. I hope nothing's wrong. You think maybe I should call Chief Dunlap?"

"Yes. Maybe. Just to be on the safe side. I'll make a few phone calls too—see if I can find her."

"Would you please do that?" Mrs. Meadows asked. "And when you do find her, tell her to call me immediately."

"I will, Mrs. Meadows." Madison hung up and stood looking at the receiver for a moment, wondering what Carrie Belle had gotten herself into. With her stomach clenched into a tight knot, she turned and gazed out the window, scanning the busy street, hoping to see Carrie Belle there.

You're getting yourself all worked up about nothing, she told herself. *Just stop it. This doesn't help.* But she couldn't shut up that little voice in her head that had nothing good to say.

Chapter 7

A cloudless morning sky drew Cameron out to explore the town. The sun gleamed in all the shop windows, and the awnings snapped in the wind. The square was busy with people preparing for a festival of some sort. They scurried up and down ladders, erected booths along the sidewalk, and hung streamers between lamp posts. The tap of hammers filled the air. In the courthouse lawn, a group of shirtless workers, fire department volunteers, hammered away at the skeleton of a bandstand. Banners were strung over the avenues, reminding the citizens to "Come and join in all the fun!" next Saturday morning.

Cameron strolled aimlessly around the square, his hands in his pockets, his belly full from a heavy breakfast at Dooley's. He felt better this morning. More than a week had passed since he'd experimented with the Tongue, and without a doubt, it had worked a curious effect on him. He felt remarkably serene, present, and in tune with the world around him. He noticed things that usually escaped him—the crisp air, the scent of flowers, the vitality of his own body. He didn't even mind the elevator music droning from the garden speakers.

Strolling past a newspaper bin, he spotted a tray of freebie newsletters.

Interested in its main story, entitled "History and the Holloway Festival," he took one and headed over to a bench beneath a shady maple tree. He turned his attention to the paper. The story told about Holloway's long-standing tradition, since 1955, when Mayor Drysner kicked off the very first festival with the unveiling of General Thomas Holloway's statue, which now stood before the courthouse. Since then, the festival had grown in popularity, with each year bigger than the last. People came from all over the South.

The article gave a small history lesson, outlining the events that led up to the battle in Holloway. The story began at the election of Lincoln in 1860, when he raised an army of seventy thousand soldiers to force South Carolina back into the Union. This caused a ripple of tension all across the nation, as most of the southern states—including Tennessee—debated whether they should secede from the Union. Fairfax County on the Cumberlands found itself split down the middle. Everyone was forced into taking a side. Meanwhile, the plateau, with its steep escarpment walls and its isolation from the rest of the world, became a no-man's land of robbers, thieves, and murderers. Eventually, most of the Union sympathizers escaped to Kentucky, at this point still a neutral zone, but some stuck around, formed pockets of resistance, and called themselves Unionist Home Guards, who resorted to guerilla warfare. This set the stage for one of the meanest battles in Tennessee.

In September 1862, a Confederate Cavalry, led by General Thomas H. Holloway, assigned with ferreting out Home Guard units from the Cumberlands, cornered a two-hundred-man faction, led by notorious Unionist Horace Doherty. The two parties formed columns and blasted away at each other for seven hours, while smaller patrols on both sides hid in the hills and took pot shots at the soldiers down below. In the end, General Holloway and his men won the battle, losing only fifty men, while leaving not a single survivor from the Home Guard. Holloway became a war hero; Doherty became a piece of decoration as they hanged him from a tree.

Cameron had just finished reading the newsletter when someone touched his shoulder, making him jump. He spun around and found Hob standing next to him, wearing a porkpie hat and a red vest.

"There you go again," said Hob with a big smile. "You about the jumpiest son of a gun I know."

Cameron grinned crookedly and rubbed the back of his head. The lump had nearly faded. "What are you up to, Hob?"

"Just killin' time before work. Say, whatcha readin' there?" Hob took the newsletter, flapped it open, then scanned a few paragraphs before he scoffed and rolled his eyes. "I see. Don't go believin' everything you read around here. Folks have a way of dodgin' the truth. Or flat out makin' it up."

Cameron frowned. "About the war?"

"About General Holloway." Hob lowered himself slowly onto the bench, gathered his thoughts, then gazed at the courthouse, where the sun rose just above its cupola, forcing him to squint. "No one ever mentions Mr. Thomas Holloway's foul disposition. He was one twisted son of a bitch. Killed a lot of folks in the name of the Confederacy, when in reality, it was just an excuse to kill a lot of folks."

"Bet that happened a lot back then," Cameron offered.

"Especially up here in the Cumberlands where no one was lookin'. But the Confederacy did know what sort of man Mr. Holloway was. I suppose it only made sense to use him for their purposes. They slapped rank on his shoulders and then pointed him in a general direction that suited them. Holloway, along with two hundred of the meanest sons of bitches you'd ever want to meet, prowled the plateau and killed most anyone they come upon, woman or child, Blue or Gray. It just didn't matter. They was bloodthirsty."

"Pretty effective though," Cameron interjected, "I mean, at least from a military standpoint. He annihilated a unit as big as his own. Except he kept most of his men."

"Yes, that's true. But it ain't the whole story. What they fail to mention is that the Home Guard ran out of ammo. Holloway and his men had a serious advantage. Maybe fifty Union solders ran for the hills. Got about half a mile, then holed themselves up at a plantation home. But Holloway found them. Ratted them out and forced them to surrender. And that's when the story gets really good."

Cameron coughed into his fist. He became painfully aware of the heat and the heavy breakfast he'd eaten earlier, which was gurgling in his belly.

"But General Holloway didn't take prisoners," Hob went on. "Instead he took those men, hogtied and stripped them, then he and a handful of his soldiers gutted the poor bastards. Spilled their insides out on the ground. Blood was standin' in pools and runnin' in little streams."

"Jesus!" Cameron leaned forward, his elbows against his knees. He gulped down air, worried he might just get sick. "That's really messed up."

"Yeah. Some hero, huh? And here's the best part. That plantation home—the Old Walker plantation, where all those men were killed—they tore it down and built the Calliope right on top of it."

"What?"

"That's a fact. Someone came in and built the Calliope right on top of the battlefield jus' a few months after they hauled off the bodies that stunk up the place. Blood hadn't even had a chance to dry when they started buildin'. Of course, she wasn't a concert hall back then, just a church—a really big one." Hob noted the exasperated look on Cameron's face before he folded his arms and then eased back on the bench, obviously satisfied with himself.

Cameron shook his head. This chilled him to the bone, especially in light of what Bloom wanted to do in that place. Even stranger was that Cameron had sensed something off about the Calliope from the start. Usually his first impressions were dead on the money. Did Bloom know about the war crimes committed there? He cleared his throat. "Some place to build a church."

"Biggest one around. But you know, she's gone through a lot of changes since then. Back in the fifties, when music went pop, a guy named Schroder came in and rebuilt the place, made it a stage for hillbilly singers. Elvis Presley, Johnny Cash, Jerry Lee Lewis—they all performed there. They packed the house with kids from Atlanta to Louisiana."

"Unbelievable." Cameron gazed in the direction of the music hall. Even though the courthouse and a handful of old buildings blocked his view, he could picture the place. "I can't believe I've never heard of the Calliope before now."

"So I hear you write a little music," said Hob.

Cameron blinked. "How'd you know that?"

"I Googled your name." Hob winked at him, got up, and stretched his back.

"You Google everyone you meet?"

"I do when they play the piano like you do. I found a few of your pieces on YouTube. I liked what I heard. Strange but interestin'."

"Hob, you're a regular sleuthhound."

"Who'd have thought, huh? Say, you get bored sometime, you ought to come by my place and jam with me. Easy to find. I live on the end of

Moonlight Drive, about a mile from here. Or better yet, come see me at Bloozy's, down on Lytle Street. I'll get you up on stage."

With a slow nod, Cameron said, "I'll give it some thought."

"You do that." Hob tipped his hat in a kind of salute, then started down the sidewalk, but he spun around with a final thought. "Oh, and you remember what I said about workin' for Bloom. Don't do nothin' foolish."

"Yeah. I got it, Hob. See ya, buddy."

After school, Charlie rode his bike across town to the Calliope, where he found Kalek waiting for him at the front doors. Kalek guided him through the dark foyer and into an even darker auditorium. Charlie had seen the inside of the Calliope only a few times, mostly for Christmas concerts. But he'd never seen it so empty.

They made their way down the center aisle toward the lighted stage. Standing beside a polished black concert grand was a tall man with white hair. He stood with his hands clasped behind his back, watching. He made Charlie nervous.

"Welcome, Charlie," said the man as Charlie followed Kalek up the small flight of stairs to the stage. "Thank you for coming on such short notice. I am Maestro Bloom."

The man considered Charlie's bruises, but rather than asking about them, he thrust his hand out and Charlie shook it. The maestro's hand was cold and his clear blue eyes bored into Charlie, making him feel like a bug under a microscope. "This is my concert hall."

"Pleased to meet you," said Charlie, sounding small and self-conscious.

"I've heard a lot of good things about you, Charlie." Bloom motioned to the piano stool. "Please. Sit down."

Intimidated, Charlie sat down, then cast a quick, hesitant glance at the piano's shiny keys.

"Mr. Kalek told you why I asked you here?"

Charlie cleared his throat and nodded. "He said you were interested in finding a new pianist for your orchestra." He kept his eyes fixed on the stage floor, avoiding Bloom's eyes.

"Something like that." Bloom drifted slowly around the piano, gliding the tips of his fingers along the instrument's smooth surface. "The truth is, I'm working on a sort of experiment." He glanced at Kalek as if sharing some inside joke, then looked back at Charlie. "It's a special project, and I need someone with your talent to help me."

Charlie's brow bunched. He hoped his face didn't show his disappointment. An experiment? Not consideration for the orchestra? "What sort of project are you talking about?"

Bloom's eyes practically glowed. "Next Friday evening, I am hosting a private performance. You see, I have investors who want very badly to hear my orchestra perform. This time, I promised them something more for their money."

Charlie was more confused than ever. He looked from Kalek to Bloom with growing uncertainty. "So what do you want from me?"

"I want you to perform for me and my guests. I have a very special composition. But I'm afraid I can't show it to you until it's time."

"What? I can't read music like that. I need practice."

The easy confident grin remained fixed across Bloom's face. "Don't worry. You'll do just fine."

The idea made Charlie worried, nearly terrified. He turned toward the auditorium's empty seats. He was good, but not that good. "I just . . . well, it's not . . ."

"I will pay you a thousand dollars for your time," Bloom interrupted. He snapped his fingers and Kalek produced an envelope. He handed it to Charlie, who took it and looked inside.

His jaw fell open when he saw the thick stack of bills. He'd never been commissioned for his work. This was a lot of money. With that kind of cash, he could buy himself a new Yamaha keyboard at the Showcase. "Gee, Mr. Bloom, this is great. But I really think I should practice first. So I can do a good job."

"As I said, it's not necessary. I trust you." Bloom put a hand on his shoulder and smiled. "Now, you have to listen carefully. You must promise me that you will not tell anyone about this. Do you understand? If you tell anyone, I will ask for my money back. This is a pact between you and me."

Hesitating, Charlie shifted his gaze from Bloom to the envelope. He gave a few quick nods. It didn't make any sense whatsoever, but that kind of money made a lot of sense—even if he couldn't rehearse. "Yeah. Okay. I promise."

"Then it's a deal." Bloom smiled and shook Charlie's hand, and then he added quietly, "I'll see you next Friday. You may run along now."

Charlie looked at Kalek, then got up and started slowly across the stage, glancing over his shoulder a few times to make sure they weren't going to jump him. They'd just stuffed a grand into his pocket without getting anything in return? He scurried down the steps, down the main aisle, and hurried excitedly to the exit.

Throughout the morning hours, Madison had stapled "missing person" flyers to nearly every telephone pole in Holloway before going to her shop for lunch. Without an appetite, she sat at the table in the back room and picked at her chicken salad, unenthused. When the bell over the front door chimed, she dumped the remainder of her lunch into the trash and rushed out into the showroom, hoping to find Carrie. Instead, she found her cousin, Charlie Witt, standing in the doorway, his face bruised and puffy. A scabby crack perforated his lips. He looked as though someone had beaten him pretty good.

"Charlie?" she said, pressing a hand to her mouth. "What the hell happened?"

"Ah, Mad, it's nothing." He shut the door behind him.

"Nothing my ass! Who did this to you?"

He sat down on a stool beside the cash register, and Madison shook her head with a sigh. "Charlie, when are you going to start standing up for yourself?"

With a shrug, he turned his attention to the *Vanity Fair* lying on the counter and started flipping through its pages.

It was always the same with him. Drama just sort of surrounded his life. Poor little Charlie had always been the topic of rumors, beginning when Dory had gotten pregnant with him. She wasn't married at the time and didn't even know who the father was. When Charlie got a little older, everyone noticed that he seemed a little strange. He'd become intensely shy, and it got so bad by age twelve that Dory took him to a therapist in Nashville, believing that his shyness was some sort of neurosis. But then the therapist had apparently probed too deeply and Dory decided to end it. Madison's mother and a few others were mighty suspicious of Dory's friend, Howard, who came along only a year after Charlie had been born. Everyone was convinced that Howard's drinking and violent disposition had something to do with Charlie's shyness.

"So guess what happened today?" he said, shoving the magazine aside. "I went for an audition."

"An audition?" Madison said with a smile. "For who?"

He tossed the hair out of his eyes and leaned back on the stool. "So get this. Yesterday, this guy by the name of Mr. Kalek comes by the school, looking for a piano player, and guess who Mr. Farrell recommends to him?"

"Hmm," she said playfully. "I can't imagine."

He sniffed. "So today I went and tried out, and they want me."

"Who wants you?" she pressed, wondering if maybe a scout from a prestigious university had taken interest in him.

His chest visibly swelled. "The Holloway Chamber Orchestra."

"What?" she blurted. She folded her arms over her chest, feeling suddenly uncomfortable. "What do they want with you?"

"They want me to play for them." He frowned and drew his shoulders up, assuming a defensive posture. "Mr. Bloom thinks I'm really good."

She didn't like it. The Calliope? "Since when did they start auditioning, anyways?"

He shrugged. "Since never. That's why this is so cool." Sighing, he settled back on his stool. "Besides," he added gloatingly, "he paid me."

"He paid you?"

A flash of regret crossed his face. "Yeah, well, don't go and say anything to anyone. But yeah. He paid me. Thousand bucks just to start."

Madison realized she was scowling and tried to smile. "Well, that's great, I guess. I always knew someone would take an interest in you. But this—I just don't like it. Did you tell your mom and dad about it?"

He frowned. "They wouldn't care, even if I did. Besides, it's none of their business. I graduate in the spring, and then I'm getting the hell out of here."

"Well, you just be careful. Mr. Bloom is a very strange man. And the other musicians in that orchestra—have you seen them? Most of them are old fogies. I would think you'd prefer working with people your own age."

He shrugged. "People my own age don't even know I exist." He rubbed the bruise along his jaw. "Except the ones who want to beat me up."

A moment of uncomfortable silence passed between them, and Charlie dropped his gaze to the counter, embarrassed, when his eyes fixed on a sheet of paper near the register. "Hey, is that Carrie Belle?"

She looked down at the stack of flyers and nodded. "Carrie's disappeared. Been gone for almost a week now. I'm surprised you didn't know. It's been all over the news."

"Wow. That sucks."

"Yeah, it does." She didn't like his tone. It was too casual. She handed him a stack of flyers and said, "Here, post these at school, will ya?"

"Me? Oh, no. No thanks." He hopped off the stool and started toward the door, his face bent into a grimace. "I hope you find her. But I gotta go."

He opened the door and dashed outside. Madison followed. Hopping onto his bike, Charlie darted up Frontier Street toward the square.

She watched until he disappeared from her sight, and then a shiver came over her. It wasn't like him not to offer his help. He seemed so withdrawn. *Why in hell does the orchestra want Charlie, anyways? He's good, but not that good. It feels wrong.*

Everything felt terribly wrong.

Chapter 8

Just after midnight on the eighteenth of August, Marie Williams woke from a nightmare. She reached for George but found his side of the bed empty. *No*, she thought bitterly, her George was gone for the week. Some sort of company training in Richmond. She sighed at this. Just great.

She sat up and folded her arms over her chest. She'd had an awful dream in which she'd been hurrying down a dark alley with cold brick walls and a single streetlamp at its end. But her escape was blocked by a single man, standing at the opening, with a pale face and dark holes for eyes. He carried a musical instrument like she'd never seen before, a twist of metal with sharp edges that extended beyond his head. The sight of him had stopped Marie in mid-step, and she'd prepared to run the opposite way when music came rushing down the alleyway like water through a canal. His song was dark and brooding, and she'd known instinctively what it was: a funeral dirge. Someone was going to die.

Death is coming to you and your son . . .

Marie rubbed her eyes. The dream still had her frightened. She looked to the window, where moonlight made the curtains glow. Maybe someone was outside or a radio was playing somewhere. Maybe she was being ridiculous.

Still, she climbed out of bed, nearly stomping on a bottle of Popov that she'd left on the floor, and staggered over to the window to toss the curtains aside. Outside the flood lamp hanging on the corner of the garage lit up the backyard, where heavy foot traffic had worn away the grass and a few rusty tools lay scattered in the soft dirt. And then she saw her little boy, Hank. He was standing in front of Baloo's doghouse. He wore his blue Scooby-Doo pajamas and his feet were bare. Something about his posture—the dead-hang of his arms, the rigid angle of his back, the sideways tilt of his head—gave her a sudden chill. He had the look of someone in a deep trance.

God, is he sleepwalking?

A chill crawled down her spine as she hurried out of the bedroom. She moved blindly down the dark hallway. Vague memories of her dream and that nightmarish music turned her anxiety into fear. She rounded the corner and found the back door standing wide open.

She stepped outside. The night was warm and moist, with a few puffs of fog settling in the grass. "Hank?" she hissed at him, not wanting to wake the neighbors. "Hank!" she said again, this time louder.

Hank turned, the floodlight sparkling in his eyes. He wore a dazed expression, with his mouth hanging ajar.

God, she thought with a shudder, *he looks like a zombie.* "You get inside right this minute. You're scaring me."

He raised his right arm and pointed a loose finger behind him at Baloo's doghouse.

"Momma," he said slowly, "you hear it, Momma? It's in Baloo's house."

She stepped off the back porch and into the cool grass. "No, baby, I don't hear anything. Let's go inside and get some sleep, huh?"

She'd reached the bald spot before the garage when a rumbling growl brought her to a stop. Her eyes fixed on the dark rectangular opening to Baloo's home. The sound wasn't Baloo. Baloo was the sweetest dog in the world.

The growling grew louder, like a lawnmower springing to life.

Marie hurried toward Hank with her heart jack-hammering in her throat. *Please, God, oh please, God!*

When Baloo stuck his head out, Marie nearly screamed.

Something had happened to Baloo. The Labrador looked mad. Drool hung in strings from his mouth. He snarled and showed the gums of his teeth, and his eyes burned bright red as pus gathered at the corners. Baloo was fifteen and his black hair had grayed, his limber gait now a clumsy hobble. Never before had she felt threatened by him. But that all changed as she stared at her dog.

Baloo's gone rabid, she thought. *Oh, Christ, he's sick.*

Only a few yards away now, she scanned the thinning grass, searching for some sort of weapon, a baseball bat, or even a rock. But she saw nothing but weeds.

Baloo lurched. The old dog moved with some newfound agility, fueled by a rabid-like power, and clamped his jaws around Hank's face.

She screamed and charged across the yard. "Baloo! No! Bad dog! Goddamn it, Baloo! Bad dog!"

She drove her body into the dog's bony flank, earning a yelp as she went sprawling face first into the tall weeds. She landed on a bicycle frame and the metal bear-claw pedals scraped the skin from her shins, bringing bright flashes across her vision. She sobbed and looked up. Baloo bared his teeth as he moved over her. She shouted at him and swung her arms, but the family dog lurched forward and sank his teeth into her throat, cutting short her agonized scream.

She heard it then, just before the darkness stole over her and carried her under. She heard the music from her dream, and she realized that Hank had also heard it.

As Baloo tore something from her throat and pulled her forward, Marie thought, *And Baloo heard it too.*

Holloway Police Station was small in size and smaller on manpower. Not including his dispatch girls, Dunlap had a team of fifteen officers. The station catered to three jail cells in the back, but Dunlap usually only locked up drunks. Most of the time, they transported any prisoners to the county jail in Willow Wood, thirty miles away. In extreme cases, such as a murder, they called in the Tennessee Bureau of Investigation or the county police; Dunlap, however, liked to maintain some control over his jurisdiction, which meant that he and Bentley handled most of their own investigations. And so far, he didn't plan on inviting anyone to help him solve Carrie Belle's disappearance.

He kept the station on high alert. This meant long hours and rotating patrols for all the officers. "No one's getting a wink of sleep until we find that little girl," Dunlap had insisted during a mandatory staff meeting on Friday. For the past week, he had personally worked the night shifts, spending most of his time on the road, patrolling the neighborhoods, always with Sergeant Bentley riding shotgun.

Tonight had been the same. Both he and Bent were on the road by sundown, hopped up on coffee as they patrolled the sprawling neighborhoods of Willow Wood and Severn, just south of the square. So far they'd seen nothing but stray dogs and cats. None of the patrols had uncovered any leads. Carrie Belle had disappeared without a trace.

Dunlap sighed as he leaned forward and folded his arms over the steering wheel. The inside of the cruiser smelled like McDonald's and sweat. "Roll down your window, Bent," he muttered as he watched the road.

His lights cut a yellow path through the darkness. Thick foliage and ash trees lined the road and formed an arch overhead.

Bent rolled down his window, kicked back in his seat, and stifled a yawn. "If you ask me, Carrie Belle done probably run away. Probably with some boy she just met." He threw a sidelong glance at Dunlap and added, "You know how it is."

Dunlap shrugged. "Maybe so. Let's head over to Stony River Park. Check the place out and then call it a night."

Bentley sighed. "Whatever you say, boss."

Pulling a U-turn in the middle of Highway 90, they started back to town. The park was ten miles up the road. Sometimes folks liked to sneak inside after closing hours. It only made sense to bust up the fun once in a while and run the trespassers out, lest he lose control of his entire town. Maybe they'd find something more than kids smoking pot. Maybe they'd find Carrie Belle.

Trees flanked either side of Cutter Avenue. A few dark houses sat away from the road, but there was nothing but crickets and frogs way out here. Up ahead was the entrance to the park, but Dunlap stopped the cruiser before they got there.

He popped his head out the window and listened.

"Whatcha got?" asked Bentley.

A chorus of barking and howling broke the night.

Dunlap ducked back inside, frowning. "Dogs. Maybe coyote too. Something's upset the whole goddamn canine population."

Outside, more dogs joined the cacophony. Howls rose into the air like bottle rockets.

Bewildered, Dunlap just shook his head. "What the hell's going on out there?"

"Probably nothing."

Dunlap glowered, convinced his deputy had the instincts of a billy goat. He thrust his head out into the warm night air and listened. It sounded like every dog on the plateau was either whining or howling. It was an eerie sound, and it made the hairs on the back of his neck stand up straight.

For some reason, the Calliope came to mind; the man they'd seen playing the violin on the front steps the other night. The Calliope wasn't far away, just beyond the back of the park, beyond the soldier cemetery.

"Well, I don't like it," Dunlap grumbled. He put the cruiser into gear and started slowly along East Cutter. "Something's not right. You count on that."

"If you say so." Bentley leaned back in his seat and closed his eyes.

The radio made a squawk. "Chief?" It was Kelley Lowell, one of their late night dispatchers. "We got a real mess on our hands . . ."

With lights flashing, the cruiser sped down the highway.

Ten minutes later, Dunlap and Bentley arrived at the Colbert place. There were two squad cars and an ambulance parked haphazardly in the backyard. It looked like Christmas back there, with the treetops painted blue and red from the emergency lights. Ernie Fowlers had already arrived and flagged them down the moment their cruiser nosed into the driveway.

Ernie came over to Dunlap's window and ducked down so he could look inside. "You're just in time," he said. His eyes were wide and frightened, his skin pasty white. The man was in his mid-thirties, yet he couldn't seem to shake off his boyish looks. "They're loading Floyd into the ambulance right now."

With a nod, Dale rolled around to the back of the house.

"Christ, what happened?" Bentley whispered.

"Told you, didn't I?" muttered Dunlap. "Said I had a bad feeling."

He stopped the car, and he and Bentley got out. Dunlap had shared countless beers back here with Floyd. Now the small screened-in porch looked almost menacing, with its door hanging on its hinges and the screen ripped open like a screaming mouth.

There were a number of men standing by the steps, Sergeant Beaumont included. The coroner, Jim Howdy, was with them. His long face looked tired in the flashing light. Farther out they were loading the gurney with Floyd's body into the back of the ambulance.

"Chief?" someone called.

He and Bent turned toward the voice, but the flashing emergency lights made it difficult to see.

Beaumont approached them. He hooked a thumb over his shoulder. "I've got Donna over there in the back of my cruiser if you wanna talk to her. She seems pretty tame. 'Course I went ahead and cuffed her."

Bentley scoffed. "You put cuffs on Donna Colbert?"

Feeling numb and somehow disconnected from reality, Dunlap stepped over to Beaumont's cruiser. He leaned into the open back window.

Donna's thin frame looked almost ghostly in the dark backseat. She sat with her back straight, her chin up. Even with her hands cuffed in her lap, she made it a point to retain some of her dignity.

"Donna," said Dunlap. "Guess I could ask what happened, but you best save it for a lawyer, I suppose."

"I ain't sorry, Dale," she said in a quivering voice. She refused to look at him. "I was just following orders. You wouldn't understand."

Frowning, he braced himself against the side of the cruiser. "Donna, who in hell ordered you to kill Floyd?"

"I told you. You wouldn't understand. Don't make no difference no how. I killed Floyd. I'm going to jail." She spoke with the dignified authority of someone who had killed in the name of justice and refused to admit guilt. "So it don't matter."

"But it does matter," Dale said in a low whisper. "It matters to me. Floyd was my friend, for Christ's sake!"

Now her head turned slowly, and her eyes glowed from the shadows. "If you must know, God told me to do it. Came through my radio. God sang to me. Told me Floyd was cheating on me and that he had to be killed. So I killed him. And I don't care what you think. It's the truth."

Feeling like the wind had just been knocked out of him, Dunlap moved slowly away from the cruiser and turned to watch his men shuffle about in the light from the porch. Over their voices he heard the thin crackle from the radio just inside the doorway, playing an old country classic, Slim Whitman's "Indian Love Call." The sprightly melody sounded eerie in the still night breeze. He wished someone would cut the thing off.

Christ almighty, he thought. *Floyd's dead and either Donna's lost her mind or the all-night DJ on WSM has been suggesting to his listeners to kill their husbands.*

Someone clapped him on the shoulder and nearly startled the piss out of him. He spun around, hands balled into fists.

Bentley stood there.

"Goddamn it, Bent. You startled me."

Bentley didn't apologize. "Chief. Just got a call from the dispatcher. We got two more dead."

Dunlap felt the blood rush from his face. "Well, who the hell is it this time?"

"Marie Williams," said Bentley, then added, "and her boy, Hank. Some sort of animal attack."

"Animal attack?" Dunlap echoed. Somehow during the night things had just sort of fallen apart, as if they were all living in a snow globe, and somebody had given it a good shaking. "Hell, the Williams place is just down the road, ain't it?"

Bentley nodded slowly. "Sure the hell is, Chief. Just down the road. You believe that? Don't make no sense, does it? Three deaths and practically neighbors."

Chapter 9

In the cul-de-sac of Orpheum Manor, Cameron sent his taxi away and turned to meet Bloom and his welcoming committee of ten men and women. Ignoring the unsettled feeling in his gut, he climbed the steps, nodding and shaking hands, all the while scrutinizing Bloom's friends. These weren't his musicians, or Echoes, as Bloom called them. While Cameron thought the term Echoes fitting for musicians, he wondered how many more people Bloom had working for him behind the scenes.

"Thank you for coming," said Bloom as he led Cameron inside. The troop followed on their heels as they moved along an eastern corridor. "The orchestra is eager to meet you. The arrival of a Tone Poet marks the end of a very long wait."

Cameron listened without saying much while he studied the various pieces of art that decorated the walls. Baroque paintings and marble statues. Glass cases displaying ancient musical relics—all of it museum-worthy. *Where does he get this stuff?* The question haunted him. Not for the first time did it occur to him that Bloom was possibly an international art thief. If so, wouldn't that make Cameron guilty by association?

They approached a set of double doors at the end of the corridor. There was a rumble of voices from the other side. Bloom went for the door handles when Cameron stopped him.

"Listen, you're not expecting me to say anything to them, are you?" Cameron asked nervously.

Bloom gave him a placating smile. "No, of course not. They need nothing from you. They want only to see the flesh and bone of their artist. They have high hopes for you, Cameron. As I said, your arrival is extremely important to them."

He threw the doors open and the voices rose to a riotous pitch. They entered an enormous banquet hall where huge crystal chandeliers hung from a vaulted ceiling and velvet curtains hid the tall windows. The entire orchestra was gathered, more than fifty men and women sitting at long banquet tables running parallel to each other. More were seated at the head table running perpendicular on a low platform at the far end of the room.

Upon seeing them, the musicians stood and applauded.

"That's for you, Cameron," Bloom said into his ear as they walked along the thick, burgundy carpet.

Cameron brandished a politician's grin as he moved through the crowd of centenarians, their bodies bent with arthritis, faces gray with sunken eyes and hollowed cheeks. While they clapped and showed their dentures, their rheumy gazes fixed him with joyless scrutiny. *Are you him?* those questioning faces seemed to ask. *Are you the Tone Poet?*

Cameron followed Bloom to the platform, where Kalek received them at the head table, all but gushing with glee as he smiled at Cameron. Though an old man in his own right, Kalek looked young in comparison to the Echoes. He motioned to two vacant chairs placed at the table's center, and Cameron and Bloom moved around to their seats as the applause continued. Without sitting, the maestro raised a hand to quiet the room, and eventually the Echoes returned to their seats.

"My dear Echoes, thank you all for coming tonight on this joyous occasion," Bloom called out. The noise faded. "I'm sure many of you already suspect what it is I have to say, and so I won't waste another moment." He paused for effect, roamed his eyes about the room, and then waved a hand at Cameron, who stood beside him. "The Tone Poet has come to Holloway!"

More applause. This time Bloom, pivoting to face Cameron, joined them. The ovation continued for several moments as Cameron nodded, waved, and mouthed his thanks. Then came silence.

"Mr. Cameron Blake," said Bloom, loudly enough so that everyone could hear as they returned again to their chairs. Cameron sat down as well, feeling his pulse thudding in his ears. "This orchestra is eternally grateful for your decision to join us. We are your humble servants in this . . . *endeavor* . . . to expand the possibilities of music, to reach further than mankind has ever thought possible." Bloom raised his arms. "This orchestra has sacrificed a great deal over the years. I know this better than anyone. But now is the moment when we must stand together. I've heard rumors—talks of leaving the orchestra, of abandoning the project. This sort of talk must end. No one is leaving. We are only a matter of weeks away from performing Armonia. I will not allow one person to disrupt what we have strived so hard to accomplish. Now is not the time for doubt. Now is the time for faith. And patience. So now, let's eat!"

At a final wave of applause, Bloom took his chair between Cameron and Kalek. It didn't take long for a low din to arise as the musicians began talking among themselves. Cameron looked down at his empty plate, considering all that Bloom had said. There was still so much he didn't understand.

A man in a white jacket appeared at his elbow to pour a glass of red wine. At the same time Cameron's plate arrived, a dish of roast beef and gravy, vegetables, and salad. The scent made his mouth water. He was ravenous.

"Cameron," said Bloom in a voice meant for everyone at their table, "I want to introduce you to my first chairs, my most valued musicians."

Bloom began his introductions, pointing out each man and woman at the table, while they each returned with a welcoming nod. Among the group was Erich Lutz, the premier flutist, and Wilhelm Piccard, the first chair clarinet. Oliver Baudelaire was the premier French horn, followed by Michael Auden, the first chair trumpet. A thin, skeletal-faced woman named Anka announced herself as the first violist, and sitting beside her was a dark-eyed Italian named Salvatore, the first oboist. Second to last was Alexander Oppenheim, a square-faced man in silver-rimmed glasses, the premier cellist.

"And finally, there is Simon," said Bloom, motioning toward the ogre of a man seated at the far end of the table. His tone suggested a certain loathing toward the man. "He's our most important violinist. Our concertmaster."

Cameron nearly choked on a mouthful of food. He recognized Simon from the nightclub.

"Simon is a living contradiction. He's mostly deaf, and yet, he has an impeccable ear. He hears what others cannot."

Unaware that he'd become the topic of conversation and that nearly everyone at the table had stopped to look at him, Simon continued eating, gorging himself with handfuls of food. Grease dribbled from his chin.

Cameron looked away.

"And there you have it," said Bloom. "The others are too many for personal introductions, but perhaps you will have an opportunity to meet them all in time."

Cameron made nods and smiles at the musicians. He turned to his plate and managed several bites of roast beef and carrots before someone interrupted the silence.

"Maestro Bloom, may I trouble you?" The request came from the end of the table. It was Oliver Baudelaire, the French horn. The black-suited figure looked almost comical with his cloud of white hair, his beaklike nose, his deeply creased face. "Many of the musicians are concerned that the Tone Poet will fail like the others. What can you say to appease our doubts about Mr. Blake?"

Cameron frowned and threw a quizzical look at the maestro.

"I understand your concerns," said Bloom, "and I assure you, Cameron Blake has shown more potential than I ever imagined. He is the Tone Poet we've been waiting for. We will perform our Symphony. It is only a matter of time."

Cameron set his fork down, confused. *There were other Tone Poets?* He looked from Bloom to the musicians, feeling powerless, confused, and worst of all, absolutely clueless.

"But you *have* promised all this before, Bloom," Baudelaire went on.

"That's enough, Oliver," said Bloom, his voice low and direct. "You've waited with me this long, dear friend. I ask only for a little longer."

"But I am tired of waiting!" Baudelaire shouted, his face suddenly an angry red as he slammed his fist against the table. "We are all tired. We want answers. Why should we trust this new Tone Poet of yours? Look at him. He's just like the others. He'll ruin everything. He'll bring us nothing but Discord."

The hall filled with whispers and sharply drawn breaths. Cameron glanced out at the people sitting at the tables; their candlelit faces drawn in surprise and even fear. At his own table, several musicians attempted to calm Baudelaire, but the old man pressed them away. Having gotten everyone's attention, he seemed almost emboldened to speak his mind.

"Need we remind you of your past failures, Maestro Bloom?" Baudelaire said, showing his teeth. "Need we remind you?" He reached for his wineglass, spilled half of it on the way to his mouth, then muttered as if to himself, "We are victims of your failures."

"Goddamn this!" Salvatore cried out suddenly, smashing his fist against the table, sending silverware flying while tipping over several glasses. "How dare you speak to Maestro Bloom this way?"

"Let him speak!" shouted Anka in a thick Slavic accent. "He has the right to say these things. We cannot endure another failure."

The room unraveled into an uproar. Shouts broke from the tables down below. Several musicians stood to thrust fingers at one another. Someone shattered a plate.

Cameron looked to Bloom, hoping he would end the arguing, but the conductor seemed unaffected. He merely sat back in his chair, eyes burning. His only response was to reach out with one hand, allowing his splayed fingers to hover just above the rim of his wineglass.

"They've forgotten their purpose," Kalek said in a low voice.

The maestro swirled the tips of his first and second fingers around the rim of his wineglass in quick and fluid motions. He did this several times before a silvery tone rang from the crystal, sharp and piercing, growing steadily louder.

"They have little faith," Bloom said. His hand went round and round above his wineglass. The thin whirring sound gathered itself into an angry pitch as snowflake-patterned ripples formed on the surface of his merlot.

Cameron grew uncomfortable. It was quite a trick, but the sound hurt his ears. He shrank back in his seat.

Suddenly a wineglass exploded like a firecracker, dousing the tablecloth with red wine. Cameron, along with several musicians, shielded his face from flying splinters of glass. Another wineglass exploded and then another. All along the table they burst, popping like a string of firecrackers.

Cameron heard a glassy chatter and looked up to find the crystal chandeliers shivering like treetops in an angry storm. "Oh shit!" he whispered, then slinked over the side of his chair, crawled beneath the table, and curled himself up, knees rammed to his chin. He shielded his ears with his hands against the ringing. Moments later the chandeliers exploded with a glassy *boom!* Glass rapped against the tabletop above him like hail.

The ringing stopped. The sudden silence left Cameron disoriented. From the edges of his table, wine flowed like blood from severed arteries.

He carefully crawled out from beneath the table and climbed back into his chair. The room looked like a warzone, with tables covered in glass, plates of food overturned. Red wine soaked the tablecloths.

Bloom remained seated in his chair. He took a sip from his wineglass—the only glass to endure the ordeal without shattering—and then set it down.

"I won't stand for this feuding any longer!" he called out in a firm voice.

The musicians sat quietly at their tables, watching him with pallid, frightened faces. Shattered glass covered everything. A few faces were actually bloodied from flying crystal fragments.

"Nor will I tolerate dissent. This is my orchestra. *Mine.*" Bloom patted his brow with a handkerchief, tossed it aside, then rose from his chair and brushed off his jacket. He gazed out at his musicians. With a curt nod, he said, "Party's over."

"What the hell happened back there?" said Cameron, breaking the silence for the first time since leaving the estate in Bloom's limousine. The maestro and Kalek both shared the backseat, their backs to the rear window. Kalek looked grayer than usual, his collar spotted with either red wine or blood.

Bloom appeared calm and collected. "It was nothing," he said with a slight shrug. "A trick."

Cameron shook his head and shifted in his seat as waves of nausea crashed over him. "No. I don't buy that. What you did back there—I've never seen anything like it. And by the way, you hurt a lot of people."

"They are *my* people," said Bloom, perfectly convinced this justified his actions. "Sometimes it is necessary to remind them of that."

Frustrated, Cameron exhaled loudly and leaned back in his seat, frowning. So much of what they were doing was still a mystery to him. What bothered him most was the growing suspicion that he'd aligned himself with the wrong kind of people. He saw warning signs everywhere. *Bloom's dangerous. I know that much.* "They said you've worked with other Tone Poets in the past." He watched the maestro's face, searching his eyes. "Why didn't you tell me?"

Bloom's face remained impassive. The last vestiges of sunlight bleeding into the tinted windows warmed his features. "Yes, there were others before you. But they were unable to Attune. You are different. I feel it. That's why you must trust me."

But that's just it, thought Cameron. *I don't trust you.*

Buildings outside the windows interrupted the incoming sunlight, causing the cab to darken momentarily. Cameron turned to look outside as the limousine entered the town square. Shops scrolled by on either side as the car swung right onto Main Street. Those old buildings, especially the courthouse with its stately brick walls and white columns, lent to his sense of solidarity, grounding him in reality. He needed that; he needed to feel like part of the normal world again.

A right turn onto a narrow side street brought them to the Cherry Tree Hotel. The limousine rolled to a stop near the sidewalk. Glad to be back, Cameron pitched the door open and climbed out. He pivoted around and found the maestro leaning forward in his seat, visible in the open doorway.

"Can I expect you to come by tomorrow night?" asked Bloom. "I want another session with the fork. You have a long way to go. More Nocturnes to write."

Sighing his frustrations, Cameron scratched the back of his head. He gazed down the empty road, considering his options. "Yeah, I don't know, Bloom. I'm not sure what I want to do. I need to think. I'm still not entirely convinced that thing's not going to give me a brain tumor or something."

"Your sarcasm worries me, Cameron," said Bloom, his tone firm and brittle. "I hear it daily from the others. They complain. They fight me every step of the way. I say let them complain. But you, Cameron—I expect more from you. You know better than anyone the magnitude of what we are doing here. This is bigger than you or me. Bigger than the orchestra or this town."

"Yeah, I know all that." The desire to compose Astral Music had haunted his entire life, had driven him here to this strange town, had consumed him for decades, which was why he couldn't walk away from Holloway, not now. And Bloom knew that.

Cameron closed his eyes and drew a deep breath. He could smell fried grease from a nearby restaurant in the air. It reminded him of his uneaten dinner.

"Until you have purged yourself of Discord, there can be no Armonia," Bloom continued. "There is no other way. You must continue your sessions with the Tongue, no matter the cost."

Cameron paced a few steps, feeling restless, wanting to kick a dent into the limo's side panel. Nothing felt right anymore. But he couldn't walk away so close to a real breakthrough.

"All right, all right," Cameron said finally. "I'll be there. But you gave me the creeps back there. No more of that shit, got me?"

"Of course."

"And no more secrets. I want to know everything."

"Deal."

Cameron rubbed his chin. "Okay. Then I'll be there."

The limousine rolled away.

With dusk clinging to the horizon, Cameron headed to the square, too restless to return to his hotel room. He couldn't get the chaos at the banquet out of his mind.

Main Street was quietly alive with people enjoying the warm evening. Couples strolled with their arms around each other. Kids sat on the courthouse steps, poring over books or tossing Frisbees on the courthouse lawn. *Peaceful here*, he thought. Not like the madness with Bloom that was sapping his energy.

He found a corner market open and bought a spiral notebook and pen, then headed out to find a bench where he would sit down and write for a bit. Composing would take his mind off things and help calm his nerves. Bloom had promised his fork would bring inspiration. Time to see if it worked.

His first session with the Tongue had had a curious effect on him. He felt lighter somehow, more relaxed, even in the light of recent events. Throughout the past few days, he'd experienced moments of intense clarity, when he became only his senses, when every touch, scent, taste, sight, or sound became overpowering. He felt it now as he sat on a bench facing the courthouse. It felt like inspiration. He opened the notebook. Creative energy coursed through his body like an electrical current, nerves tingling.

Early in his career, he'd written many of his pieces like this, like audio-hallucinations, music that rolled over him like signals from a rogue radio station. He'd learned to trust these impressions and get them down on paper. The whole process was a little bizarre and maybe romantic. Again, his interview in *Music Makers* came to mind—an interview gathered shortly after he'd won a Grammy for "Hear After."

"It's like catching a signal from outside. When I get the signal, it comes hard and fast—music from outer space, written a long time ago and just floating around out there until I catch wind of it. I write as quickly as I can and then hope to God it's not something that I heard on the radio," he'd told the interviewer.

How long had it been since he'd tapped into those impulses? Too long. Years of ignoring those strange frequencies had eventually silenced that part of his mind. Not that it had mattered much. Television studios wanted melodrama, not spirituality. But today he felt different. Those mystical radio waves were nearby. He needed only to listen. So he closed his eyes and waited.

Chapter 10

In the flagging sunlight, Madison crossed the brick plaza and hugged her flyers close to her chest. She fixed her eyes on the concert hall looming before her. Being this close to the Calliope made her anxious. Aside from the nervous flutters in her stomach, a sense of dread squeezed her chest, making it hard to breathe. She regretted coming here.

It was for Carrie Belle. Madison wanted to cover every base. Besides, her cousin worked for the orchestra now. That was reason enough.

Just two hours before, she had closed up the shop and headed out with a stack of flyers that she'd made herself. A hundred sheets of paper, each with a black and white photo of Carrie Belle's quiet smile with the big bold letters across the top: *Missing. Have you seen me?*

Madison had already posted half of these flyers around the square and tucked some beneath the windshield wipers of parked cars. She didn't follow any sort of preplanned route, and she'd ended up on Bard Street and on to the Calliope.

The hairs on the back of her neck stood, and she stopped, suddenly certain that she was not alone. She looked up at the Calliope's front doors. She saw movement from the corner of her eye and pivoted to the left, where trees fringed the plaza. A shadow loped from the bushes.

Oh God, she thought. *A wolf? A rabid coyote . . .*

She swung around, flyers clutched to her chest, and headed to Bard Street, not daring to look back at the Calliope, fighting the urge to run. Fear would only make things worse. She pretended to calm herself, taking a few deep breaths.

The animal loped down the hill and moved in front of her, crouching low, its head thrust out, muscles loaded like springs. It looked sick, with a wasted body, fur dirty and matted except for mangy areas of pink skin.

She stopped. It was a dog and he looked out of his mind.

He showed his large, pointy teeth, growling.

"Oh shit," she whimpered.

She backed up a step, heart pounding. "Oh God," she whispered. "Oh God . . ."

Panicked and numb with terror, her words caught in her throat as the dog launched in a snarling whir of fur and snapping teeth. She screamed and stumbled backwards, flyers spilling from her hands as she instinctively threw her arms over her face.

The attack never came.

She risked a glance. The dog stood before her, its legs splayed in a wide stance. She recognized him as Charlie's dog.

"Sam?" she said in a tear-choked voice. "Sam, what's the matter with you?"

The animal's eyes burned with the wild hatred of something possessed.

With a throaty growl, he lunged at her.

The music did come.

With his eyes still closed, Cameron envisioned the square, the courthouse with its columns and belfry, the tall brick buildings with cornices and big plate-glass windows, the striped awnings and old street lamps. It was the town's essence that translated into melody; the flavor of history and tradition, tobacco leaves and cornfields, small houses with white picket fences and American flags draped over porches, men in overalls and with big calloused hands.

After nearly an hour, he'd written a considerable piece.

He sat there for a while, resonating in the afterglow of inspiration. The clock over the courthouse read seven-twenty, and the sun showed only a fiery crescent above the treetops. He focused on the far corner of the square beyond the courthouse to the entrance of Bard Street. He could walk to the Calliope, maybe channel some of its strange energy into inspiration.

He followed the sidewalk to the eastern side of the square to the mouth of Bard Street. The road was as dead as ever. The small tavern, like the worst rotted tooth in a row of cavities, showed no sign of life. The place gave him the creeps. Everything about this road seemed like bad juju. He pushed himself on, keeping to the opposite side of the road as he passed the bar, thinking about Simon, who evidently haunted the place.

He got no farther than the row of dumpsters when he heard the first scream echo down the throat of the street. He stopped. When the scream came again, he broke into a mindless sprint. It wasn't until he'd crested the hill that he felt a sense of alarm for his own well-being, but by then it was too late.

The sun had fallen behind the building, casting a massive shadow across the plaza, transforming it into a plane of dark shapes. Gasping, he scanned the area. Near the fountain a dog crouched over a large bundle, only the bundle moved, and it was a woman. Her long skirt was now hiked up beyond her knees, her blue jean jacket disheveled.

She shouted, sat up, and kicked at the dog. The animal leaped forward, teeth snagging her jacket sleeve as it jerked its head back and forth, whipping her arm about. She screamed again, and the dog snarled wildly.

Cameron charged the dog, delivered a football punt into the animal's ribs, and felt its bones crack. Light with malnutrition, the dog went sprawling. It rolled a few times before it found its feet and ran yelping toward the trees until it disappeared.

Panting, Cameron turned and squatted beside the woman. "You okay? It's gone, I think."

She wiped tears from her cheeks, then put her hands over her face and sobbed openly. "Stupid goddamn dog. I can't believe he attacked me."

"He looked sick."

She slowly dropped her hands to her lap and looked into his eyes.

He meant to say something more, but forgot exactly what. Despite the shadows, he got a good look at her, and she literally struck him dumb with beauty. Her large, uncertain eyes were fearful, and a slight tremble of her lips didn't detract from her appearance. Her silky brown hair was in a ponytail with an escaped lock hanging over her brow.

"I know he was sick," she said as his gaze dropped over her. "He belongs to my cousin. Or at least he did."

He forced a swallow. He kind of felt bad for kicking the dog so hard. "Did he bite you?"

She drew her fist to her chest and inspected it carefully. Aside from a torn cuff, she'd escaped without much injury. "No. He didn't bite me." With a sigh, she dropped her hand into her lap, then shook her head as tears formed in her eyes. "God, I was so scared. He—Sam—looked like he wanted to kill me."

He sat beside her and put a hand on her shoulder. They sat quietly for about five minutes as she composed herself. Then he picked himself up, clapped the dirt from his jeans, and offered her a hand. "Come on. Let's get out of here. Before he comes back."

Despite his words, he was quite sure Sam wasn't coming back. He pulled her gently to her feet, and for a moment they stood face to face, close enough that he caught the scent of her perfume. He felt a fierce attraction to her, likely a result of the endorphins still pumping in his veins. After a long moment, she dropped her gaze. The moment shattered as she made a frustrated noise.

He looked down at his feet, where colored papers were scattered across the brick.

"Shit." She crouched and gathered her papers up.

He helped rake a number of them into a sloppy stack, then glanced at the top sheet. The black-and-white image of a young woman with a moon-shaped face and a dimpled smile looked up at him.

"Thanks for your help." She all but snatched the flyers from his hands. She stood quickly, holding the papers to her chest, and he rose to face her.

He felt awkward, as if he'd done something wrong. "Cameron Blake," he said, offering his hand again.

She gave him a thoughtful study, then said in a small voice, "Madison Taylor. Thanks for helping me." She shook his hand.

He had the feeling that she wanted to leave. He couldn't blame her.

"Listen. Could I buy you a cup of coffee or something? I know you must be shaken up pretty badly."

Her eyes searched his face. "No thanks. I think I just need to go home and sleep it off."

"Right." He gave a defeated smile. She started to turn when he added, "Could I at least walk you back? Just to make sure you get back safely."

A smile touched her face and she looked him in the eye. "Yeah. Okay. I'd like that."

Side by side, they walked down the dark stretch of Bard Street, passing between abandoned storefronts, moving from one cone of light to the next, both of them glancing at the dark windows of the darkened shops. Only two streetlamps, spaced at twenty yards, interrupted the darkness squeezed into the narrow side street. The real shock came when Madison wound her arm around his and walked beside him.

"You don't mind, do you?" she asked in a trembling voice.

"No. Not at all." He looked at her. "You okay?"

"Just really rattled. I don't know why I went to that place," she said, referring to the Calliope. "I hate it there. And I hate this road. It gives me the creeps. They need to do something with it. Put up more lights for starters."

He waited a beat, then said, "Is that a friend of yours—the girl in the flyer?"

She nodded. "She works for me. She's disappeared."

"Sorry to hear that." They fell quiet and the silence rolled over them. They could hardly see in front of themselves now. Only a neon sign buzzed in the tavern's window at the end of the road, but its hazy blue light did little to comfort him. He wished he hadn't mentioned the flyer.

"I've been putting these things up for hours now," she said, waving the stack of colored papers. "I was just about to call it a night but then I decided to go up to the Calliope. Stupid idea."

"Pretty strange place, isn't it?"

"That's an understatement."

They reached the lower slope of the road, where the Bard Street Tavern was slotted among the row of historic buildings. Its blue door made it stand out from the others, matching the blue sign buzzing in its single window. Both of them gave the place a wary look as they passed it, making sure to stay on the opposite side of the road. The blare of country music escaped through its curtained window.

Then they were out of the dark road and in the safety of the square, where the feverish light from the Karma Koffee shop on the corner spilled across the sidewalk. The square was well lit. Garden lamps surrounded the courthouse and shone on its walls, while tiny lights glowed in the pear trees along the sidewalks. Soft jazz purred from hidden outdoor speakers. Cameron breathed a little easier. It felt safer. Even if that was only an illusion. Still, Madison kept a firm grip on his arm, and he pretended not to notice. Following the sidewalk to the left, they met a crisp evening breeze. Their shadows floated like apparitions across the shop windows.

"It's a nice town," Cameron said.

"If you don't mind getting mauled by wild animals." She dropped her gaze and muttered, "Sorry. I'm usually not this nasty." When she looked up at him, a little warmth had colored her cheeks. "You don't live here, do you?"

"Nope." He almost mentioned that he'd come here to work, but she obviously had bad feelings about the Calliope, and he didn't feel like explaining himself. "I'm here on a break. I needed the fresh air. That sort of thing."

She nodded, and after a short pause, she said, "Now I remember. I saw you outside the courthouse a few weeks ago. You were carrying a duffle bag on your back. You looked . . . lost."

"That was probably me."

"So, what do you do back home?"

"I write music," he said, then added, "I guess you could say I'm a composer."

"No kidding?" She gave him a sidelong gaze. "That's neat. Have you written anything that I would have heard?"

He shrugged. "Maybe."

"Like what?"

He cleared his throat, feeling suddenly self-conscious. He always did whenever someone quizzed him about his professional life. "I wrote a piece called 'Hear After.' I published it just before I got into television."

She stopped near the inset door of the Totem Tobacco, where the big, stony-faced wooden chief stood. "No way. You're putting me on, right?"

He shook his head with a hesitant smile. Most people he told this to had never heard the piece, didn't know it by name, or were genuinely surprised. Madison looked almost frightened.

"Can this day get any weirder?" she said more to herself, smiling slightly.

"I take it you know the song?" Even in the dim light he could see that her cheeks were glowing red, her eyes faintly watery.

"If you only knew."

Her look of almost gratitude pleased him. "Thanks. I like hearing that."

"No. Honestly. That song changed my life." Bewildered, she looked him in the eye, as if seeing something there she hadn't noticed before.

He almost flinched at her intensity.

"This is so bizarre," she whispered.

He didn't press her. She took his hand and pulled him after her. They passed several more shops, then turned onto Frontier Street, where a number of shops lined the road.

"That's my shop on the corner," she said, pointing out a small shop, lit by a single porch lamp. "It's not much, but it's mine."

"I like it," he said with an approving smile.

They walked the next two blocks, arm in arm, like old friends. When they reached the gravel driveway, they fell victim to an awkward silence. Cameron didn't quite know how to proceed; he felt almost guilty for wanting to ask Madison for a date as she'd nearly been ripped apart by a wild animal only half an hour earlier.

"I wish we could've met on better terms," he said, turning to face her.

She shied away. "Well, now you know where I work. If you're over this way tomorrow, maybe you could come and say hello. Unfortunately, I only sell women's apparel. But then again . . ." she made a face, "you never know."

"That's right. I could probably use a new blouse."

She gave a lopsided grin, but it lasted for only a fleeting moment before her face took on a more somber expression. "Thanks for saving me back there," she said. Their eyes met for a moment—a very long moment—and Cameron's stomach did a cartwheel. "I owe you big time."

Before he could say anything more, she turned and hurried away, leaving him grinning like a fool. He went back up the street toward the square with his hands in his pockets, deep in thought, her perfume lingering about him.

Chapter 11

The fork's ringing burrowed into Cameron's ears, something alive and powerful. The pitch lowered, sinking to an abysmal drone, sucking the light from the study, and an inky darkness swallowed up the room, including Maestro Bloom who sat on the opposite side of the table.

A vision unfolded. He glimpsed the vast hall of some ancient gothic cathedral, with soaring stone walls and pointed archways and windows. Noisy with the steady tapping of hammers, it smelled of blood and musty air. Ribbons of entrails stretched overhead and festooned the walls. By the light of candles mounted on iron stands, twenty men dressed in brown robes worked at several stations scattered throughout the hall. Some of the workers used crude hammers to beat metal into strange forms. Others worked on a kind of loom, where one man sat on a chair that moved back and forth on runners while he fed tissue into large wheels that spun and wove it into string.

Cameron knew this had happened a long time ago, in a foreign country, in an abbey high in the mountains. A group of men had been touched by divine inspiration, and they'd built the Archetypes to communicate with God.

Just as suddenly as it came, the vision went away, and he found himself, naked and alone, in a dark room with polished stone floors. Frightened, he crouched and wrapped his arms around his knees, shielding himself from the cold that lapped against his skin. He noticed something clenched tightly in one fist and opened his hand. He was holding the tuning fork. It glowed dimly, sending warm vibrations pulsing down his arm.

Something whispered in the darkness.

He caught his breath and held the fork over his head, using its somber blue glow to drive back the shadows. Underfoot was shimmering black stone, and things moved beyond the light, crouching shapes that scuttled back and forth in palsied movements.

He stepped forward for a better look, and all but one of the creatures scurried away. The remaining creature faced him, the light shimmering against its black, hairless form. The size of an average dog, it squatted like a man, but moved on all fours. Its shiny skin was pulled taut over the bones of spindly appendages and knobby joints, making the creature resemble the instruments beneath the Calliope, as if somehow sharing the same origin.

The demon raised its head and hissed. Cameron nearly fell over himself. It had black pits for eyes and a great maw lined with jagged teeth. The face was flat, with bands of crisscrossed scar tissue for a nose, glistening with mucus. More of them gathered to either side of the creature, hissing and snapping their teeth like rattlesnakes.

"Stay back!" Cameron shouted, waving the fork in wide arcs. It continued to glow and vibrate. He felt its weight, but he no longer heard its low ringing. Either it had stopped or his ears had grown accustomed.

Wet feet slapped on the marble and one of the creatures penetrated the blue light of the fork. Crawling on all fours, it resembled the others, except that its head was disproportionate to the rest of its body. The face was that of a whey-faced boy of about ten years with thick blond hair and soft cheeks. The eyes gleamed like black marbles, regarding Cameron as he shuffled back in horror. He knew the face.

"Oh, God, Brent," he whispered. "What'd they do to you?"

The thing that looked like Brent scuttled closer, moving in fluid, catlike motions. Its ribs pressed against its flanks, covered with a froglike skin that swelled and contracted with each raspy breath. It stopped, crouched, and thrust its head forward. Its mouth dropped open, lips curling back as it loosed an ear-shattering scream. Cameron was forced to stagger back, his hands covering his ears. This did nothing to dilute the shriek, like a thousand fingernails ripping across a chalkboard. He rammed his fingers into his ears and clamped his teeth shut, groaning to endure the assault, but it soon overcame him. He dropped to his knees, crying out.

As the creature screamed, its jaws dislocated and widened to python-like proportions. Brent's face split open at the sides, beneath the jawbone, revealing oily black skin underneath. The lips curled back from tooth and gum until the bone showed.

"Stop it!" Cameron shouted. "Fucking stop it!"

But the creature had no intention of stopping. When he thought the sound would drive him insane, Cameron noticed something peculiar about the caterwauling. It was no monotone, single-noted scream rising and falling in pitch, but a whole chorus. The demon was singing to him— atonal and discordant—but a song nonetheless. And it was a familiar song.

The nightmare dissolved. Sitting at the table, with Bloom across from him, Cameron still held the fork with his thumb and forefinger. It continued giving off its hellish pitch. The music, however, continued to ring in his ear.

"Quick! I need something to write with!"

Bloom leaned across the table and touched a stack of paper and a pen, already prepared.

Letting the fork fall to the table, Cameron picked up the pen and started to write. His hand moved the pen and strange shapes sprang across the blank page like magic. Circles enclosed circles. Strange symbols filled the gaps. Words of an unknown language appeared in the corners. The music came without a single thought, as if he were channeling the whole thing. Every line, straight as an arrow, every circle, perfect.

He felt a certain tension release itself as he wrote. He almost laughed. He'd kept the pain so long, allowing it to resonate, that those dark and pervasive vibrations had rooted themselves in his sound aura. As he encoded those discordant vibrations into strange symbols, the energy loosed its hold over him, breaking its grip.

He finished the work in an hour and shoved the papers aside, not wanting to look at them any longer, as if in doing so he might become sick with it again. He was exhausted and soaked in sweat, with his shirt stuck to his back.

Bloom took the music and examined it quietly. "Discord. Look at this. Beautiful."

Sagging in his chair, Cameron leaned forward against the table, feeling wasted, overcome with bitter guilt. "I want that burned," he muttered through gnashed teeth. "Makes me sick to look at it."

"Don't be foolish. Why would we do a thing like that?" Bloom attempted an appeasing smile, but it came off as patronizing. "Astral Music is special, even the discordant works. You'll see when we perform it tomorrow night."

Cameron blinked out of his daze. "What are you talking about? Tomorrow night? What gives you the right?"

The maestro rose from his chair. "This piece is more important than you can possibly imagine. You must trust me. Everything will make sense in time."

"Where are you going? You still owe me an explanation. I want to know about the other Tone Poets."

"That will have to wait. You need rest, and I have things I must tend to."

"I want answers!" Cameron slammed the table with his fist, causing the tuning fork to jump. The room seemed to tilt on its side. Exhaustion was setting in. He could hardly keep his eyes open.

Bloom had already turned away. He paused at the door, his back to the room, his head cocked slightly. "I admire your courage. It was not easy, what you did this evening. But now it's time to heal. I'll tell my driver to take you back to your hotel. Tomorrow at sundown—meet me at the Calliope. I will show you something extraordinary. It will change everything."

Cameron sighed, leaned back in his chair, and rubbed his eyes with his hands, too tired to argue anymore.

A worn dirt path followed a wide creek through lush forest, teeming with life and color. Moss carpeted the rocks, and lichens crusted the soaring cliffs rising up on either side of them. As he followed behind Madison at a strong pace, Cameron's mind eventually fell silent. The hike was doing wonders for his nerves. He couldn't remember feeling so relaxed and in tune with the world around him. The smell of earth, pine, and river water made his head spin. The music of birdsongs lightened his spirit. It was the perfect day for a picnic.

"So when did you say you were going back home?" Madison asked, glancing over a shoulder at him, her tone deceptively indifferent.

"Not sure yet." He bit his lip. "I guess as long as it takes."

"To do what?"

"I don't know. Find a little direction, I suppose. I'm reconsidering my career."

"You work in television, right?"

Cameron sucked down air as they climbed a hill. "Yeah. For the past six years. Nighttime dramas. That sort of thing. But I don't think I'll be doing that anymore."

"No?" She stopped and turned to face him. "Why not? Sounds like a pretty good gig to me. I bet it pays pretty good too." She stopped herself, blushed, and added, "I don't know why I said that."

"Don't get me wrong; the money's fine," he said. "But it's not about money for me. Not anymore."

"Then what's it about?"

He shrugged. "I always thought I'd do something more important with my life."

Wiping the sweat from her brow, Madison nodded, then started on her way again. "I know exactly what you mean." They walked for a mile or so until they reached the waterfall. Just as she'd promised, the place was breathtaking. The water plummeted from a thirty-foot drop in a deafening roar, crashing into a green pond, surrounded on all sides by thick foliage and sun-dappled rocks. The rocky banks were all aglow with splashes of green moss.

Taking off her backpack, Madison edged up to the pond and crouched down on a flat rock. She pulled off her sneakers and socks.

"So tell me something," she said, looking up at him. "Why did you really come to Holloway? And don't tell me you came just for the fresh air."

An embarrassed smile touched the corners of his mouth. He'd dodged this same question the night he'd first met her. He'd hoped to keep his real reasons a secret, at least for a while. "Well, that wasn't a complete fib. I mean, I do need the air."

"Keep going."

Cameron scratched the back of his head, hiding his discomfort. "Well, I came to compose for the Holloway Orchestra."

Her eyes widened. She rose to her feet. "Really," she said flatly.

He looked away. "I'm working with Maestro Bloom. He approached me with a deal that I just couldn't pass up."

Madison gave a smile that wasn't really a smile at all. "He's got you, too, huh? Geez, that guy's busy."

"What do you mean?"

She shrugged. "My cousin told me the same thing. Said they offered him a job."

A sudden rush of blood reddened Cameron's face, and he turned his head away, hoping his alarm didn't show. "Well, Bloom's certainly ambitious," he said dismissively, hoping she wouldn't probe any further.

She didn't. Instead, she waded into the water. A ways out, she called over her shoulder, "You comin'?"

Cameron looked at the clear pond. The morning's sultry heat had reduced him to a sweaty mess. Gnats and other unfortunate insects were stuck to his throat. His sweat-soaked shirt clung to his chest. A dip in the pond sounded like heaven.

As he started to take off his shoes, Madison splashed farther out, until the water reached her thighs. She made a *brrr* sound and folded her arms over her chest. "It's a little cold."

Carefully balancing on pointy rocks, he fumbled his way into the water, finding it colder than she'd let on. "Cold, my ass, This is freezing!"

She giggled. "Come on. It's not that bad!"

As he drew closer, she motioned for him to follow, and they waded toward the waterfall. After a few steps, he reached for her hand. She gave it, smiled at him, then dropped her eyes. Cameron felt his heart tremble.

They marched on. Ten yards ahead, the waterfall met the pond in a thunderous mist that billowed and swirled. A river-scented gust of wind tossed their hair into their faces. For a moment, they fell silent. Then he felt her eyes on him. The roaring water fell mute, and only his pulse drummed in his ears as he turned and drew her close. He leaned forward, slowly, giving her a moment to retreat if she wanted. She didn't resist.

Soft and gentle at first, their kiss seemed to draw energy from the falls. Cameron wrapped his arms around her waist, pressing himself firmly against her. Every atom in his body seemed to accelerate, collide, and fuse with hers.

When the kiss ended, they turned and watched the waterfall, and neither said a word.

Kalek and several others met Cameron at the Calliope's front doors at sundown. Kalek felt less of a shepherd to this flock; in a former time, he'd been their preacher. Then, when Bloom was born from the tuba, these previous church members took their direction from him instead. They, like Kalek, had continued to follow this extraordinary man who had tapped into an otherworldly realm. They, too, were also old, some slightly crippled in limb, but just as eager to follow and obey.

Except for a few overhead lights, the foyer remained cloaked in darkness. Off to either side of the wide lobby were more musicians, all watching with quiet anticipation. Kalek grinned as he guided Cameron quietly down the thick carpet toward the central auditorium doors. The warm lights and careful silence evoked a strange, almost church-like sense of reverence.

Kalek looked over at him. "Maestro Bloom is quite taken by you. He believes you are vastly talented."

"I don't think it's my talent he wants," said Cameron. Whatever it was he'd written in that discordant trance had nothing to do with talent, not as he knew it. "What I did last night, did that have anything to do with art?"

"Oh, I certainly believe so. It's not easy facing our demons. But you did it. And you captured that expression on paper. Isn't that the definition of art?"

Cameron shrugged. "If you say so."

They pressed through the swinging doors and into the auditorium. The seating area was dark, but the stage glowed with a soft illumination, and they moved down the aisle toward it. Onstage, several men were wrestling with a large black piano.

Bloom stood nearby, watching and directing. "Move it nearer the edge."

Cameron knew the hideous instrument. They'd brought it out from the Calliope's basement. One of Bloom's Archetypes. The Dragon.

Maestro Bloom looked down as they approached. "Oh, good!" he called. "Join me, would you, Cameron? Our guest will be arriving soon."

"What guest?" Cameron called back.

Bloom ignored him, returning his attention to the piano.

Cameron frowned, but Kalek nudged him gently along. They mounted the steps to the left of the stage.

"I know you have questions," Bloom said as they crossed to him, not even looking at them. "But I encourage you to keep those questions in abeyance for now. Mr. Kalek, I want you to wait outside for Mr. Witt. He'll be here shortly. Bring him here the moment he arrives."

"Yes, of course." Kalek descended the steps and headed back the way they'd just come.

"Mr. Witt?" said Cameron.

The maestro ignored him and raised a hand and shouted to his men, "That's fine there! Leave it and get out of my sight!"

The men backed away, and Cameron got a closer look at the Dragon. The thing looked like the fossil of some nightmare creature, with the contour of its back following the impressions of an intricate skeletal structure and a spinal cord that stretched across its length. The polished black skull mounted over middle-C leered straight ahead with a mouthful of knives.

"I suppose this has something to do with the music I wrote last night?" Cameron's voice quivered with uncertainty.

Bloom placed a hand on his shoulder and led him away from the instrument. "Yes, it does. The Astral Music you wrote last night will usher in our newest member to this orchestra."

"Another musician? He's coming here? Tonight?"

"That's right. He's an extraordinary talent, a master pianist. His arrival will make this orchestra complete."

They stopped at the edge of the stage and Cameron faced him. "I don't understand. What does Astral Music have to do with anything?"

Bloom raised a hand. "Again, I must ask you to wait. You will have your answers soon." He nodded toward the dark seating area. "The Calliope seems restless these days. I think she's starting to waken."

A cool draft wafted over them, strong enough to flutter their hair. A shiver raced down Cameron's spine and he hugged himself.

Bloom threw him an amused grin. "Oh, don't let the place unnerve you. There's nothing to be afraid of here. Nothing but drafts and settling boards."

A thought occurred to Cameron. *The Calliope . . . she's as haunted as they come. A hotspot for spiritual activity.*

The central auditorium doors flew open and Kalek strode in with a tall, gangly teenager at his side.

"Please tell me that's not our new pianist," Cameron moaned. "Christ's sake, Bloom. He's just a kid!"

Kalek led his guest onto the stage. The boy looked nervously about as he cleared the top step. He had a narrow, weasel-like face, with a pair of horn-rimmed glasses balanced on the ridge of a long nose. Blossoms of acne marred his cheeks, and his long hair had a greasy sheen.

Probably still a virgin, thought Cameron. *Probably shitting his pants too.*

Bloom stepped forward and shook the kid's hand. "Charlie. Thank you for coming."

Charlie got his first look at the Dragon and paled. "What is that?" he asked in a shaky whisper.

"Only a piano, Charlie." Bloom spoke carefully, not wanting to frighten the boy. "No matter how lifelike it seems." He turned and quickly beckoned Cameron over to them. "Charlie, I want you to meet our renowned composer. This is Cameron Blake. He wrote the piece that you will perform for us this evening."

Cameron shook the kid's clammy hand. Charlie's brow relaxed some when Cameron looked into his eyes, sensing something there that made him feel safer. This only increased Cameron's guilt over the matter.

Bloom's footfalls echoed heavily as he walked briskly to the piano, then turned to face them. He rested one hand on the piano's back. "Will someone please get the lights?" he said, barely throwing his voice.

Suddenly the stage went dark, as if the world had vanished beneath their feet. A cone of light sliced through the darkness at an angle and fell on the Dragon. The polished black material that covered its frame looked wet and fleshy, and the skull watched them with a malicious grin, its eye sockets filled with shadows. The Dragon seemed to spring to life.

"Come over here, boy," Bloom said. "I assure you, it won't bite."

Reluctantly, Charlie stepped forward, his eyes fixed on that snarling demon skull, arms hanging loosely at his sides. Bloom motioned for him to take a seat on the bench. Charlie hesitated.

Cameron couldn't blame him.

"The Dragon is a special instrument," Bloom said in a cool, instructive tone. "There is only one of these in the entire world. It is capable of producing sounds that no other instrument can produce."

Charlie scratched the back of his neck, obviously deep in thought, then reluctantly lowered himself onto the bench.

The aged, haggard faces of several musicians appeared toward the rear of the piano, just outside the cone of light.

Cameron, growing more uneasy by the moment, also moved in closer. *The kid wasn't old enough . . . for what?* he asked himself. They weren't exactly breaking any laws here. Still, it felt wrong.

"Beautiful, isn't she?" Bloom said to the boy, as he placed a sheet of crumpled paper on a bracket above and behind the mounted skull.

Charlie stared at it, his brow drawn in worry. "I don't know what this is," he said, slowly shaking his head. "This doesn't make any sense to me."

Cameron moved in for a closer look. He wanted to see it for himself as he remembered little of the tuning fork–induced nightmare, or the work he'd produced under its spell. There had been some hellish semblance of music in that dream and writing it down proved the only way to wake up from it. Any hopes he had of remembering that night died the moment he peered over Charlie's shoulder.

He recognized the cryptic notation only because he'd seen similar works in his dream journal. All of it drawn by a hand much more delicate than his own, meaning nothing to him, as if he'd channeled the whole thing by automatic handwriting.

Bloom propped himself against the piano and grinned at Cameron, then turned his eyes to the boy. "The notation will undoubtedly seem strange to you, but if you let go—if you give yourself over to the music—you will find that you can read this just as easily as you would a page from a book."

Cameron felt that the words were also aimed at him. "What are you talking about, Bloom?" he asked scathingly. "You can't expect him to play that."

Impatience shimmered in Bloom's eyes as he fixed a threatening gaze on Cameron. "On the contrary, anyone with the slightest musical ability can play it."

"So why did you choose me?" Charlie wondered in a petulant tone.

Bloom looked at the kid and the intensity left his face. "I chose you for a number of reasons. First, you are the best pianist in this godforsaken town. Second, and most importantly, because I knew that I could count on you. I've had my eye on you for a long time. I see how the other boys treat you. They don't understand you. They don't understand your talent. But after tonight, things are going to change, Charlie."

Charlie's voice seemed small for his size. "How?"

"Once you play that music before you," said Bloom, "you will never hear music the same way again. The music will lead you to a spiritual awakening."

Cameron threw his hands up. "What the hell are you talking about, Bloom? You're filling this kid's head with bullshit." He clutched Charlie's shoulder and looked him in the eyes. "Listen, man, you don't have to do this. Christ, I don't even know what we're doing here."

Behind his thick spectacles, Charlie's eyes grew wide with uncertainty. His mouth moved as if he wanted to say something but couldn't get his tongue to work.

"That's right, Charlie," Bloom said in a voice loud enough to echo out into the auditorium. "Go home. Back to your pathetic life. To parents who hate you. Peers who don't respect you. I see the bruises on your face . . ."

The kid's head snapped around to meet the maestro's gaze. Cameron recognized the desperation in the boy's movements, the way he looked back and forth between the men, like a drowning victim groping for a line.

Bloom let his words sink in for a moment before he continued. "Or you can stay and take part in something important. Something special. Something that has never been done."

"You don't have to do this," Cameron interjected, but he knew Bloom had won the kid over. He could tell by the way Charlie drew himself up, fortified.

"It will change me?" Charlie's question sounded more like a plea.

Grinning coldly, Bloom glanced at Cameron, then said, "Most definitely."

There was a long pause. Then the kid nodded and said, "Tell me what to do."

Nothing happened for a long time.

Sitting quietly at the piano, Charlie waited with his back slouched, his fingers touching the keys, eyes fixed on the music, as if waiting for it to suddenly make sense—exactly as Bloom had told him.

Cameron paced the stage with his hands on his hips, a bitter smile slashed across his face, his mind racing. *This is ridiculous. Irresponsible. We're fucking with this kid's head. What am I doing here?* Finally he spun around and looked at Bloom. "I can't do this. We need to stop. Right now."

A piercing note cut across him. Mouth still open, his eyes went to Charlie, who looked over his shoulder at them, his face holding an uncertain smile.

"I think . . . I think I got it," he said.

Bloom nodded. "Okay, then, Charlie. Let's have it."

The kid returned his gaze to the keyboard and adjusted his glasses. His posture crumbled, his back bent like a question mark, and then he played a chord. The piano produced a strange sound, not entirely unnatural, at least not at first. But there was a subtle undertone, felt more than heard. As Charlie's hands started to tear up and down the keyboard, a frantic melody tried to take shape. But the piece was unpredictable and at times convoluted, resisting any attempt Cameron's mind made to grab hold of it and make sense out of it.

Even so, the music was eerily familiar.

At that moment a thought sprang to mind. It was Madison's voice: *My cousin told me the same thing. Said they offered him a job.*

"Oh God," Cameron whispered.

The piano began to open up, like a blossoming flower, as each of the two planks forming its lid raised slowly by the hinges at the outer edges. Parting at the dividing spine that ran down the piano's back, the planks swung upward like sections of a drawbridge. Inside were syrupy cobwebs that clung to the underside of each plank, falling in viscous ribbons down into the piano's inner workings.

Cameron's stomach tightened as his panic mounted. He could hardly breathe. But if Charlie shared his terror, he didn't show it. The kid continued to rip his hands across the keys, hammering out the alien music, seemingly oblivious to the piano's unfolding.

"Stop!" Cameron shouted. "Charlie! For Christ's sake, stop!"

But Charlie didn't stop. He was a puppet on strings. When he threw his head back and screamed, Cameron rushed forward to help, but one of Bloom's men grabbed his arm and held him in place. He tried breaking free, but the maestro moved in front of him and shook his head.

"Don't interfere, Cameron," he said, his voice barely competing with the horrid sounds coming from the piano. "This must be done."

Scowling, Cameron wrenched his arm free and stepped past the maestro. No one tried to stop him. By now, the piano's lids had opened as far as they would go, each raised at an angle like spreading wings. Curious, he looked down into the instrument's casing, expecting to see the typical arrangement of felt hammers, strings, and sound boards. Instead, he gazed into what seemed like an eviscerated corpse with its ribcage cracked and forced open. A thin translucent film covered what looked like a framework of bones, assembled in a kind of captain's wheel design, with each bony spoke radiating outward from a central hub. In the gaps were what appeared to be human organs, ligaments, and ropes of entrails. Silver strings were threaded throughout the entire affair, spanning from one side of the frame to the other.

"What the fuck is going on?" Cameron shouted.

The music stopped suddenly. Several wires snapped free with violent pinging sounds. Cameron threw his hands up to shield his face and staggered back until he was out of the radius of whiplashing strings.

Charlie just sat there, his head rolled back, gawking, until one of the breaking wires whipped him across the face and sent his glasses flying off. He merely pressed a hand to his cheek to stop the blood and watched.

A moan echoed across the stage.

Hands still raised to ward off snapping wires, Cameron moved closer until he could see down into the opened back of the instrument, beneath the sheet of translucent membrane, and the inner mechanics of human bones, ligaments, and wire. Two hands pushed their way through the parts until the palms pressed against the membrane. The film stretched like rubber, the fingers tearing through and ripping open a large hole. Suddenly the bloody face of a man appeared, eyes round and wide with panic. The mouth opened and a wild, hellish scream bellowed out.

Paralyzed with horror, Cameron staggered and dropped to his knees, still watching.

Two arms reached up from within the piano, hands gripping either side of the frame. A man hoisted himself up to his waist, face turned toward the ceiling. Naked and covered in viscera and placenta and all the birth stuff of the universe, the man's pale chest hitched with each pull of breath.

"Welcome back, old friend," said Bloom, standing with his arms crossed, his expression unflustered.

The man in the piano continued gasping for breath, his back arched, the muscles in his arms rigid, hands tight on the edges of the frame. Shoulder-length hair, black and blood soaked, framed his narrow face.

"I fulfilled my promise," Bloom went on. "Now you must fulfill your end of the bargain."

Cameron climbed to his feet and staggered toward the stage's edge, bewildered and unable to break his gaze from the man standing halfway out of the piano. When he glanced beneath the instrument, expecting to see the man's legs protruding from the underbelly of the case, he saw only empty space. *Like a goddamn magic trick*, he thought. *An optical illusion. At least the kid seems all right.*

Charlie sat slumped on the piano bench, his arms hanging between his knees. A thin gash broke the skin of his face from cheek bone to chin, bleeding freely; otherwise, he looked fine, if somewhat dumbfounded.

"My God, Bloom," Cameron gasped, shaking his head but unable to look away from the piano. "What did we do? Why didn't you warn me?" His voice grew steadily higher in repulsion and fear as he reached the edge of the stage.

"This is the pianist we've been waiting for, Cameron," said Bloom, his voice calm and soothing. "He's been gone a long time. But you've brought him back. Now this orchestra is complete."

The blood-covered man drew a wheezy breath, threw his head back as he spread wide his long, sinewy arms, and gave a triumphant howl.

This broke Cameron's trance. His feet nearly slipped beneath him as he spun around and leaped from the stage into the seating area, his stomach heaving. He didn't look back as he bolted up the far aisle, nor did anyone try to stop him as he plowed through the swinging doors into the lobby.

It was raining by the time Cameron finished packing and returned to the square with his duffel bag on his back. Unable to find a taxi, he walked east along Main Street. The rain fell in cold sheets, forcing him into a stoop, with his head bent against the downpour. A mile or so out, he plunged into a soupy darkness. Shops gave way to small homes, spread out in widening intervals amid thick woods along the road.

A set of headlights, blurred by the rain, appeared on the road behind him. He turned and thumbed for a ride. The car slowed as it approached, then came to a stop beside him. It was a Bentley stretch limousine. With an angry shake of the head, Cameron turned and walked away.

The Bentley followed. When the back door opened with a muffled click, he stopped and looked. The interior remained dark, and for a heart-stopping moment, Cameron half expected the blood-covered face of the resurrected musician to appear.

But the face that eventually appeared belonged to Maestro Bloom.

"Cameron, please get in," he said carefully, almost fatherly.

Cameron only stood in the rain, contemplating. He threw a final, longing glance down the highway, considering the few short miles to the next town.

But he couldn't leave; not after seeing so much. Not with so many questions chasing around in his head. His gaze turned to the open car door, knowing already what he would do. With a sigh, he tossed his duffel bag inside and then followed.

Shivering, he settled into the leather seat and pulled his door shut. The limo rolled back onto the street. Bloom said nothing, staring straight ahead.

Cameron was first to break the silence. "What the hell happened back there?"

"A miracle," Bloom said simply.

"You could have at least warned me."

"And what would you have said?" Bloom asked in a flat, casual tone. "If I told you that we were going to bring a man back from the other side, would you have believed me?"

Clenching his teeth, Cameron shifted around in his seat so that he could look Bloom in the eye. "Who the fuck is he?"

"His name is Christofori. At one time he served as pianist for my orchestra. He was my most valued musician. Then one night he slit his throat and took his own life. But I knew a secret. Though he destroyed his body, some part of him lived on, trapped in a prison of Discord, a perpetual nightmare. And so when tonight our young Mr. Witt performed the Nocturne, Christofori heard it, and he came running like a hungry dog to the clanging dinner bell. The moment he emerged, his soul remembered the frequency of its former physical mass, and he once again became whole."

Cameron sat back, feeling deflated. He stared out the window at the dark buildings gliding past and wondered how long he would allow Bloom to guide him into the dark unknown. *Jesus Christ, what have I gotten myself into?*

"There are things that I must tell you about the orchestra," said Bloom quietly, "things that I could not tell you before. But now you've seen; now you understand the power behind the music. And now you are ready to learn more."

By now they were back at the town square, heading toward Cameron's hotel. He shrank into his seat, suddenly exhausted, and too tired to resist. Too tired to leave.

The world had begun to unravel, and nothing would ever be the same.

SECOND MOVEMENT
The Echoes

Lo! 'tis a gala night
Within the lonesome latter years!
An angel throng, bewinged, bedight
In veils, and drowned in tears,
Sit in a theatre, to see
A play of hopes and fears,
While the orchestra breathes fitfully
The music of the spheres.

–Edgar Allan Poe, Ligeia

Chapter 1

Holloway went through changes in the early weeks of September following Christofori's return. There seemed to exist a certain undertone of tension and discontent. People didn't talk about the change, and most weren't even aware of it, aside from an occasional suspicion. But it was there, like a slight discordant ringing in the ears, an agitation.

The police station became inundated with reports of domestic disputes, public disturbances, spousal abuse, and home burglaries. The people were acting more strangely each day.

The police reports were disturbing.

Terry Kaplan, an insurance agent at Fundamental, received an email including several scandalous pictures of his wife Annie, forty-year-old mother of two, having sex with three guys from the paper mill. That afternoon Terry sent his kids to his sister's house, and when Annie got home, he attacked her. He would have likely killed her, had his neighbor, Mel Kirkland, not called the police after hearing her screams. When the police arrived, Annie had come running out of the house, smeared in blood, wearing nothing but a pair of blue panties, begging the officers to save her.

There was Gary Lewis, a recovering alcoholic and father of two beautiful daughters, who quit his job without a second's notice and went on a week-long drinking binge. It ended when Sergeant Bentley found him face down in the cedar chip playground of Oak Fort Memorial. Gary had apparently drunk himself to death.

Then there was "Mooch" Gupton, who'd come back from the Iraq war and used his disability checks (he'd lost his hearing as a result of a roadside bomb) to purchase a small shack out on Memorial Drive. Mooch never bothered a soul. But that didn't stop Pete Wilkerson from blowing his chest open with a Remington twelve-gauge when he caught Mooch stealing apples from his orchard. When the chief arrived several hours later to investigate the scene, Pete insisted that it'd been an accident. He'd mistaken Mooch for a bear.

The town vandals also became inspired. Someone spray-painted "Fuck You" on the brick walls of the Presbyterian church. Two houses a block away from Bernie High went up in flames a day apart from each other. Meanwhile, some kids went driving around town, bashing mailboxes with baseball bats. It was a mess, and the seemingly disparate occurrences left Chief Dunlap with a feeling of hopelessness. A cop from the LAPD probably wouldn't flinch. But for Dunlap, it just didn't jibe. Things didn't happen like that in Holloway.

Only Bloom, and those closest to him, knew the reason for the sudden chaos. From the beginning, he'd suspected something like this would happen. There were side effects from conjuring vibrations powerful enough to open doors. The effect on the environment and the people was purely incidental. Performing Cameron's Astral Music with the Archetypes had created a powerful field of dark vibrations, and they needed somewhere to go. The echoes seeped into the woodwork and the earth like a toxic spill. The Calliope resonated with it, and the people within a few miles' radius felt it in their bones.

Cameron's two-mile trek to Oak Fort Memorial Park left him sweat-soaked in the noonday sun. The walk relaxed his muscles and churned his blood. He felt energized and ready to work on his nearly completed "Symphony of Holloway."

The thing had nearly consumed him these past few weeks. At least, it did when he wasn't spending time with Madison. In many ways, she'd become his muse, inspiring him. In fact, he often credited her with his newfound creativity, when in truth, he knew better. The real inspiration came from his sessions with the Tongue; while it dragged him through horrific dreams, it also proved therapeutic, and in the aftermath of writing his Nocturnes, he'd become a vessel of overwhelming creativity. He'd even come to welcome the fork's hellish pitch. The bottom line was that he was working again, writing music with a kind of fervor that had become unfamiliar to him over the past ten years. Attuning was everything Bloom had promised, and more.

He slid off his backpack and retrieved a bottle of water from it. Taking a swig, he moved deeper into the park. The entry road carried him past a miniature wooden fort that stood on a sea of cedar chips, where children squealed as they spilled down the slides, hung from the nets, and chased each other. He could tell at a glance that the kids were playing war—probably reenacting the Battle of Holloway. It was harmless, but it rubbed him wrong. Those kids had no idea of the horror that'd taken place here. Beyond the playground was the pond and then, beyond the next hill, the sun-bleached battlefield, where fences made from crude beams of timber ran along the perimeter. Antique cannons on wagon wheels sat poised at various points along the paved pathway. Several signs were posted along the trail, describing battles and providing biographical tidbits about generals and war heroes.

The steady crack of musket fire, the choking black clouds of gun smoke. Men dying in the grass, while cannon blasts drowned out their screams. That was the reality of the town's history.

Eventually, he reached the memorial cemetery and passed through the opened gate. He followed the main path through the weather-worn headstones to the short rock wall that extended across the cemetery's perimeter. He slid off his backpack, found his notebook inside, and sat down. He'd made it a habit to come here each morning and work. It beat sitting in his stuffy hotel room. Besides, the cemetery inspired him, with its memories of the dead, and more importantly, its view of the Calliope, which sat at the top of the hill about a mile away like some grim overseer. He couldn't have picked a better place to write a symphony about Holloway.

He flipped through the pages, arriving at the place where he'd left off. A quick scan of the work brought him up to speed. The piece had grown progressively darker. It couldn't be helped. It was Holloway's tragic history. The Symphony had changed considerably from those first inspired sessions. What had begun as a kind of grand American narrative was now something much darker. He no longer understood it himself, but he'd stayed honest to the work.

More than two weeks had passed since Charlie Witt had performed the Astral Music, setting Christofori free from his personal prison of hell. Since then, Cameron had learned the full story of Bloom's orchestra. Bloom had told it to him in pieces over several evenings, while they sat together on the mansion's stone terrace, looking down at the Cumberland Gorge.

"When I was a young man, a friend introduced me to a secret organization called the Musicians Guild," Bloom had told him. "The Guild owned a small museum outside Vienna, overlooking the Danube where they kept a storehouse of priceless musical instruments. I was immediately intrigued by the Guild, not only because of their collection, but because of their knowledge. Their library of books and secret letters all pointed to one single idea—an idea that I had always suspected, that music is magic, and that it has power. So I joined the Guild, and then they revealed a secret, the Archetypes, kept hidden in the basement for hundreds of years."

On this first night, they had sat in large iron chairs near the terrace's wooden railing. Only a few insect-repellent candles burned on the table beside them, and the inky darkness swallowed them both up. In that light, Bloom's relaxed yet regal outline could be seen, one leg draped over the other, shoulders square, arms relaxed on his chair's armrests.

"By the time I became a member, the Guild suffered from a detrimental case of boredom," Bloom said. "They were old and restless. They no longer believed the Archetypes had any power whatsoever. Some of them suggested that the Guild had been formed out of superstition and was irrelevant for the modern age. Nearly every meeting ended in a heated debate about what should be done with the instruments. Some wanted to call the news media and share our secret with the world. Some wanted to sell them. And then there were those like me who wanted to go on doing their job and keep them hidden.

"It was I who suggested we end the debate and simply play the damn things. 'Perform Armonia and see for ourselves,' I told them. The bastards were horrified by the thought." Bloom smiled quietly to himself as he stared up at the sprawl of stars in the vaulted night sky. "They came up with a thousand reasons why it was impossible. Where would we find an orchestra? Who would conduct it? But I pushed back. I told them that I would do all the work. I would form an orchestra, find a Tone Poet who could write Astral Music, and even conduct the Symphony. The Guild members were reluctant at first, but they eventually gave in. The next several years I focused my efforts on putting together an orchestra. I traveled the world, collecting musicians, convincing them to push the limits of their musical abilities. At the same time, I searched for a Tone Poet, someone like you who could write the unknowable music. In just two years I had my orchestra. But finding a Tone Poet was another matter. It took me another two years before I heard a rumor about a man who had heard the music of God."

Cameron, half drunk from the expensive wine that Bloom kept pouring, sat forward, irresistibly alert. He felt he was hearing his own story unfold. "Who was he?"

"I found him in an asylum overlooking Lake Geneva. His name was Luca Verdel. Like you, a near-death experience led to a profound interlude with the Divine. But he'd been overwhelmed with the experience, and over the years, it had slowly driven him insane."

Cameron cleared his throat uneasily. He knew the feeling. He knew how an experience like that plucked at the seams of sanity until the whole thing threatened to unravel.

"The asylum," Bloom had continued, "kept the man in a small room with a single window and an old piano with its strings clipped. I found him naked, wasted away, banging away at the silent keys, his fingernails bloody splinters. I accused the institution of negligence, and I demanded to take custody of the man. After months of negotiations, the sanitarium awarded me custody.

"I brought Verdel to our museum in Vienna, where we began sessions with the Tongue. I had hoped to Attune him, but he was far too gone for that. Each session played out the same way. Luca would listen to the tuning fork until its Discord filled his head with nightmares. But instead of writing, he would get up and leave the room. I realized too late that he was using the fork to nurture his demons, rather than exorcise them. This was, of course, a blatant abuse of the tuning fork. Without artistic catharsis, the Discord made him sicker.

"I was angry, of course. I knew Luca Verdel would never Attune, but I wanted my Symphony, and so I allowed my desires to override my discretion. I forced the matter. I told the Guild that we were ready. A week later I led the orchestra in our first Symphony of Astral Music."

The revelation forced the air from Cameron's lungs. He paced the terrace. "Why did you keep this from me?"

"I had my reasons," said Bloom, a warning in his tone.

Cameron bit back his anger. "So what happened then?"

Bloom's eyes lost focus as he recalled some frightful memory. "A nightmare. Complete terror. Verdel harbored dark secrets. From the moment we began, I felt his sickness—his Discord—spread through me. There was a moment, I think, when I could have stopped the Symphony, but I was too curious, and I let it continue. Rather than tapping into Armonia, we tapped into something . . . else. Complete Discord. Filth."

The air chilled. Cameron sat down, suddenly spooked.

Bloom blinked and then fixed his eyes on Cameron. "I assure you, we do not want a reoccurrence of that night. That's why our sessions with the Tongue are necessary. We must be absolutely certain that we rid all discordance from your astral body. You must Attune, or you cannot give us Armonia."

Cameron shook his head, considering the insanity of it all. He closed his eyes and rubbed the bridge of his nose with his thumb and forefinger. "Why are we doing this? Didn't you already learn your lesson? I mean, I'm not a religious guy, but if I were, I'd think we were fucking with things that we shouldn't be fucking with."

"Isn't that the beauty of it—this act of divine trespass?" Bloom grinned. "I think you and I are both intrigued by the idea of unveiling the secrets of the universe. Besides, it didn't kill us before, even when it probably should have. But this time will be different."

"Why should I believe that?"

"Because you are different. You are Attuning. I can feel it. And so can you. This is destiny. We were brought together for this purpose. Imagine it, Cameron. If we get it right—and I think we will—we will touch the Divine, and the experience will transcend anything man has ever known. This is the true religious experience. This is what poets and gurus have only tasted since the beginning of time. I'm talking about a transcendent moment in the history of mankind—a moment when man creates a bridge to God. Can we possibly turn away from that?"

There had been no denying his curiosity after that. Cameron was sold.

So they had conducted more sessions with the Tongue, more nightmares relived, all in the name of Attuning. Those nightmares continued to haunt him afterwards. He woke sometimes in the middle of the night with the violent feedback-squeal of the fork ringing in his ears. It seemed to have some effect on his moods, too, giving him the highs and lows of a manic-depressive. He couldn't help wonder how much more he could withstand before snapping like Luca Verdel.

But the Tongue had helped him too. He couldn't deny that. Not just with the Astral Music, but with his personal music. Like what he was writing now.

A breeze whispered through the cemetery trees and Cameron looked down at the sprawl of notes across the notebook paper in his lap. He was in way over his head. He couldn't ignore the dangers, both physical and mental. Maybe even spiritual too. He had every reason to leave.

But the truth was he couldn't leave. Not yet. No matter how insane things got, he couldn't shake the feeling of purpose—that he was following some sort of predetermined course. Destiny. When the music welled up inside him, he set his pen to paper and started to write.

"Ah, Mr. Kalek," said Bloom as the old man trundled into his office. He leaned back in his chair and spread his arms amiably. "I've been expecting you. You seem to be on your own schedule these days."

The old man huffed as he moved over to an armchair and dropped into it. His wispy hair fell over his heavily wrinkled brow. His face was sallow, with dark pools beneath his eyes. "I apologize. I've been busy."

Bloom's eyes narrowed as he played with a pencil. "You look worn to the bone. Shall I get you a drink?"

"No," said Kalek, flapping a hand in the air. "No booze. Not tonight."

"Is everything all right, Alfred?" asked Bloom with great affection.

"I'm fine," Kalek wheezed. "Everything is fine. Just tired, is all."

Bloom knew better. He'd long ago lost confidence in Kalek, and this disappointed him. At one time, the old man had followed him with nearly religious fervor, more so than the other former church members did. Kalek had once proven himself an adroit businessman, resourceful and astute, and for more than a decade had overseen Bloom's entire estate. He had helped sell a trove of stolen artifacts—not an easy task. He'd also worked out the arrangements for the Calliope and the old sanitarium. Kalek had successfully kept the show running for all these years, but somewhere along the way, he'd lost faith, and now doubt had curled up in the old man's brain like a parasite. Of course, Kalek never gave voice to his doubt. But Bloom knew it was there.

It didn't matter. The show was nearing its conclusion, and Kalek had outlived his potential. Bloom asked him, "We have come a long way, have we not, old friend?"

Kalek nodded. "Yes. We certainly have."

"Hard to believe that we are merely weeks away from accomplishing what we set out to do more than a decade ago." He watched Kalek's face for any sign of doubt, worry, or something worse, and he found it there, like a shadow slipping over the old man's face.

Kalek seemed to sense Bloom's concern. He dropped his head. "Simon worries me. The man is deranged. I don't trust him."

"Where is this coming from?"

"He's an abomination." Kalek's thin frame trembled beneath his jacket. When Bloom made a displeased face, he quickly added, "I'm worried he will jeopardize everything we've worked for. We can't let him out of our sight. He should be locked down, hidden from public, before he hurts someone."

"Simon rarely leaves the estate," said Bloom casually.

"Oh, I doubt that. I doubt that very much."

Bloom waved a petulant hand. "I'm not concerned about Simon." He adjusted the sleeves of his jacket. "Now, as I recall, you've been keeping a close watch on Cameron Blake. Surely you must have seen something that we can use."

The tension rushed from Kalek's muscles, leaving him slumped in his chair. He scratched his unshaven face. "I don't have anything to tell you. He keeps to himself, mostly."

"But what does he do with his time?"

Kalek shrugged. "He writes."

The maestro said nothing for several moments. He finally nodded to himself. "All right. Keep a close eye on him. Follow him. Find out what he does when he's not working. I want to know everything about him."

The old man nodded and started to get up.

"Oh, and Kalek?"

"Yes, Maestro?"

"Don't forget why we are doing this. Stay strong for me, old friend. We have only a little further before we rest."

With a tired nod, Kalek turned and left the office.

Chapter 2

"**I** finished it," Cameron said, handing the notebook to Bloom.

The two men followed along the mansion corridor where the air-conditioned air lapped at Cameron's neck, causing him to shiver. He didn't mind. He'd spent most of the day outside in the heat, working on the Symphony. The project had swallowed him whole. Only when he'd finished did he realize that he was late for his visit with Bloom. He hadn't even had time to clean up before racing to the estate.

"What is this?" said Bloom, slowing some as he flipped through the pages.

"The symphony I told you about. I finished."

"Ah! The new project. I'm excited about this, Cameron." He snapped the notebook shut and gave a wry smile. "Didn't I tell you? Didn't I say that pushing the boundaries of music would lead you to higher grounds as an artist? You've found inspiration. Tell me more about this symphony."

Cameron scratched the back of his head, feeling oddly self-conscious. "I chose Holloway as the backdrop. It seemed like a good subject."

"Yes, Holloway has a fascinating history. It should do well for a subject."

They began walking again. For a short while neither said a word, with only the tapping of their footfalls interrupting their silence.

"Holloway Festival will be here in just a few weeks," said Bloom. "I was hoping to give the orchestra a chance to perform. This will be perfect."

"You should probably give it a listen before you get your hopes up."

They turned another corner and entered through a set of doors, leading them into a large anteroom where burgundy drapes hung over tall windows and rows of leather bound books climbed the walls. Across the room, a man stood facing away from them, eyes fixed on the piano, hands locked behind his back. Tall, slender, and wearing a black suit, he looked like a vulture waiting for something to die.

The man did not turn until Bloom cleared his throat. Then he spun around as if to pounce, regarding them both with large, almond-shaped eyes. He was handsome, with a narrow face, angular cheekbones, and a high brow. His long black hair nearly touched his shoulders, framing a striking yet somehow lifeless face.

"Christofori," said Bloom, taking a step farther into the room. "I've brought our composer. I wanted you to meet him. This is Cameron Blake."

Hands still clasped behind him, the pianist took a step forward and sized Cameron up with a single glance. He looked at Bloom. "You are late," he said in a hoarse whisper, a thick Italian accent flavoring his tone. "I expected you hours ago."

"I see that you are feeling better," Bloom said crisply. "You should be back to your old self soon enough." He looked through a set of open double doors leading into an adjoining bedroom.

Cameron followed his gaze and glimpsed at a four-post bed beyond the doors. A woman lay curled on her side on a tangle of sheets. She didn't move.

"I trust she is only sleeping," Bloom said.

Cameron looked at him, puzzled, until it occurred to him that something might be wrong with the woman. He felt a rush of panic as he looked back at her. She lay perfectly still. Too still.

Christofori moved over to the doors and pulled them shut. "My guest is very tired," he said, turning to face them as he put his back to the doors. He allowed a quiet smile. "She had a long night."

He crossed the room and stopped to stare at Cameron, who backed a step.

The man looked normal enough, but Cameron couldn't shake the initial image of him, covered in blood and birthstuff, rising up from the opened back of the Dragon.

Cameron's face belied his disgust and the musician suddenly scowled at him.

"You don't look much like a Tone Poet," Christofori said. "What makes you think you can deliver Armonia to us?"

With an unaffected shrug, Cameron said smugly, "The boss seems to think so."

After searching Cameron a moment longer, Christofori turned to face Bloom. His eyes fell to the briefcase hanging from Bloom's right hand. "Maestro, that wouldn't be the music you promised, would it?"

"I had every reason to burn them," Bloom said coldly. Then he held the briefcase in the air between them. "I should have, the way you left us so quickly."

A kind of hungry desperation burned in Christofori's eyes. His nostrils flared as he ran his tongue wetly across his bottom lip. He took the briefcase from Bloom's hands and sat down on a nearby sofa. He placed it on the coffee table before him and released the hasps with a snap.

"My God," he whispered as the case opened and he sorted through the brittle sheet music. His mouth quivered. "Is it all here? Every piece?"

"All of it."

Christofori fell silent as he fluttered through the pages, pausing at various moments to appreciate a forgotten work before moving to the next. His face held a look of religious awe.

Bloom continued. "I have kept these for you as an act of friendship. I expect you will return the favor. You must promise me that you will not leave this orchestra before we perform Armonia. We cannot do so without you."

"Despite our differences, I have always been loyal . . . to the music. I wish to hear Armonia as much as you. But you must not fail us again. I cannot endure that. You must promise me this."

Bloom flinched slightly, eyes narrowing. "We will not fail this time. I assure you."

The musician's dark eyes gazed inward, weighing and measuring. Finally he said, "I will stay."

Bloom left and Cameron followed, but he hesitated before stepping out the door. He looked toward the bedroom doors, wondering about the woman, but Christofori now stood in his line of sight, his brow raised, as if daring Cameron to press the matter.

With a slight nod, Cameron turned away.

Silently, the two men walked the dark hallways, moving deeper into the house. With twilight setting, the estate felt like a mausoleum, with shadows playing tricks on Cameron's eyes, their footfalls echoing like knuckles rapping on the wall of a tomb.

"What was all that about?" Cameron said once they were far enough away from the musician's room.

Bloom wore a tight smile. "Christofori has something of a fetish for rare music, particularly ensembles written by psychopaths and murderers. These musical nightmares express the darkest of the human condition. They give sound to man's greatest fears. Before Christofori took his own life, his audiences paid fortunes to hear them."

"Charming," Cameron said with a smirk.

"He is fortunate that I had the foresight to keep them."

"I'm sure."

Soon they reached the door at the end of the hallway, and Cameron tasted acid at the back of his throat. Time for another session with Bloom's tuning fork. Just thinking about it made his head spin.

"This is our fourth session," said Bloom. "More than halfway there. Seven chakras; seven sessions."

"I want to do this. But I–I feel like this is killing me," Cameron said flatly.

Bloom looked at him with a quiet smile. "I suppose, in a way, it is."

At that moment, the door opened as if on its own, with Kalek standing on the other side, smiling tightly. "Good to see you again, Mr. Blake. Everything is prepared."

Cameron's taxi came to a stop before a shack of a building with a flat tin roof and a front porch with wooden railings. Beer signs buzzed in the windows. The word "Bloozy's" glowed in big blue neon letters on the front of the bar. The place was busy, with maybe forty cars parked in its gravel lot.

"This is it," said Buzz, looking in the rearview with an amiable grin. The driver was in a boonie hat and a chambray shirt, and his car reeked of cigarette smoke and body odor. "Wish I could join you."

"Anytime, Buzz." Cameron slapped a twenty into the man's hand and got out.

The balmy night air rang with music and wild laughter. He crunched across the gravel, feeling tired, not sure if he was really up to this. It'd only been a few hours since his session with the Tongue, and his head still swam with the fork's sickening tone and its dark hallucinations. In its aftermath, he'd written music that made Stravinsky's "Rite of Spring" sound like a child's lullaby, and still he had more Nocturnes to compose, more Discord to uproot, as his soul was apparently wrought with it. He stepped into the bar and stood at the door for a moment, allowing his eyes to adjust to the dark, smoky lights. The noise was deafening. Over the heads of the crowd, he spotted a stage at the opposite end of the barroom where a trio of black musicians grooved to a slow, spicy tune. The lead singer, as big and burly as a grizzly bear, eked mournful sounds from his guitar, while the trumpeter to his left drew himself up and blew a somber cry. The keyboardist to the right let loose a shower of high notes. The music jabbed a hot poker into the pit of Cameron's stomach, and he smiled despite himself. It was good music. For the first time in weeks he felt grounded. The smell of beer and cigarettes suited him just fine. This was real, visceral stuff.

His eyes happened on a man sitting on the stage steps, a guitar cradled in his lap. He almost didn't recognize Hob in his gray vest, rayon slacks, and porkpie hat, cocked at an angle on his head. Smiling, Cameron made his way to the bar. He ordered two Budweisers from an attractive female bartender who looked like an African queen, with her head wrap, black curls, and large golden hoop earrings. With a bottle in each hand, he worked his way over to the stage.

Hob didn't see him at first. He was too entranced by the music, eyes shut, head bobbing to the rhythm, his hands keeping time on the side of his guitar.

"Hob!" Cameron shouted, competing with the music.

Hob jerked his head up, startled, and looked up at Cameron with his brow knotted into a frown. He smiled, as if knowing all along that Cameron would eventually visit him.

"Well, if it ain't Jerry Lee Lewis himself," Hob said with a wide grin. "How you doin', man?"

"Good to see you," said Cameron, handing Hob a Budweiser.

Hob gave him a look of solemn gratitude before he took the bottle and sipped it. "Now that's mighty nice of you. Say, you just in time. Me and Boots is just about to go on—five, maybe six minutes from now. Why don't you join us? You can use Pap's keyboard. He won't mind."

Cameron shook his head and waved his hands defensively. "Oh no, I'm just here to listen."

Boots came over and clapped a hand on Hob's shoulder. "Hob, you just about ready?"

"I'm always ready." He motioned toward Cameron and said, "This here's Cameron Blake. You remember me talkin' 'bout him, don't you?"

"Oh, yeah," said Boots. "I hear you play some mean keys."

Offering a humble smile, Cameron shook his head and said, "Contrary to what Hob will tell you, I'm not much of a musician. I write—that's the easy part. I let guys like you do all the hard work."

"Don't listen to him," Hob interjected playfully. "I'm tryin' to get him up there with us, but somethin' tells me the boy's chicken."

"Is that right?" Boots knitted his brow. "Come on up with us. Ain't nothin' to be scared about. We just here to have some fun."

On stage, the band ended their song, and the trumpeter wished everyone a good night. Moments later, the sweaty musicians thundered down the steps, passing through Hob, Boots, and Cameron.

"That's our cue," said Boots.

Hob tipped back his beer and drank half of it in a single swallow. Then he caught Cameron's eye and tipped his chin toward the stage. "Come on, man. Whatcha got to lose?"

Hob bounded up on stage and adjusted the microphone stand. Boots followed him up. "Holloway, lookin' good out there," Hob said in a deep, rich voice. "We gonna slow things down a little just now. But first, I want to welcome a friend of mine up to the stage. Name's Cameron Blake. Plays a mean piano. Paps . . . if it's okay with you?"

"Okay by me," Paps called from the crowd.

Cameron shook his head. He didn't want to perform. He just wanted to drink his beer, get a nice buzz, and go home.

"Only problem is," Hob went on, "this boy's kinda shy. Let's see if we can get him up here."

Applause and whistles filled the bar. Though Cameron kept on shaking his head, the crowd heckled him on. It went on for a few moments until he finally caved. He hopped up the steps and gave a reluctant wave to the crowd once the spotlight found him. He went over to the electric Yamaha keyboard and took a seat. Sweat had already begun to drip down his face. Whistles came at him like bottle rockets. Boots winked at him.

Hob, his guitar hanging at his hip, fluttered his fingers along the strings and conjured up a bluesy phrase. Boots answered back. A few excited whistles and shouts of praise came from the audience. When Hob nodded at him, Cameron reluctantly picked up Hob's slow rhythm and found the scale. Soon the magic happened: a smooth and intuitive melody. Losing himself to the sound, Cameron allowed his fingers to explore the keys. And it sounded good. It felt good. Worries vanished. Fears and disappointments lost their potency. Performing the blues for an audience worked like a drug, and he let go.

After their brief but welcome session—the crowd had given them an impressive ovation—Cameron, Hob, and Boots slid into a dark booth at the back of the bar and ordered a pitcher of Pabst Blue Ribbon. Beneath a dim lamp that hovered above them, the three men drank and grinned with satisfaction. They made small talk for a little while, and then Boots threw a few bills on the table and called it quits.

"You done real good out there, Cameron," he said with a wide grin. "I hope we can do this again in the future."

"Me too," Cameron said, clapping the man's meaty shoulder.

After Boots left, Hob dug a crumpled cigarette pack from his front pocket, shook one out, and lit it between his lips. He drew from it with his eyes closed and rested his head against the back of his bench, looking like a man savoring the afterglow of good sex. "You know, you ain't so bad for a white boy."

Cameron raised his mug. "I'll drink to that."

"You decide to stay in Holloway for a while, we could make this a legitimate act." He poured frothy beer into his mug and then Cameron's, spilling copious amounts on the table. When he sat back in his seat, he held Cameron with a quiet gaze before speaking. "So, what's up with Mr. Bloom these days?"

"Interesting guy."

Breathing smoke from his nostrils, Hob tilted his head. "You can say that again. By the way, that song I heard you playin' the first day I met you, where'd you learn that?"

Cameron frowned, searching his memory. He shrugged. "Honestly, I don't remember. Why?"

"It's just that, well . . ." Hob stopped himself, smiling sheepishly, and then waved a dismissive hand. "I best keep my mouth shut. You might think I lost my damn mind."

"Try me."

"Well, that song . . . it sounded like something me and my wife used to sing during our shows." He chuckled hesitantly.

"Is that right? I wish I could remember it. Maybe I hit my head harder than I thought."

Hob's smile left his face. "It scared the hell out of me. See, unless you caught us at one of our shows, which I doubt, there's no way you could have heard it. We never recorded it. I don't sing it anymore. And Clara . . . well, Clara's been dead for six years."

Cameron dropped his gaze and scratched his jaw, uncomfortable with the implications of this conversation. After a moment of reflection, he said, "Maybe you just heard what you wanted to hear."

Hob looked disappointed. "Yeah. Maybe."

Cameron drained the rest of his beer. He shifted in his seat, feeling bad. "Hey, maybe I picked up something. You know? Psychic impressions. That sort of thing. Honestly, I did feel . . . something."

The light returned to Hob's eyes and he grinned quietly, knowingly. He managed a quiet laugh. "I like you. You're all right."

Cameron toasted him with his mug. "Right back atcha."

The waitress came over with another pitcher of beer, and they refilled their mugs, talking about nothing in particular while they drank. After a few jokes, Hob became withdrawn.

He fixed Cameron with a suspicious gaze. "Will you be honest with me?"

"Okay. Sure."

"Your work with Maestro Bloom—that wouldn't have anything to do with those instruments in the basement, would it?"

A long, silent moment passed before Cameron asked uneasily, "You know about those?"

"I been the Calliope's janitor for ten years. You think she can keep a secret like that from me?"

"Does Bloom know you've seen them?"

"Hell no. Mr. Kalek promised to fire me if I ever so much as stepped a foot in that basement." Hob slid his glass to the side, then leaned forward with his arms folded on the table. "Listen, I got a good thing goin' there. I show up two, maybe three times a week, and I work my own schedule. Don't nobody tell me what to do. Mr. Kalek pays me to stay invisible, and every week I get a paycheck in the mail. And it's a good enough paycheck. But I'll tell you somethin': that Calliope is bad news. Got some bad energy trapped in her boards. Some days you can almost hear it, hissin' like a radio that's lost its signal."

Cameron shivered. In truth, he'd had a bad feeling from the moment he stepped foot into the Calliope, which only grew worse when he'd gone into its basement. "That place is strange, isn't it?"

"Oh, it's strange all right. Trust me. And strange shit happens there all the time. Like you playin' a song that you ain't never heard before and that, without a doubt in my mind, was written by a woman who has been gone now for a very long time." When Cameron didn't dispute it, Hob continued. "So back to my original question. You obviously know about the instruments. I just want to know: What's Bloom plannin' on doin' with them?"

Part of Cameron wanted to tell Hob everything, from his near-death experience, to Bloom's desire to capture the Astral Music and play it on those twisted instruments of his. But another part of him refused to talk. This had nothing to do with Hob. "You know, he showed them to me," he said, eyes focusing on a burning cigarette stub in the ashtray. "They're interesting to look at, but not a whole lot more. I mean, they're antiques. Not a one of them could carry a clean note." He paused before meeting Hob's gaze again, and when he did, his stomach clenched.

Hob's eyes were hard and piercing, his nostrils flaring as his lips formed a straight line. "You too, huh?"

Cameron felt a stab of guilt for lying.

"These days it seems like everyone is more interested in keepin' secrets than anything else. I suppose I can't blame you. I mean, we hardly know each other."

"Hob—"

"Like I said, I like you. I think Clara likes you too. I think she channeled through you in order to tell me somethin'. Maybe she wants me to look out for you. Maybe even warn you. That's why I'm gonna tell you this, and I want you to listen to me closely." He leaned forward, his voice dropping to a whisper. "I don't know what business you got with Bloom. But whatever it is, ain't nothin' good gonna come out of it. Not the Calliope. Not those instruments in her basement. You mixed up with the wrong crowd."

The two men fell silent. Cameron held the man's gaze for as long as he could before dropping his eyes. He felt suddenly drained. He wanted nothing more than to go back to his own bed in San Diego and forget he'd ever come to this strange town. "I gotta go, Hob," he finally said. "I appreciate everything. I really do."

Hob sneered and shook his head. "You ain't heard a word I said all night."

Cameron rose, dug a twenty from his back pocket, and tossed it on the table. "Thanks for the talk," he said. "Let's do this again sometime." With that, he left Hob sitting alone at the table, sulking over his beer.

It was past eleven at night when Charlie let himself inside the large home on Gravis Avenue. It didn't surprise him to find most of the lights on. He knew the routine. It was Friday night and that meant he'd find his mother, Dory, in the den, watching late night dramas in her silver nightgown, half sloshed on vodka martinis. His stepdad would be passed out drunk in his leather recliner in the upstairs room, Fox News on the TV. That's how they kept the marriage going. Neither could stand the other's company, and so they retired to their own holes and drank themselves unconscious.

The moment Charlie walked inside, his mother hurried out into the foyer in her nightgown, her eyes wide and hopeful. She shouted over her shoulder, "Howard, he's home!"

She rushed over to Charlie, but she stopped before she reached him. "Oh, God, Charlie?" she said, clapping her hands over her mouth. "What's wrong with you?"

He liked that she saw it. He was different now. He felt different. It was Cameron Blake's music—it had changed him. He could feel it, and it showed.

Heavy footfalls drew Charlie from his thoughts. His stepfather, a short man with a heavy gut in blue pajamas, squeezed into the vestibule. His broad face was flushed from alcohol and anger. For a moment, both his mom and Howard stood with horror stamped on their faces as they blocked Charlie's path.

"Christ Almighty, what the hell happened to you?" Howard growled. Sour whiskey lingered on his breath. He looked at Dory. "The kid's on dope. Probably stoned out of his mind for the past three days."

He grabbed Charlie's arm by the elbow and held it up so he could inspect for needle marks. Seeing none, he let the arm fall. "What are you on, boy? Just tell us."

Charlie didn't bother with an explanation. They didn't deserve one. And he no longer needed them. Following the days of his rebirth, he'd moved into a small room within the sanitarium on Bloom's estate. It was small and dark with holes in the walls that allowed rats to come and go. It suited him just fine. Things were changing. He didn't care for worldly comforts anymore. Food became bland; he ate only once a day. Sunlight irritated his skin. Soap made him nauseous. Most days he just stayed in his room, curtains drawn, staring at the wall, occasionally getting up to relieve himself in the bathroom at the other end of the hallway. Sometimes he just urinated in the corner.

Joining the orchestra gave meaning to his life. Not that he served an actual role within the ensemble. As a musician, he'd done all he could for them once he resurrected Christofori. But there were other ways he could help them as they prepared for their great Symphony, of which Charlie knew little, aside from it's importance to the musicians.

Without a word he pressed past his mother and charged upstairs to his bedroom.

His stepfather followed him to the first step, where he stood by the balustrade. "You ain't fooling anyone, Charlie! I know what this is. You're goddamn lucky we haven't called the cops yet." He looked at Dory. "Crystal meth, I'd bet. Did you see his eyes? My God, he's stoned out of his goddamn gourd."

Upstairs, Charlie shut his bedroom door behind him. His mother had tidied up his room—which he always hated—making his bed and leaving a pile of folded clothes on the chair. He found a backpack in the closet, dumped the books, then stuffed it with jeans and t-shirts. Before leaving, he stopped in front of the mirror and looked at himself. It was true. He looked like death. He no longer wore his glasses after they'd shattered that night at the Calliope, and he was bloodlessly pale. His long hair fell in greasy tangles to his shoulders and he'd grown. He was nothing like the old, nerdy Charlie that everyone picked on. No, this was better. He grinned at himself but it looked more like a snarl, and it would have made his mother scream had she seen it.

When he returned downstairs, his parents were waiting for him. They looked at his bags with astonishment. His mother shook with worry, but his stepfather grew red in the face and trundled into his path.

"Howard, for Christ's sake!" Dory shouted. "Do something!"

"Now that's enough!" Howard shouted at Charlie, aiming a finger at the upstairs loft. "You turn your ass around and go back upstairs or I'm calling the goddamn cops."

Enraged, Charlie shoved his stepdad against the wall and pinned him there with his forearm. Leaning close to his ear, he growled, "Leave me . . . the fuck . . . alone."

"I'll call the police!" his old man wheezed. "You hear me? I'll have you put in jail."

"You don't have the balls," Charlie snarled. He stepped away, shot his mother a warning glance, then stormed out the front door.

Chapter 3

Cameron and Madison returned to the waterfall later that September on a day of cool breezes and abundant sunshine, a climate too exquisite to squander inside. With a cooler packed with food and drinks, including a bottle of wine and two plastic wine cups, they followed the same trail, only this time they took a rocky path beyond the waterfall. Madison claimed it was a secret path, and Cameron doubted if it were a path at all.

At some points it became dangerous, and they had to climb. But she moved confidently ahead, familiar with each rock and root, as she led him higher and higher. The payoff was worth it; a private overlook where a massive flat boulder provided a ledge for them to sit down and relax. From here, they had a spectacular view of the waterfall.

While Madison rummaged a blanket from her backpack, Cameron stood at the edge, hands on his hips, and whistled at the sight. Then he turned and helped her spread the blanket across the smooth rock. Together, they sat with their arms draped over their knees, while the sun dried the sweat from their faces.

"Isn't this wonderful?" She kept her eyes closed against the sun, and Cameron stole a long glance at her face, wanting to stare at her for hours. When she blinked her eyes open, he looked away, embarrassed. She seemed not to notice.

"Sometimes I come here to get away," she said. "Read a book or just meditate. It's private. No one bothers you."

"Is that so?" Grinning mischievously, Cameron leaned over for a kiss.

She didn't resist when their lips met, nor when their tongues explored one another. He drew her closer, with one arm wrapped about her back, and kissed the crook of her neck. He breathed her in, tasted her, immersed himself in all the physical wonders of Madison Taylor. With his back to the blanket, the smooth but hard rock beneath, he pulled her on top of him as their hands moved over each other's bodies.

"Oh God, Cameron," she whispered as he ran his hands beneath her shirt. She wasn't wearing a bra, and his thumbs explored the puckered skin of her nipples. "Maybe we should slow down," she managed between gasps.

He looked up at her. "You said it was private here."

"That's not what I'm worried about. If you don't stop, I'm going to do something I might regret."

Blood throbbed in his groin while she searched his eyes. She must have found whatever she was looking for. Suddenly she slipped her shirt over her head. Cameron swallowed and lowered his gaze to the small swells of her breasts, exquisitely shaped. She bent forward for a kiss. He returned it. Her tongue probed deep into his mouth. He slid his fingers through her hair, his heart lurching into overdrive as she quietly unfastened his shorts. He did the same for her. Soon they were both undressed and tangled up in each other's arms. He ran his tongue down the slope of her throat, tasted the salt of her skin while exploring her breasts. Her scent filled his head as her hair spilled over him like a shower of feathers.

Then he slid himself inside her. His toes curled with the pleasure of it all. She gave a little cry and bit his shoulder. He clenched his eyes shut, then opened them wide, and the world went away. There was only their pleasure and the rushing of the waterfall. It filled his ears and became the sound of his blood roaring through his veins. It was fast and fierce lovemaking, and it ended all too soon.

Afterwards, Cameron lay on his back with one arm under his head. Madison was curled up next to him. They fell silent as the sun shone down on them. He dozed for a moment, for how long, he couldn't say.

She woke him with a question. "So what kind of work are you doing with the orchestra?"

"It's complicated," he said flatly. He felt ashamed. He'd never mentioned

Charlie. Her cousin. It was much more complicated than he could ever explain.

"Try me," she insisted.

He sat up with his arms draped over his knees and gazed out at the vast canopy of forest beneath them. He found a rock with his fingers and tossed it over the side of the ledge. He let the silence go on for several moments as he prepared to talk. Until now, he'd lived a secret life, doing things that he knew would never make sense to the rest of the world. And with the exception of Hob, he'd kept it all to himself. He never thought he'd actually explain his actions.

"Bloom found me in L.A. Told me he was working on a special project and needed someone with my background."

"Why your background?"

He looked at her for a moment and wondered if he really wanted to tell her. But he already knew the answer. He wanted it more than anything. He'd been going at this alone far too long. He'd held back from telling Hob. Bloom and Kalek didn't count. It was always business with those two, and they kept secrets.

Finally, he looked at her and said, "Because I've heard the Astral Music."

"Astral Music? What the heck is that?"

He told his story. He began with the car wreck and the music he heard during his four minutes of death. He talked about his subsequent obsession with the near-death music during his college years and how it had driven away his first wife. He talked about Bloom's visit to L.A. and their agreement to work together. Once he finished, his ears burned with embarrassment.

"That sure is quite a story," she said a little uneasily. She tried to smile but failed miserably. Her eyes danced left and right before fixing directly on him.

"You think I'm crazy," he said.

She brought her knees to her chin and folded her arms around her legs. "I don't think you're crazy. It's just, I don't like Bloom. He's weird. He keeps the Calliope so secretive. And his orchestra, have you seen them? Well, of course you have—they're all so really, really strange."

"I know it," said Cameron. "But they want the same thing I want. And I'm closer than I've ever been. I can feel it. Besides, things are already getting better for me. I'm really on top of things. I feel tremendous—even inspired. Would you believe I just wrote a symphony? I finished it in just a few weeks. And it's good . . . I think." He smiled, but caught the worry lines crossing her brow and changed his tone. Taking her hands into his own, he said, "Listen, I know it sounds strange, but I could really use a friend right now."

Her eyes searched his face. "Well, I just hope you know what you're doing."

"Me too."

It was past midnight and Charlie lay with his hands folded beneath his head on the stiff Army-issue cot, staring up and watching a tiny spider scuttle across the cracked ceiling. He'd watched the spider for maybe an hour, waiting for sleep to take him. His room at the end of the eastern wing of the sanitarium's first floor was not much bigger than a walk-in closet and hot as an oven. He didn't care; he liked it here. This was his new home.

Ignoring the beads of sweat forming on his upper lip, he closed his eyes, wanting to sleep, but he could hear through the walls. The musicians who shared the building with him never slept. At any point of the night he heard wild laughter or sobs. Most of the Echoes sat in their stinking dorm rooms and played music through all hours of the night so that the halls echoed cacophony. Bloom's orchestra was a strange bunch, all right. They all shared the same cold black eyes, like the eyes of sharks, detached and vicious.

They reminded him of vampires. A coven of bloodsuckers. It was a recurring thought. Maybe tonight they'd try to eat him. The thought sent his heart galloping in his chest. He rolled over onto his side and buried his face in his pillow. He thought about his mother, wondered if she worried for him, and felt the sting of loneliness before shoving the thought away. He had to watch out for thoughts like that. They would tear him apart if he let them. Those thoughts belonged to the old Charlie, and the old Charlie was dead.

He closed his eyes and imagined himself standing on the stage of a lavish concert hall.

Lights shone in his eyes. In the dark seats below, hundreds of men and women, dressed in a fashion belonging to another age, watched with quiet anticipation. He was dreaming. That had to be it.

Notes tinkled behind him, and he turned to find Christofori, sitting before his piano, ensconced in the beam of a spotlight. Charlie watched as the man began storming through a wildly complex piece. Maybe it wasn't his dream; maybe it was Christofori's dream.

Dressed all in black, his face glowing like bones, Christofori looked like a sinister mortician sitting before a coffin on its bier, his fingers scurrying. His music sounded like a funeral dirge.

Charlie covered his ears against it. Tears filled his eyes.

A dizzying menagerie of scenes spun through his mind—all of Christofori, of Bloom, of sometime long past when the fashion world was draped in regency gowns and candelabras. All through it the spinning continued, the dirge trudging mournfully, and the gasps of pleasure or pain from women.

And Bloom's voice whispering "soul" and "music." When Christofori moved at the piano and the dream slowed, scrawls of bloody writing among the notes on the sheet music focused in Charlie's view.

Christofori was suddenly gone. Charlie turned around, dizzy and nauseated from the whir of dreaming, and there he saw the elegantly thin pianist. A claw-footed porcelain bathtub. The pianist soaked in the water there, a look of despair on his now gaunt face. Charlie frowned as the man dropped a hand to the side of the tub. His fingers searched for something on the floor. Eventually he found the straight razor. The water sloshed as he brought the edge up to his eyes and allowed the light to slide across its length. He lowered it to his neck, blade glinting at his throat.

Charlie gaped. He charged forward with a hand raised. "No!"

He woke with a start. He couldn't stop shivering, and when the tears came, he didn't try to stop them but instead covered his face with his hands and cried himself to sleep.

Chapter 4

On Saturday, more than two thousand people flooded the town square to celebrate Holloway Festival.

This beat last year's turnout by several hundred. The crowd got going around ten in the morning, and by noon it could barely fit on Main Street. Bells jangled and firecrackers popped. The smells of frying grease, sugar, and cooked meat hung in the air. At the booths lining the sidewalks, children got their faces painted and visitors could get their caricatures drawn for three dollars—except all the artist's portraits looked the same, though no one had the gall to tell him. Cameron especially liked the old-fashioned red popcorn wagons that smelled of butter.

He and Madison made their way through the crowds and vendors, both of them breathing in the carnival smells of cotton candy and funnel cakes, hotdogs, and hamburgers. When they passed a small brass quartet in the gazebo behind the courthouse, Cameron grinned. He felt like a kid all over again. It was a good feeling.

"You know, I didn't think places like this existed anymore," he said. "I keep expecting to see Andy Griffith drive by in a '65 Ford Mayberry squad car."

"Are you poking fun?" Madison asked.

"No way. I love it."

A whirlwind swarmed in his stomach as she gave him a suspicious grin. She had a warm openness about her and a kind of childish glow that made him want to scoop her up and smother her with kisses. She wore a tight red t-shirt and khaki shorts, her hair drawn back and braided.

"If you're impressed with this," she said, "you should see this place during Christmas. It's like Whoville."

The distant sound of applause and trumpets and a thudding bass drum drew their attention to the western side of the square where the crowd had thickened. Madison looked at him with wide-eyed excitement.

"They're starting the parade." She slipped her hand into his and pulled him toward the gathering crowd. "Let's go watch!"

He allowed her to lead him through the bustle, and when they reached the corner of Bard and Main, they found a clearing beside a streetlamp where they had a view of the oncoming parade floats. Cheers rose from farther down the street. Cameron paid only a passing glance to the banner flapping overhead reading *Free Public Concert with the Holloway Chamber Orchestra, Saturday, 7:00 p.m.*

"Would you believe that I was valedictorian my senior year?" said Madison.

He blinked and looked at her.

She raised a brow, as if daring him to argue the point. When he didn't, she added, "I got a float all to myself."

"I'm impressed."

She shrugged. "It was pretty embarrassing."

"I bet you ate it up."

She gave him a crooked smile. "Maybe a little."

She slipped her hand into his and his heartbeat quickened. Madison Taylor was quite possibly the most beautiful woman he'd ever known, and to think that he had found her here, in a forgotten town where no one would ever think to look.

"You know, they do this thing every year," she said quietly. "I love it, but I also think it's sort of dumb. I mean, what are we celebrating? Some general won a battle 150-odd years ago. So what? It's not like the South won the war or anything. Besides, shouldn't we find something better to celebrate than a massacre?"

"Good point," he said. General Holloway's disturbing war story sprang to mind.

She pointed suddenly to the mouth of Church Street where a huge float came lumbering into the square. "Oh, look! Here comes the parade!"

Fire engines and police cars blared sirens as the parade floats clambered into the square. Bernie High School had several floats, flanked by the marching band, manned with cheerleaders and the football team. Even their paper mache mascot, that looked suspiciously like Tony the Tiger, had its own exclusive float. The Ledbetter Library followed, with its staff dressed in *Alice in Wonderland* costumes. Perhaps the most interesting part, at least for Cameron, was the squad of men dressed as Confederate soldiers, armed with antique rifles, satchels, and other nineteenth century military accoutrement. This troupe was headed by a four-man band that played a little ditty with flutes and snare drums.

For no reason, Madison's hand became a vise grip on his arm. He turned to find her frozen in place, her face drawn with worry. He followed her gaze across the street to find Simon standing in a crowd of parade watchers, his bald head and missing ears making him stand out. A leather strap ran diagonally across his chest, bunching his sports jacket, and a worn leather satchel hung at his hip.

Cameron's eyes widened. *The son of a bitch found my satchel.*

"That guy gives me the creeps," Madison said, keeping her voice low. "You think we could maybe find another place to stand?"

He tried to smile, then took her by the hand and led her away from the floats, going against the crowd. After a moment, he glanced over his shoulder and found her face drawn into a tight, worried expression. For some reason he felt almost frightened for her, and in that same moment, a deep desire to protect her. Suddenly he drew her close and kissed her. For a moment, the world fell mute as all external noise broke around them like river rapids against rock. Nothing now but heavily drawn breaths and thudding heartbeats.

The kiss ended with her suddenly pulling back, her eyes wide with surprise.

"Where did that come from?"

He grinned sheepishly and shrugged. "Got carried away. Sorry."

She smiled. "Don't apologize. I liked it." She squeezed his hand. "Let's get back to the shop."

"Whoa, girl, that's it." Chief Dunlap gave Splinter's rein a good tug as he guided his horse into the shade beneath a pear tree in Frontier Bank's back parking lot. He'd come back here to get away from the crowd, but there was nowhere to hide. Even now, as he stroked the flank of his Tennessee Walker, several children swarmed him, wanting to pet the horse. Splinter whinnied as their little hands reached for her bridle.

"Boys and girls," Dunlap said, sitting high above them on his caramel-colored horse. He looked down on their little faces. "Ya'll might want to give Splinter here a rest. She's a little hot and tired."

There were a few mournful groans, but the kids backed off. Dunlap gave them a parting smile and patted Splinter's head as the children hurried away. He knew that once he let a few kids pet his horse, he'd end up having to hand out pony rides.

With a cluck, he nudged Splinter with his knees, and she clopped out of the shade and crossed the parking lot, where the heat rippled off the tarmac. Mounted officers weren't the norm in town, but the mayor insisted for the festival. The animals were good for deterring fights and unruly behavior, but they left big cakes of manure in the middle of the road.

This year they had something else to worry about. Just the day before, Bill Tillman, a garbage man with Fairfax County Waste, had found Carrie Belle's purse in a dumpster on Bard Street. Her billfold, including forty dollars, was still inside. This troubled Dunlap a great deal. No longer did he think Carrie Belle had simply run away. If that were the case, she sure as hell wouldn't have thrown away forty bucks. This pointed to even grimmer case scenarios, like abduction and all the nastiness that went with it.

Dunlap sighed. In his heart, he believed something terrible had happened. At this point, he could only speculate, but he could dream up some nasty possibilities. He told none of these things to Linda Meadows when he'd met with her the day before. But the woman had seen it in his eyes. Her little girl was gone and wasn't coming back.

Once out of the bank's parking lot, he nudged his way through the crowded sidewalk toward Beethoven's Closet. The crowd watched him as if he were himself some sort of parade float. He gazed quietly at them. Families, elderly folks, kids with stars and butterflies painted on their cheeks and brows. He dreaded the thought that there might be a killer among them.

He headed over to where some of the visitors had camped out with picnic blankets on the grassy lawn of Beethoven's Closet to watch the parade. Several people scattered as his horse trotted onto the grass, coming up gracefully from the ditch. He saw Madison and a man watching, too, and they scurried aside to avoid getting trampled.

"Good Lord, Dale!" Madison snapped. "You should be walking that animal. You're gonna hurt somebody."

"We're doing just fine," the officer returned, jerking the reins and bringing his horse to a halt, glancing at the man with her. "Who's your friend?" he said with his best nonchalant smile.

The man stepped forward and offered his hand. "Cameron Blake."

"That horse of yours better not make a mess on my lawn, or I'll have you pickin' it up with a plastic bag," Madison interjected.

As if on cue, the horse crapped in her yard, earning gagging sounds from a few of the nearby picnickers. Madison rolled her eyes. "Dale, please tell me something good."

The playful light in the officer's face dimmed. He sighed and nodded toward the shop. "Why don't we step inside? I'll tie Splinter up to the porch post."

The air-conditioned shop was a welcomed break from the summer heat. It was a cozy atmosphere, scented with soaps, incenses, and perfumes. They gathered in the foyer, where Dunlap sat next to Madison on the overstuffed sofa, while Cameron propped himself against a window ledge. There was no easy way to say it, but Dunlap put it as gently as he could, seeing that Madison didn't seem to mind getting personal news with Cameron present.

"So you found her purse . . . in a dumpster," Madison said flatly, letting the words resonate. She buried her face in her hands. "Jesus, Dale, what does that tell you?"

Dunlap shook his head slowly, his bushy white hair a sweaty mess from his helmet. "Nothing good. But right now we can only speculate."

Cameron moved out of Madison's way as she stood and drew the curtains, shutting out the light and the outside noises. She returned to the sofa and Dunlap patted her knee. His heart ached for her. In many ways, he felt almost like a father to her. Always had.

Dunlap cleared his throat, glancing at Cameron. "You're in town for the festival?"

"Actually, no. I'm here on business. Just for a few months."

Dunlap's bushy brows went up. "What sort of business?"

"I'm a composer," Cameron said with a hint of reluctance. "Mr. Bloom commissioned me to write a symphony for his orchestra. They're performing one of my works at the Calliope tonight, actually."

Regarding him quietly, Dunlap scratched at his whiskers. Cameron looked like a nice enough fellow, but then again, he was a stranger, and right now, Dunlap suspected everyone, especially strangers.

"Bloom's about the strangest son of a bitch I ever met," said Dunlap, making a sour face. "He hardly ever comes out of his shell. Unless he's got something to gain. I see him every now and then at town council meetings. He likes to grease the skids. He's got Mayor Finny in his back pocket. Finny puts him up on a goddamn pedestal just because Bloom dumps a lot of money into this town. The rest of us are just expected to leave him alone. But he gives me a bad feeling."

"From what I've seen, Bloom's not interested in anything that doesn't involve music," Cameron said.

"Strange lot," Dunlap said.

Cameron gave an easy smile. "Very strange, maybe."

The chief stood with a grunt. "Before I get out of here, I've got to ask, Cameron. August sixth. It was a Wednesday night. Do you remember what you were doing?"

Cameron sighed and considered for a moment, counting the days. "Well, let's see. I got into town on the third of August, I think. So that means I would have been . . ." He blinked. "I suppose I would've been with Maestro Bloom. We were working that night."

Dunlap nodded. "Okay then. Thanks." He and Madison said their goodbyes, and then just before he left for the festival, he turned back to her. "By the way, the dumpster where we found Carrie's purse sits on Bard Street, just down the road from the Calliope. I don't trust Bloom. Or his musicians. You just might want to watch yourself." He glanced to Cameron. "And you let me know if you see something out of the ordinary."

Cameron nodded, meeting Dunlap's probing gaze without flinching. "Yes, of course."

Dunlap left, found Splinter grazing on ornamental grass near the side of the shop, and swung back into the saddle.

Chapter 5

The festival ended at sundown, with the exception of a few drunken stragglers who kept the party going with laughter and belligerent shouts. The vending carts were gone. The shop windows were dark. The air, calm and balmy, rang with country music, spilling from a bar on the square.

Cameron and Madison held hands as they followed the slow migration up along Bard Street toward the Calliope. When they reached the plaza, both fell silent, and cold apprehension squeezed his insides.

Madison whispered, "This place gives me the creeps."

"I know you hate it here. That's one of the reasons why I never mentioned tonight's show."

"Yeah, right." She gave him a wry smile. "You were probably planning on bringing someone else."

He laughed. "No. It's not that. The truth is I hadn't planned on coming tonight myself. I didn't think I was ready. I still don't."

"Ready for what?"

"I've been writing crap for so long, for other people, that I almost forgot how to write something . . . honest. So forgive me if I'm a little nervous about falling on my face."

"You know something? I don't understand you."

With a firm hold on her hand, he led her up the steps and into Calliope, where a large crowd had gathered in the foyer. Surprisingly, Bloom had staffed the venue with about fifteen high school students, dressed in red vests and bowties, who worked the front doors and ticket booth. After waiting in a twenty-minute line for tickets, which sold for ten bucks each, they climbed the stairs to the balcony and found their pew toward the far right corner. Not the best seat in the house, but good enough.

"I'm pretty sure you could have gotten better seats for half the cost," Madison said with a playful sigh. "Seeing as though you wrote the thing."

"Shut it, sister," Cameron chided, but his smile faded when he turned his attention to the stage, hidden behind drawn red velvet curtains. He'd nearly convinced himself that he had nothing to worry about. But now he wasn't so sure. Behind those curtains waited Bloom's Echoes, musicians capable of magic, of resurrection, of God only knew what else.

When the auditorium lights went out, a hush fell over the crowd, and in all that silence and darkness, a single beam of light slashed through it and shone down on Maestro Bloom, dressed in tuxedo tails, standing before the curtains.

"Ladies and gentlemen," he said, allowing his voice to echo almost preternaturally across the auditorium. "Thank you for joining us tonight on this very special occasion. It was here, 151 years ago, that the great General Holloway defeated his enemy, fighting bravely, valiantly, and with great precision. Many died that day. The blood of both opponents soiled the land beneath us. These were men who died fighting for what they believed in. Tonight, we honor General Holloway, but even more so, we honor history, as well as those who fought and died for our freedom."

Applause filled the auditorium.

"In just a few short moments," Bloom went on, "this orchestra will perform a new symphony, composed by the renowned composer, Cameron Blake, who has written a piece exclusively for you . . . for the citizens of this lovely town. Tonight, I give you 'The Symphony of Holloway.'"

Behind him, the curtains withdrew, slowly revealing the orchestra as the maestro turned to face it. Lights from overhead shone down on the fifty musicians gathered there. Seated with their instruments poised, the musicians looked like ancient mummies, with blanched faces, skeletal grins, and sunken eyes. Light shimmered in wisps of white hair. That they wore tuxedos and evening gowns only contributed to the absurdity of it all.

Bloom's baton flashed, catching the light overhead, and the symphony began.

The music was playful at first, with rolling snare drums and flighty lilts from the flutes that evoked impressions of colonial America. The strings and woodwinds painted sprawling landscapes of golden wheat fields, mountains, and gurgling streams, while the syncopated high notes of the violins showed a busy colony bustling with proud Americans who worked hard from sunup to sundown, a rough age of God, religion, innocence, and idealism.

But then the mood darkened, as if signifying an approaching storm, and with a sudden slash of his baton, Bloom started the war.

Trumpets pressed their way to the forefront like infantrymen, while the bass drums pounded a foreboding tattoo. Hooves trampled the earth. Cymbals crashed and the theater shook with mock cannon fire. Soldiers fought and died on an imaginary battlefield, while men shouted as they charged their enemy with their long rifles.

Cameron listened with a growing sense of pride. This was a powerful and epic score. He'd captured the town's history and brought it to life with rich colors and an emotional depth that he'd never imagined himself capable of doing. This was surely his best work to date. And it was all because of Bloom's training.

The music ended. For a moment, there was only a stunned silence, but then came the applause, and it filled the concert hall. Cameron laughed a little despite himself.

Madison turned to him with tears in her eyes. She gripped his arm excitedly and whispered, "Cameron, it's wonderful."

He squeezed her hand and returned her smile. Bloom waited for the audience to quiet before he spoke into his microphone. "We hope you enjoyed tonight's performance," he said in his smooth, velveteen voice. "But before we leave you, the orchestra wishes to share one last piece. Please listen as a trio will now perform a Nocturne written by Mr. Cameron Blake."

With a little bow, Bloom left his podium at the same moment that three musicians emerged to the forefront of the orchestra. There were two men in tuxedos, carrying strange black violins with oblong necks and gothic scrollwork. The men flanked a single woman, old like them, with short cropped white hair and a sunken face. Her long black evening dress hung awkwardly on her frail and shapeless body. Her instrument was even more bizarre; while it resembled a bassoon, it had the look of a tangle of black metal tubing with serpentine loops and wriggles. Bloom's Archetypes.

"What the hell are they doing?" Cameron hissed, straightening in his chair.

Madison looked at him, frowning. "What's wrong?"

He only shook his head. He didn't want to scare her. But the thing was that he was already scared. *They wouldn't dare play those things in public, would they?*

And then the music—if it could be called that—began. The bassoon sounded like a braying lamb. The violins gave off wild, frenzied peels. The song had no melody; it was simply a panicked soundscape, like something from a horror movie.

"Cameron?" Madison moaned, but her voice sounded miles away. "I don't like this." She clamped her hands over her ears and looked at him with terror-filled eyes. "What's happening?"

Helplessly, he turned and gripped her shoulders and shook his head. He didn't know why Bloom would do this. Why had they kept this a secret from him? *I'll kill the son of a bitch.*

As the music continued, becoming even more dark and menacing, Cameron leaned over and covered her ears with his own hands. He'd hope to protect her from the noise, but it didn't work. As he watched, Madison's eyes rolled back in her head to show their whites and her mouth hung ajar.

"Don't listen to it," he shouted, pressing his forehead against hers. "Don't listen!"

There was a flash of light onstage. Then a powerful wind stirred within the auditorium. Grimacing, Cameron looked up to find the air above him filled with smoke, or something like smoke, with tendrils that stretched and wormed toward the stage, moving with the subtle motion of reeds caught in an underwater current. The air crackled, and the metallic scent of ozone stung his nostrils. The Calliope's ceiling became a star shower, with sparks bursting across the auditorium. Meanwhile on stage, a wreath of mist enveloped the trio and the orchestra behind them.

He drew Madison close. Her body quivered against his. *What in Christ's name is happening?*

Then the music arrived at some incomprehensible conclusion, a chorus of inhuman screams, and the overhead lights exploded like firecrackers. Glass showered the stage and darkness enveloped the musicians. And then there was silence.

In the quiet aftermath, the massive red curtains squeaked on their runners as someone backstage pulled their ropes to draw them across the stage, hiding the orchestra from the audience. Once drawn, the curtains fluttered, and Bloom stepped through to stand in a single beam of light.

"Ladies and gentlemen," he said in his smooth, baritone voice. "We hope you enjoyed tonight's symphony. And we thank you."

Arms straight at his sides, he took a little bow and then disappeared between the folds in the curtains.

The lights came on, but rather than applause, an uncomfortable quiet pervaded the auditorium. Gently shrugging Madison's head from his shoulder, Cameron got up and pivoted in a circle as he looked all around him. Something was wrong. No one moved, not at first; they looked as if they'd been lulled to sleep.

The people began to stir, and he crouched down before Madison and shook her gently by the arms. "Mad? Wake up."

She blinked her eyes open and looked at him sleepily. She frowned. "Oh, did I fall asleep?"

"I think you must have." He glanced over her shoulder. Most everyone had woken now, and that was a good thing. He didn't want her to see. He wanted her to believe that she had alone fallen asleep. Only now did sobbing children interrupt the quiet. People were standing up and making their way to the aisle.

He looked at her again. "You want to get out of here?"

With a tiny nod, she said, "Yeah. Okay."

The audience roused itself from its daze. Many were moving sluggishly for the exit doors. Cameron helped Madison to her feet. She swayed drunkenly, and he took her by the hand and guided her into the aisle, where they joined the heavy flow of people. All around them were vacant eyes and slack jaws.

As they shuffled along, he glanced over his shoulder at the enormous red curtains blocking his view of the stage. *What were the Echoes hiding?*

"You're upset," she said, catching him off guard. "Didn't you like the show?"

He met her gaze. "No, I'm fine."

He searched her face, wondering what she remembered. Not much, obviously, or she would show some sort of horror, or religious awe. She and everyone else had already forgotten the music. The clouds of ether. The lightshow. They were clueless to what had just happened. *Good thing, too*, he thought, *or they'd all be running mad in the streets.*

They left the auditorium, and he practically dragged Madison through the lobby.

"Are you mad at me for falling asleep?" she asked.

"I'm not mad. And don't worry. You didn't miss much."

Warm night air found them when they stepped outside. A steady flow of people spilled down the steps into the plaza. With the landing crowded, he took her to the side, out of the way of traffic, and she only looked at him with wide-eyed confusion. He grimaced, wanting to comfort her, but he couldn't yet.

"Listen," he said. "I want to talk to Bloom. Why don't I call you a cab?"

Her eyes widened even more, and he saw real terror there. She grabbed his arm and shook her head. "No, Cameron. Don't leave me. I don't want to be by myself tonight."

He nodded. "Okay. Then will you wait for me? I have to talk to Bloom. You can wait out here."

Her eyes became unfocused, and for a brief moment she looked like a scared little girl. Then she gave a defiant shake of her head and said, "I'll wait. But not too long, okay? Promise me?"

Closing his eyes, Cameron pressed his lips to her forehead, tasting her warmth, and held the kiss. "I promise."

Cameron took an employee corridor to the backstage area, where he found the narrow passages crowded with men and women dressed in formal attire.

Guests of Bloom's, he assumed, though he'd never seen them before and they weren't the old congregational members who'd followed Kalek from his former church. He'd caught them celebrating. Every one of them had a glass of champagne, and their excited voices and laughter rang throughout the hallways. They hardly took notice of Cameron as he walked through them.

He slowed his step when a man, standing with one hand in his pocket, raised his glass in a toast and then winked, as if he shared a secret with Cameron. It made no sense to him. He hurried onward, even as a chill scurried down his spine. *What the hell was that all about?* Something was wrong here.

Then a sudden realization stopped him mid-step. Catching his breath, he braced himself against the wall, trembling with panic. *Oh my God. You got to be shitting me.*

It wasn't possible. It couldn't be them. It just couldn't.

They watched him, grinning. Some raised their glasses in a silent toast. And they were . . . younger.

And he recognized them.

No, no, no. This is all wrong. All wrong! Setting his jaw, Cameron hurried to Bloom's office. The door stood open, and he stepped inside, finding the room crowded with more musicians. Like those in the hallway, they beamed with youthful smiles, obviously luxuriating in the restored vigor of their bodies. They gabbed and laughed uproariously at their own jokes. Kalek and Christofori were among them, sitting in armchairs among others he didn't recognize.

Bloom sat behind his desk. Even he looked different somehow. Younger, maybe. The angles of his face were sharper. More defined.

"Well, well," called the maestro, eyes twinkling as his arms unfurled. "Here he is now, the star of the show. Come inside, Cameron. We were just talking about you."

The room fell silent as Cameron marched to Bloom's desk and planted his hands on its edge, leaning forward. "You son of a bitch. What did you do?"

The maestro regarded him with quiet guardedness. "Look around you. Isn't it evident?"

"Oh, I understand, all right. You used the whole fucking town to make them younger. It was a dirty trick. You lied to me!"

"Would you have allowed it, had I told you?" Bloom paused and looked at him pointedly. "No, of course not. I knew you wouldn't understand, and so I didn't tell you. But as I've said in the past, we must take the necessary steps before we perform Armonia. This was one of them. I did what I had to do. And now this orchestra has the strength to perform our Divine Symphony."

Disgusted, Cameron looked about the room, meeting the gaze of each musician standing around him. A beautiful woman with sharp features and black short-cropped hair. A craggy-faced man with stiff white hair that fell to his shoulders. He felt a chill scurry down his spine as he recognized them. The same faces, only decades younger, a bewildering transformation. Once again the orchestra had defied reason and reconfigured the physical world around them.

And with my music.

"Yes, look at them," said Bloom. "Look at what we've accomplished. The musicians are young again, stronger than ever, and prepared for the greatest performance of their lives. And rest assured. No one was hurt tonight. I only took what was needed. They won't remember tomorrow. Oh, they might experience a slight fatigue, but that is all."

"You've gone too far!" Cameron shot back. "This is unethical and borderline criminal. Those aren't animals out there. They're people. You can't just do what you want with them! For Christ's sake, can't you see how fucked up this is?"

"Whose side are you on?" someone said behind him.

Cameron turned around as Christofori rose from his seat. The man brushed his long raven-black hair from his face, revealing a snarl. "Either you are a part of this orchestra, or you are our adversary. One of these days you will have to decide."

"Christofori is right," said the man named Lutz, standing with his arms folded toward the back of the room. While much younger now, he looked similar, with long white hair falling just below his ears. "The ends justify the means. You must trust Maestro Bloom, just as we must trust him."

"Thank you, Christofori, Lutz," said Bloom. "I'm sure our composer understands. Don't you, Cameron? We are one orchestra. There must not be conflict among us."

"Then stop doing this shit behind my back," Cameron snapped at him.

Bloom nodded. "Fair enough. And so now the orchestra is ready to perform the Symphony. So tell me, Cameron. Are *you* ready?"

Cameron stormed out of the office.

He found Madison outside, looking small and frightened, where she sat on the top step with her arms folded beneath her breasts and her hair covering most of her face.

They spoke very little as they walked back to Beethoven's Closet. Cameron was glad to find a stream of people milling along Bard Street, having come from the Calliope. The last thing he wanted to do was escort Madison alone. Not tonight. When they arrived at her shop twenty minutes later, he helped her into her Honda, parked in the driveway. He insisted on driving, and she didn't protest. The truth was he didn't trust her to drive. She still looked dazed, and he wanted to keep an eye on her for a while to make sure Bloom's little trick didn't have a greater effect than he'd let on.

One thing was certain. The music hadn't affected him in the same manner. In fact, he felt good, except for a slight ringing in his ears, but even that had quieted somewhat.

"I told you already," said Madison, not bothering to hide her frustration. "I'm fine. Why do you keep asking me that?"

Drawing her legs beneath her on the sofa and wrapping her arms around her knees, she eyed Cameron skeptically. It'd been a long night, but she already felt better, here in her living room, among the comforts of her own home, the warmth of her favorite sofa, the bookshelves crammed with her favorite books. Cameron paced the room. He looked tired, with dark rings beneath his eyes. He still seemed deeply troubled about tonight's concert. He must have really thought that it stunk.

I still can't believe I fell asleep.

This bothered her too. She'd been wide awake when the show started. The first two hours had been terrific. But then the three musicians had come out . . . and she couldn't remember anything after that. With a shiver, she tugged her robe close about herself and dropped her gaze.

"Actually," she said. "Now that you mention it, I do feel sort of strange. Tired."

He sat down with her and rubbed her shoulder. "Could I stay here tonight?"

She gave him a feeble smile. She liked the thought. Yes, she wanted him to stay. But her own doubts chased the smile away. She knew he didn't intend to stay in Holloway. He would leave her as soon as he finished his work with Bloom. She sighed heavily. No, she couldn't depend on him to keep her safe from the unnerving sensation running through her.

He kissed her, as if reading her mind. She gave in, allowing him to fold himself around her. Before long, her pajama top came off, as if by itself, and she returned him the favor with a smile, then scaled the ridges of his chest with her hands. The rest of their clothes came off just as easily with the rush of intimacy, and when he slid inside of her, she bit into his shoulder as every nerve resonated with the pleasure of it.

"What am I doing with you?" she moaned, running her fingers through his hair. "You're just going to leave me."

He didn't say anything more, and she didn't press. Instead she chose to focus on the pleasure of their lovemaking, rather than the fears that begged for her attention. His kisses subdued her worries, at least momentarily, and they finished in a heated, noisy climax that left them both sweat-soaked and exhausted on the sofa.

Sometime later they went upstairs and crawled into bed. For a long while, she lay quietly in Cameron's arms. The room glowed by the moonlight from the window. The rhythm of his breathing had slowed. He was almost asleep. But not her. Her mind wandered.

She saw with perfect clarity the trio of musicians taking the stage with their strange black instruments shimmering beneath the lights. But the music

. . . she couldn't remember it, not a single note. From then she recalled only faded images. Flashes of light. Cameron shouting. Hands covering her ears.

A dream, she decided. Nothing more. *I fell asleep. So why do I feel so . . . strange?*

She sat up, holding the sheet to her breasts, and said, "Cam? Did something . . . happen tonight?"

He didn't answer her. She couldn't see his face but felt his eyes on her. Then she had an epiphany. Cameron's experiments with Bloom. His Astral Music. All this had something to do with why she had holes in her memory of tonight's concert.

"Something did happen tonight," she said. "Didn't it?"

Finally, he shook his head from side to side and muttered, "Nothing happened."

With a sigh, she swept the hair from her face and tucked it behind an ear. Something had happened tonight, she felt sure of it now, had known it from the moment the concert had ended. *And he knows.*

"Please talk to me," she said in a voice choked with desperation. Dread coiled itself around her, threatening to snap her bones. "Nothing makes sense. And if you know something, then goddamn it, I need you to tell me!"

Sighing, he sat up, drawing his knees to his chest. He opened his mouth to speak but then stopped himself.

"They played that music for us, didn't they?" she said, tired of dancing around the truth. She searched his face, hidden in shadows.

Something flashed in his eyes and his gaze dropped. "I don't know what to tell you."

"You can start with the truth!" She drew away from him, avoiding his touch. "That music . . . it did something to me. To everyone there. And you were part of it!"

"Now just wait a minute!"

"No, you wait a minute. I don't know what sort of game you're playing. You and that goddamn orchestra are up to something."

"That's not true."

She paused. "You're lying. I can hear it in your voice."

"Madison—"

"I think you should leave."

A flash of anger, then Cameron snapped the covers back and hopped out of bed. Without turning on a light, he found his clothes draped over a chair and started to dress. He didn't say anything for a moment, but his movements were harsh, almost violent. He moved toward the door but stopped. "I care about you," he said in a quiet voice. "But everything is . . . upside down right now."

He left the room.

She listened to him go as tears sprang to her eyes. Clutching the blanket to her chest, she gave a troubled sigh. She knew he would never choose her over Bloom and his ghastly orchestra.

Chapter 6

The next morning, Hob found the Calliope shrouded in gray fog. The surrounding trees and even the building seemed to sag beneath its weight. The gray seemed to seep inside, and the place seemed especially brooding as he entered. He whistled as he walked the back corridors, as if to drive away his sense of dread. It didn't work.

He turned on all the lights as he made his way to his supply closet.

Over the past eleven years, he'd developed an intimate knowledge of the Calliope. It came with cleaning all her secret places. From day one, the building had spooked him with its strange sounds, its clunking heating ducts, creaking boards, and yawning rafters. Sometimes he heard even stranger sounds, like whispers, or music. It hadn't been like this before Bloom and his orchestra came. But lately the place throbbed like a sore toe. This morning, that feeling was almost palpable.

Hob reached the supply closet. The narrow room stank of bleach and cleaning solvents. Shelves of chemicals lined the walls. Push brooms and dingy mops leaned against the corners. He heaped bottles of cleaners onto his pushcart, then filled a mop bucket with water from the tap and rolled it out into the corridor.

From what he'd seen, last night's concert had drawn out an impressive crowd, and that meant trash on the floor, scuffed-up tiles, piss around the urinals, and so forth. He expected long hours, but he didn't mind so much. Most days he just dusted for the sake of appearances.

He rounded a corner with his cart and jerked to a stop. A woman stood just before the stage door at the end of the long corridor. At least, that had been his first impression. But the hallway was empty now. Fluorescent lights flickered overhead.

"Anybody here?" he called. His voice went echoing out into empty space.

After a moment, he shook himself and pressed forward. He found it best to pretend these sort of things didn't happen, merely tricks of light. In moments he was through the door and out onto the stage.

The stage lights shone warmly on him as he stopped about ten feet from the edge, where there were new scuffmarks on the floor. He squatted down beside his cart and reached for a cleaning agent. A can of Spot Shot fell from the top tray, rolling away from him. Muttering, he rose up, knees popping. Another bottle fell from the cart.

He frowned. He hadn't even touched it.

Then the cart started jittering. It shook the cans and bottles from its top like a dog shaking off fleas.

Hob swallowed and slowly reached out a hand to steady it. "Okay, now," he said to the empty auditorium, trying his best to sound confident. "I see whatcha doin.' You tryin' to frighten me. I thought we had an understandin'–"

The words caught in his throat as the air turned to ice all around him. The pushcart began trembling violently, even with his hand gripping its handle. He backed away. The pushcart tottered from side to side. Bottles rolled about his feet.

Sweet God almighty, what the hell is goin' on?

The pushcart made an angry dash at him. He jumped out of its way. The cart shot over the edge of the stage and crashed into the third row of pews.

Hob looked into the dark auditorium. He was no longer alone.

Hundreds of Civil War soldiers sat in the pews, wearing blue and gray uniforms, their faces bloated, flaps of skin hanging from their foreheads and chins, each illuminated by some inner effulgence.

They sat quietly, as if waiting for a show.

Hob staggered backwards and tripped over a can. He fell hard on his backside and a sharp pain shot up his spine. "Sweet Jesus!"

He picked himself up and ran.

You know what you supposed to do. You've known all along.

Hob closed his eyes to the voice in his head. He rapped his knuckles against the door of room 104 at the Cherry Tree Hotel and then waited.

Something thudded behind the door.

"Cameron? You in there? Open up, man. It's Hob. I gotta talk to you."

Leaning against the wall, Hob squeezed his eyes tighter shut. Images of swollen corpses wearing antiquated soldier uniforms filled his head. He shivered. He would never go back there. His first few years working at the Calliope had been inconsequential, working for the city, getting paid scraps.

Then came Bloom and his entourage. The concert hall's entire staff of fifteen men and women had been cordially invited to get out. Hob had taken the news especially personally; with Clara sick, and the hospital bills growing, they'd depended on that paycheck. Losing his job just wasn't an option. So the day after the staff had cleared out, Hob had returned to the Calliope, bent on having it out with the snooty brass that had fired him. That had been the first time he met with Alfred Kalek, the orchestra's executive manager.

Kalek had listened to Hob's complaints, and then he'd done something completely unsuspected: he'd offered Hob a job. The Calliope needed one janitor, and one who wouldn't ask questions.

Hob had, of course, agreed to the specific instructions laid out that day and had enjoyed the perks of assuming the role of executive janitor ever since. But then things changed. The Calliope changed. In just a few weeks, the building began thrumming with bad vibes. Shadows stirred and voices whispered his name.

Everything changed when Clara died.

The following evening, Hob had broken two of his promises to Kalek. First, he'd snuck into the Calliope after sundown. Second, he'd gone down to the basement, and for the first time, he'd seen the dark instruments, those twisted shapes that seemed almost alive with a cold, unnatural energy.

He opened his eyes to see the hotel door, as he waited for Cameron.

He should have left the Calliope when he saw those mangled instruments, but he'd stayed to keep an eye on Bloom. He'd forced himself to forget about the instruments.

But then Cameron Blake came along and played Clara's song out of the blue. Hob understood now. She'd been trying to communicate with him.

Following a click, the door opened, breaking Hob's thoughts from the past.

Cameron stood just inside the room in shadows, wearing only a pair of jogging pants. He was a mess, with his hair uncombed and dark pools beneath his eyes.

Squinting against the sunlight, he asked, "What's going on, Hob? What time is it?"

"I need to talk to you."

Cameron hesitated, turned, and led Hob into his room.

The place was dark and stuffy, with a queen bed shoved against the wall, a dresser, a writing table. The curtains were drawn. A muted television mounted up high provided most of the room's light. There was barely enough room for a guest.

"Didn't happen to bring some coffee with you?" said Cameron, as he lowered himself onto the corner of his bed. He nodded toward the chair across from him and said, "Have a seat, Hob."

Hob shook his head. "Can't sit. Too shaken up to sit."

The pleasant, but tired, grin dissipated from Cameron's face. "What's going on, pal?"

With his hands in his pockets, Hob drifted over to the big window and drew back its curtains, letting in a great flood of light. Without turning, he started to talk, letting the surreal story of the soldiers escape him.

Cameron flinched as the account unfolded, and in that moment, Hob knew everything he needed to know. *This son of a bitch has got something to do with it. Him and Bloom and those goddamn instruments. Somehow they're all connected.* "I got to know," he pressed. "What's Bloom up to down there in that basement? You two been up to somethin'. Those instruments . . . what's the story?"

Scratching the back of his head, Cameron paced by the window, refusing to look at him. "I can't talk about that, Hob. I'm sorry, man. But I just can't."

"Can't talk about it, huh?" Hob snorted and shook his head. For the first time since he'd seen the ghosts that morning, his knees had stopped shaking. Now he just wanted to hit something—preferably Cameron Blake. "You blind or somethin'? Bloom's got you in some bad shit. You up to your knees in it."

His head hanging, Cameron turned around. "Listen. Why don't you take a few weeks off? I'll talk to Bloom. I'll tell him you needed a break or something."

"Like hell. Somethin's going down at the Calliope. And I'm gonna do somethin' about it."

"Like what?" Cameron shouted, gesturing wildly with his arms. He plopped down on the corner of his bed. "Okay. You're right. I don't understand everything that's going on up there. He's been . . . experimenting. I can't say more. But I can tell you one thing." He looked up and met Hob's eyes. "Bloom's not going to like someone snooping around in his business."

"You're afraid of him," said Hob, nodding slowly. It made sense now. "Well, not me. I'm the goddamn custodian. The cleanup guy." He went for the door and threw it open, letting sunlight inside. He glanced over his shoulder. "I've got to do what I feel is right. If you won't help me, then I'll do it on my own."

He stepped outside and shut the door just as Cameron said something, pleading with him. But Hob didn't hear it. Squinting against the sun, he started down the steps, wondering just how he'd make good on his promises.

Beethoven's Closet looked like a bruise in the sullen morning light, with its windows dark, its curtains shut. A "Sorry, We're Closed" sign in the door window. Frowning, Cameron twisted the doorknob and found it locked. After ten and still closed. It didn't make sense. *I should have stayed last night. Should have made sure she was okay.*

Exasperated, he turned and faced the rain, watching as several cars splashed down the road on their way to the square. He shivered with worry. *Maybe something's wrong.* No, Bloom had prepared him for this, had warned him that the audience would suffer some sort of hangover. Madison was probably just sleeping it off. He'd give her a few hours and then drop by her place and check up on her. Just to make sure.

The rain fell harder.

He sighed and thought about Hob's ghosts. *The Calliope seems restless these days. I think she's starting to waken*, Bloom had once told him. Was this what he'd meant? Cameron didn't like it.

He wanted—needed—to leave Holloway. Put it behind him. Bloom had given him every reason to run. Last night was a dirty trick, played on the whole unsuspecting town, including Madison, and they'd used one of Cameron's Nocturnes to do it. Chills scurried down his spine as he imagined the men and women gathered outside Bloom's office last night. Smooth faces and smirking eyes. They'd made themselves younger by stealing something vital from the audience. Sure, Bloom promised no one had gotten hurt, but how could he know for certain?

If I stay, I put everyone around me in danger. This has got to stop. But leaving would have its consequences too. For starters, there was Madison. How could he leave her? He'd fallen hard for her. But things were more complicated than they ought to be—because of Bloom, the Astral Music. Then again, he always managed to complicate things. Still, he couldn't simply walk away. *I could ask her to come with me.*

True, but what about the Symphony? Could he walk away now that they were so close to actualizing his lifelong pursuit? Bloom finally had his orchestra, vital, talented, and capable. Cameron's Attuning was all that remained.

Bloom and his orchestra were cold. Selfish. Unnatural. *I can't ignore this. I can't pretend they have good intentions.*

The question, then, was why he still chose to stick around. From the moment he'd arrived, Bloom had more or less dragged him by the ears. Every time he thought about walking away, Bloom reeled him back in. But it wasn't all Bloom. A deep curiosity lingered at the back of Cameron's mind. Always had. The Astral Music was somehow integral to the loss of his family. Without a doubt, performing Armonia would give him closure. It would make sense of everything, and for that reason he could not leave Holloway. Not now.

His focus returned to the shop. With his hands shoved in his pockets and his head lowered, he left the protection of the awning and walked into the rain.

Kalek wrenched open the Beachum Sanitarium door and stepped into its rundown foyer.

A reception counter ran along the far wall. A clue to the building's past. In fact, a close eye could discern all kinds of clues to the rooms that had once served as solariums: tables once used for crude operations and electrotherapy treatments, and bathrooms equipped with Vichy showers. Despite the recent reconstruction efforts, the sanitarium remembered itself. A few coats of paint couldn't hide the stench of the sick and deranged. Nor could it conceal the rot at its foundations. Rats scurrying in the walls. Blackbirds nesting in the attic. Any honest health code inspector would have deemed the place uninhabitable, but Bloom had thrown enough money around to ward off prying eyes.

From the lobby, Kalek stepped into the main corridor. It was wide enough to drive a car through. The hallway was painted a dreary avocado green. Along the walls were narrow doors with tiny windows, looking into rooms that would have long ago provided lodging for dying patients. Kalek could almost hear their faint moans.

No, he corrected himself. *That's them—that's their music.*

In fact, the corridor echoed with faint clamor. This happened every night. The sanitarium's corridors became tonal sewers as fifty musicians sat alone in their filthy rooms and played their instruments. Eventually, the sounds from their separate performances came together and flooded the halls with unsettling cacophony. Tonal garbage.

They did this as an act of musical healing, a necessary plight of their condition. The Echoes used music to sustain themselves. They drew nourishment from it. And Kalek had seen what happened to the Echoes if they didn't. They dried up like petrified corpses, like sacks of flesh and bone left out to dry in the desert sun.

But they no longer needed to heal themselves. Last night at the Calliope,

Blake's Nocturne, performed for a full house, had changed everything. The concert had allowed the Echoes to rejuvenate, to draw the life force from hundreds of men, women, and children. That kind of sustenance would keep them going for another fifty years. So why did they continue to serenade themselves?

I have to see them, he thought. *I have to see them for myself.*

He soon reached a wide staircase with a polished wooden railing. For a moment he stood at the first step, looking up to the banister above him. Somewhere on the second floor, a violin resounded like a lunatic's laughter. Begrudgingly, he climbed. At the top landing, he entered another dimly lit corridor, where the naked bulbs flickered. The music was louder here. Kalek's eyes wandered to a door on his left, where the sounds of a violin squeezed from the room behind it.

He went to the door and reluctantly pressed it open an inch. Peering into the dark room beyond, he found a circle of burning candles on the floor. Pungent incense covered a musky odor. At the center of the circle sat Simon, the violinist, perched on a wooden stool with his violin pressed to his chin. Naked except for a pair of dirty black slacks, his body swayed as he sawed at the strings with his horsehair bow, teasing out a somber melody.

Kalek's eyes widened in surprise. In a single night, the man had become youthful. His skin was now pink and plump. While still considerably heavy, his belly no longer distributed itself in flabby folds around his waist. His face was now round and boyish, with deep-set eyes that radiated with a wild intensity. Of course, the rejuvenation had not restored the hair on his head or the lobes to his ears. *But by God, the bastard's young again.* Kalek swallowed painfully. *He's no more than thirty-five years old.*

A quivering dog, nearly hairless and so skinny that its ribs poked at its flanks, hobbled into the ring of candles and settled at the foot of Simon's stool. A golden retriever, the dog was poorly nurtured, with a bristly coat of fur riddled with the mange. When it fixed Kalek with a rabid gaze, he stifled a shout. The shriveled dog looked demonic, with eyes filmed over with cataracts and a mouth drawn into a hideous snarl. Its entire frame quivered.

"Dear Lord!" Kalek moaned.

Simon blinked his eyes open and looked directly at Kalek. He stopped his music making. Before Kalek could draw away from the door, Simon spread his lips into an ugly grin, showing a mouthful of crooked teeth.

"I learned a new song," he whispered.

It was the first time Kalek had ever heard the man speak.

Simon raised a spiral notebook and shook it. "Would you like me to play it for you?"

Kalek shook his head. He'd listened to the Echoes perform a thousand times. They were the best musicians in the world, and most times he enjoyed listening to them, especially when they settled into some harmless composition by Mahler or Strauss. But as a rule, he left the room when Simon played alone. The man's lunacy had a way of manifesting itself into his melodies.

"I . . . ah . . . no thank you, Simon," said Kalek. "I just wanted to–"

In a single, practiced motion, Simon dragged his bow across the strings, lurching into a solo before Kalek could stop him. A brooding melody filled Kalek's head. All at once, the wind went out of him. His chest hurt, and his heart felt as if it would pop like an overinflated balloon.

He held his head in his hands and bolted for the door. Simon's eerie music and laughter followed him out.

Chapter 7

Four nights had passed since she'd last seen Cameron, and this left a bad feeling in her stomach. Would she ever see him again? For all she knew, he'd left town already.

I overreacted, Madison thought. *I know it now. I fell asleep at that damn concert. Had a bad dream. Blamed it on Cameron. And now he's gone.*

Standing at the window of her shop, she gave a sigh and gazed longingly outside. A curtain of gray hung over the front yard. Streams of water surged along the drainage ditch that lined the roadside and trees sagged with waterlogged branches. It'd been raining for several days.

She exhaled heavily. Was it any coincidence that the outside world looked how she felt on the inside? She watched a green Volvo nose into the gravel driveway. A woman in a blue rain jacket and plastic rain bonnet got out. She wrestled against the wind and hurried along the stepping stones to the shop's front porch. The cowbell clattered as the door opened and the woman stepped inside.

Forcing a smile, Madison skirted around the counter to greet her guest when she stopped in surprise. Though only a silhouette in the doorway, she recognized her.

"Mrs. Meadows?" she asked, feeling her heart sink. "What are you doing here?"

Linda Meadows shivered but said nothing. Her raincoat had failed to keep her completely dry. Her gray hair hung in soggy curtains, framing her long, strained face. Already in her early sixties, she looked frightfully old, as if all the worry and stress had stolen ten years from her. Carrie Belle had often talked about Mrs. Meadows—her foster mother—as being too old to handle someone like her. Whether or not this was true, Linda was certainly too old to wrestle with something like this.

"I–I wanted to come by," Linda sobbed. Her mascara-smeared eyes darted about the room, as if hoping to find Carrie Belle—as if she'd simply been hiding. "I was hoping that I might find something . . . something to remind me of my Carrie Belle."

Madison hugged her for a moment, noting the birdlike thinness of Linda's body, the cloying smell of her perfume. The woman's despair hung about her like something physical, and Madison felt a sudden stab of guilt at her own self-centered worries.

"Oh, Mrs. Meadows," she said. "I'm so sorry."

Linda's gaze dropped as she shook her head. "She's gone. She's not coming back. I feel somehow . . . responsible."

"Don't talk like that," said Madison. "We don't know anything at this point. And whatever's going on—it's no one's fault." She pointed to the armchair in the front foyer, where she'd cried her own tears for Carrie Belle just the other day. "Do you want to sit down?"

Linda shook her head. "I can't stay. I didn't come to cry. I've been doing plenty of that lately." She sniffed, wiped her nose with a wadded Kleenex, then drew her shoulders up as if to gather herself. "The reason I came was to ask you for a favor."

"Anything you need."

"I think I know who did it—who took Carrie Belle."

Madison took her hand and squeezed it tightly. "Who, Mrs. Meadows? Who took Carrie Belle?"

"It was the men in that orchestra."

Madison started as if slapped in the face. Her knees felt weak. She hadn't considered this before. Those musicians were too old to pose a threat. "Mrs. Meadows," she said carefully, "if you know something, then you really should talk to Chief Dunlap."

"No," Linda said, shaking her head defiantly. "I don't trust him. He wouldn't know his ass from a hole in the ground. He hasn't done a thing to help find my Carrie Belle. Why should I start trusting him now?"

Wringing her hands, she walked over to the window. Rain pelted the glass. She watched for a while. Outside thunder rumbled. "I can't explain how I know it," she said in a dreamy voice, her back to Madison. "But I do know it."

She turned, meeting Madison's gaze, and said, "The night of the symphony, I had a vision. I saw one of them—the fat one with the bald head—I saw what he did to her." She made an effort at swallowing as her lips trembled. She whispered, "He did something . . . horrible."

Madison blinked. She wondered if Mrs. Meadows had become delusional. *Who can blame the poor thing, with all that she's gone through?* But then, in a way, Madison believed her, and so she guessed they had both lost their minds.

"The orchestra took Carrie Belle," Linda said in a husky voice. She set her jaw in determination, her mouth tightened. "They took her from me, and I need your help to prove it."

Around two that afternoon, as the cool rain came down over Holloway, Chief Dunlap stepped into the Calliope's lobby and shook his yellow slicker dry. His visit was unannounced; even so, Kalek surprised him by greeting him at the door. Kalek was a strange old man and he seemed nervous, but then Dunlap had a feeling this was the man's natural disposition.

"I'm here to see your boss man," said Dunlap, looking Kalek hard in the eye. "Will you take me to him?"

Kalek nodded, half bowing. They traversed a long white corridor that Dunlap had never seen before; it ran alongside the auditorium and had white linoleum and a drop ceiling. Along the way, Kalek gently prodded Dunlap about the nature of his visit, but the chief ignored him. Dunlap had been meaning to speak with Bloom ever since Carrie Belle's purse had turned up not a quarter of a mile down the road from the Calliope. Of course, the location of this evidence didn't exactly incriminate Bloom and his orchestra. Bloom did, however, have a small army of musicians working for him, and he kept them hidden away like a dark secret. No one ever saw them around town, and they rarely left their dormitory, the old Beachum Sanitarium—a place no one in his right mind would stay. Bottom line: that bunch was strange and anti-social. But were they killers? Dunlap didn't think so. Bloom's group of fogies were too old to harm anybody.

At least, that's what he thought until recently.

"You know, I never really liked this place," Dunlap told the old man as they reached the end of the corridor. "Gives me the goddamn creeps. Wasn't always like that. Long time ago I used to come here as a little boy, back when they used this place as a concert stage for hillbilly singers—what you'd call country music singers nowadays. I saw Elvis Presley here. Place went batshit."

Kalek looked at him with a bemused, somewhat forced grin. "How interesting!"

The old man's false excitement gave Dunlap a bad taste in his mouth. "Now the place feels like a goddamn morgue."

Moments later they arrived at Bloom's dimly lit office. The room had a sophisticated look to it, with its leather-bound books and mahogany paneled walls. A little too polished for Dunlap's taste. Bloom, sitting at his desk, looked a little too thrilled by this unannounced visit.

"Chief Dunlap!" said Bloom. He slid his work to the side as he smiled. "How nice to see you. I wish you would have called first. I would have had a better welcome party."

"Oh, Mr. Kalek was good as anything, I suppose," said the chief. He turned to look at the old man, but Kalek had already left the room.

Bloom rose from his chair to shake the chief's hand, and Dunlap studied him. The conductor seemed out of place in Holloway. Somehow too big for Holloway. And he wore a smile that didn't reach his eyes. Something about meeting the maestro's cold gaze made him wish he'd brought Bentley.

Bloom motioned to an armchair. "Please, have a seat. What brings you here this afternoon?"

Dunlap looked down at the chair, decided against it, and faced Bloom, who had already returned to his chair. "Bloom, I've got a missing girl. Carrie Belle Meadows. She disappeared on August six, and I'm getting desperate. So

I'm leaving no stone unturned. Which is why I came to see you. You seen anything out of the ordinary?"

"Dreadful," said Bloom, leaning back and looking exasperated. "And you have no leads to go by?"

"Well, we got one." Dunlap quickly responded. "We found her purse in a dumpster not far from here."

"Curious. But surely you don't think anyone here had anything to do with her disappearance?"

"No. I don't think that. Not yet, anyways." Dunlap let his gaze wander to the rows of leather books behind Bloom's desk. "I spoke with a guy by the name of Cameron Blake the other day. He's been working with you?"

"That's right. He has. Is there something wrong? Surely you don't think Mr. Blake–"

With a dismissive wave, Dunlap cut him off. "I'm not accusing anyone. I'm just covering all the bases. Said he was working with you on the sixth of August, the night Carrie Belle disappeared. Can you verify that?"

Bloom rubbed his chin thoughtfully, his eyes distant. "The sixth of August," he echoed. "Would that have been a Wednesday night?"

"That's right."

"Then, yes, I can verify that he was here that night. He's been composing music for my orchestra for the past few months." The maestro leaned forward, the corners of his mouth formed a quiet smile. "I'll share a secret with you, Chief Dunlap. Mr. Blake is composing something very special for this orchestra—something likely to become a masterpiece. This means good things for Holloway, I can assure you. Such a work is likely to put Holloway on the map."

"Is that right?" said Dunlap with mock enthusiasm. "Well, now, that is exciting. And here I was worried about a possible murderer on the loose in Holloway." He tucked his thumbs beneath his belt, considered Bloom for a moment longer, then turned and started for the door. "You be sure to keep your eyes open for anything suspicious," he called over his shoulder.

"I certainly will."

The Ledbetter Public Library sat hidden behind Fairmont Elementary, about two miles west of the square. The two-story brick building was nondescript, with a flat roof and bland windows, and it seemed to shrink with each year. The moment Madison stepped in through the door, the smell of dust and old books brought back a heap of memories. She'd loved coming here as a kid, usually on Saturday mornings with her mother. Madison would always leave with a stack of books, most of which she would never read. She couldn't remember her last visit. She only hoped she didn't owe overdue fees on any books.

Aside from its modern flourishes, the library looked the same. *God, it hasn't changed a bit*, she thought. She remembered Mrs. Westmire, the gentle-faced librarian, who used to sit in a rocking chair and read stories like *The Wind in the Willows* or *The Velveteen Rabbit*.

When a mother and daughter squeezed by, Madison got out of the way and walked toward the counter, lost in her own thoughts of shared moments with her mother. So many memories, and so much had stayed the same. But there were new touches as well, like the cluster of computers, most of them occupied by teenagers, and the shelves of DVDs and Blu-rays. The huge card catalog cabinet had been toted away, probably to sit in a museum somewhere, or more likely, a junkyard.

"Can I help you find something?" asked a man standing behind the counter, scanning through a stack of books. In his late thirties, he was short and wiry. Bright blue eyes behind thick-rimmed glasses. His hair was black and shaggy, matching his beard.

Turning, she stepped up to the counter and found his nametag among the flowered design of his Hawaiian shirt. "Hi, Steve," she said, "I need to search through some old local newspapers, maybe ten years or older. I didn't know if I needed to use the microfiche or something?"

He smiled at her. "Well, now. That probably won't help. The old fiche there's a dinosaur. Besides, we've got most of that scanned into a database. There's a computer upstairs that's hooked in directly. It's got access to just about every newspaper published here in the past forty years."

She nodded, feeling a little excited. "That's what I'm looking for. Thanks."

"Hold on," he said, setting aside a stack of books. "I better come with you. Just in case you need some help."

Steve led her upstairs to the less exciting stuff where rows of reference books, bibliographies, and encyclopedias lined the room.

"That's the one right there," he said, pointing to a lonely computer tucked away in a quiet nook. As they approached, Steve pulled out a chair and motioned her to sit down.

Madison did so. Steve stood next to her and explained how she could search the database. He spent a few more moments on the details and then left her to fend for herself.

Madison bent closer, adjusting her glasses as she scanned the screen. She first typed "Maestro Bloom" in the main search box, then added "Holloway Orchestra." After a moment, several articles popped up. She clicked on the first titled, "Holloway to House its Own Orchestra" by Carol Sells.

Madison read to herself.

> It isn't often that Holloway, our cozy little town in the hills, has the good fortune of receiving such renowned artisans as Maestro Leonin Bloom, who has recently purchased the Calliope and is gearing up to renovate the historically significant theater. Mr. Bloom, critically regarded as one of the finest modern conductors in England, intends to bring an entire ensemble with him. His musicians, an eclectic group, are also renowned for their talents. "We are fortunate to find a place like the Calliope," said Mr. Bloom. "Holloway, with its beauty, its insularity, and its rich history, will serve as the perfect home for this orchestra. We thank the people for sharing its city with us and look forward to sharing our musical wonders with them."

Madison skimmed the article further on.

> Maestro Bloom, an art dealer of rare instruments and musical compositions, has purchased the estate and hopes to revitalize the Calliope for a new generation of music

lovers. "We believe that our symphonies will put the city of Holloway on the map," he said. "We do expect to draw guests from around the country, but not for the sake of profit. We do this for the sake of art."

With a sigh, Madison sat back from the screen and rubbed her eyes. *Why would Bloom choose to bring his orchestra here?* In the past five years, the Calliope had catered only two or three concerts a year. Surely that couldn't pay for the upkeep or the allowances of all those musicians.

She didn't quite know what she was looking for. There was something strange about the orchestra. That was all she knew.

Maybe she could convince Cameron to disassociate himself from it.

She closed her eyes and recalled her last conversation with Charlie, when he'd come by to tell her that he'd joined the orchestra. Her younger cousin had been flattered when one of Bloom's employees had come to his school, searching for a pianist. *What was his name?*

Kalek.

She leaned forward, typed in the name, and waited. The cursor blinked several times and then the result showed: *One item found.*

She clicked on the link, and the screen filled with a page from the *Herald* that showed a photograph of an old steepled church perched on a hilltop. Accompanying the photo was a very strange header. Someone coughed, and she jumped in her seat. She looked over her shoulder. *Go on, you big weenie,* she thought to herself. *You've already come this far.* Drawing a breath, she leaned forward and started to read.

"Church Falls Prey to Hallucinations, Several Guests Say," the next article by Andrea Arthur claimed. Madison read on.

> May fifth marked opening day for a small church in Fairfax County, where unexplained events, and possible mass hysteria, ended the sermon and resulted in one high school student in Nashville's Parsons Psychiatric Ward. The Church of Harmony Hill was created by Reverend Alfred Kalek, a veteran Holloway Baptist preacher who left his parish three

years ago after his wife's death and his subsequent attempted suicide. When Kalek announced his intent to begin a new parish, many in the community were skeptical of the idea, questioning Kalek's radical views and believing they would clash with the more traditional religious beliefs of the local community.

"I thought he was crazy from the start," said Wilma Burlington, who served as one of Kalek's nurses at Peach Grove Hospital, where Kalek spent a month recovering from a self-inflicted shot to the head. Burlington claims that Mr. Kalek obsessed about music he heard during a near-death experience and that he hoped to start a church that incorporated this strange music into its core dogma. "He told us that once he got better, he planned on starting a church where they read music books instead of the Bible," said Burlington. "He was so strange. I never really believed him."

An uneasy feeling came over Madison, but she continued reading.

While no one was certain of Kalek's religious views, one thing was certain: they were not prepared for what happened that Sunday. Though the events of that day are still unclear, many believe that Kalek drugged his parish with psychedelic narcotics. According to Bill Moore, a lifelong resident of Holloway who attended the sermon, the hallucinations began once the musicians, visiting from Bernie High School, began playing. "I never heard anything like it," said Moore. "Once the music started, I felt strange, like I was drunk. The music sounded strange, too, and then something happened; I can't understand it."

Madison gasped, reading silently about Joshua Hill—who became a resident at Parson's Psychiatric in Nashville afterwards—and about Reverend

Kalek. Grimacing, Madison folded her arms over her stomach in an attempt to suppress her nausea as she read of the naked man who magically appeared during the sermon. *What the hell really happened there? Either Kalek drugged everyone, or he put on a show to freak everyone out. Or both. Either way, Kalek is obviously a lunatic.* Equally as troubling was Kalek's belief that he'd heard music during a near-death experience.

Just like Cameron, she thought. Only Kalek had constructed an entire dogma around that music. And now they were both working for Bloom.

Her eyes returned to the grainy black-and-white photo at the top of the screen. At first she'd thought the church looked like every other Southern church on the plateau. But now the image had adopted a somewhat haunted look about it.

She shivered and pressed the print button.

Chapter 8

For the third day in a row, a heavy rain fell with no end in sight. Rather than resist the dreadful weather, Cameron took a two-hour walk in the rain to the Oak Fort Memorial Park. Fortunately, the rain had stopped by the time he reached the soldier cemetery.

He entered beneath an arch in the rock wall and stood at the top of a hill. The land sloped away, crisscrossed with rows of headstones in neat diagonals, shaded with fir trees. He followed the main path through the cemetery, and after several yards he reached the central hub, where Old Glory flapped at the top of a tall white flagpole. At its base, two black powder cannons sat beside a pyramid of cannonballs. He found a place to sit on a flat grave marker, then retrieved his pen and notebook from his bag and waited.

This had been the site of a Civil War massacre. This was a place of death. Undoubtedly, this sort of atmosphere would fuel his creativity. Each morning came with an irrepressible urge to write music. This was the sort of fire that kept junkies running back to their suppliers. And he'd been intoxicated with inspiration. The past few days he'd done nothing but write in frenzied artistic bursts. In his hotel room, the coffee shop, or anywhere that offered a quiet nook.

The Tongue is changing me. Refining me, like smelting ore, drawing the impurities to the top.

Those sessions with the fork—writing the Nocturnes—had awakened something inside of him, removed some sort of blockage from a creative artery. As a result, he'd become more attuned with the world around him.

Each time he sat to write, he produced what he supposed were masterpieces. He'd composed more works than he had written in a decade. Bloom had made good on his promises. Inspiration alone kept him from leaving Holloway.

Not once during this time did he visit the orchestra. That stunt at the Calliope had angered him, and he wanted Bloom to know it, to let him squirm a little.

He stayed away from Madison, too, although for entirely different reasons. He was worried about her. Over the past few days he'd visited her shop, had stood in the rain and watched her window, breathless each time he caught sight of her. From all appearances, she'd recovered from the orchestra's performance, just as Bloom promised, and he wanted desperately to talk to her, to make sure she was okay. But a guilty conscience kept him from going inside. Things were too confused. Best to keep her out of it, to leave her alone.

Still he missed her terribly, and he'd come here, to the seclusion of the cemetery, to have it out with his conflicted emotions, to channel these feelings into a song, to write a song for Madison Taylor. Then maybe she would understand, and maybe he would too.

After sundown, Bloozy's drew a sparse turnout.

The barroom's quiet was interrupted with bouts of laughter, while jazz trumpets squawked from hidden speakers. No one on stage tonight, just Paps's electric piano and a few barstools. Dark faces regarded Cameron as he moved toward the bar, where he located Hob in his porkpie hat, wedged between Boots and a few friends, all of them laughing about something—all but Hob, who seemed beside himself, withdrawn.

Cameron tapped him on the shoulder. Hob turned and looked at him with something between surprise and distaste.

"I need a word with you," said Cameron. He glanced at Boots, who was giving them a prying look. He added, "In private."

Hob gazed at him coolly. "I got nothin' to say to you."

"I wanted to talk about the orchestra," Cameron returned, knowing this would get the man's attention. It did. Taking his bottle of Coors, Hob gestured at a vacant table near the bar and started away with Cameron following. They sat down across from each other. Empty beer bottles littered the tabletop. Hob lit a cigarette, then folded his arms over his chest and stared quietly, perhaps replaying their last conversation.

"All right man," sad Hob, "You got my ear. What you got to say?"

Glancing both ways, Cameron leaned forward and said, "Do you believe in God, Hob?"

This certainly got Hob's attention. He drew his brow in stunned amusement. "What the hell kind of question is that?"

"You wanted to know what the orchestra's up to, well, I'm telling you. They're experimenting with music, playing shit you've never dreamed of—a different kind of music. The kind of shit you hear when you die. Spiritual music."

Closing an eye against a wisp of smoke, Hob regarded him quietly. "If I hadn't seen those instruments, I'd think you'd gone crazy. Still not so sure."

"Those instruments can play sounds that don't even exist. Create music that does . . . things."

"Does things? Like what?"

"I'm not entirely sure yet. But those ghosts you saw in the Calliope—I'm pretty sure it's all connected."

"Like I said before. You mixed up in some bad shit. It's all wrong somehow. I've worked there long enough to know. I can feel it. And you can too. I can tell by lookin' at you."

"No, you're wrong." Cameron retorted. This was something he'd wrestled with from day one. Was it wrong to tamper with nature? Maybe. And in some ways, his work with Bloom did feel wrong. But there was something else too: a sense of purpose, a feeling of destiny, and that felt far from wrong. "This thing is bigger than me, Hob. It's important. I've spent my whole life waiting for this moment. It's like I'm supposed to be here."

Shadows stirred across Hob's brow, then he gave a scornful grin. "Oh, I get it. You think God wants you here. Like you is Moses, just doin' what God wants. Well, I think that's bullshit, and I don't want anything more to do with you."

Cameron flinched, stung. Sure, he'd expected a reaction like this, but it still hurt. He'd managed to isolate himself in just a few short days. Madison had shut him out. Bloom had betrayed his confidence. And now Hob wanted to part ways.

With a pained nod, Cameron said, "Then will you do me one last favor?"

"A favor?" Hob scoffed. "Apparently you ain't heard a word I said."

"Can you get me on stage tonight? I'll need a guitar too."

Hob twisted his face in disbelief. "Man, I had to drag your ass up there last time. What gives?"

Cameron gave a despondent shrug. "I've been writing some new stuff, and I've got nobody to share it with."

This almost got through to Hob. His eyes registered something like empathy. But then his expression soured. "Nah, man. I don't think so."

Cameron fidgeted, scratched the back of his neck, nodded. "Yeah, all right, I got it."

Hob eyed him a moment longer, swallowed the last of his beer, then got up without a word and disappeared into the crowd.

To hell with it, thought Cameron. He left the table and started to the exit. He didn't need Hob. He didn't need anybody. *I'm on my own in this.*

A microphone squelched, and Cameron turned to find Hob standing at the microphone on stage, his guitar slung over his shoulder.

"Ladies and gentlemen, I got a special treat for you," said Hob in his smoky radio voice. "I'm gonna turn it over to a friend of mine for just a minute. Some of you met Cameron Blake before. He played here a few weeks ago. Anyhow, Cameron has somethin' he'd like to share with us, so let's welcome him up to the stage."

The crowd responded with a somewhat unenthused burst of whistles, hoots, and applause. Caught off guard, Cameron swallowed nervously, listening to the blood thudding in his ears. *Well, you asked for it*, he told himself.

"You out there, Cameron?" Shielding his eyes from the stage lights, Hob searched for him.

Cameron raised a reluctant hand as he pressed his way toward the stage.

"There he is!" Hob called, then added jovially, "Thought you done left. Come on up here and show us what you got."

As soon as Cameron stamped onto the stage, Hob handed him his guitar, a polished Fender. Cameron slung the strap over his neck, cradling the instrument in his arms. He moved up to the microphone and gazed at the dark faces. The applause faded, leaving a heavy silence. His ears burned with sudden embarrassment. He adjusted the microphone to buy himself some time, cringing when it squealed. The guitar felt heavy and strange in his arms.

Grinning, Hob pivoted to look at him. A look of concern flashed in his eyes. Under his breath, he said, "It's all yours, Cameron."

Cameron's gaze lingered on the expectant faces below him. He closed his eyes to shut them out. Listened for echoes of that strange music he'd heard once before at the Calliope. Nothing now but silence, broken by a few muffled coughs. The clink of bottles.

Come on, damn it. Beads of sweat formed on his brow. *Where is it?*

The music came in a sudden rush of understanding. His eyes flew open as his curled fingers found the notes. He strummed a slow, bluesy rhythm, matched with a woeful melody, a sound like the sullen mood of a broken heart; a lonely person sitting alone at a smoky bar. The song did not belong to him. Though he'd caught a few phrases during his first visit to the Calliope, tonight's performance was nonetheless culled from thin air, unrehearsed, each note a discovery. He didn't miss a beat.

From the corner of his eye, he glimpsed Hob, standing in the shadows onstage, his face bent with something between awe and bereavement. Cameron caught his eye. They stared quietly at each other for a moment, understanding passed between them. Finally, Hob went to the piano, sat down, ripped out a few high notes. Together, they brought the song to life, a song written by a woman long dead.

Outside the bar later that night, standing in the dark, Cameron filled his lungs with the warm night, feeling the inspiration tingling in his body. He felt like an instrument. Like a tuning fork. God, he felt good. Shoving his hands in his pockets, he started across the gravel parking lot when the door flew open, and Hob came bolting outside.

"Say, man, will you hold up a damn minute?" Even in the sullen light, Hob looked shaken. "That was real cute. You tryin' to get me spooked, playin' Clara's song like that?"

"No, man. I'm trying to reach you."

"I knew I wasn't crazy. I heard you playin' that the first day I met you at the Calliope."

Cameron sighed, shook his head, smiled to himself. "It scared the shit out of me, too, at first. This discovery—this connection between sound and spirit. I want to learn more. And only Bloom can teach me."

"But the guy's fucked up," Hob insisted. "Why can't you see that?"

"Maybe I do. But it doesn't matter. I'm not doing this for him. I'm doing this for me. This is what I'm supposed to do."

Hob rubbed his chin. His eyes were wide. Finally, he shook his head, turned away. "You ask too much out of me."

"Then at least do me this one favor," said Cameron. "Stay away from the Calliope. Don't interfere."

A sadness filled Hob's eyes. Slowly, he shook his head, dropped his gaze. Then he went back to the door and opened it. Noise from within spilled out onto the front porch. Hob threw him a final glance.

"I'll stay away . . . for now," said Hob. "I just hope you know what the hell you gettin' yourself into."

Just past midnight, seven Echoes stood on a hilltop overlooking Bill Atwater's farm, home to more than thirty sleeping cattle, its landscape interrupted by the dark shapes of sleeping cows and hay bells. To Charlie Witt, also in attendance, the sky looked incredibly large, like a star-studded glass bowl clapped over this quiet sanctuary. A breeze stirred across the open field, stinking of manure.

The Echoes stood silent and unseen, except for the occasional glint of moonlight from their polished instruments.

Charlie waited breathlessly. The land rolled away from them, dropping in a smooth slope toward flatter land, giving way to a barn and silo, then a stone house sitting on the banks of a stream, its windows all dark.

Of all the changes Christofori's return had wrought, the musician named

Eris was most affected. Even brittle with age and nearly insane after the pianist had committed suicide, she'd revived—in spirit, at least—upon his return. He'd been just as eager to reunite with her. Now with her rejuvenated youth from the concert at the Calliope, she was again lovely. She moved forward from the group, hips swaying, a wraith in a black dress. In her arms she carried the metal coils of her nightmare bassoon. She blew into the instrument's mouthpiece and a hollow note climbed into the air, like wind cutting around an eave. The other musicians joined her and soon a sullen song expanded across the hilltop, a chorus of ghostly voices. Lightning flashed across the horizon.

As if summoned, a handful of cows ambled up the grassy slope, moving closer until they stood obediently before the musicians.

The melody grew grim, a death's song.

The largest cow trudged to the front of its group, udders sagging near the grass. She raised her head, whipping her tail in agitation. Charlie's eyes lowered to the cow's convulsing belly where muscles rippled, contracted. Fluids spilled from the udders and other openings. Then the flesh gave, like a torn garbage bag, dumping her innards. Ropes of intestines spilled onto the earth with slippery quickness. Even while her belly hung in loose curtains, the bovine continued standing for a moment longer before she fell over on her side.

Still playing her strange music, Eris moved over to the mound of gore. In the grass at her feet, the entrails became animated, thrashing like a nest of snakes, curling into loops, writhing in the muck.

Charlie staggered, dropped to his knees, hands locked over his mouth. He watched the tendrils coil themselves about the fallen carcass and then contract, snapping bones, squeezing blood from muscle, and then consuming the very body that had once served as their home.

Viscera. That was the name Christofori had given them when he hinted earlier at details of Eris's talents. Charlie wasn't quite sure what he'd meant, but now he fully understood with sickening clarity. They had brought a truck, now sitting at the base of the hill, with empty metal drums in the back, to capture these . . . things. Bloom's instructions echoed in Charlie's ears: *We must prepare for our final symphony. We must protect our Calliope.*

Suddenly a light shone directly into Charlie's eyes.

"All right, you sons of bitches," said a deep, frightened voice. "I want to see hands. If not, I swear to God I will shoot you."

The music stopped and the Echoes turned to face the man. Charlie knew who he was, and also knew it was too late.

Oh no, Mr. Atwater, thought Charlie. *You shouldn't have come.*

Chapter 9

"This is it," said Dunlap as he swung right onto Padget Road, a narrow gravel road lined with poplar trees and deeply rutted trenches.

As the cruiser jostled along the rough surface, Bentley rolled down the passenger window, allowing the cool morning air inside. "So Bill Atwater just up and disappeared in the middle of the night," said Bentley, throwing the chief an amused grin. "Sounds like he's up to something, don't it?"

Ignoring him, Dunlap peered through the dusty window, trying to read the numbers on mailboxes as most of the houses were nearly out of sight. He didn't find Atwater's disappearance as amusing. Kelley Lowell, working as dispatcher for the morning shift, reported the incident. Apparently, Janie Atwater had gone to bed with her husband curled up at her side, and when she'd woken this morning, she'd found an empty bed.

"I mean, if you ask me, Bill's probably seeing someone on the side. Probably meant to sneak out and do his thing before his wife woke up, then ended up falling asleep. Happens all the time. Usually the wife don't want to believe it, that's all."

The chief fixed Bentley with a cold stare. "She found his shoes by the bed and his car sittin' in the driveway."

Bentley's smile faded. "Well, now that's strange."

The driveway stretched along a good quarter mile of golf ball–sized gravel that slapped against the oil pan. The ranch house sat at the top of a hill, with a blue sedan parked in the drive and an old red pickup sitting up on blocks. As they approached, the front door opened. A woman wearing a green robe over her nightgown stepped outside, her arms crossed over her chest.

"Is that Janie?" Bentley said, leaning forward on the dash.

Dunlap hunched over the wheel, squinting. "That's her all right."

"She don't look so good."

Bent was right. Janie's face was ruddy and swollen, as if she'd been crying. As Dunlap brought the cruiser to a halt and nudged open his door, Janie raced across the yard, her face twisted up, "Something got my cows, Chief!" she shouted. "There's blood everywhere. And I think Bill might be dead!"

Dunlap glanced over at Bentley, then hefted himself out of the cruiser. When Janie came over, he clutched her by the elbows and forced her to look at him. "Slow down, Janie. I can't understand you if you don't slow down."

"There's dead cows all over the field," she said again.

Dead cows? Kelley hadn't mentioned this, nor had she mentioned Janie was damn near hysterical, which meant that Janie must have found something since she'd reported her husband missing. "Well, did you see Bill or not?"

A look of wild despair shone in her eyes as she shook her head. "I don't know," she said. "I–I couldn't tell."

Couldn't tell?

When Bentley stepped alongside him, Dunlap nodded toward the rear of the house and said in a raspy whisper, "Go on and have a look, Bent. I'm right behind you."

Clutching Janie's delicate shoulder, Dunlap looked her in the eye and said calmly, "Can I leave you alone for a minute? I need to go have a look. Why don't you sit down?"

With an almost childish shake of the head, she clutched at his arm, but he pressed her hands away, forcing her to sit on the porch step.

He hurried after Bentley, moving in ungainly strides up the hillside. The pasture rolled out in a smooth incline for nearly fifty yards before evening out again. By the time he reached the barn and silo perched on the ridge, he was sweating buckets and gasping for breath. He found Bentley over by the barn, bent over, hands planted on his knees. When Bentley saw him, he raised a hand and shouted, "Holy Jesus Christ, Chief. We got ourselves a situation."

"Well no shit, Sherlock," Dunlap grunted.

He reached the ridge, and before Bentley could say anything more, the acrid smell of blood slapped him in the face with almost physical force. His belly, full of eggs and bacon, churned. The hilltop buzzed with what must have been a million flies. And then he saw the cattle about twenty yards out. Blood fanned out across the wheat-colored grass. Maybe twenty bovines were lying on their sides, torn open, their bellies emptied.

"Jesus!" Chief Dunlap groaned, burying his face within the crook of his arm. "What in God's name did this?"

After a moment, Dunlap worked up his nerve and trudged forward across the grassy ridge until he was standing next to Bentley, who pointed at a large carcass. The brown and white spotted skin of its underbelly had been sliced so that its ribs were exposed. There didn't seem to be anything left inside, as if someone had cut the animal open, then gutted it.

"Who would do something like this?" said Dunlap, using his boot to kick back a flap of skin.

"No, Chief," said Bentley, pointing to something farther away. "You don't understand. I think I found Bill."

Chief Dunlap knew he'd be sick before looking at the lump in the grass. He didn't want to look. He could smell the horror without any need to see it. He held his breath, closed his eyes, then opened them slowly. "Holy Christ," he said, planting his hands on his knees, head sagging.

Bentley staggered, dropped to his backside.

"Don't do it, Bent," Dunlap said with little hope.

Bentley did it anyway. He crawled as far away from Bill's splayed body as he could, then threw up his breakfast in the tall weeds. The gagging sounds made it all the worse.

Bill Atwater lay on his back in the witch grass, his arms spread at his sides, his face seemingly sculpted from paraffin wax, eyes gaping, lips drawn in a frozen snarl. Atwater was most certainly dead, and while Dunlap could not determine the cause of death, he imagined it had something to do with the man's stomach. Bill's Peterbilt t-shirt wasn't large enough to cover his grossly distended abdomen, looking like a fleshy hot air balloon. The farmer's mouth was gaping open, as if he'd died singing an opera. The grass was soaked beneath him.

"Oh, God," said Bentley, sitting down, his knees drawn up to his chin. "What in hell happened to him?"

"Beats the shit out of me," Dunlap said, shaking his head. "Why don't you get down there and call Kelley. Tell her we got a possible homicide. We'll need Dewey to get some fingerprints." He touched his mouth, then added, "Call animal control too."

Bentley staggered to his feet. His face looked whiter than Bill's. Straw and dirt were in his hair. "We gonna call the county boys for this one, or the Bureau?"

"Neither," said Dunlap. Most certainly not the Tennessee Bureau of Investigation; he hated those slick types. And the last time he'd seen Sheriff Parker, he'd told the man to kiss his ass. "I think we should take care of this one by ourselves."

Bentley searched the chief's face for a long moment, obviously wanting to offer his input, but he eventually kept his opinions to himself. When Bentley turned to go, Dunlap grabbed his arm. "Oh, and Bentley . . . pull yourself together, for Christ's sake. Janie's feeling bad enough as it is."

His sergeant nodded, slicked his hair back with both hands, wiped the string of bile hanging from his chin, and then started down the hill.

Friday ended Cameron's hiatus from Bloom. He went to Orpheum Manor, and Bloom greeted him with an unctuous smile, a desire to appease him. Just as Cameron hoped, his absence seemed to have driven home his point. No more tricks. No more lies. Still, he made his position known the moment they sat at the round table inside the treasure room.

"You've got two weeks," Cameron told Bloom as Kalek drew the curtains and left the room. "After that I'm leaving."

Sitting at the round table, with the room's priceless artifacts pressing in on all sides and oil portraits watching them with knowing eyes, Bloom slid the oak box over to Cameron and urged him to open it. Cameron tried to hide his sudden and irresistible urge the moment he looked at the Tongue, nestled in its dark velvet bed. God, he wanted this. Despite its trance-induced nightmares, its horrifying hallucinations, he actually wanted this.

Bloom obviously misread his anticipation for something else, hesitation, maybe. "I told you from the beginning. The process of Attuning is difficult. But what we are striving for here is an act of self-actualization—an act of transformation and spiritual growth. Until you reach a state of harmonic perfection, you will never recall Armonia. For this reason, you rid yourself of Discord. You must compose your final Nocturne. And then you will become Attuned . . . and transformed."

Cameron plucked the Tongue from its box, held it up to the candlelight. His hand trembled. With a sudden thump, he rapped the metal fork against the side of the table, and in moments the discordant vibrations filled his head. His teeth jittered and blood spilled from his nostrils. Darkness swirled about him and swallowed him up.

Time passed. He wasn't sure how much, aware only of the agony that threatened to engulf him and never let him go.

And then, someone was shouting. No, the shout belonged to him. He snapped awake from his nightmare still sitting at the table. Bloom sat across from him. Blinking against blurred vision, Cameron made out shapes in the room's dark recesses. A stockpile of priceless works of art, he realized. Stolen treasures. From a museum. Bloom made his fortune by stealing priceless treasures and then selling them. That's how he funded his orchestra. The Calliope, the sanitarium, Orpheum Manor—all of it bought with stolen art.

"Cameron," came a low, velvety voice from the darkness. Bloom's face moved forward. The light from the candle flickered in his eyes. "The Nocturne—you must write it down."

In sudden realization, Cameron didn't want to write. To write the music meant recognizing a part of himself that he hated—a part of himself that scared him. He wanted nothing to do with it.

"I don't want to," he pleaded. His head swam. He wanted to sleep. "Don't make me do this."

"Write the damn music," Bloom persisted, this time in a low growl.

"No!"

Bloom slammed his fist against the table. "If you don't write, you will make yourself sick. Now do it!"

"I told you I'm done with this shit!"

Cameron stood and pitched the table over on its side. The tuning fork went clattering across the marble tile. He staggered drunkenly for a door that seemed impossibly far away. A buzzing pierced his ears like thousands of flies. He kicked and stumbled over something. The doorway loomed closer. He slammed a shoulder into the doorframe, then spilled out into a hallway.

Bloom's voice followed him. Closer and closer. An echo in his ear.

Understand this. The fork has drawn Discord to the forefront of your mind. It will remain there until you get rid of it. Eventually you must write this thing.

Trembling, blinking the sweat from his eyes, Cameron slammed into a wall and then another. A painting clattered to the floor.

"You've come further than anyone I've ever known," Bloom's dislocated voice continued, following him down the long, long hallway. "You will Attune. And we will have Armonia."

Chapter 10

Madison waited for several minutes before Dory Witt opened the door a crack, just enough to look outside.

Dory wore a blue robe over a pajama top, though it was almost noon. The woman looked haggard, with deep creases around her eyes and mouth, her hair a frizzy red rat's nest on her head. She looked ghastly thin too.

Good God, thought Madison. *Has everyone in this town lost it?*

Dory looked at her, frowning, as if she didn't recognize her right away. Then she opened the door a little farther and poked her head out. "Madison? Well, what in blazes are you doing here?"

"I wanted to talk to Charlie."

Dory furrowed her brow. Her countenance gloomed over and her eyes became deadpan, her mouth forming a single line. "What's he done now?" she said in a somber tone.

"Oh, no, it's nothing that he's done," Madison said quickly. "It's just that, the last time I saw him, he told me that he'd started working for the orchestra, and I haven't seen him since."

"Neither have we," said Dory, raising a brow. "Why don't you come inside?"

At the kitchen table, they sipped coffee several hours old, exchanging small talk, and Madison couldn't help but notice the piles of dishes in the sink, the stacks of unopened mail on the counter. Dory usually kept the place tidy. Then there was the collection of half-empty bottles on the bar. It looked like Dory and Uncle Howard were hitting the bottle pretty hard.

Madison reached across the table and placed her hand over Dory's. "What's going on? Where's Charlie?"

Pursing her lips, Dory slurped her coffee, then shook her head. "He's been gone for weeks now. Charlie's not welcome here anymore. Howard's still mad at him."

"But why?"

Dory's red-rimmed eyes fixed on her. "Charlie's changed. He's not the same boy anymore. He . . ." She swallowed and once again her face went deadpan. "He attacked us."

"Attacked you?" Madison covered her mouth with a trembling hand. "My God, what happened?"

With a shrug, the woman put her mug aside, stared blankly at the wall, and let the story tumble from her.

"Did you call the police?" Madison asked, shocked at the account.

"No." Dory frowned as tears glistened in her eyes. "Howard wanted to. But I begged him. Told him that Charlie's only two months away from turning eighteen. If he wants to leave, well then . . ." she faded off, then shrugged. "He can do what he wants."

They both heard the sound of a car pulling into the driveway and looked to the window. A black Cadillac sat in the driveway.

"That's Howard," said Dory. She looked sadly at Madison and touched her arm. "You should probably go. Howard's not doing well these days. If he even hears Charlie's name, well, he throws an absolute fit, and I–I just don't want to go through it again."

Nodding, Madison leaned forward and hugged her aunt. Then she got up and headed for the door. "You keep your head up, Aunt Dory. Everything will be okay. I promise."

Dory gave a tiny nod, and Madison let herself out, wondering if she'd made a mistake. She couldn't make a promise like that. Not here. Not now.

Outside, she trotted down the front steps just as Howard hefted himself from his car. He scowled at her as she approached.

"Howard, how are you?" she said, grinning forcibly.

"You seen that little bastard around?" he snapped, jowls flapping. He thrust a fat finger at her. "If you have, you tell him that he's not welcome around here anymore. I've had it with him. Got that?"

Scowling, Madison backed away from him, confounded and angry. "You know, Charlie's going through a hard time right now. I think you ought to watch how you treat him. He's just a kid."

"My ass. He'll be eighteen in a few months."

She put her hands on her hips. "Well, until that time is up, he's your responsibility."

"Fine then!" he shouted. "Tell him to come on back home. He's got two months. And after that his ass is back out on the street. You tell him that, you got me? You tell him that!"

Madison stormed out of the yard. *I should slap that fat bastard.* She'd never liked him. She'd always blamed him for making Charlie's life so impossibly difficult. Seeing him like this today only reminded her how much she loathed him. *Mean son of a bitch. No wonder Charlie finally got the hell out of there.*

The next day, Madison drove to her shop at a slow crawl, hunkered over the wheel, trying to see through the windshield as the wipers swatted ineffectually at the rain. She had no reason to go to the shop at this hour, with only one hour left before closing time. Still, she felt the need to check in. Make sure everything was in place.

And Cameron. Maybe he'd left a note . . .

Somehow, she'd managed to sleep an entire day away. It wasn't like her to do a thing like that, at least, not since college. *Maybe I'm getting sick.*

Oddly enough, she still felt tired, after so many hours of sleep. An awful, unsatisfying sleep that lasted all day, plagued by nightmares and strange music. She'd woken several times expecting to see Cameron, only to find herself alone in bed, and then falling sadly beneath another wave of sleep.

The jerk hasn't called in nearly a week. Any other guy she would have kicked to the curb. But what she felt wasn't exactly anger. She felt a great deal of worry too. Something had happened that night at the Calliope.

Bloom and his entire orchestra were up to something nasty. And to make matters worse, Charlie was involved with it. *What the hell is going on around here?*

She parked in the driveway of her shop and got out. It was a race across the front lawn as rain pelted her until she reached the covering of her porch. She jammed the key into the lock and then noticed a fold of paper tucked into the doorjamb, protected in a Ziploc bag. Frowning, she plucked it free. Her heart skipped a beat when she saw Cameron's name scrawled across its face.

She shouldered the door open and stepped inside. The clatter of the cowbell over the door drew Mozart out to greet her. She squatted down, patted his head, and then went about turning on the lights. After shaking out her wet jacket, she went over to the counter and sat down with Cameron's letter.

Not a letter. A song.

Several pages of written music, each note penned with almost mechanical precision, each symbol like a tiny drawing. At the top was her name, written in elegant letters. Was this the title? She flipped the papers over and found a note.

Madison, I'm sorry for falling off the face of the Earth. I guess I needed some time to myself. Don't hate me, okay? I'll call you soon. Promise. By the way, I wrote you something. Next time I see you, I'll play it for you.

Cameron

She dropped the papers to her side and went to the window, watching the gray light coming from outside.

"What the hell, Cameron?" she whispered. Tears stung her eyes. She hated him for making her feel this way. An emotional rollercoaster. How long did he hope to keep stringing her along?

Sniffing, she flipped the pages over and looked at the music. A song just for her. Despite her frustrations, she couldn't help but smile a little. No one had ever written her a song before, and the fact that Cameron Blake, the composer of her favorite song, had written it for her . . . well, now, that topped just about everything.

She couldn't wait to see him again. "Cameron," she whispered. "You asshole."

With her arms folded, she turned to resolutely stare out the window.

"Hello? Is anybody here?"

Madison's voice bounced off the walls as she moved slowly across the dark lobby, the maroon carpet padding her footfalls. She passed the concession stand and gazed up at the dark chandeliers. Her stomach twisted. A voice in her head begged her to leave.

She'd come to the Calliope on a whim. She hadn't expected to find the doors open. Without even thinking, she'd let herself inside, something she'd never dreamed of doing. But there was a good chance she might find Charlie here, or Cameron, and that gave her courage.

"Is anybody here?"

Her words sounded timid. She looked down at the sheets of music in her hand, the song Cameron had written her. She'd come hoping to talk to Charlie. She needed to see him, not only to ask him to play the music—which she wanted desperately to hear—but to make sure that everything was all right. But now this all seemed like a really bad idea.

When she reached the auditorium doors, she heard piano music and felt a great relief. *Is that Charlie? Yes, maybe.* But the moment she pressed the doors open and the sounds poured over her, she knew that this dark and complex music came from a talent that far exceeded her cousin.

Still, she walked into the auditorium. She felt vertigo from the room's vastness, with its soaring ceiling, its tiers of empty seats all spilling toward the stage. And there she found the musician, a man in a black suit sitting before a piano.

She saw Christofori and was instantly mesmerized by not only his talent and flourish as he played, but by his very appearance. His sweep of black hair at the nape of his neck, his long thin arms reaching for the next note on the piano keys—all lent something refined to him, something absolutely compelling in his exaggerated motions. He played stooped over, his spine bent in a graceful arc, arms moved in fluid, swan-like motions. He played with his entire body.

Watching him was almost hypnotic, moving on an untouched level.

Without even thinking, Madison started forward down the center aisle while the notes swirled about her like an armada of butterflies, romantic, enthralling, sweeping her into her fantasies.

Moments before she reached the end of the aisle, he stopped, stood, and spun around so quickly that he nearly knocked over his stool. His eyes fixed on her with an almost physical intensity.

"Hello?" he said in a heavily accented voice. "Can I help you?"

She cleared her throat, startled by his attention and dramatic magnetism. "Yes, please, I'm–I'm," she stammered, feeling a little scared, as if he'd caught her eavesdropping. "I'm looking for someone. Charlie Witt." Her words came out much too fast. "Do you know him?"

"Charlie. Of course." A tight smile formed at the corners of his finely sculpted mouth.

What's that accent? she thought. *Italian, maybe.* But that wasn't quite it either.

"Please. Come up so I can see you better."

She hesitated. "No thank you. I was just . . ."

He leaped down from the stage with the litheness of a cat, then grinned as he moved toward her. She took a step back, her heart beating wildly. The man was more than just handsome. He was beautiful, with that narrow face and skin the color of marble. He stepped closer.

Madison stood her ground, determined not to let him intimidate her.

"My name is Christofori," he said in a smooth voice. "And who are you?"

"My name's Madison Taylor," she said, feigning confidence, although her voice was too loud and went echoing across the auditorium. "I'm Charlie's cousin."

"Ah, his cousin. I see."

Moving closer, he brushed her cheek with the backs of his fingers. Madison flinched, shocked by such forwardness. She didn't quite know how to handle how vulnerable he made her feel. She cleared her throat. "I'm sorry. I really don't have much time. Could you just tell me where to find Charlie?"

"You have very pretty eyes," he mused.

Only now did she notice the condition of his skin, its near translucence, so thin she could see the veins and arteries crawling like ivy up along the sides of his face. She bit her lip, nodded, then forced a smile. "You know what? Maybe I'll come back tomorrow."

The amusement left Christofori's face, eyes narrowing. For one moment, he looked angry, even violent. "Leaving so soon?"

She shrugged. "I have someone waiting for me in the car outside."

"I understand." His gaze dropped, seeing something in her hand that caused him to tilt his head in a curious gesture. "What is that?"

Before she realized what he wanted, the man plucked the folded papers from her hand. She'd completely forgotten about them.

"What is this?" he said again, that amused grin resurfaced, then grew wider. His eyes scanned the music—Cameron's music—then he met her gaze. "This is fantastic. Who is the composer?"

"Just a . . . a friend."

"A friend? Oh, I don't buy that." Once again his eyes peered into her, as if he wanted to read her mind. "Would you mind if I played it?"

Caught off guard, she frowned. For some reason, the idea struck her as almost offensive. The music belonged to her. A gift from Cameron. Something private and intimate. This Christofori had no business playing it.

"No," she said, shaking her head. "That's not necessary."

"Oh, come now. Let's have a listen, shall we? It'll be fun."

He turned and leaped onto the stage, even more catlike than before, then moved like a shadow before tucking himself into position at his piano. Placing Cameron's music above the keys, he dove into the music before she could protest.

She wanted to scream at him. He had no right. But her anger vanished the moment the music began. A shower of tinkling notes fell all around her, notes as graceful and simple as butterflies, as light as dandelion puffs.

She stood frozen. The melody blossomed. Sweet, simple, and somehow familiar. It moved her deeply, brought tears to her eyes. It was as if she'd heard this music all her life, as if she'd been humming it to herself since childhood. Cameron had somehow known this about her, had plucked it from her head. It was her song; the melody of her life. She started weeping. Tears as hot as steam spilled down her face. Her breath hitched in her throat. *Oh, Cameron. It's beautiful. I love it. I love it.*

But her joy soon ended. *This man—this stranger—how dare he play this?* She wanted him to stop. But she couldn't speak. She just stood there, just let this thing happen to her. Finally she managed, "Please . . . would you stop?"

He either didn't hear her or didn't care. The music went on, both plucking at her heartstrings and at the same time infuriating her. Balling her hands into fists, she finally shouted, "Goddamn it! That's enough! I said stop!"

This got through to the musician. He stopped in mid-melodic phrase, and silence filled the empty auditorium. It was suddenly too quiet. Her heartbeat thundered in her ears.

"Just please . . ." she whispered, cupping her hands over her mouth. "No more."

Taking the music, Christofori walked to the edge of the stage, then crouched and held the papers out to her. "He loves you very much."

She hesitated, then moved forward, quickly snatching the papers from his hand. She'd had enough of this. It was time to go.

"I think I know who wrote this. I recognize Mr. Blake's work. It sounds like him. It is quite nice, isn't it?" His eyes twinkled with amusement, and then he whispered, "Thank you very much. I enjoyed that."

Clenching her teeth, feeling the blood hot in her cheeks, she said, "If you see Charlie, tell him I was here."

Then she was hurrying up the main aisle, forcing herself not to look back. By the time she reached the doors, she was nearly running, and Christofori had started playing again.

That night, Kalek went again to the sanitarium, only this time he visited the theater, Bloom's final touch to the dormitory.

At one time the makeshift theater had served as a cafeteria. It was one of the sanitarium's larger rooms. Carpeted planks bolted to the walls helped with the acoustics. Maybe fifty chairs were formed into neat rows before the stage. Sometimes the maestro entertained here, but most times Bloom spent his time here alone, listening as one of his musicians performed for him.

This was never an act of musical appreciation, Kalek had long ago discovered, but rather an act of necessity. Somehow the music kept Bloom stable. Attuned. Without this weekly ritual, the maestro became a nervous, imbalanced mess, and left unchecked, his condition made him violently ill. His body withered, his skin wrinkled, his limbs trembled. Kalek had seen this only once and hoped never to see it again.

Kalek marched into the dimly lit theater and spotted Bloom sitting with Christofori at the front row. The stage was empty. At the sound of his entrance, both men turned to watch him.

The maestro called out, "Alfred, we were just talking about you."

Hesitating for a heartbeat, the old man plodded toward the two. A woman appeared onstage, wearing black, glowing like a wraith beneath the stage lights. A swanlike creature, she stood tall and lithe, with a long neck, pale skin, and almond-shaped eyes. Raven-black hair cropped short spilled over the angular planes of her face. He hesitated, unable to put a name with that face until his memory sped up.

Eris wasn't as he recalled her, as Christofori's long-lost love, the woman who'd pined over him—and then went mad—after his bloody suicide. She'd come back from her near-comatose state of fragile, rigid mental lapse and was, like all the musicians, younger.

My God, how beautiful, he thought. He'd not seen Eris since her transformation from the concert, only the rumors of her new loveliness. The old woman had shed her age like a snake shedding skin. She carried a bassoon across her hip, hanging from a shoulder strap. The lights gleamed against its metalwork, its silver ivy crawlers of valves and keys.

No. Not a bassoon. She had an Archetype. As Kalek forced himself forward, Eris began playing a song of sepulchral tones and low vibrations. He sat down in the chair next to Bloom. "You were talking about me?" he asked, feigning a curious grin.

The music became only background noise.

With his eyes fixed on the stage, Bloom said, "You have failed us, Alfred."

"Failed you?" Kalek made a wounded frown as fear welled up from his belly, and his tongue grew parched. "What do you mean? What did I do?"

"It's what you didn't do," said Bloom. "I gave you a simple task. You were to watch Mr. Blake and learn about him."

"But I've done what you asked me to do!"

"Then where is he?" Christofori interjected as he leaned forward to get a look at the old man.

Kalek blinked. So preoccupied with his fears and contemplations, he'd shirked his duties by staying drunk most of the time. "He's . . . around. I would know if he tried to leave."

"Very well. And what about Madison Taylor? Why haven't you told me about her?"

Kalek's eyes grew wide. That was a name he'd hoped to keep secret from Bloom. "I–I didn't think it was necessary."

"Is that right?" The corners of Bloom's mouth turned up in amusement. "Did I not give you adequate instructions? Did I not instruct you to tell me everything about Cameron Blake?"

Kalek dropped his gaze. Shortly after Cameron arrived in Holloway, Bloom had ordered Kalek to keep a constant surveillance on the Tone Poet. The reason had been twofold: first, to ensure that Cameron did not leave; second, to learn about the man's personal habits in hopes of uncovering something that might be useful down the road. So Kalek had spent each night following the man around town, to the bars where he drank, the diners where he ate. Then one afternoon he'd followed Cameron to a small boutique just off the square, where a young woman had accompanied him onto the front porch. That had been his first glimpse of Madison Taylor. She was young, charming, and prettier than any other girl in Holloway. He shrugged. "I didn't think she mattered."

"I never asked for your opinion," Bloom snapped. "You were to watch Cameron and learn about him. About the people he deals with. Nothing more."

"The little whore came to the Calliope," said Christofori, his voice heavy with arrogance. "Blake wrote her a song. She wanted Cousin Charlie to play it for her."

"She came to you?" Kalek croaked.

"Incidentally," Bloom said, "Blake's music revealed a great deal about their relationship."

"I don't understand," said Kalek. "What could you have possibly learned?"

Christofori fixed Kalek with an impatient glower. "Are you daft, old man? Have you forgotten who I am, and what I can do? I can read volumes into any composition. Every piece of music acts as a confession of the artist's soul. This work was no different. Blake's fears, his need for acceptance, his anger— all of it was there, underscoring his feelings for that woman."

"But why should we care about that?" Kalek forced himself to speak calmly.

"Why should we care?" Bloom barked, baffled at Kalek's failure to make the connection. "This is what we've been waiting for. The final piece of the puzzle."

"But how do you mean?"

Bloom grinned darkly. "Madison Taylor is going to inspire Cameron Blake to compose his final Nocturne. His Dirge."

Kalek shrank in his chair. Just as he'd feared, Bloom wanted to exploit Cameron's love for Madison. *Oh, the poor girl.* Such a pretty girl, with eyes so much like those of his deceased wife that it had rocked him to the core. "But Blake will write this on his own. I know it!"

Christofori stood up and stabbed a finger at him. "I am sick of hearing this weasel speak! You are not worth the air you breathe!"

Kalek gasped and looked to Bloom for support, but the maestro's face was expressionless. Never before did Bloom allow the musicians to talk to him like this. Why didn't he come to Kalek's assistance now? Filled with a mixture of dread and anger, Kalek rose from his chair and walked around Bloom to stand before Christofori.

"How dare you?" he shrieked. "I've devoted my life to this orchestra! I've done nothing but make sacrifices from the moment I brought the maestro back!"

Trembling, he looked once more to Maestro Bloom, hoping this had finally gotten his attention, but he saw only cold estrangement.

Bloom had abandoned him.

Over the span of a decade, Bloom had treated him with the gentle respect of a caring son to his father. Kalek had gotten the sense that Bloom considered him as something of a father figure for having aided in his rebirth. But there was nothing of that warmth now.

He knows, thought Kalek, struck with certain horror. *He knows that I am dissident, that I will kill myself before I participate in Armonia.*

The music ended, and Bloom stood from his chair, clapping loudly. In a kind of stupor, Kalek looked once more at Christofori. There was a dangerous smirk on the pianist's face.

Onstage, Eris gave a curt bow before gliding back into the shadows.

Bloom turned, clamped a hand on Kalek's shoulder, and looked directly into his eyes. "I know you betray in thought, old friend," he said in a calm and far too relaxed voice, a slight grin playing at his lips. "I know you think about killing me. About killing yourself. But you must understand. The wheels are turning; the machine is in motion. You cannot stop it now. If I did not owe you my life, I would kill you now. But you and I are in this together," he said, leaning closer, "and I want you there when I stand before God."

Chapter 11

A brooding mood had taken hold of Cameron. He'd lost count of the days since he'd refused to write the Nocturne.

But the thing was still inside him, manifesting itself as a ringing in his ears, an agitation in his muscles. Something had gone terribly wrong. What was worse, the fevered inspiration had passed. Now the world had gone mute, had lost its music. All that remained was the ringing in his ears. His creativity had crashed. Fear paralyzed him.

Standing in the inky darkness outside the Bard Street Tavern with his hands in his pockets, a hoodie hiding most of his face, he stared at the neon sign in its single window. He needed a drink like nobody's business.

He closed his eyes and felt a terrific dreariness take hold of him. He wanted to leave Holloway, wanted to hide himself. But there was no escaping this thing. He had to finish, and that meant confronting himself. That meant writing the Nocturne. And if he didn't, the ringing in his ears would eventually rot out his brain.

He went inside, only to find it unbearably noisy in the dark barroom. An old Hank Williams, Jr. song played from hidden speakers. A handful of twenty-somethings occupied the pool table. The noise of the place made him sick, set his nerves on edge.

He squeezed his way to the bar and took a vacant stool between two strangers. He waited ten long minutes before the bartender came to take his order. He thought his head might split open from all the noise pollution.

"What can I getcha?" said the bartender.

Cameron bit down the retort that came to mind at the delay. "Jack on the rocks."

The bartender went away, and Cameron leaned forward, set his elbows on the bar, and covered his ears with his hands. He lowered his head, shut his ears. *The goddamn noise.*

Someone broke the balls at the pool table and it sounded like a cannon blast.

Cameron jerked up and turned to face the stage, half expecting to find Simon sitting up there on his stool. The bartender returned with his drink. Cameron took a sip, and someone bumped into him. Turning halfway around on his stool, he met the eyes of a short man in a blue jean jacket and a John Deere trucker hat. He'd seen him before.

"Sorry, friend," said the man, showing his blackened teeth in what looked like a smile.

He pressed his way closer and Cameron caught a whiff of day-old trash and cigarette smoke.

"Say, didn't I see you here a few weeks ago? You came to hear him play. Simon, I mean."

"So what?" Cameron muttered.

The man wheezed a laugh and clutched his shoulder as if they were best friends. "That's what I say. So what?" Still laughing, he squeezed in closer. "Now listen. I'd bet he plays tonight. But it won't happen 'til some of these assholes clear out. He don't like crowds, ya see. He's shy."

Cameron shrugged. "I didn't come here for that."

"Is that right?" There was a laugh hiding in the man's eyes, as if they shared something more. "Don't worry, partner. I won't tell. We keep a good secret 'round here."

Troubled about the way the man smiled at him, Cameron returned to his drink and folded his arms on the bar, hoping the man would go away. Instead, an arm draped his shoulders.

"Maybe we get lucky tonight," said the stranger in a phlegmy whisper. "Maybe them two honeys at the end of the bar hang around a bit longer, until Simon comes out and plays us a tune."

Cameron glanced sideways as the man nodded at two young women who were drinking together at the counter end.

"That'd be something, wouldn't it? Simon will make 'em go all frothy between the thighs. Just a few songs and those little whores will spread their legs for the whole bunch of us." The man uttered a quiet laugh and added, "Just like last time."

Suddenly alarmed, Cameron swiftly pivoted to face the man's jaundiced eyes. "What are you talking about?" he whispered.

"You know what I'm talking about." For a moment the old man seemed almost sober. "Everyone here knows what I'm talking about, except them jokers at the pool table, and them little honeys there. Everyone knows." His gnarled hand clutched Cameron's shoulder as he laughed. "Including you."

"Take your hand off me," Cameron growled. The ringing in his ears had started up again and his heart thudded louder in his chest.

The man backed away.

Cameron got up, dug a ten out of his pocket and threw it on the bar. When he turned around, the old man stood in his way, smiling.

"Where you goin'? You gonna miss all the fun."

Without thinking, Cameron threw a fist into the man's face, crunching the guy's nose like eggshell. The man spun back and crashed into a nearby table, scattering the chairs. The table flipped and the man disappeared beneath it.

The bar went quiet. The younger guys at the pool table howled with sudden laughter. One of them shouted, "Holy shit! Did you see that?"

Cameron found himself standing with his hands balled into fists, blinking as if he'd just woken up. He looked about the barroom, meeting the stunned gazes of a dozen onlookers.

Behind him, the bartender half climbed over the bar, looked down at the mess of chairs, arms, and legs, and shook his head.

"Harley, get your ass up!" he shouted. Then he looked narrowly at Cameron and said in a low southern drawl, "And you can get the fuck out of my bar."

Madison dreamed of Christofori. He sat at his piano, leaning slightly forward, his beautiful black hair framing his pallid face. She stood behind him, her hands on his shoulders, watching as his hands moved nimbly along the keys, while lovely, familiar music washed over her.

Had Christofori written this for her? If so, it was wonderful, and it resonated inside her, warm between her legs. She stroked the man's hair, kissed his cheek.

Make love to me, Christofori.

A thumping sound woke Madison from the dream. For a while, she lay in bed, listening, unable to identify the sound at first.

Someone was knocking on the door.

She fumbled in the dark until she found the alarm clock. It was past three in the morning. *They found Carrie Belle,* she thought. An image of Carrie's naked and bloated body floating down Stony Creek flashed across her mind's eye. Just like in her dreams. Wrapping herself in a bathrobe, she went downstairs.

The knocking started again. Madison unlocked the door and opened it an inch. Cameron was standing on her front porch, wearing a rain-soaked hoodie. He looked bad, unshaven, with pasty-white skin. She gave a reproachful shake of her head. It'd been two weeks since she last saw him.

"You're a real bastard," she said. "You know that?"

He shook his head and shrugged an apologetic gesture.

A sudden rush of emotions engulfed her and she stepped onto the porch and wrapped her arms around him, then kissed his mouth. "Oh, Cameron," she whispered, framing his face with her hands, covering his face with kisses. She breathed him in, tasted the salt of his skin. "I was worried. I thought maybe you'd left me."

"I'm sorry," he said as they went inside, arms around each other. He managed to shut the door behind him with a foot. "I wanted to see you. I really did. But I–I couldn't. You got my note at least?"

"Of course I did." She kissed him again with a small smile. "Thank you for the song."

"Like I said, when I get a chance, I'll play it for you."

She closed her eyes, recalling her dream, disquieted by Christofori's intrusion there. The man repulsed her, so why had she dreamed of him? She chased the thought away. "I'm glad you came. I've needed to talk to you."

He nodded, dropped his gaze, then wiped his face with his hand. "Yeah. Me too."

"You want a towel?"

"No. I'm fine."

"Let's go sit down in the kitchen," she said. No reason to soak the sofa. "I'll make us some coffee." She grabbed for his hand, intending to pull him along, but at her touch he jerked back with a hiss. "What's wrong?" she said.

He tucked his hand in his armpit. "It's nothing."

She frowned and went for his hand again. A playful struggle ensued, but she finally had his hand and got a look at the busted knuckles. "Please tell me you didn't get into a fight."

He wrenched his hand free. "I had a long night."

"I'd say so." She folded her arms over her chest.

"The guy deserved it," he added.

"Tell me why. What did he do?"

He opened his mouth to say something, then changed his mind.

She grinned knowingly, then reached for his hand again, and this time he let her inspect it. The knuckle was bruised and swollen, the skin split and crusted with blood.

"This looks bad," she said quietly. "We should disinfect it. I'll get some peroxide."

She ushered him to the kitchen, fetching her medicine box from beneath the sink. She gave him a few aspirins and then sat him down at the table, where she went to work cleaning and dressing the wound with a Band-Aid. She'd just about finished when he stole a kiss.

She gave him a little smile. It was a good kiss, and she needed it badly. "I'm sorry about kicking you out the other night. I was just . . ."

He shushed her with a peck to her cheek.

"I just don't know what to think anymore," she said, her voice thick with desperation. Tears stung her eyes. "I mean, everything's just so . . . so confusing right now. And, well, look at you, Cameron. You look like hell."

He shrugged. "I've been . . . working through things. That's all."

She shook her head. It sounded like he'd been spending more time with Bloom, no doubt. She wanted to tell him about Kalek and the hysterics at his church, but she stopped herself. Cameron would get defensive, and then they'd argue, and eventually he would leave. She didn't want that. She needed him too much tonight. In the morning, she would tell him everything. In the morning, she could say everything on her mind.

But not now. Not tonight.

An angry noise—like acoustic feedback—ripped Cameron from his sleep. Clapping his hands against his ears, he sat up, all too aware of Madison's presence, and gave a silent scream against the blaring sound. The pain of it drove him out of bed. He tried to stand but collapsed. Pressing his back against a wall by the nightstand, his fingers shoved deep into his ears, he waited for the noise to subside.

Madison suddenly appeared, crouching before him, hair hanging in her face, eyes wide with worry. She mouthed frantic words he couldn't hear.

Reluctantly, he brought his hands away from his ears and inspected his palms, warm and wet with his own blood. Bloom had warned him about this.

This is happening because I refused to write the Nocturne.

Madison shouted something else. This time he could hear her.

"Cameron? Oh, my God, Cameron! You're bleeding!"

He closed his eyes, swallowed, tried to calm himself. Tremors shook his body. *Bloom and that goddamn tuning fork—it's making me sick. God knows what I've done to myself.* Here in Madison's bedroom, where everything made so much sense, the idea of Attuning or performing Armonia seemed utterly insane. *Why did I do this to myself?*

"Cameron?" Madison's voice was clearer now, frightened.

"I'm fine," he muttered.

"You are *not* fine."

Feeling queasy, he climbed to his feet and staggered into the bathroom and flipped the light switch. The blaze of bright lights hurt his eyes. The mirror over the sink showed a haggard face. Blood stains colored the collar of his white undershirt. Wincing, he stepped closer to the mirror. His ears were ringed with blood and more of it oozed down his neck. The noise hadn't stopped yet, but it was easing some. *What the hell is happening to me?*

His knees weak, he braced himself against the sink. Only then did he catch Madison's reflection. She stood in the doorway behind him, wearing a white tank top and panties, her arms folded over her breasts.

"You need a doctor," she said in a low voice.

"No. Not tonight." He turned on the tap and waited for cold water. The worry hardened into a rock in the pit of his belly. He knew what he had to do. Bloom had warned that he would suffer for not finishing what he'd started. He splashed his face.

She handed him a hand towel, and he dried himself with it, then he turned to face her. The noise had stopped.

"I just need to sleep," he said, trying to sound optimistic.

"I'm worried about you."

You've held on to this anger for so long, said Bloom's voice inside his head. *By now it has become a part of you. If you don't write the Nocturne, it will eventually kill you.*

He stepped closer and planted a kiss on Madison's forehead. "We'll deal with it tomorrow. Okay? I promise."

She consented but insisted she clean his neck with a warm washcloth. She worked quietly, and he avoided her gaze. Once finished, they went back to bed and held each other, and Cameron went to sleep.

Chapter 12

After knocking several times, Charlie pressed his face against the tiny window set within the front door of Beethoven's Closet. He cupped his hands around his face so he could see inside and make sure the place was empty. This was all just a precaution. He'd been watching from across the street for the last hour, scoping out the place, and not a single person had come or gone. For some reason, Madison had decided not to open the shop today, which struck him as unusual, seeing that she rarely took a day to herself, especially on a weekday. *Maybe something's happened to her.* He shrugged inwardly. The question vanished the moment it arrived. These days his mind didn't function like it had in the past. He didn't feel like his old self. Emotions no longer flowed into his conscious mind. In some ways, he'd shed that old part of himself, and it felt pretty good.

He glanced over his shoulder and then gripped the doorknob. In one hand he held a large brass key, a spare to the shop, given to him by his aunt several years ago. He fit it into the door lock.

It was a cool October morning when Madison visited the old chapel, the Church of Harmony Hill. After falling into disrepair over the years, the structure, perched there on its hill, looked like something that died a long time ago. Its baseboards were green with moss, and ivy scaled its clapboards like varicose veins along the legs of an old man. The roof sagged and the windows were cracked and shattered.

Hugging herself, she stood before it and fought an overwhelming desire to turn around and leave. Her eyes fixed warily on the front door. It hadn't been difficult finding the place. She'd discovered the address on her home computer. A quick search had turned up a number of forums, where people discussed what had happened at the church. Among those posts was the mention of a sixteen-year-old boy named Joshua Hill who had been hospitalized following the sermon and spent ten years at a mental ward in Nashville. The details of that day were shrouded in myth. Demons, aliens, psychedelic drugs, mass hysteria—pundits had come up with all kinds of ways to explain what had happened here.

She climbed the shaky front steps and tried the door. The knob turned easily enough, but the door wouldn't open. It had warped over the years, jamming itself into the frame. After ramming it two or three times with her shoulder, it flew open.

She took a moment to look into that yawning doorway before stepping inside the dark foyer. It smelled dank inside. Too dark to see. She willed herself forward, taking careful steps. The floorboards creaked underfoot as she went to the dark doorway at the back wall.

She felt ill the moment she stepped into the dark chapel, as if its squalor penetrated the pores of her skin. It was a long rectangular room with a vaulted ceiling and walls decorated with stained glass windows. Pews lined the wide central aisle. There was a stage at the far end of the chapel where a cedar podium jutted up from the rotted carpet.

Drawing dank air into her lungs, she started down the central aisle. The place reeked of moist earth and rotting leaves. Rays of dusty light came through the busted windows, but the place seemed to crawl with shadows. *God, please don't let there be rats.*

As she walked, she let her eyes wander about the chapel, searching for a clue that might shed light on what had happened here a decade ago. Her gaze rested on an ocular stained glass window set high into the far wall. The window portrayed the Second Coming of Christ, sitting on his throne with one hand raised in a kingly gesture. Flanking the Savior were several golden-haired angels armed with trumpets and conjuring what must surely be an inspired theme song. *The theme for* Rocky, *maybe.* A rock had taken out most of Christ's face.

She reached the stage and mounted the steps. Moving behind the pulpit, she gazed down the length of the chapel, back toward the way she'd come, and for one fleeting moment, she forgot herself. Memories of her childhood came bubbling to the surface of her mind. She remembered Sunday worship at Bethel Baptist with her parents. Those were good times, with friends and community and silly songs. It hadn't been until her sophomore year at Keystone State University that a philosophy professor had encouraged her to reconsider her religious beliefs. After that her faith had died out like a flame in a harsh wind. The loss had stung something terrible. But once she'd become disenchanted, there was no going back.

It was easier then, she thought. *I miss it. I miss believing in something.*

A loud bang caused her to jump a little. From here she had an expansive view of the chapel and could see all the pews, all of them empty. Except they weren't all empty. From the corner of her eye, she glimpsed the face of an old woman seated in one of the pews.

A shock surged through her body. Staggering back, she clamped her hands over her mouth to stifle a scream. But there was no need. When she looked directly at the seated woman she saw nothing but shadows. The woman had disappeared, as if she'd never been there in the first place.

No, she thought, shaking her head. *There was someone sitting there. An old woman. I didn't imagine her.*

"Who's here?" she called.

Heart hammering dangerously at her ribs, she listened. It was difficult to see the rear of the chapel because only a few dusty sunbeams angled in through the windows, and they illuminated only what they touched, leaving everything else in shadows. And there were a lot of shadows. The wind howled against the eaves outside. It was a ghostly sound. Maybe she was imagining things.

Hopping down from the stage, she started up the central aisle, fixing her eyes on the open doorway. It seemed miles away. And even worse, she felt as if someone was just behind her, reaching out to grab her.

It would have been so much easier to run. She moved along at a restrained clip, just as cool and calm as one could expect, given the circumstances. Something scraped the floorboards behind her, a sound like claws against wood, and then something rushed across the aisle behind her.

With a start, she swung around, but it was gone, disappearing beneath the pews to her right. She couldn't pawn it off on her imagination this time. Something was in the chapel with her—something as big as a dog and as nimble as a deer. She held her breath. Something scrambled beneath the pews. Madison followed the sound, pivoting until she once again faced the open doorway, realizing the animal was going to cut her off.

She sprinted, panic-driven, and had nearly reached the doorway when a squat, black shape darted into her path, tripping her. She sprawled to the floor hard enough to make her hands go numb. For a moment she just lay there as her heart hammered away and stars burst in the darkness behind her closed eyelids. She tried frantically to catch her breath, opening her eyes, ignoring the splinters in her palms. Her ears rang, even as they trained on the background noises.

Something behind her growled like nothing she'd ever heard before. Fear kept her glued to the floor, but slowly she turned, looking over her shoulder.

The sallow face of an old woman stared back at her.

She was in her seventies, with short, silver hair that swept back from her brow. Sunken eyes and deep creases topped her scowling mouth of paper-thin lips. She looked almost grandmotherly, but that ended at the base of her skull. The neck—long and sinewy—belonged to something inhuman entirely, something squat on a four-legged body. The creature was the size of a small child, with frog-like skin, black and clammy.

A monster.

The absurdity mentally knocked Madison off balance, and she gave a horrid moan. She twisted around and scooted a yard away.

The creature was a knot of tightly wound muscles, ready to pounce, lightning quick. It moved closer, its old lady face hanging close to the floor as it grinned a mouthful of square, yellowed teeth.

"Get away from me!" Madison screamed and kicked out with one sneaker.

The creature scampered back, dodging the blow, seemingly offended by the affront.

Madison scooted farther back.

The creature threw its head back and sang out a scream.

Madison's panicked brain rattled. *The goddamn bitch is singing.*

It was a song. Formed from a complex range of undulating pitches, from whooping cries to rumbling groans, the crooning reminded her of a whale song, only played backwards. Nightmare music, stirring painful images in Madison: her parents rotting in their coffins, Carrie Belle's bloated body festering in a hole in the earth, a rape in a barroom, a slashed wrist, a scream.

"Stop it!" she whimpered, tears spilling down her face. The crooning scrambled her overwhelmed nervous system. She managed a slight shake of her head as she clamped her hands over her ears and screamed. "Stop it! Please stop! Please, please . . ."

Sobbing, she crawled toward the door on her hands and knees, her palms stinging from splinters. Her muscles were mush, and the exit seemed miles away. Behind her the creature howled its deranged song.

Somewhere far away a window exploded with a hellish crash.

Oh, God—please don't let me die here, Madison prayed as she crawled another yard. Suddenly before her were two legs clad in black trousers. She stopped and looked up, holding her breath. The face of a man in his mid-seventies looked down at her behind his glasses. Older now, but she still recognized Reverend Alfred Kalek.

"Help me!" she cried.

He stepped past her and sent a kick into the creature's face. A woman's scream followed.

Madison turned in time to see the creature scamper back, its claws clicking against the floorboards. The thing spun in a frenzied circle before facing its attacker, teeth bared, shoulders drawn, hissing a catlike warning.

The reverend didn't seem the slightest bit vexed.

"How dare you, Alfred?" came a trembling, brittle voice from the old lady's face, sounding perfectly human. "Kick me like some kind of dog?"

Alfred raised a fist. "That's enough, Judith! Get out of here before I hurt you. You understand? Get out!"

Madison could hardly believe it when the creature went scurrying away, only to cast one last hurtful glance over its shoulder before disappearing into the pews.

"You saved my life," Madison whimpered as she rose to her knees. A sob welled in her chest. Reaching toward her savior, she shuffled on her knees, took one of the man's gnarled hands, then pressed her lips to his knuckles as the sobs came. "Thank you, oh, thank you!"

Kalek jerked his hand free and said dryly, "You're trespassing."

His response galvanized Madison. She sniffed and wiped her face. "You're him," she said in a quivering voice. "You're Reverend Kalek."

"Why are you here?"

She got clumsily to her feet and found her balance. "What was that thing?"

His scowl deepened. "You have no right to be here."

"Is it still here?" She looked around as she began to tremble.

He turned his back on her and walked toward the door.

She followed after him, thinking it best to keep close. That creature was still in here somewhere and this man could somehow control it.

"This church has been defiled," he said in a quiet, hoarse voice. He swung around, an ugly scowl twisting his face. "I asked you a question, Miss Taylor. What are you doing here?"

She gaped at him. "How do you know my name?"

"The Oppari. They're flesh eaters, you know. It would be sucking on your bones right now if I hadn't followed you here."

"I read about this place in the paper," she said, still trembling. "You were the preacher here. People said you drugged your parish. But that's not true, is it? Something did happen here that day. Something . . . terrible."

His watery eyes filled with regret. He paced for a moment with one hand slapped to his forehead. "It was my fault. I never wanted anything bad to happen. I thought God wanted them to hear it."

"Hear what?"

He shook his head. "A song. I heard it when I died and left my body. I wrote it down when I recovered. Later, I brought in the high school band to perform it for my church. I thought God wanted me to play it for the parish. I was tricked." He scowled. "And now my soul is damned."

Chills ran down her spine. His story sounded so much like Cameron's. Bloom had collected both men.

"Cameron heard music too," she said. "He told me so. Said he and Bloom were writing a symphony."

"A symphony?" he scoffed. "That's just a word. You wouldn't understand. And I don't have time to explain."

"Then help me understand. Please!"

Something scraped the floorboards in the darkness trapped between nearby pews. The creature—the Oppari—was drawing closer.

Madison's panic returned. Grabbing Kalek's arm, she gave him a final pleading look. "Is Cameron in some sort of trouble?"

His lips curled into grimace. Stepping closer, he whispered, "You want to know what they're doing out there? They're trespassing. They think they can just hop the fence into Heaven while no one's looking. Well, they won't get away with it, I'm here to tell you."

She shook her head. "I don't understand."

"I said you wouldn't."

She exhaled a harsh breath. He talked like a lunatic, in metaphors and cloaked language. "The newspaper said a man was here that day when everyone went crazy. Said he appeared out of nowhere . . . Who was he?"

The anger vanished from his eyes as they shadowed over with regret. "I can't talk about that. Don't you understand?"

"Who was it, Reverend? Tell me!"

Finally, defeated, he said, "It was him. It was Maestro Bloom."

The visions were random, overwhelming, fluttering before Cameron's eyes. He saw his mother glaring at him with a bloody face, whispering, "God has something special planned for you. . . . God has a plan . . ."

He saw the creature with his brother's head. He saw himself covered in blood.

Then the visions ended, and he found himself standing in the chamber beneath the Calliope. He had undergone a ghastly transformation, and now . . .

Oh God! he thought. *What happened to me?*

Somehow he'd become trapped in the body of a six-year-old boy. Chilly air lapped over his naked body and he hugged himself for warmth. A single blue light shone down on him and at its fringes he saw the Archetypes, completely surrounding him. Like nightmare creatures, the things quivered, chattered, and mewed. Some slashed their tails or scuttled about like spiders. Pivoting in a circle on the slippery marble floor, Cameron sobbed, watching as they drew closer.

Leaping back, he slammed into someone standing behind him and cried out. Whipping around, he found Bloom, twice his size now. The man's eyes were pools of darkness as the blue light haloed his hair.

In the quivering voice of a child, Cameron said, "I'm cold."

Bloom stepped closer, and when he spoke, his voice echoed and multiplied in an unsettling distortion of itself. "What is it that keeps the truth hidden from you, Cameron? What pain do you hold so dear that you fear losing?"

"I don't know what you are talking about!"

"It's here in this room with us, Cameron—anger, fear, pain. See it and know it now."

Cameron shook his head and retreated a step, attempting to hide his nakedness with his arms and hands. "Leave me alone!"

Bloom moved toward him, his eyes glowing a subtle blue. "What are you keeping hidden in your heart?"

Pain scrambled up the contours of Cameron's chest, and he snarled and made fists with his hands. Suddenly the rage took him. He stood straight, no longer caring about his nudity. "I said leave me alone!" he shouted. "You want to know why I'm so angry? I'll tell you why. I hate it here. I hate it! It wasn't fair. God let them die. Mom was already sick! She was going to die anyway. But that wasn't good enough. So He killed her and then He killed my brother and my dad too. And then He let me live so I could blame myself!"

Tears sprang to his eyes and he buried his face in the crook of his arm, then sat down hard on the cold stone floor beneath him. When he broke into sobbing fits, Maestro Bloom squatted down and touched his shoulder.

"I think I understand now, Cameron," he said with paternal calm. "It is understandable, this anger you hold toward God. You have every right to harbor such hatred."

Cameron blinked the tears from his eyes. He felt frightened that someone should know such an awful secret. "Please don't tell," he said as shivers wracked his small frame and tears ran down his face. "Please, please, please don't tell . . ."

Bloom smiled and patted Cameron's shoulder, radiating with fatherly warmth that seemed so uncharacteristic of him. "Your secret is safe with me. To be honest with you, I have often felt the same anger. I, too, have suffered divine injustices. And I have also blamed God for them."

Catching his breath, Cameron looked into the man's eyes and for the first time found honesty lurking there. Bloom had made himself transparent. The man truly felt empathy for Cameron's anger toward God. He understood and did not judge.

This quiet moment passed between them. A shared moment of warmth and understanding.

Then Bloom remembered himself, ruffled Cameron's hair, and stood up.

Cameron looked up at him, his face full of trust.

"You have held on to this anger long enough, Cameron," said Bloom. "It is time to let it go. You don't have to forgive the universe for its callous nature, for taking your family away from you and pinning the blame on you. But you must deal with this pain of yours. Are you ready to do this?"

Cameron, choked with a sob, nodded.

"Good." Bloom placed a hand on his shoulder. "I will show you how. You must confront the thing that hurts you most. All you have to do is turn around—turn and face your hatred."

Alarms rang in Cameron's head as Bloom pressed his right shoulder, causing him to spin around. He fought against it, all the while feeling a presence behind him. There was something waiting for him in the dark. He was terrified. He didn't dare turn.

"You must," Bloom insisted, as if reading his thoughts. "Don't be afraid, Cameron. After all, it is your anger. You created this."

Cameron drew a quivering breath. "No!" he whimpered. "Don't make me!"

"Do it now, Cameron."

Something sinister burned in the man's eyes, and Cameron felt a sudden stab of fear. He shook his head and said again, "No! I don't want to turn around. I don't want to!"

With a start, Cameron snapped awake and jumped from his chair, knocking it over to clatter on the hardwood floor of Bloom's study. A sound rang in his ears, a quick droning that reached all the way down to his toes. For one terrible moment, he lost himself. He couldn't remember where he was or what he'd been doing. Gasping, he blinked the sweat from his eyes and searched the room, certain that shadows and snarling demons had overrun the place.

Then he remembered. He'd come back to Bloom's estate. He'd asked for this—to once again listen to the fork and suffer its nightmares.

Across from him, the maestro sat at the table with his legs crossed and his hands folded in his lap. He looked quietly at Cameron, his eyes dark and scrutinizing. He motioned to the scattered papers on the table. "Another failure."

Cameron looked at the papers scattered across the table. He'd nearly forgotten. This whole thing had been a hallucination, a nightmare. And he'd been tasked to face it head on.

"Oh," he muttered. He righted his chair and sat down heavily. The muscles in his legs trembled and he was dying of thirst.

"I took you to that dark place," said Bloom. "I showed you the core of your Discord. But you were not ready. Obviously, it frightens you too much."

"Yeah, well, you should try it sometime." Cameron touched his face, finding it wet with tears. Embarrassed, he hurriedly dried his eyes with his sleeve. "It's a miserable experience."

"If it is any consolation, you went very deep this time."

"It didn't happen," Cameron said flatly. "I didn't Attune."

"No. You did not."

"I remember some of it," he said, looking at Bloom. "I saw the Archetypes. And you were there. I think . . . I think I dreamed of myself as a kid."

"I'm afraid that we have more work to do," said Bloom. He seemed reluctant to talk about the vision. "Until you uproot the Discord of your sound aura, you will never Attune, and any efforts to bring forth Armonia will result in failure. Until you free yourself of your Discord, there can be no Divine Symphony."

Cameron got up with great care. His body ached and his ears rang dully.

The maestro crossed his arms over his chest and raised a hand to his chin, fingers exploring the lines around his mouth. Deep crevices stretched across his brow as his eyes went blank with inward concentration. "It seems to me you are holding on to your anger. You fear letting it go. This pain of yours—it seems very important to you."

"Look, I'm trying. I don't know what you want from me. If I'm resistant on some subconscious level," Cameron shrugged, "well, then I don't exactly have a say-so in the matter, right?"

Bloom's eyes narrowed. "Let us not forget why we are doing this. The Astral Music opens doors—we've already seen that. But we've only seen the effects of minor works. We can't even imagine what lies in store for us, should we perform Armonia. What will we see when we ride the waves of sound to the Center of all the Universes?"

Cameron's eyes widened as he considered the possibilities. Bloom nodded curtly. "I will have my limo waiting to take you home," he said. "Go home. Get some rest. You'll need it. Tomorrow, we try again."

Chapter 13

On the way back to town, Madison called Cameron's room on her cell phone and hid her relief when he answered. She had asked him to meet her at the courthouse gazebo, skillfully sidestepping his probing questions.

"Just be there," she'd said, ending the call without so much as a goodbye.

When she pulled her Honda into the lot near the gazebo some twenty minutes later, she found him waiting there as promised.

"You're early," she said as she clomped up the steps.

Cameron nodded. "You sounded . . . anxious."

"I was . . . I am."

Her heart ached when she met his eyes. He looked run-dry, like the day after a drinking binge. He wore a pair of worn jeans and a button-down Oxford with its tails out. He was pale and thin, and dark around the eyes. It had only been a day since she'd last seen him. "You look like hell."

"Well, that makes two of us," said Cameron as he eyed the torn fabric around her knees. "What the hell happened to you?"

"I fell."

"You fell?"

He looked worried, and she felt a bitter joy in that. *Good*, she thought. *Let him worry.* It was, after all, partially his fault. She wouldn't have gone and nearly gotten herself killed if he'd been honest with her from the start.

She walked to the opposite railing and looked out across the street at the row of quiet shops. She'd chosen the gazebo because it was mostly hidden.

Sunshine, air, and privacy. Just the place to discuss matters such as insane reverends and creatures with human faces.

She turned to him when tears suddenly sprang to her eyes. She shook her head and clamped a hand over her mouth. The sobs came, shaking her whole body, and she couldn't stop it. She hurt in so many places, inside and out.

He hurried over to her and grasped her hands, squeezing them firmly.

"Talk to me," he whispered.

She snorted, wiped her nose with her sleeve, then looked coolly into his eyes. "I did some research. Found some interesting things about your friends at the Calliope."

Something flitted across Cameron's face. His concern dissolved, became a look of suspicion. "What are you talking about?"

"That man named Alfred Kalek. He works for Bloom. Did you know he had a church about ten years ago?"

"I . . ." He shook his head, his face drawn into a baffled frown. "I mean, he never told me. And why should I care anyway?"

"Well, you should. Something really strange happened there. It was in the newspapers. People went crazy. Mass hysteria and everything."

He rubbed his mouth, obviously upset.

"The church is in Willow Wood, about half an hour from here," she went on. "I drove to it this morning. Just to check it out."

She told him the whole story, about the creature, the attack, and Kalek. The blood drained from Cameron's face as he listened. He propped himself against a post and stared off at the shops across the street. When she finished her story, he let a handful of moments pass before turning to face her.

"You're sure it wasn't some kind of animal?" he shrugged. "Maybe something escaped from the zoo."

"You mean like a baboon or something?" Madison gave a highly annoyed laugh. She almost wanted to slap him for saying something so idiotic. "Jesus Christ, Cameron. Don't you think I'd know if a zoo animal attacked me? Give me a little credit."

"I'm just saying . . . I'm sure it was dark in there." He folded his arms over his chest. "Are you sure it was Kalek?"

"It was him, all right. I found a picture of him on the 'Net." She rubbed her eyes and then added, "If he hadn't come, I don't know what would have happened to me."

He touched her arm. This last statement seemed to bring the gravity of the situation to a head for him. "This is why I wanted us to take some time away from each other," he said. "I was afraid you might get hurt."

"Well, I did get hurt." Her face twisted suddenly, an involuntary act as tears stung her eyes. "In more ways than one. Do you even know what sort of people you're working with? My God, Cameron, if only you'd seen that thing!"

He drew her into his arms and pressed his lips against her brow. She relaxed some. She wanted to resist him, knowing that they'd resolved nothing, that their relationship remained uncertain, that he just wanted her to stop crying. But it did make her feel better. She needed him, simple as that, and for the moment, she had him near. Maybe it was foolish to hope for more.

After a moment, she cleared her throat and said, "And that's not all. Kalek told me something else . . . about what really happened at his church."

Now he pulled back some so he could look her in the eye. "What do you mean?"

Pursing her lips, she looked off to the distance. An hour ago, standing in the moldy remains of that destitute chapel, she'd been willing to believe everything the old man had told her. But now, out here in the sunshine and fresh air, it all seemed crazy. "He told me about a song he wrote . . . something he heard during a near-death experience. Same as you. Only, when he got the high school band to play it during Sunday morning service at his church, something happened. A man appeared. It was Bloom," she whispered, afraid some passerby might hear her. "He just . . . appeared."

"Appeared?" Cameron drew his brow in an almost comical expression of disbelief. "What the hell is that supposed to mean?"

"I mean he just appeared. Out of fucking nowhere."

He made a face, turned his gaze inward, then braced himself against the railing. "I shouldn't have dragged you into this."

"Too late for that." She met his gaze and glimpsed a great deal of pain hiding behind his eyes. Folding her arms over her chest, she added in a quiet voice, "And you know what? I can't help but wonder if Bloom's musicians had something to do with Carrie Belle's disappearance."

He looked away as his eyes relayed a flicker of realization.

She'd seen that shadow pass over him. "Do you know something, Cameron?"

He looked at her earnestly. "No. I wish I did."

"Then can you at least tell me what's going on? Can you please just be honest with me? Just this once?"

He searched her face, obviously wrestling within himself. Finally, he sighed and gave a reluctant nod. "All right," he said. "Okay. I'll tell you what I know."

For the next hour or so they walked and talked, and he told her everything. By the time they reached Yarborough Elementary on Kensington Street, Madison felt sick with dread.

"If that tuning fork of his makes you sick," she said and held her hands out, as if she shouldn't even have to ask such a ridiculous question, "then why in hell would you go on using it?"

An uncomfortable smile touched his face. "Because it helps too."

"It doesn't sound like it's helped anything."

Now the quiet smile had disappeared and he blushed with embarrassment. "For a long time I carried around a lot of pain and anger, and well, sometimes the only way to free yourself of something like this is to . . ." he shrugged, "rid it from your system. Piss it out, like a kidney stone. And that's just what I did. I mean, you should have seen some of the stuff I wrote during those sessions. It was really awful."

A shiver stopped her in mid-stride. She folded her arms over her chest and shook her head. "I don't like this, Cameron. It scares me. It's wrong. Just like the thing at Kalek's church."

This got through to him. He put a hand on her shoulder and looked her in the eyes. "I think I know that now."

"The night of the concert," she said, holding his gaze. "They played one of your Nocturnes, didn't they?"

When he didn't respond, she socked him on the shoulder. "I knew it!" She felt both relieved and angry; relief because she wasn't crazy, angry because Bloom and his musical miscreants had tricked the entire town. "Something happened that night. I knew it wasn't just in my head!"

"I wanted to tell you," he said quietly. "Bloom never told me his plan. I swear it. I wouldn't have let them do it. I wouldn't have brought you there."

"So what in hell did he do to us?" she shot back.

He scratched the back of his head as he turned his gaze to the small brick elementary school. He could hear laughter from the playground around back. "I don't know. Nothing terrible. But . . ."

"But what?"

"Somehow they . . ." he shook his head, as if he himself didn't believe it. "I don't know how they did it . . . but they got younger."

"Younger?" She frowned and shook her head. "What the hell does that mean?"

"It means that each musician shed about thirty years." He gave an exasperated shake of his head. "Whatever he did that night at the Calliope—whatever they took from the crowd—it made the musicians young again."

Her stomach cramped. She wrapped her arms around her belly and grimaced. The day's horrors struck her like a blow. Shaking her head slowly, she said, "How could you let something like this happen?"

"I don't know," he said, shaking his head in quiet desperation. "I just don't know how it got this far."

When he reached for her, she swatted his hand away, her anger in force again, and then twirled in a clumsy circle, searching for a place to sit down. "Oh my God. I can't take this. I don't know what to believe anymore. And you! You're just as much a part of this as anyone else in that orchestra."

He got a firm hold of her elbow and pulled her close despite her resistance and wrapped his arms around her. Eventually she relented, emotions succumbing to his touch. He planted a kiss on her forehead and made shushing sounds.

"Everything is okay, Madison," he said. "It's over. I'm making sure of that."

"How? Are you going to the police?"

"No. Nothing like that. Dunlap would never believe us, and you know it."

She tried to pull away from him, but he tightened his hold on her. "Then what are you going to do?"

"I don't know. I'll think of something."

She shivered and closed her eyes. "I'm scared, Cameron. I'm scared, and I don't know what to think."

"Then let me handle it. I'll think of something."

By the time they arrived at Madison's house, she felt haggard with aftershock, and Cameron had to practically carry her inside. She asked him to wait while she took a shower. She needed time to think.

Afterward, she found him lying in her bed, atop the blanket, watching television. When she crawled in beside him, he looked at her quietly for a moment, then said, "Listen, I want to ask you something."

"Okay," she said, though the word came loaded with uncertainty.

"I want you to come with me to San Diego."

She drew back, frowning. "What are you talking about? I can't do that. This is my home."

"I know. But I'm worried about you. This town . . . it's got problems. It's not good for you. Come away with me."

"You're afraid of Bloom. Why don't we just go to the police?"

"I told you already. The police can't help. Bloom's got everyone in this town wrapped around his finger. I think the best thing to do is just get the hell out of Holloway before anyone knows better."

She swallowed the lump in her throat. She'd known that this moment would come. She'd been expecting it. Even so, it hurt her to think that they'd reached the end of the road.

"You'd like it in San Diego," he went on. "I've got plenty of money for both of us. And let's face it. Your shop would do better in California. I mean, think of the possibilities. What do a bunch of country hicks know about fashion anyway, right?"

"Those country hicks happen to be my friends and family."

He sighed. "Okay. I'm sorry. That wasn't funny. I just . . . I just think you're better off coming with me."

She drew a trembling breath, squeezed his hands, then blinked back tears. "No, Cameron. And it's not because I don't care about you, because I do. But this is my home. I've worked hard to build a life here." *I can't believe I'm saying this.*

He fell silent for a long moment. Then he said, "I know. I shouldn't have asked."

"No." She smiled, moved in closer. "I'm glad you asked."

He rolled over toward her, kissed her on the mouth, pressed his forehead against hers. "I love you," he whispered. "But I can't stay. Eventually, I have to go."

She shushed him with another kiss, then whispered, "I know. Just stay with me for a while, okay?"

He agreed, and she fell asleep shortly afterward, aware of his warmth, of his weight in the bed beside her. He never bothered getting under the covers with her, and she knew he would not be there when she woke up.

The following afternoon brought a shivery rain to Holloway. It spattered Simon's hairless scalp as he trudged across the front yard of Beethoven's Closet, his violin case swinging from one fist. He tromped up the porch steps and then opened the door with the key he'd gotten from Charlie.

He stepped inside. With only a faint light seeping in through the windows, he easily submerged himself in darkness. Blue shadows crawled along the floor and over his face and hands. The outside light shone brightest on the register counter, and he went over to it and set his violin case down, then unlatched the hasps. Opening the lid, Simon drew a sharp breath. He was a simple man, with elemental emotions, ranging from lust to hunger to fear and rarely anything between. But when he stared down at the strange black instrument nestled in its velvet-lined bedding, he experienced something akin to religious awe.

He drew a breath of perfume-sweetened air, a scent that made him think of the woman who'd wandered into his bar only a few months ago, only to succumb to his music and give herself to countless men. With a shiver, he drew the instrument from its case, and waited.

Buzz was as friendly as ever. When he saw Cameron, he got out of the taxicab, tipping the brim of his cargo hat. Cameron felt right at home as he hopped into the backseat of the yellow Chevrolet Caprice. By now, not having a car was grating on his nerves. But he had no desire to rent a car, and it wasn't too much of a burden to just pick up the phone and call Buzz or his brother Kevin. One of them would invariably rush over to pick him up. They always drove similar cars, both relics from the nineties, both reeking of cigarette smoke and McDonald's French fries.

"Where to, partner?" Buzz said from the front.

Cameron gave him the address that he'd gotten from Madison in one of her Google searches.

Half an hour later, Buzz parked the taxi on the side of the road. Just up the hill, a country cabin sat nestled in a copse of ash and poplars. The house had the look of a modified A-frame, with a wraparound porch and a wooden staircase. A stone chimney ran straight up its center, splitting its face in two, with large triangular windows at either side. Like the house in *The Amityville Horror*, thought Cameron.

Buzz promised to wait in the driveway while Cameron did what he needed to do. Cameron made it worth his time by giving him a fifty.

After climbing the staircase to the top landing of Kalek's porch, pausing a moment to consider the fantastic view of the neighboring hillside, he knocked on the front door, but no one answered. He glanced at the windows, but thick curtains kept him from spying inside. The place looked empty, and this left him feeling desperate. Just in case, he went around to the side doors and knocked again. Still no one answered.

"Shit," he muttered. He turned to go when he glimpsed a ghostly face in the window. He jumped in surprise, then laughed at himself when the door swung open.

Kalek appeared in the doorway. "What are you doing here?"

Still a little jittery, Cameron cleared his throat and said, "I came to talk. About Bloom. About your church."

Kalek's brow rose in surprise, but then his scowl resurfaced and he started to shut the door. Cameron stuck his foot in to keep the door from shutting, then gave it a shove hard enough to send the old man staggering back into his home.

Cameron followed inside and shut the door behind him.

"Who do you think you are?" Kalek cried out.

It was dark inside, something Cameron hadn't prepared himself for, and for a moment he couldn't see anything beyond Kalek. The old man stood before him, snarling like a trapped animal.

"Now hold on a minute!" Cameron raised his hands to show they were empty. "I didn't come here to hurt you. I just want you to tell me what attacked Madison."

Kalek shuffled back a few steps with his hands balled into fists and his wiry frame trembling with anger.

"You saved Madison's life," Cameron said. "So if anything, I owe you one."

"And this is how you repay me? By forcing your way into my home?"

"You wouldn't have let me in without a little push."

The old man sighed and shook his head. His shoulders slumped as the tension left his muscles. "This wouldn't have happened if you hadn't gotten her involved," he said in much calmer voice. "Maestro Bloom warned you not to tell outsiders about us."

Cameron risked a glance around the spacious living room. Heavy curtains covered the large windows. Beams stretched overhead, interrupting his view of the lofted ceiling. The place was furnished with leather sofas and loveseats. A muted television on the far wall streamed endless footage from CNN. Evidently, Bloom paid Kalek enough to live comfortably.

There was a round table placed in the corner before the entrance to the kitchen. Cameron nodded to it. "Why don't we sit down? You look like you're about to fall over."

The old man stewed for a minute longer. Then he licked his lips and said, "Are you alone?"

"Just me and the taxi down below."

"Maestro Bloom would not appreciate me talking to you. You know this, don't you?"

Cameron shrugged. "Yeah, well, right now I don't give a shit about what he thinks."

Kalek's face soured noticeably. He gave a dismissive swat with his hand, moved over to the table, and dropped himself into a chair, folding his arms. Cameron took the chair across from him and waited quietly.

"That creature is an entity of Discord," said Kalek. "Maestro Bloom calls them Oppari. Sometimes they slip through when a powerfully discordant piece is played. They have a tendency to take the physical form of a painful memory. In this case, the Oppari wears the face of my wife. So I suppose I'm responsible for it."

"You? What do you have to do with all this?"

"Plenty." Kalek fetched a pack of Marlboros from his breast pocket, tucked one between his lips, and lit it. His face went lax as he drew. "I lost my wife to an aneurysm and she died in our church. I was so mad that I decided to take my own life. I parked my car in the garage and took my .22 pistol and shot myself." He touched a spot of white to the right of his brow, half hidden beneath his hair. "I left my body, and that's when I heard it—not the armada of singing whales that you heard, not the Voice of God—but instead something terrifying. Imagine the sound of your ears ringing after you hear the blast of a gun. Only the ringing was in my soul."

Frowning, Cameron leaned forward, searching Kalek's haggard face. The way he described this sound called to mind the Tongue. Cameron wondered if they were somehow connected.

"Maybe I glimpsed Hell," Kalek continued in a strained voice as he blew a cloud of smoke. "Or maybe it was a realm of Discord, just like Bloom says. I'm not sure if there's a difference. Anyhow, I think I would have stayed there for a long time, maybe forever, had my neighbor not discovered me and saved my life. During my recovery at the hospital, after waking from a nightmare, I wrote down what I remembered of the death music. I must have been still asleep because I don't know how to read music, much less write it. Yet when I woke the next morning I found . . . music."

His watery eyes fixed on Cameron. "I don't know why I did this. I suppose, subconsciously, it was a sort of admission of guilt. I didn't want to forget it. I didn't want to hide from it. And even though I escaped, nothing could change the fact that I had strayed from God. So I did the only sensible thing for a man with the knowledge that his soul is hellbound." He paused and gave a full smile. "I started my own church."

Kalek went on to tell his story in great detail from the beginning to the grisly end.

"Again, I don't know why I did it," he confessed with a kind of disbelieving laugh. "I suppose I felt like I could atone for my sins. By performing this music for everyone to hear, I was letting go of my awful secret. I was showing everyone the imperfections of my soul. I'd hoped to start over. Do you understand? Get it out in the open and go from there." He scoffed at his own stupidity and snuffed out his cigarette. "It didn't happen that way."

Cameron nodded in half understanding, half sickened rapture.

Kalek chortled quietly to himself. "My music freed Bloom, just as your music freed Christofori. Only, Bloom didn't need an Archetype for his own resurrection; he is stronger than the others."

Cameron shook his head, striving to make sense of it all. He went to the fireplace and supported himself against its mantle, cluttered with religious knickknacks and silver-framed photographs. "Why didn't anyone tell me?"

"I could write a book about things that Maestro Bloom has not told you."

"You're a Tone Poet, aren't you?"

"I'm not anything."

"Don't bullshit me. All this time I thought I was alone."

"You are alone," Kalek said bitterly, dropping his gaze as if ashamed of himself. "We may both be Tone Poets, but we are not of the same keel. You heard Heaven; I heard Hell. That makes us different in my book."

Cameron stowed this away for later. He had more things to work through and it was getting late. Already a half hour had passed since Buzz had agreed to sit tight. Hopefully Buzz was a man of his word. It would be one miserable hike back to town. "So what happened to Bloom before you pulled his ass out of thin air?"

"Before the resurrection?" Kalek gave a sinister grin, eyes narrowing, his voice just above a whisper. "He was murdered."

"Murdered? By who?"

"By a group of curators for a private museum."

"The Musicians Guild," Cameron said, recalling an earlier conversation with Bloom.

"He told you about them, did he? Well, the Guild hunted down Bloom and his Echoes after they performed their blasphemous Symphony. Most of the Echoes got away. But not Bloom. They trapped him and burned him alive. All they managed to do was destroy his body. His twisted soul had no place to go, you see. And that's how he came back."

"And after he came back," said Cameron as he walked slowly to the table, "Bloom returned to that museum, didn't he? He went back and took the instruments."

"You bet your ass he did. The moment he regained his strength, he looted that museum. Took his instruments and enough treasures to make himself a fortune on the black market. He burned the rest."

Standing over the old man, Cameron bent forward with his hands on the table and said between his teeth, "What did Bloom do to them, Kalek? What did he do to the Guild?"

A look of anguish twisted the reverend's face as he grimaced. "He murdered them," he whispered. "And I helped. We brought Erich Lutz with us, one of Bloom's Echoes. His Pied Piper. Lutz walked straight into that museum with a river of rats in his wake. They massacred the Guildsmen." He covered his face with a trembling hand. "I saw it happen. I saw their corpses, still seated at the table, with their faces chewed off . . . only a few strips of meat still cleaving to the bone." A sob rattled from his throat and then he added, "I have their blood on my hands."

Cameron paced the room as the hardwood creaked beneath his feet. So there it was. He'd spent the last weeks working with a cold-blooded murderer. *Jesus Christ, I'm in deep with these criminals.* He stood before a window that overlooked a forested hillside and said, "Why did the Guild kill Maestro Bloom?"

Kalek slowly rose and crossed the room to Cameron, his back hunkered over as if he hardly had the strength to walk. His scowl deepened and he said, "Because he committed a crime against God. Because he and his entire orchestra are an abomination. And I am just as guilty. These musicians . . . they thrive on Discord. They celebrate death and base desires. The one called Simon, for example. Just the other day I went to Bloom's sanitarium. Made an accidental turn into Simon's upstairs bedroom. Pornography was taped all over his walls. And there was Simon, playing his violin, and the things his music told me . . ."

"Like what?" Cameron heard himself say, though he didn't really want to know.

"He raped a woman, once. Oh, maybe he's not the one who did the physical act, but it was his music that seduced that little girl into whoring herself out to all those men. They took her onstage before God and everyone." He paused and added, "I think they might have killed her."

Cameron's eyes widened as he clapped a hand over his mouth. His thoughts turned to Carrie Belle, and then to his fight at Bard Street Tavern. *Just a few songs and those little whores will spread their legs for the whole bunch of us*, the man had told him.

"Oh, my God," he muttered. He staggered to the door and wrenched it open. He'd heard enough for one night. "What the hell have I gotten myself into?"

"More than you realize," Kalek said behind him. A hint of amusement in his brittle voice. "More than you realize."

Chapter 14

Madison woke and Cameron wasn't there. A brick settled in her stomach. She sat up in bed, wincing at the ache in her muscles. Faint sunlight pressed against the windowpanes and cast her room in shades of red and orange, but it told her nothing about the time. Was it dusk or dawn? She looked over at the empty bed and could still hear Cameron's voice.

I love you. But I can't stay.

Her mood darkened until she could hardly breathe. He was gone, and she had nothing left. Nothing but nightmares.

Snap out of it, Madison. This time it was her voice. *Maybe it's not too late. Maybe he's still here in town. Tell him you changed your mind. That you want to go away with him.* This sudden sense of urgency got her out of bed.

She drove around Holloway searching for him. She stopped by his hotel first, but he never answered his door. She cruised around the square a few times, but that turned out to be fruitless. She finally considered a visit to the Calliope, but the thought of Christofori's smug grin gave her the creeps. *"Let's have a listen, shall we? It'll be fun."* She didn't want to go back there. Not ever again.

"Goddamn it, Cameron," she said under her breath when she came to a stop at a red light. "Where in hell are you? You're the only asshole in America without a cell phone."

She didn't know where to go or what to do. *He won't leave,* she told herself. *He'll come back to say goodbye, and then I'll tell him. I'll go with him to California. Anywhere. Because . . . Oh God . . . because I love him.*

But first things first. She couldn't leave her shop without a goodbye. Just long enough to clean out the cash register. Set the security system. Put a makeshift "Closed until Further Notice" sign in the window.

Five minutes later, she parked her Honda in the Closet's driveway. Nightfall had come and her shop looked strange in the dark. It'd been two days since she'd opened for business. Not even a sign in the window to let her shoppers know. She'd basically abandoned the place. Besides a handful of loyal customers, who would care if she never opened again?

The truth was, the shop didn't matter much to anyone. Madison had tried so relentlessly hard. She'd shouldered the burden all alone, fighting every step of the way just to stay afloat, always a gulp away from drowning.

No, not alone. Carrie Belle had helped.

Bands of pressure clamped around her at the thought of Carrie. Could she leave with Carrie's face still plastered on a missing person flyer? Carrie's disappearance was one of the reasons why she wanted to get out fast. Things were falling apart in Holloway. And the more she thought about it, the more she shared Mrs. Meadows's suspicions. Maybe one of the musicians had done something to Carrie, something terrible, and that meant there was a killer on the loose. It was time to throw in the towel—and not just on her shop, but on Holloway.

Sorry, Dad. I tried. I really did. It just . . . it just didn't work out.

Madison got out of her car and crossed the lawn to the front porch. She stopped when she noticed the outside light had gone out. Certain she'd left it on—she always did—she climbed to the top step and inspected the bulb when a dreadful feeling washed over her. Her gaze shifted to the doorway, to its single dark window. She drew an uneasy breath. Something was wrong. It was a feeling more than anything else, a voice that told her to go home. *Go home now.* She nearly took the advice. But she only needed a few minutes, just long enough to close out the register and put a sign in the window.

She dug in her purse for her keys but stopped when she heard a song playing from somewhere within the shop. She recognized the sullen timbre of a violin. She knew the song too. Cameron had written it for her. It was her song, and someone was in her shop, serenading her.

The door creaked slowly open all by itself, revealing the dark hollow inside.

Run, Mad, the panicky voice in her head told her.

But the music was so warm, so familiar, and wrapping itself around her, like embracing arms.

A new voice—a voice belonging to a man—spoke to her in soft whispers. "I'm here, inside. Come inside. I want to show you something."

"Cameron?" She frowned. "Cameron. is that you?"

"Yes. It's me. Come inside."

She took a hesitant step forward, then another. She wanted badly to see Cameron, to find him inside the shop, playing the song that he'd written for her. She passed into the open doorway and into the front room of her shop. The lights were off, but someone had lit hundreds of candles, placed in parallel lines to the left and right of her, following away from her like runway lights.

Wait a minute. Where am I?

The room transformed. She found herself standing in the central aisle of an impossibly large auditorium, flanked by wooden pews, while the candles followed the blood-red carpet all the way down to the stage.

She staggered, pressed a hand against her forehead.

Oh no. I know this place. The Calliope.

Her feet moved her forward. She shook her head, but the music filled her brain. It wouldn't leave her alone. She couldn't think.

Nor was she alone. Onstage, Christofori sat at his piano. He didn't even look down at her as his hands raced up and down the keys, playing the song that Cameron had written for her. The music of her soul.

It's a trick, she told herself. *I have to get out of here.*

But she drifted on, summoned by that wonderful melody that knew so much about her, and before she approached the stage, the pews on either side of her belched sudden plumes of flame. Great walls of fire rose up to the ceiling, trapping her. The heat struck her like a slap across the face. Her skin blistered and burst. The pain was tremendous. She screamed and shadows unfurled like great wings above her, stretching over the aisle to form an arc, a dark tunnel that led to the stage, to the pianist, and ultimately, to her song.

A tumid moon hung in the sky when Kalek arrived at what remained of the Church of Harmony Hill.

Once inside, he forged a path through the gutted building, kicking through boards with rusted nails and crunching over broken glass. By the time he entered the foul-smelling chapel, his shirt was damp with sweat. He shone his flashlight on the empty pews, then fanned the beam from left to right.

He slowly walked down the main aisle toward the stage at the room's opposite end, breathing through his nose to sniff her out.

"Judith?" he called. His voice sounded thin. The air stank, ripe with decay. She was near. "Are you here? I want to talk to you."

For the past eighteen years, he'd managed to keep Judith—or whatever part of her that lived here in the chapel—a secret from everyone, including Bloom. To this day, he still wasn't completely sure what it was. The Judith Monster was Oppari, he knew that much, a demon from some realm of dark vibrations. Sometimes they appeared when the Echoes performed powerful pieces of Discord. But the Judith Monster was different. She had the face of his wife and that made him partial to the damn thing—and responsible for it. After all, the creature had manifested the same day the high school band had performed his music; the same day Maestro Bloom had appeared. He believed the creature contained a part of Judith, a vestige of her spirit, a piece of her ego that he'd salvaged from death.

I made her. She's a product of my work. The work of a demented Tone Poet.

Of course, that had been Bloom's assessment. Bloom had long ago dismissed the possibility that Kalek could compose Armonia for the orchestra.

"My dear Mr. Kalek, you are filled with dissonance. Even if the Voice of God is trapped inside you, it is buried beneath your suffering and your disillusionment with reality." Bloom's words stung even now.

Yes, perhaps the state of his soul kept him from composing Armonia, but he'd been well enough to bring about the resurrection of Maestro Bloom, and of course, the Judith Monster.

"Judith?" he called as he moved down the center aisle. The beam of his flashlight trembled. "Come out so I can see you."

He heard the strange purring before Judith's head poked around one of the pews. His light shined full on her face, hovering close to the floor. She looked at him with those wide, familiar eyes, filled with uncertainty. He groaned at the sight of her. With just her head exposed, she was the spitting image of his wife. But then the Judith Monster broke cover and revealed her squat, doglike shape.

He gave a sad smile and said, "There you are, dear." He sighed, then slipped off the small backpack he wore strapped over one shoulder. He reached inside and found the Ziploc-sealed sirloin. "I thought you might be hungry, so I brought you something to eat."

He stepped forward and ripped open the plastic seal with his fingers. Judith mewed, a high-pitched sound of desperation. Her talons clicked against the floorboards as she moved forward. Her long neck carried her head forward, drool spilling down her chin.

"Come here, dear," he said, lowering into a crouch. He held the steak out, letting it drip, while in his opposite hand, he gripped a butcher knife, hidden behind his back. "Come have a bite."

Hunkering low, the creature moved closer, watching him as she sniffed the air. She moved closer. Her long tongue uncurled from her gaping jaws and slid along the slab of meat. She mewed excitedly and scuttled closer. Her head snapped out and half the steak disappeared into her mouth. She gobbled violently while Kalek held on.

"That's it," he whispered as tears stung his eyes. "That's it. Have all you need, my love. I'm sorry I did this to you. It's time to end it now."

Tightening his grip on the butcher knife in his left hand, he brought the blade down in a chopping motion, snapping through brittle bone at the back of Judith's head, where the base of her skull met with the nape of her long neck. The Judith Monster threw her head back and screamed, her jaws distending. The effect was like a thousand foghorns blasting in Kalek's ears. He reeled backwards and fell as the creature spun in manic circles until eventually slumping to the floor.

Rolling onto his belly, he crawled over to her, as she lay on her side, gasping for breath. Already regretting what he had done, he reached forward and placed a hand on her brow. Her eyes rolled up to meet his. There was no anger; only confusion.

She gasped, licked her lips, and whispered, "Alfred? What have you done? Why did you do this to me?" But then the air escaped her throat with a hiss, and she sank like a deflated tire.

"Oh, no, Judith!" He caressed her cheek with his hand. "I'm so sorry. So, so, so sorry. Please forgive me."

The creature's eyes glared vacantly ahead as blood spilled from her nose. Kalek shook his head and sobbed. On his knees, he brought his face close to hers, pressing his lips against her cold, leathery brow.

"Forgive me," he said again. And again. And again.

Cameron snapped wide awake, alone and disoriented and surrounded by a silence so thick it seemed tangible. At first, he couldn't locate himself. Then he remembered. He'd come back to his hotel room after visiting Kalek, fallen into a pleasant slumber filled with dreams of Madison. She'd liked the song he wrote for her, felt it in her very bones, and then she'd grown icy-cold beside him.

No, wait. He'd first stopped at Bloozey's, hoping to find Hob, but Hob hadn't been there. So he'd had a few drinks. Strong ones. After that, he'd come back to the hotel and passed out.

I shouldn't have left her, he thought, sick with guilt. *She's probably scared out of her goddamn mind.*

The sudden shriek of a siren broke the silence and he got up and went to his window to close it, but he hesitated. The siren sharpened his dream of Madison in his mind, a dream that had already started to fade. But that feeling of dread resonated. He leaned half his body out of his second story window. From his limited view, he could just barely glimpse the square. Emergency lights flashed onto a few third-story windows and washed against the courthouse cupola.

He drew back inside, then sat down on his bed, rubbing his chin. Just a fire. Things burned all the time.

So then why did he feel so anxious?

His dream of Madison had felt so real, so detailed, down to the scent of salt on her skin, the perfume that she wore, the touch of her spine beneath his hands. *I don't blame you . . . I need you to know that.* He looked at the window, listening to the sirens. Those fire trucks were heading south of the square—in the direction of Beethoven's Closet.

He had to make sure.

He entered the square just as a fire engine and an ambulance squeezed into the narrow streets. When the two vehicles swerved onto Frontier Street, Cameron stopped and stared at them, his nervousness growing.

He quickened his pace and cut across the courthouse lawn, to the empty Main Street, and finally onto the next street, where he saw great spiraling flames reaching high into the dark sky. Beethoven's Closet was on fire.

Cameron slowed just for a moment as the realization knocked the wind from his lungs. "No!"

He sprinted the final hundred yards.

A crowd of onlookers formed a wall about the scene. Emergency vehicles were parked haphazardly in the road, lights flashing. Men in police uniforms moved between the vehicles, while on the lawn several firemen joined to each other by jacketed hoses sent arcs of water spraying toward the burning building.

Panting, Cameron shoved his way through the crowd until he was on the lawn of Beethoven's Closet. A window shattered and several firemen shouted at each other. Cameron groaned, only now glimpsing the ambulance parked near the road. Moving toward it were two men in blue uniforms rolling a yellow collapsible gurney between them. A body lay on the gurney, partially covered by a blue sheet, a breathing mask strapped firmly to its face.

Cameron shoved his way to the ambulance. The medics loaded the gurney into its rear.

Please, it can't be her, he thought. *It can't be her.*

He nearly knocked over a policeman standing in his way. Frowning, the cop shoved him back and thrust a finger at him. "Sir, get behind the police tape right now."

Cameron blinked and looked into the young face of a newly recruited officer.

"Listen," he said, aiming a finger at the ambulance, "I have to see who's on that gurney. You understand? I have to."

The officer shook his head. "Not possible. I need you to get back on the road."

Cameron blinked the tears out of his eyes and moved forward. When the officer grabbed his shoulder, Cameron slammed his fist into the guy's nose.

"Goddamn it!" The cop clamped both hands over his nose and mouth.

Cameron, just as surprised at what he'd done, watched the man stagger back a few steps. He wondered if maybe he should try to help him, when something hard and blunt slammed into his side. Sparks exploded in his head. The wind rushed out of him in a forced *oof.* Then he felt the cool grass beneath him. Gasping and gritting his teeth, he tried desperately to catch his breath, but the task proved too difficult. He looked up and found two shiny black boots planted in the grass before him. His eyes followed those boots up to a pair of thick, uniform-clad legs, then a pair of muscular arms folded over a wide chest, and finally, a pair of angry blue eyes.

"You just struck an officer of the law," said the officer. "Your ass is grass."

For a moment Cameron expected one of the man's boots to crash into his nose and snap his jaw. The stomp never came.

"What the hell is going on over here?" Chief Dunlap shouted.

Cameron, crouched over in the grass with his arms buckled around his stomach, recognized the voice, but he sounded miles away, and Cameron didn't look up.

"Can't you see we got enough to worry about already?" Dunlap sounded close to tears. He stopped before Cameron and hunched over with his hands on his knees. "Bentley, what the hell's going on here?"

"This dope just punched Preston in the face," Bentley said. "So I took him down."

"Oh, for Christ's sake." The chief fixed his gaze on Cameron. "Blake, what the hell's wrong with you? You want to go to jail? You think that will make things better?"

"It's not her, is it, Chief?" Cameron rasped, rocking back and forth. "Please. Tell me it's not her."

Red strobe lights flashed across the chief's craggy face and shone in his eyes, red and puffy beneath his bushy brows. Slowly, the man shook his head and said, "Wish I could, son."

Cameron dropped his head and grimaced. "Oh, Jesus," he sobbed between gritted teeth. "Oh, God . . ."

"Come on," Dunlap said and gripped his upper arm. "Get up before we make a scene . . . as if we ain't already done that."

With the chief's help, Cameron climbed to his feet.

Bentley pointed a finger in his face and said, "You want me to cuff him, Chief?"

"What I want is for you to get those people off this lawn," Dunlap barked back. "That way the firemen can do their goddamn job."

"But, Chief! You ain't gonna let him get away with this, are you? He struck an officer of the law!"

"You heard me!" Dunlap snapped. "Now get on out of here."

Shaking his head, Bentley went away.

The doors of the ambulance shut with a muffled thud. The paramedics hopped into the cab and then the vehicle found its way off the lawn. Then the ambulance turned on its sirens and filled the night with alarmed gales as it ambled back toward the square. Oddly, it didn't seem in much of a hurry.

"He's right. I should throw your ass in jail," said Dunlap. "But I won't. I know how much she liked you."

Cameron looked at Dunlap, eyes wide as he tried to make sense of the chief's last comment and why he'd used the past tense. "What are you saying? Is she . . . is she going to make it, Chief?"

Dunlap shook his head. "No. I don't think so. She . . . um . . . she . . ." Unable to finish his sentence, he clamped a trembling hand over his eyes and waited. When he spoke again, he said his words quickly. "She wasn't breathing. She was already gone."

Cameron's face crumpled into a silent sob. He'd talked to her only a few hours ago. She'd been radiating with life. Things weren't supposed to work this way. People didn't just flash out of existence like blown lightbulbs. The absoluteness of it all overwhelmed him.

"She was like a daughter to me," Dunlap went on, talking to no one in particular, making Cameron feel as if he were eavesdropping. "I promised her daddy I'd take care of her. And now this . . ."

"What happened?"

Dunlap blinked, confused, and regarded Cameron like a stranger. "What in hell does it look like? Fire took her."

"But why . . . why was she here in the first place? It's already past nine, for Christ's sake. She closes her shop at six."

The chief gave a hopeless shrug as he turned toward the smoldering building. The firemen had gotten the flames down to a manageable state, but they had a ways to go before putting out the fire completely. Thick clouds of harsh, putrid smoke hung in the air, most of it settling over the lawn and causing several men to collapse into coughing fits. The onlookers had begun shuffling back to avoid breathing smoke.

"I don't know why this happened," Dunlap said, bringing the pitch of his voice up a few notches to hide his pain. He sighed. "I suspect it was an accident. These old houses burn like matchsticks."

Cameron watched the fire, the silhouettes of firemen, the rising clouds of smoke. Several men had gone inside to strangle out the remaining flames. He stared at the scene but registered nothing.

This was no accident. It stank of something deliberate, something aimed at him, perhaps the result of having learned too much.

One of the firemen stomped out of the shop's open doorway with what looked like a purse hanging from his fist. No, not a purse, but a leather satchel, and even from this distance, Cameron recognized it—the same one that Simon had confiscated.

Distantly, Cameron registered Dunlap's voice. The guy, working on autopilot now, had been talking for the last few minutes.

"Anyway," Dunlap was saying, "I'd like you to come by the station tomorrow, a matter of procedure, you understand."

Nodding absently, Cameron walked dazedly toward the fireman across the yard, toward a mound of items salvaged from the fire, his satchel lying on top. Careful not to burn himself on its metal buckles, he grabbed the satchel's strap and raised it. Covered in smoke resin but otherwise unharmed, the bag had escaped the fire and made it back into his hands.

"You looking for memorabilia?" someone shouted at him.

He looked up to find Bentley standing not five feet away with his arms folded over his chest.

Bentley must have read something in Cameron's expression because the officer's eyes darkened with suspicion. "Whatcha got there?"

"It's mine," said Cameron. He cleared his throat. "I left it here a few days back."

"Then take it and get the hell out of here," Bentley said, pointing toward the road. "We got enough help around here, thank you very much."

Cameron nodded and turned away. His chest squeezed tightly around his lungs as he crossed the yard and ducked beneath the police tape.

He lost himself in the dark street, feeling more rundown than he'd ever felt before.

Chapter 15

The taxi rolled to a stop before the wide steps of Orpheum Manor. Cameron gazed at the house's dark facade, with its windows spilling lights across the front driveway, illuminating a handful of sleek cars sitting along the curb.

"The son of a bitch is having a party," he muttered in disbelief. "You believe that?"

Acid boiling in his stomach, he leaned forward with a fifty-dollar bill in hand and met Buzz's eyes in the rearview mirror. "I need you to wait here a few minutes. I got some business to take care of inside, and I need to make sure you're here when I come back out."

Buzz shifted around in his seat and regarded him with a sober look. "Nope," he said and jerked the brim of his boonie hat down low on his brow. "I don't want your money. Not tonight, buddy. This one's on me."

Cameron shrugged and muttered, "Suit yourself." Truth was, he didn't need any favors—not from Buzz, not from anybody. He shoved his door open.

"You know, I don't pretend to know you all that well," Buzz said, meeting his gaze again in the rearview mirror as he leisurely lit a cigarette. "But I do know one thing for certain: you look madder than a bobcat in a piss fire. You got a look in your eye, and, buddy, I seen that look before. A cousin of mine had it right before he shot the sorry bastard who slept with his wife." He exhaled a cloud of smoke out of the window. "I hate to think you might go and do something just as stupid. Think about it first. Don't let whatever happened tonight ruin you for good."

"Yeah, thanks, Buzz," Cameron said. "Now don't forget. Be a friend and wait outside the gate. Will you do that for me?"

The cabbie shrugged. "Suit yourself. But don't say I didn't warn you."

Cameron got out and watched as the old Chevy turned around and started down the long driveway. Just outside the gates, the brake lights came on, casting a sullen red glow among the low hanging fir branches. Satisfied, Cameron adjusted the satchel's strap on his shoulder and turned to face the house. Snatches of music rode the breeze. No one slept here; even the old sanitarium and the outer carriage houses showed signs of festivities. They were celebrating—celebrating—while Madison lay in a sliding drawer in the morgue. Cameron wanted answers. He wanted to hurt someone.

He walked to the top steps and pushed through the unlocked door, expecting to find Kalek. An empty foyer greeted him. Music and laughter floated down the halls. A small bald man with brown skin and glasses entered into the foyer. His face tightened with shock until a look of recognition brightened his eyes.

"Oh, Mr. Blake," he said with a thick Indian accent. "We were not expecting you this evening."

"Where's Kalek?"

"Mr. Kalek is not here." He offered a slight smile. "Would you like me to tell the maestro that you have arrived?"

"That won't be necessary." He looked around for something to use as a weapon. Seeing the fireplace at the far wall, he went over and picked a heavy iron poker from its stand. He hefted its weight before brandishing it like a sword. Catching the man watching him, he threw him a shark's grin. "That ought to do it."

"Do what?"

Cameron started down the main corridor with the poker in one fist and the satchel swinging at his side.

The doorman hurried after him. "Mr. Blake! Please stop! I insist!"

The wide corridor took Cameron past the television room, the lavish living room, the closed kitchen to his left, and finally the double doors leading into the dining room. He paused with his hand gripping the door handle. For a moment his rage subsided, leaving him to wonder what exactly he planned to do and why he hadn't told the chief about Simon and his satchel. Gales of laughter resounded behind the doors and the anger rushed back into his system. He took a step back and kicked the doors crashing open.

All laughter stopped as he charged into the large room. Roughly twenty guests sat about the stretched dining table, watching him with open-mouthed surprise.

He recognized most of them—the orchestra's First Chairs. Maestro Bloom sat at the head of the table, looking least surprised of all. At the end of the table near where Cameron stood, Simon sat in a chair, hunkered over a plate of food, eating with his bare hands.

"Cameron?" said Bloom as he rose slowly from his chair. His gaze hardened when he saw the fireplace poker. "I didn't expect you here tonight."

Cameron strode to the table, the poker propped on one shoulder. Several musicians shrank away from him when they noticed the rage in his eyes. Only Simon, his face buried in handfuls of food, failed to see him approach.

Cameron swung the poker, a meaty thwack sounding against the man's bald head. Squealing with surprise, Simon grabbed his scalp, jumped up, and spun in wild circles, dashing plates of food to the floor. Blood spilled between his fingers.

Cameron gawked in horror at the injury.

Several men pounced on him. The poker clanged to the floor and then someone grabbed Cameron's wrists and forced his arms behind his back. Another man behind him locked an iron-like arm around his throat, cutting off his air. Cameron fought with all his strength, kicking and shaking his head, even as he was hoisted off the ground.

"What have you done?" Bloom shouted from the end of the table. "How dare you come into my home and attack my guests?"

"You let it happen, didn't you?" Cameron managed. The arm around his throat made it nearly impossible to talk. He gnashed his teeth and growled. Tendons bulged in his neck. "You let him kill her!"

"What are you talking about, Cameron?" Bloom said with quiet exasperation. "Have you lost your mind?"

"She was innocent, for Christ's sake!" Tears stung Cameron's eyes.

"Cameron," the maestro boomed, straightening to his full height. "Calm yourself! I don't have a clue what you are talking about. What happened? Someone you know was hurt?"

"She had nothing to do with us!"

"Cameron, who are you talking about?"

"Madison," he rasped, flinching as he said her name out loud. Fresh tears spilled down his face. "Madison Taylor."

Raising his hands in baffled surrender, Bloom looked down at Christofori, still seated in his chair. Christofori merely shrugged and sipped from his glass of wine.

"I've never even heard of this woman," Bloom said. "Why would I want someone to hurt her?"

Cameron stopped struggling against the tangle of arms holding him. Bloom had a point. He had no motive to kill Madison; even if she had known too much about him, she hadn't exactly posed a threat to him. Besides, Bloom would never risk driving Cameron away. This didn't add up.

"Your dog over there," Cameron said, nodding to Simon, who had finally plopped down on the floor with his back to the wall, his cracked head cradled in his blood-laced fingers. "He set fire to her shop. He killed her. And I'd bet it's not the first time he's done something like this."

"Simon?" Bloom's face contorted as he gazed at the sulking musician, then looked again to Cameron. "But are you sure?"

Cameron glanced to the soot-blackened satchel, now lying on the floor, where it had fallen after the musicians jumped him. "I'm sure of it. There's the proof. They found it inside her shop."

The maestro stepped around the table and walked over to the bag. "What is it?" he asked, sounding genuinely concerned.

"I kept my music in it. At least, I used to."

"You're certain—?"

"I'm sure. I saw him with it during the festival. He must have had it when he snuck into her shop, which he torched."

"That seems unlikely," said Bloom. "I never saw Simon with this."

"He had it," Cameron snapped. "Maybe I'm wrong about you. Maybe you didn't have anything to do with this, but that mother-fucker over there in the corner—he did have something to do with it. There's not a doubt in my mind."

Bloom returned to his chair and dropped into it. He sighed and shook his head, his troubled gaze resting on Simon. "My God," he whispered, covering his eyes with a trembling hand. "Simon, what have you done?"

The room fell quiet. Cameron freed his arms from his detainers, who no longer seemed worried about him, and went to where his satchel lay on the floor. He slung its strap over one shoulder and headed to the doors.

"Then it's over, Cameron?" Bloom called after him. "You're throwing in the towel?"

Cameron stopped in his tracks. Surprised, he turned, shaking his head. "Are you kidding me? She was burned alive! As far as I'm concerned, our project died with her." He pointed at Simon. "And that mother-fucker's going to jail. I'm making damn sure of it."

No one challenged him as he moved again for the doors. He paused, adding, "And another thing. You're a liar. Why didn't you tell me about your condition? About the church? About the museum?"

The musicians shifted uneasily in their chairs.

Bloom leaned back in his seat, frowning as his eyes shifted back and forth until finally brightening with sudden comprehension. "Ah, I think I understand. Mr. Kalek spoke with you, didn't he? He told you all about this orchestra—all the terrible things we've done and so on."

"He told me enough," said Cameron.

Bloom spread his hands in a submissive gesture. "Will you at least allow me to defend myself? You must understand that Mr. Kalek is a dear friend, but he has become unreliable over the years—delusional, even."

"You abused the Archetypes, didn't you?" Cameron challenged. "You deliberately tapped into Discord."

"Nonsense."

"It made you all sick," Cameron went on. "Didn't it? It changed you from the inside out. That's why you brought me here—so I could fix you."

"Enough of this!" Bloom shouted, slammed his fist against the table, and leaped to his feet. "You don't know a thing about this orchestra. Kalek has distorted the truth. He is trying to undermine all that I have worked for!"

"You've done that yourself." Cameron backed toward the door, a rush of adrenaline shoring him up. "What about that tuning fork of yours? I never needed to listen to it, did I? That thing made me sick. And for what? I'm not any closer to composing Armonia than the day I asked for your help."

"I suppose you believe yourself the expert now?" Bloom asked indignantly.

Cameron turned his back on him. "Shove it up your ass, Bloom. I'm done here. I'm going home."

"After everything I've done for you—this is how you will repay me?" Bloom shouted.

Cameron paid no attention to Bloom's sudden tantrum as he stormed down the corridor and then out through the front door.

By the time he walked the length of the driveway and jumped into the back of Buzz's taxi, he was trembling and covered in sweat.

Buzz took a quiet look at him and then drove on without saying a word.

The police station was located in an old brick building on College Street just a few blocks from the square. The building's tall windows, facing the road, were all covered with blinds. Nonetheless, the place looked open for business, and the chief's Dodge Durango was parked at the curb.

Cameron stepped into the front lobby. The place had a subdued atmosphere, draped in blandness. From behind a Plexiglas window opposite him, a woman watched him with a stolid expression that echoed the room's colorless aura.

"Help you with something?" she said through a vent fixed in the window.

He cleared his throat. "I'd like to talk to Chief Dunlap."

"Your name?"

He told her.

"He expecting you?"

"No. But he'll want to hear what I have to say."

The woman stared at him with quiet petulance before picking up a phone and punching a few buttons. After a moment she spoke to someone on the opposite end and then hung up. "Chief said he'll be right out. You can have a seat."

Cameron sat down but didn't have to wait long before a door swung open and Dunlap stepped out, looking haggard and aged.

"Mr. Blake?" he said, hitching up his belt. "What's going on? Didn't I tell you to come see me tomorrow?"

Cameron stood and adjusted the shoulder strap of his satchel. "I need to talk to you. In private."

Dunlap sighed through his nose. "How important is it? I've got reports to write and papers to file and—"

"Trust me. It's plenty important."

"Well, then, come on back."

They followed a narrow corridor that passed several offices before entering the record-keeping room crowded with large file cabinets and cubicles, most of which were presently empty. They continued to the door in the far wall that led into the chief's office.

"Have a seat," said Dunlap, as he settled into his leather chair.

Cameron sat down on a creaky wooden chair and glanced around the office. The small room was a mess, with heaps of paper on the desk and stacks of books on the cabinets. Important-looking documents were tacked to corkboards. Toward the back wall, his eyes went to a framed photo of Madison. He'd nearly forgotten how close they'd been. Watching him with tired eyes, Dunlap sat back in his chair with his elbows resting on the armrests. Cameron couldn't help but feel sorry for the guy. Dunlap had known Madison for decades; Cameron had only known her for a couple of months.

"First off, I'm sorry for your loss," said Dunlap. The skin beneath his eyes hung in great fleshy wrinkles. "The two of you were getting close, sounded like to me. The last time we spoke, she had some nice things to say about you. Matter of fact, that's why I'm not putting you under the microscope right now."

"Well, I appreciate hearing that."

Dunlap nodded slowly and sighed. "Well, let's hear it. Whatcha got for me?"

Before Cameron could speak, someone tapped at the door and then pressed it open. Bentley stepped inside, his brow drawn. Cameron groaned under his breath and turned back to Dunlap.

Dunlap said, "What do you want, Bent?"

"Saw Mr. Blake come inside, and I was curious what he had to say," said Bentley, sounding like a miffed, defiant teenager.

Dunlap grimaced and conceded. "Fine. Come on in and sit down. But, Bent, I'm warning you, I'm not in the mood for any lip from you. Mr. Blake here's been through hell tonight."

"I suppose we all have," said Bentley as he stepped inside and sat on the corner of Dunlap's desk with his arms folded across his chest, accusing eyes boring holes into Cameron's forehead. "He's not the only one who had feelings for Miss Taylor."

Cameron knitted his brow with sudden comprehension. Bentley had had feelings for Madison. Maybe more. With a sigh, Cameron placed the satchel on Dunlap's desk.

The chief stared at it, smoothing his mustache with his thumb and forefinger. "What is it?"

"I seen it earlier tonight," said Bentley. "He took it from the shop."

"That's right," said Cameron. "It's mine. Had it for years." He went on to explain about throwing it away and spotting Simon with it at the festival. "That's why, when I found it in Madison's shop tonight, I knew."

"What are you saying?" Dunlap asked carefully.

"I think Simon had something to do with that fire. And I think that if you went and searched his room at Beachum Sanitarium, you'd find some curious things."

"Now hold on a goddamn minute," said Dunlap. "I just got done searching that place with the fire marshal. He didn't see any evidence of arson. He seemed pretty convinced that faulty wiring caused Madison's shop to burn down." He wearily regarded Cameron. "Believe me, I want to play the blame game too. This is a pointless death. A goddamn tragedy. It'd be easier to point the finger at someone." He rubbed his nose and paused. "And why didn't you say something about this earlier tonight? Now you gone and tampered with evidence."

"I don't know," Cameron said quietly. "I wanted to be sure."

Sighing, Dunlap drew the satchel closer to him. After a moment of sifting through the crumpled sheets of music and scribbled notes inside, he looked up and shrugged. "So it's got your name on a few papers. At the very least I can pin this stuff to you. But not Simon. Did anyone else see him with it?"

"No, probably not." Cameron sighed, his gaze going to his trembling hands. "But he's got something to do with it. I swear to it. And there's more. I think he had something to do with Carrie Belle."

"What?" Dunlap's face a mask of bewilderment. He leaned forward. "What do you know? What's Bloom up to? What's been going on up there?"

Cameron shrugged despondently, breathing a sigh as he drew a vivid memory of Madison's face. "Just do me a favor and go have a look. Will you please do that for me? For Madison?"

Dunlap again smoothed his mustache as he stared blankly at the far wall. "Hell, I s'pose it's worth a look."

Satisfied, Cameron clapped his hands against his knees and got to his feet. "Then I'll leave you to it. And you can have the bag—the music inside, too, if you want." He didn't mention his journal, tucked beneath his belt at the small of his back, hidden by his shirt. The journal had miraculously come back to him; it was his and belonged to no one else. Nor was he finished with it.

He started for the door, but stopped when something that Kalek had mentioned came back to him. "Oh, by the way, Simon's room is on the second floor. His walls—they're covered with dirty pictures."

"Dirty pictures," Dunlap echoed. "Cute."

"And there's one more thing. Bloom's musicians . . . they won't look the same. Not now. They've . . . changed."

This earned a look of bewildered amusement from Dunlap and Bentley. Bentley asked, "What the hell's that supposed to mean?"

"Let's just say, they look a hell of a lot younger these days." Cameron wrenched the door open. "Just look for the guy with no ears. He's the killer. I bet my life on it."

"Where in hell do you think you're going?" Bentley hopped to his feet.

"Unless you got a problem with it, Chief," said Cameron, not bothering to look at the sergeant, "I'm going back to San Diego. I've had enough of this town to last me a lifetime."

The taxi rolled to a stop and its headlights shone on a barrier gate arm reaching across the road. A sign read, "Park Closed from Sunset to Sunrise."

Buzz parked the car on the dark paved road with walls of cypress and oak trees pressing close to either side. Not a street lamp for miles.

"This is as far as she goes," Buzz said over his shoulder. "If you want, I can kick back and sleep for a few hours. Give you a little time to do . . . whatever you need to do."

Cameron looked down at the journal in his lap, salvaged from the satchel now in Dunlap's care, dirtied from Simon's touch. Then he clasped the man's shoulder. "That won't be necessary, Buzz. I owe you one, pal."

He opened his door and got out. The air was warm and fragrant. And quiet. He started for the barrier when Buzz leaned out the window and called after him.

"Now, you don't expect me to just leave you out here, do you? Hell, it's more 'n fifteen miles back to town."

"I can handle myself," Cameron called back as he moved into the path of the headlights. "I've got at least twenty miles left in these sneakers."

With a petulant wave of his hand, Buzz ducked back inside. It took the Chevrolet several attempts to turn around in the narrow lane.

Cameron paid him no attention as he climbed over the barrier arm. Soon, not even the car's brake lights were visible through the trees. The darkness thickened and enshrouded him. He walked on, crunching over gravel. In moments the road led him to a parking area with tall lamps shining down on the bare tarmac. Remembering his earlier visit here with Madison, he followed the railing until he reached the iron staircase that zigzagged its way down the cliff, descending into darkness. He leaned over the railing for a look, but it was impossible to see the bottom.

Should've brought a flashlight, he thought. *I'm shit out of luck if I break a leg. Or worse.*

He managed the stairs without falling, and when he reached the bottom, he started along a moonlit path deeper into the forest. The dark was almost crippling, but eventually his eyes grew accustomed, and soon the black woods formed into inky blue shapes, rock clusters, shrubs, and tree trunks. The hike got easier once he reached the stream, which glowed like a vein of silver as it wound its way deeper into the forest. Soon he could hear the roar of the Shawnee Falls far in the distance.

Half an hour later, he reached a wooden bridge, then he left the trodden path, remembering Madison's directions, and found his way to the waterfall.

Near the pond, he balanced himself precariously on shattered rocks that encircled the water. The rush and roar of the falls were nearly deafening, and the billowing air lapped wetly at his face. Walking became treacherous, with jagged rocks, slick with moss, and nothing but moonlight to see by. Still, he proceeded on all fours in a kind of spider crawl as he moved along the water's edge until reaching the opposite side of the falls. When he reached the high bank, he hoisted himself up by grabbing handfuls of roots and grass.

In the light of day, Madison's secret path had been difficult; in the dark, it was deadly. Using anything he could grab hold of, he made his way up the incline. When he finally reached the ledge at the top, he was breathless, scraped, and bleeding. Knocking the dirt from his hands, he stood daringly at the edge of the cliff. Off to his right, the falls thundered. Below him, treetops covered themselves with frosty moonlight.

He felt her then; her presence almost palpable. The scent of her perfume. The ringing of her laughter. Tears sprang to his eyes; the air rushed from his chest. "Oh God," he sobbed, dropping to his knees, his hands bracketing the sides of his head. "Madison, I'm so sorry. Please . . . forgive me."

The pain was unbearable, a crushing weight against his chest. The sting of guilt made it all the worse. *Oh God, I lost her. I lost her and I–I'm responsible. I led Simon to her. She died because of me.*

A nasty buzzing rang suddenly in his ears, violent and mind-numbing. His eyes gaped with understanding. Bloom's tuning fork was working in him, had been since the beginning. And now this pain, sudden and searing, acted as a catalyst.

The Discord had surfaced, demanding release.

"We compose Nocturnes," he heard Bloom say, his voice startlingly clear in Cameron's mind.

Crying out, he clamped his hands over his ears, moving dangerously close to the edge. He didn't care. Nothing mattered outside of this blind, demonic sound.

"Oh, Jesus," he moaned. "What's happening to me?"

The ringing unfurled and became a black symphony, expanding across the horizon of his mind. This was a grand orchestration, a nocturne of sepulchral melodies, swollen with emotional poison. The music, formed of sounds somehow fluid and natural, was so familiar that it frightened him, encompassing a lifetime of fear, pain, and anger, as if all the discordant currents of his subconscious mind suddenly manifested as music.

"Write it down, Cameron."

Memories surfaced like snapshots: the car wreck, his mother's shattered face, his brother's legs jutting from a maw of steel, past loves, abandoned friends. His memories shouted accusations at him: *You selfish bastard. All you care about is your work. . . . You're chasing a goddamn fantasy. . . . But what about me, Cameron? What about me?*

Finally, he saw Madison, lying next to him, giggling and wide-eyed, her light-brown hair scattered across her face. For a moment they stared lovingly into each others' eyes, but then her smile sobered. She whispered: *I think I'm falling in love with you.* Then her face constricted in horror, and her eyes widened before their surfaces blistered and boiled and erupted in a cough of flames.

Again it was Bloom's voice. *"Write it down and be free of it."*

Still on his knees, he reached to the small of his back, under his shirt, where he'd tucked his journal beneath his belt. He jerked it free and splayed it open on the rock before him. He flipped to what he hoped to be a blank page, smoothed it flat, then started to write. It was dark but he didn't need light. He wrote with his eyes closed. The music flowed through him. His pen raced to capture it. Fast and furious, he plotted page after page of the strange otherworldly music.

This went on for several hours, until the rising sun brightened the horizon, and the forest began waking up all around him. He didn't stop until he'd completed his dark masterpiece.

His Dirge.

The walk back to the park entrance proved much easier in the daylight, even with an aching body and a head filled with a violent ringing sound.

He couldn't remember much of the night before. What he'd experienced seemed as distant and removed as a dream, or a drugged hallucination. But he had his journal, and he had his Dirge. And he was ready to go home.

But first things first: he still had the fifteen-mile walk back to town ahead of him, and his head swam with exhaustion just thinking about it. Dripping with sweat, he arrived at the barrier gate arm. His heart leaped in his chest when he found Buzz's yellow Chevy parked on the side of the road.

God love him. Cameron laughed under his breath and shook his head. *The son of a bitch waited.*

He walked over to the car. Buzz was kicked back in the driver's seat, his boonie hat shielding his face from the morning sun. One long-toed foot hung out of the driver's side window. Cameron rapped his knuckles against the rooftop.

Buzz gave a start. The hat fell away, and he regarded Cameron with puffy eyes.

"Oh, hey there," he said with a groggy smile. His thick beard was a wooly mess. "Didn't expect you back so soon."

"I thought I told you to go home."

"And leave you out here all by yourself?" Buzz snorted. "Not on my watch."

Shaking his head again, Cameron walked around to the passenger door, wrenched it open, and hopped inside. The car smelled worse than usual, likely a result of Buzz's shoes and socks scatted across his floorboard, but this hardly mattered now.

"I can't tell you how happy I am right now," Cameron said, grinning.

"I don't know why you stuck around, Buzz, but I could kiss you right now."

Buzz held his hands up. "Nope. Not necessary." The man leaned forward, fetched his shoes and socks and started dressing his feet. "So anyways, I got to thinking to myself, 'Damn, that guy's crazy if he thinks he's gonna walk all the way back to town.' I mean, I can't imagine walking that far myself, except maybe when I was in the Army, and even then . . ."

Listening with only one ear, Cameron leaned back in his seat and shut his eyes, grateful that Buzz had thought to wait for him. During last night's . . . excitement . . . he hadn't given much thought to his escape strategy. If Buzz hadn't waited around, he didn't know what he would have done.

"Anyhow," said Buzz as he plopped his hat over his thick, curly hair. "That's neither here nor there."

He keyed the ignition, but the engine wheezed desperately without catching. The two men stared at each other, neither saying a word. Buzz gave it a moment and then tried again. This time the engine caught and rumbled to life.

They shared a nervous laugh before Buzz gassed it.

The Overtone

I celebrate myself, and sing myself,
And what I assume you shall assume,
For every atom belonging to me as good belongs to you.

–Walt Whitman, *Song of Myself*

The physical world is vibration, quanta, but vibrations of what? To the eye, form and color; to the ear, sound; to the nose, scent; to the fingers, touch. But these are all different languages for the same thing, different qualities of sensitivity, different dimensions of consciousness.

–Alan Watts, *The Joyous Cosmology*

Chapter 1

From the Nashville airport, Cameron caught the one p.m. Delta flight bound for San Diego. The window seat in first class on the Airbus A320 gave him a chance to clear his mind while making out shapes in the clouds. It felt safer up here. The world seemed somehow manageable, tranquil even. The farther he got away from Holloway, the crazier it all seemed: Bloom and his Echoes; the music you hear when you die; Armonia. It was all so . . . dreamlike.

Except Madison. *She was real. And I lost her.*

With a heavy sigh, he looked down at the journal in his lap. He flipped to its final pages where he'd written his Dirge. He had this—this one piece of music, his triumph, the end of a journey, his demons exorcised—to remind him of what he'd experienced in Holloway. Out there on the gorge, he'd composed a celebration of pain and anguish, an accusation aimed at God, a work of almost Satanic wickedness. If ever he had struggled to accept himself as a true artist, that struggle had ended there. He'd written a goddamn masterpiece. Even if he had sold his soul to achieve it.

Take that to the fucking bank.

And if Bloom was right, then the Dirge meant he had somehow fixed himself, exorcised the demons. Completed his therapy. Attuned.

So why didn't he feel any different? He knew the answer: *Because it didn't work.*

At the San Diego airport, he had just a moment to enjoy the warm, balmy air before ducking into a taxi. The driver followed Harbor Drive along the coastline, and Cameron watched the world pass by his window. Things were much different here. The people, the glassy skyscrapers, the swaying palm trees, the hotels and strip clubs, and the sailboats drifting in the bay.

This city was far from the quiet world of Holloway. He felt like a stranger here, and the feeling only intensified when the taxi dropped him off in front of his home on Barrett Street.

For a short while, he stood on his front lawn with his duffel bag planted on the ground at his feet. He stared with strange eyes at his swanky little house by the sea, a work of eccentric taste, with stucco walls and Spanish tile roofing. Little Mediterranean flourishes and stone walkways. He could hardly remember life here before Holloway.

Inside, he felt even more out of place as he moved from room to room, each lavishly decorated with hand-tufted Indian rugs, leather sofas, marble coffee tables, and cherry and oak cabinets and dressers. Walls of glass panels presented an expansive view of the surf behind his house. Guitars autographed by Eddie Van Halen and Neil Diamond hung on the wall. Curio cabinets showcased awards with his name on brass plaques. Framed pictures of him and his friends.

No. Not me. Some other guy. I've . . . changed.

He was still left with a hollow feeling, an unredeemed feeling. He hadn't Attuned, and it had left him plagued with the same demons from his childhood. Something was still unfinished.

He ignored the feeling. What he'd left when he had fled Holloway could stay there.

The feeling was unsettling, almost frightening, and when he caught his reflection in the gold records that lined the living room wall, he faced a powerful realization: the old Cameron Blake had been replaced by someone else, a man with rugged features and world-weary eyes. Certainly, he was a stranger here, a trespasser, and this house, with all its stuff, belonged to a man who had somehow vanished into thin air.

In the dining room, he found a blue square of paper slapped onto the refrigerator, a note from Camilla, his cleaning lady. Evidently, she'd come by several times in the past months to clean the place. By the fourth visit she'd realized that he had not come home, and so she had little to do but air out the rooms. She finished her letter with reproach, and he could hear her clipped English: "You know, if you going to leave town for a while, you can at least tell some people where you are going to. I hope nothing bad has happened."

He crumpled the note, thinking that, yes, bad things had indeed happened, but it was all over now. He was done with Holloway, done with chasing dreams; what remained of him, however, was questionable.

After a hot shower to wash off the grime from the past two days, he stepped out onto the back porch with a cold beer and sat on a splintered step to watch the setting sun do wonderful things to the sea. Slowly, a great fire spread across the horizon. The warm air brushed against his face. Beyond the shore, the swells were painted in sullen blue pastels before they crashed against the beach and turned to milk. He had missed the ocean. He breathed in the smell of salt, drank a deep swallow of his beer, and fantasized about the delicious sleep that lay ahead.

Something startled him from his meditation. He turned to gaze up at the weird hanging wind chimes as they chattered their strange music. They rattled and gave off glassy peals. He shivered. The ugly things were somehow the only thing familiar about this place—the only things that seemed to connect him with everything he'd been through in Holloway.

He listened for a while until the sun went down. Their resonating chatter was so beautiful and peculiar. He must have dozed a little because he dreamed of a bulging cocoon, clinging to a leafy branch. The thing trembled for a moment before splitting open, a hole filled with twitching legs. Then butterfly wings unfurled.

He didn't recall going inside or climbing into bed or falling to sleep.

It's my fault that little girl died, thought Kalek as he pinned the note to the breast pocket of his jacket. It made him look rather silly, like a package under a Christmas tree, but it hardly mattered. Nothing did anymore. *And she looked so much like my Judith.*

With a heavy sigh, he positioned himself in the center of the room where a chair stood beneath the loop of a hanging noose, dangling from a ceiling beam. He climbed the chair and then tugged the rope, making sure it would hold his weight. Once satisfied, he poked his head through the loop and tightened it around his throat until the coarse strands bit into the soft skin of his neck.

Tears blurred his vision as his gaze swept across his spacious living room. Bloom's money had paid for this cabin. The place lacked warmth. Had Judith lived here with him, she would have livened up the atmosphere with color and ambiance. She would have thrown dinner parties and get-togethers. Life without her had become meaningless.

His eyes went to his reflection in a tall window on the opposite side of the room. He looked neat and trim in his favorite black suit, what little remained of his hair combed over his ears. Only the note pinned to his breast pocket seemed out of place. He couldn't see the words in his dim reflection, but he knew the lines by heart. He'd gone to great pains to get it right, to say everything he wanted to say.

Maestro Bloom, consider this my resignation. I've decided not to join you in your attempt to meet God. I no longer believe in what we have worked on all these years to achieve. From the start, I wanted only to see my wife again, and now I fear that I never will, as she will certainly be in a better place than where I'm going. I hope your orchestra fails. I myself have begged the Good Lord to forgive me, but I don't think He will. Goodbye.

Kalek tightened the noose with a quick jerk. Tears lined in his eyes. Readying himself, he spoke in a firm voice to the empty room.

"Before you judge me too harshly, oh Lord, please consider this: You have been hard on me. Very, very hard on me."

With that, he kicked the chair out from beneath him. He dropped and the rope cinched violently around his throat. Kalek gagged as his body shook with spasms, his feet kicking at the air. His eyes widened as the blood thumped at his temples. Hot urine ran down his leg.

Then darkness washed over him, and Kalek welcomed it.

Chapter 2

At five-thirty on Monday morning, the crisp sunlight broke the horizon and spread rapidly across the Calliope's plaza, finding the cool blue pool of the penny fountain, and then, just a few feet away, Hob. He sat on a concrete bench leaning his elbows on his knees, head hanging low. He looked much older in the dawn light. Even the chocolate tones of his face had turned an ashen gray.

A cigarette burned between the knuckles of two trembling fingers. He drew from it, his eyes on the concert hall. After a moment he closed his eyes and listened, or at least imagined, the subtle vibrations rolling like black waves from its red brick walls. The place acted like an electric transformer, causing the silver fillings in his teeth to rattle. The Calliope had changed. The orchestra had transformed her into something dark and brooding. They'd drawn out her bad juju. They'd amplified her negative energy.

Trembling, he drained the last of his coffee and shook his head decisively. He couldn't do it. He just couldn't bring himself to go inside. This had been the fourth morning in a row that he'd watched the sunrise mirrored in the building's glass panes, the fourth morning that he couldn't muster the courage to go beyond its front doors.

He stood up, preparing to go home, when the low rumbling of an approaching car caught his ear. His head snapped toward the entrance of the plaza as a black sedan topped the hill. Moments later another black sedan followed, then a limousine. Soon the small convoy had crossed the plaza, moving toward the front steps of the Calliope. Any second they would roll right past him.

He dropped down behind the concrete bench, scampering on his hands and knees to the backside of the fountain's basin, and hid himself. With his back to the circular wall, he waited for his heart to stop knocking. Only now did it occur to him how foolish he must look . . . or guilty. If someone had seen him they might just think he had a reason to hide. But he worked here. He had every right to be here.

Safely hidden, he peeked over the basin's rim.

The three black cars had parked before the Calliope's front steps. Sunlight glinted off their dusty black hoods and tinted windows. Several doors opened all at once and a handful of men climbed out.

Hob didn't recognize any of them. Just like Bloom's musicians, they wore black suits, but the resemblance ended there. These weren't the bent-backed senior citizens of Bloom's orchestra; these guys were young and lithe.

Maestro Bloom climbed out from the limousine. Hob recognized his thick white hair, the confident poise of his shoulders. He pointed to the second vehicle, said something to his men, then marched up the Calliope's front steps with a long-haired man following at his side. When they reached the landing, Bloom paused, stiffened, then spun on his heels to gaze across the plaza.

Hob dropped behind the fountain before Bloom could see him.

He waited five minutes, though it seemed like an hour, and then mustered the nerve to risk a glance.

The landing was vacant. Bloom had gone inside, but his men remained down by the vehicles, most of them gathered around the middle sedan, where two of the men were dragging something large from the backseat. It was a bundle wrapped in white sheets, maybe six feet long. They hauled it up the steps with one man on each end.

"What the hell?" Hob whispered, keeping low.

The bundle disappeared into the Calliope along with the men. Moments later all three vehicles started up.

Hob pressed himself against the basin and waited. Soon the small convoy made a circle around the plaza and then disappeared to the vacant parking lot behind the Calliope.

In the quiet aftermath, Hob trembled with panic. He had to go to the chief. He had to call someone for help. He wanted to think that bundle was a piece of furniture, but he knew better.

But the police had no business with the Calliope; the hall was more or less outside their jurisdiction, considering Bloom had the mayor in his back pocket. Anyway, it was he—Washington Hob—who served as head janitor. This was his mess to clean.

Having the plaza all to himself again, he stood up, brushed the dirt from his knees, and started toward the auditorium. A small inner voice begged him to go home and pretend he never saw anything. But he couldn't do that. For reasons beyond his understanding, the ghosts of his past had dragged him into the affairs of the Calliope. He wouldn't cower away from it.

He climbed the Calliope's front steps, confident that the powers-that-be would grant him safe passage into that awful place. "Clara, baby," he muttered before opening the doors, "I sure hope we know what we're doin.'"

Hob managed to sneak upstairs without getting caught. From the second floor corridor, he let himself onto the balcony, where numerous rows of pews crowded the sloped tier suspended high above the auditorium floor. Standing at the top of the aisle, completely exposed, he had a perfect view of the stage, teeming now with men in black suits beneath the bright lights.

Hob dropped into a crouch and scurried to the knee-wall at the end of the aisle, hiding himself beneath the railing. After a moment he raised up just enough to see over the ledge.

Onstage, Bloom emerged from his workers to stand over the body of a dead man, lying spread-eagled on his back, a sheet spread beneath him.

Even at this distance, Hob recognized Kalek's gaunt face, so pale that it almost glowed beneath the stage lights. Hob stifled a scream.

Bloom squatted beside Kalek. In a thin voice that nearly dissipated before reaching the balcony, he said, "What have you done to yourself, old friend?"

Hob shuddered. He didn't like the way Bloom sounded. Too calm, too relaxed. But at least one thing was certain: Kalek had taken his own life. Still, this didn't explain why Bloom had brought his body here. "Look at the mess you've made," Bloom went on. "You know I can't allow you to leave me, don't you? The orchestra needs you. I need you." With a sigh, he rose up, then turned to face the others. "Mr. Maas," he said, "will you please come forward?"

A tall man with a young, brooding face and wide shoulders moved into the spotlight. He carried an instrument, only he wore it around his arm, like a spiraling snake, spanning from shoulder to wrist, where its end opened, forming the shape of a bell. Hob had seen other instruments like these the night when he'd sneaked down into the basement. Somehow these instruments were responsible for everything wrong with this place . . . with this whole town.

Bloom laid a hand on the musician's shoulder and spoke to him in a low voice that barely reached Hob's strained ear. It sounded like, "Bring him back to me, Maas."

The musician looked down at Kalek's corpse and said somberly, "I will do my best, Maestro."

Hob cringed, watching as Maas thrust his head forward and pressed his lips to a mouthpiece of his instrument. Its opposite end intoned a low, reedy sound that expanded across the auditorium, taking the form of a funeral dirge.

Hob shivered. What possible reason would they have in playing this music for old man Kalek? He didn't know and didn't care. It was time to leave. But when he tried to get up, a lethargy gripped him. The world shifted about him. He found himself standing over a coffin. Inside was Clara's cancer-wasted body. The hollow shell of the woman he had loved lay on a bed of silk; puffy head, sallow face, and lovely dark skin had gone to an ashen gray.

Oh, my Lord, he begged with a sob. *Don't make me live this again. Please not again!*

Clara's corpse opened her eyes. Her lips parted, tearing free of the stitches that had until now kept them sewn together. "They gonna ruin it, Hob," she said in a gurgled voice. "They gonna ruin the whole show. You gotta stop 'em."

Hob snapped out of his dream with a jerk of his head. The music still played. He blinked away the vision, frightened and confused. He looked again to the stage, where the tall musician played his funeral dirge while the others watched. The end of his black instrument began spewing a thick fog that writhed and eddied as it stretched across the stage to engulf Kalek's body. Tendrils of the stuff reached up along Kalek's sallow face, penetrating his gaping mouth and nostrils. The corpse convulsed, arms and legs flopped and thudded against the polished floorboards, pelvis thrusting until its back nearly snapped.

A ragged scream erupted from Kalek's throat.

The music stopped.

Hob's eyes widened, then he crouched low. He didn't risk another look, but instead started up the carpeted aisle on his hands and knees. In his wild panic, the air seemed somehow thinner. The exit doors seemed miles away. He scrambled there and made his way outside, praying he wasn't seen by anyone, his old legs churning as fast as he could make them go.

No. My car—I left it parked out back, he thought, breathless. *They'll know I was here. Then they'll come for me.* His stomach twisted into a knot as he fled the lawn and stumbled into the deep of the woods. Without a doubt, some serious weirdness was going on at the Calliope. *To hell with the car. To hell with the job. To hell with this town.*

He was getting out.

But as he hurried down to where he knew the smooth dirt path picked up, it was Clara's voice he heard, Clara singing her same song: *Burn it down, Sugar. Burn the whole thing down.*

His legs slowed. He needed to think. Going home wasn't an option. His best bet was to hitch a ride to Willow Wood. Find a motel and lay low for a while. And then, when the moment was right, he'd come back to the Calliope and clean house, as best as he could. That was his job, after all. Always had been.

These are delicate moments. Our situation is a house of cards. We must tread lightly . . .

Bloom stood alone on the stage facing the empty pews of his concert hall. Only the stage glowed with light. The rest was dark. For a long while, he meditated, listening to the whispers of the past, the desperation of ghosts, the screams of long-ago massacres. The Calliope remembered everything. The voices of the dead were trapped forever in its very foundations.

Eight hours had passed since the trespasser had fled. Eight hours since a small team of Echoes had gone after the janitor. And still no word. This troubled him a great deal. So much depended on finding the man. If he went to the police . . .

He sighed and ordered his mind to silence.

After the incident, Bloom had gathered his musicians and rehearsed them at the Calliope for nearly six hours. They'd played the gamut of classics, from Haydn to Brahms to Wagner. Christofori performed Béla Bartók's "Four Dirges" and even treated them to a masterful performance of Franz Liszt's No. 5, "Feux Follets," on his grand piano. They ended with one of Bloom's favorites, Gustav Mahler's "Das Lied von der Erde," while Salvatore sang passionately, *"Dunkel ist das Leben, ist der Tod." Dark is life, is death.* The effect was calming on the maestro.

These private performances were more than ritual; they served something vital to their nature by keeping the Echoes sane. Momentarily Attuned. Without it, the musicians lost hold on reality. They withered as Discordance gnawed at their brains, just as Eris had demonstrated until rescued by the resurrected Christofori with love beyond death. A corpse was what she had nearly become by leaving the orchestra. For this reason, Bloom rehearsed his musicians on a near-daily basis. Today had been no exception. But the rehearsal could not go on forever.

Now, alone with himself, his body still alive from their music-making, Maestro Bloom listened to the Calliope while he considered things. How he wanted to free himself—and his Echoes, of course—from these fleshy prisons, from suffering. These mortal bodies. And he was close.

Things had gone horribly wrong, and it had started with Madison Taylor. The order to have her killed had been a bold but necessary move. Cameron had made clear his inability to exorcise his final demon and compose his Dirge. It had become glaringly obvious that the man needed a little push, a little inspiration, and so he had forced Bloom's hand. Liberation egged on by Madison's great tragedy.

But something had gone wrong. Simon had left behind evidence. And then Cameron had disappeared. Kalek had hanged himself. Now this janitor issue . . .

The backstage door opened and Christofori strode out onto the brightly lit stage to stand beside Bloom and gaze out at the empty seats. He did not speak for a long moment.

"The musicians are back at the estate," he finally said. "And our search party is still out."

Bloom folded his arms. "You told Simon to put that deplorable dog out of its misery?" It wasn't mercy that made him give the order; the mangy golden retriever howled at night and would perhaps draw attention. Also, it liked to escape and scavenge.

"Yes." Christofori allowed a small nod. "But he won't do it. He seems to have made a strong friendship with the animal."

Bloom considered this. "Then we best leave it alone. But there's something wrong with that dog. Simon's been filling its head with Noise, I think."

Christofori folded his arms and nodded. "Indeed he has."

The maestro checked his watch. It was nearly seven p.m. "Mr. Washington Hob should have been relieved of duty months ago, before he grew bold enough to sneak around as he did. The fact that he still has access to the Calliope is indicative of Mr. Kalek's flagging mental stability. Now we risk total exposure."

"I don't believe so, Maestro," Christofori said in a low voice. "Even if the janitor goes to the authorities, they would never believe him. Besides, what crime have we committed? We brought a man back from the dead—we didn't murder him."

"Nonetheless, I suspect Cameron went to the police before he left, and they will come for Simon soon enough. As a matter of protocol, they will want to investigate the Calliope and the orchestra. The last thing we need right now is to provide more kindling for the fire."

"I still don't understand why we allowed the Tone Poet to leave Holloway," said Christofori in a quiet voice.

Bloom knew the pianist was too smart to directly challenge him. He grinned and said, "It is all part of the plan. Cameron needed a final push to compose his Dirge, and I am certain he has accomplished this. Any day now he will become Attuned. But he will need time to understand what this means. Time to understand his true nature. Once he has succeeded there, we will retrieve him. Until then, it is best we give him space."

A sob from behind caused the two men to turn and look at Kalek. The old man sat slumped on a wooden chair at the center of the stage with his arms hanging between his knees. His body shook with sobs. This had been going on for twenty minutes now.

Bloom wanted to drive his fist into the man's face. He hated Kalek for what he'd done. The old man had given his allegiance, had promised to serve the orchestra, only to betray him with this suicide.

Moving to stand over the man, Bloom raised the old man's chin with two fingers and looked into his cold, rheumy eyes now full of fear and confusion. He tittered sadly. Alfred Kalek was lost to him. Lobes of the man's brain had starved of oxygen after his self-inflicted strangulation, but enough remained of the man to suffer, to know his punishment.

"I'm sorry I had to do this, old friend," Bloom simpered. "But you knew I would never allow you to leave me. We are in this together. We must see this thing through."

It gave Bloom only a small satisfaction, knowing the depth of Kalek's suffering. No one was going to leave him, not now, when they were so close to performing the Symphony. It was precisely this reason that he'd brought Kalek back. And to ask a question.

"What did you tell him, Kalek?" Bloom said evenly. "What did you tell him about my orchestra?"

Kalek uttered something. Rank breath escaped his parted lips. The man's eyes filled with tears. Obviously, he couldn't talk just yet. But he could listen.

"Mr. Blake has . . . disappeared from us," Bloom said with easy calm. "I have reason to think that he went home to California. But no matter. He can't hide from me. I will bring him back when he is ready. And there is nothing in this world to stop me from orchestrating Armonia. Nothing in this world."

"Maestro Bloom," said Christofori, standing nearby. "If the janitor goes to the police . . ."

"No. I don't think he will do that," Bloom said. "No one will believe him. Nonetheless, we must prepare ourselves. Once Blake has had time to Attune, we will need to retrieve him."

"But how will we know when he is ready?"

Bloom grinned. "Simple. We will ask him."

Chapter 3

October wore on and San Diego settled into its terrifically mild climate, so pleasant that Cameron spent most of his time outside, enduring his marathon walks along the coastline so often that the sun scorched his face, arms, and legs. He walked the beaches of the Bay and followed Silver Strand Boulevard into Coronado Island. He made long excursions to nearby parks, like Chula Vista and Marina View, always keeping to himself, always alone.

Aside from the occasional conversations with his neighbor, Gary, or his calls to Camilla, his cleaning lady, to cancel her services, he'd kept his distance from the rest of the world. But his solitude failed to ease his mind. He'd become a stranger to himself and the world around him, disassociated and unresponsive.

What he had abandoned in Holloway had left a void in him. There was no denying that. His chance at ridding himself of his past haunting of Astral Music was gone. That had been his decision when he left Bloom.

Several weeks had passed since he'd returned home, and yet he felt incomplete here. Holloway had changed him. His work with Bloom and his sessions with the Tongue had fractured his sense of self. By assigning sound to his torment and then trapping those discordant imprints by way of ink and paper, he had mended some very old wounds. But who was he now without the familiar suffering of his ego? Discord had been a part of his core identity, and without those darker tones, he hardly recognized himself. He'd gone through some sort of psychological crisis, a complete crash-and-burn of the ego. His perception had shifted with such force that it left him depressed and disoriented. A hole remained where he'd harbored a lifetime of endless pain. How was that for irony?

Of course, writing the Nocturnes did not liberate him from emotion or free him from suffering. Madison occupied his every waking thought. He blamed himself for her death. She had died for no other reason than that she'd known him, and that realization alone kept him awake at night. But it was safe to say that he no longer experienced pain in the same way as he had before. The part of him that fed from misery had gone away. His new self experienced sorrow in an altogether different manner. No longer did the beast of pain leave its bones buried in his mind; now, it remained exposed in the light of consciousness. And that made all the difference in the world.

Writing his Nocturnes, and more importantly, his Dirge, was supposed to change everything. *Attuned, you will never be the same again. You will know how to hear the universe, and when you can do that, you will hear the music of God.*

No, he didn't hear God. He heard nothing at all.

One more thing continued to plague his thoughts: Armonia, the sound signature of creation itself. For all its mystery and promise, Armonia had offered him something akin to divine purpose, and giving up when he'd gotten so close was devastating. It was these same thoughts that circulated daily through his brain, making him restless.

The only thing that eased his mind was the wind chime that still hung from a back porch rafter. How many hours had he stood beneath that strange cascade of seashells, bone fragments, and metal scraps? Waiting for a revelation that would make sense of everything? The chimes, however, never fulfilled their promise. They weren't enough. He wasn't even sure Attuning would have given him his much-needed closure, but it had been his only chance.

At least he had his music to keep him grounded. He spent countless hours in his home studio. When he sat down to write, a river of melodies poured out of him. For days on end he explored different sounds to correlate with his run of emotions. He felt sharper and more creative than ever before.

Ultimately, his work proved cathartic. How better to deal with his grief and despair?

But eventually his weeks of solitude became too much to bear. He needed the conversation of friends; he needed to share his work. The only problem was who to contact. Sure, he had friends—he had friends for all occasions. Fellow composers and associates from the university where he sometimes picked up classes to teach. None of those people appealed to him now.

As a last resort, he called Barbara Hughes and regretted doing so the moment she answered her phone. She'd been thrilled to hear from him and bombarded him with questions about his "sabbatical" as she called it. She wanted to know everything and jumped from question to reproach. He listened to her ramble on, and when he finally got around to offering some semblance of an explanation, she stopped him. No, dinner, a long dinner, and then they'd talk for hours. Maybe more.

He knew what she meant by "more" and he didn't want her that way now. No one would replace Madison.

He didn't tell her that. Dinner it was, but he hadn't set a date.

Somehow he didn't think anyone outside of Holloway or inside his current list of friends would understand what he'd been through. He mollified her with promises to listen to every deal she could throw at him.

Still, it left him empty.

October 26, roughly two weeks after Madison's death, Chief Dunlap went to the Bloom estate. He brought Bentley with him; Bentley still thought this whole thing was legitimate. Of course it wasn't.

Dunlap hadn't bothered acquiring a warrant from Judge Bowman, and so he decided to go off-radar and have a look around the old compound without any lawful reason to do so. He'd get around to telling Bentley, eventually.

When they arrived, they found the iron gates open. Dunlap tried the callbox, but when no one responded, he shrugged and drove on inside. They soon passed into the estate grounds, with its manicured hills and tall pines and sturdy oaks. Soon they passed before Bloom's mansion, which looked like something medieval, hewn from rocks and trees. He followed the road around to the back of the estate property, to the old Beachum Sanitarium, standing with its back to the bluff and the Stony River.

"Shit, ain't that place ugly?" Bentley mumbled beside him.

Dunlap glanced at him and slowed down a little. Bentley was right. The place looked like literal Hell. Cameron Blake had begged him to investigate the sanitarium, and now that he was here, Dunlap couldn't remember why he'd waited so long. Mostly, he had wanted to believe Blake had it all wrong about Madison's death.

No, it was easier to throw Cameron's satchel in a desk drawer and try to forget about the whole thing, chalk it up to old wiring.

But some things couldn't be ignored. He'd seen her body; he'd seen the way most of her clothes had burned away, revealing flanks of charred and blistered skin. The flames had melted most of her hair away and left her bald except for a few bristly tufts. Legs and arms turned black and charred. Smelled like overcooked meat. No way for someone that gold-hearted to die.

There was something else, too—something the county fire marshal who'd investigated had mentioned that kept coming up in his thoughts: no point of origin for the fire was found. All fires start somewhere—a faulty wire, a coffee pot, a cigarette that fell on the floor—but not this time. It was like the fire started everywhere all at once.

Dunlap parked his cruiser before the sanitarium, then he and Bentley got out and met at the front bumper. Bentley hooked his thumbs in his belt and squinted up at the building. "You sure you wanna go in there?"

The sanitarium loomed over the surrounding treetops, peering back at them in ominous warning. No wonder this place had become the stuff of nightmares for the kids of Holloway.

Dunlap left Bentley standing at the car and went up to the rickety front porch. He knocked on the large oak door and when no one answered, he tried the knob. The door was unlocked.

"These sons of bitches don't much care for security, do they boss?" said Bentley, joining him.

"No, guess not," Dunlap drawled. "Well, let's get this over with."

The sanitarium's interior was about as charming as the outside. There were long corridors with olive green walls and matching linoleum. Naked fluorescent lights stuttered, and there was chicken wire in the windows. The building housed maybe thirty rooms. Fortunately, Cameron had given them two decisive clues: a room somewhere upstairs with girly magazine cutouts covering the walls. So they climbed the main staircase to the second floor and went nosing around until they found a room that fit the bill.

The bedroom resembled a small prison cell, with gray walls and a single dirty window. A soiled mattress rested on a steel frame that had been shoved up against one corner. On the wall above the dresser and mirror were twenty or so pages ripped from girly mags. And the place had a smell, like fish and rotting trash, so strong that it forced them to bury their faces in the crooks of their arms.

"This is it," said Dunlap, his voice muffled by his arm. "Let's see what we can find."

They searched for almost half an hour. Such a tiny room didn't have that many hiding places. They tossed the mattress over on its side. Nothing but trash and more skin magazines there. They emptied the dresser drawers, which were sparse, and then rummaged through the closet. Lastly, they kicked through stinking piles of dirty clothes left in the corners. But they found nothing to suggest that Simon had anything to do with the murder of Carrie Belle Meadows or Madison Taylor.

They'd just about given up the search when Dunlap's eye caught something that he'd at first overlooked. There was a small rip along one side of the mattress. He went over, stuck two fingers into the incision, and rooted around for a moment before he fished out a pair of cotton panties. They were stained with what looked like blood.

"Maybe that son of bitch was right after all," Dunlap said, referring to Cameron Blake, of course, who'd been on his mind a lot lately. Dunlap turned and showed Bentley the undergarment, dangling from a single finger. "Tell me something, Bent. This look normal to you?"

Dunlap got his search warrant and arrived at the Calliope after sundown with Bentley and four of his men. They found the doors unlocked and let themselves in. With drawn weapons, they crossed the lobby, and when they reached the auditorium doors, Dunlap shushed them all with a wave of his hand and gently pressed the doors open.

A beautiful symphony washed over them as they all stepped inside. A full orchestra occupied the stage. There must have been fifty musicians, all of them dressed to the teeth in dark clothes. Bloom stood before them on his podium, keeping time by the gentle motions of his hands.

Dunlap pressed his way ahead of the others and motioned for his men to hold fast. Something struck him as strange about the whole thing. A roaring symphony. An epic performance. And yet, the orchestra didn't have an audience; not a single guest was seated in the pews. The orchestra played exclusively for themselves. Dunlap supposed this could all just be an elaborate rehearsal, but who rehearsed like this? This couldn't be a mere rehearsal; they were doing it for themselves. He'd caught them in the middle of a kind of musical masturbation. It bothered him.

Something else bothered him too. He'd never seen these musicians before. What happened to the old folks that Bloom kept employed—the freakishly old men and women who lived up there at the sanitarium? These men and women were in their thirties, at their prime.

But Cameron warned me about this, didn't he? Said they'd be younger.

With a sudden flourish of his right hand, Bloom stopped his orchestra and snapped around on his dais. He looked directly at Chief Dunlap, who shivered when a cold chill scurried down his spine.

Bloom smiled amiably and spread his arms in a welcoming gesture. "Chief Dunlap!" he called as he stepped to the edge of the stage. "To what do we owe this visit?"

"Howdy, Mr. Bloom," said Dunlap as he placed a hand on the butt of his revolver. "Sorry to interrupt, but I'm afraid I've got some business to tend to."

"Business?" Bloom replied. "What sort of business?"

Taking some pleasure in ignoring Bloom, Dunlap lumbered closer to the stage with Bentley now at his side. Both searched the orchestra for Simon. *Just look for the guy with no ears,* Cameron had told him. *He's the killer.*

"I see him right there," said Bentley and aimed a finger at a man standing with his violin hanging from one fist.

Dunlap nodded, made a gesture to his officers, and sent them storming the stage.

"What is the meaning of this?" Bloom called as he watched the officers grab Simon by his arms and haul him out of his chair. Simon gave a swine-like squeal and attempted to wrench his arms free. One of the policemen went sprawling into the other musicians. Several more officers pounced on Simon. They wrestled him to the floor, burying Simon.

Bloom turned a pleading eye to Dunlap. "Chief Dunlap, I hope you know what you are doing. What has Simon done to deserve this treatment?"

Dunlap nodded. *Good. He called him Simon.* "We have reason to believe that your man over there is behind the disappearance of Carrie Belle Meadows," he called up. "We're taking him in for questioning."

"Absurd!" Bloom retorted. "Simon is harmless."

"We'll see about that."

Over on the stage, the men had gotten cuffs on Simon, who bellowed great childish sobs as they jerked him to his feet.

Dunlap couldn't take his eyes off the musicians. Cameron's words went round and round in his head: *Let's just say, they look a hell of a lot younger these days.* But that was bullshit. Bloom just hired new musicians; nothing abnormal about that. Even so, Dunlap felt dreadful as he looked at them. An odd tension covered every face. They looked alert, as if anticipating a call to action, especially the long-haired pianist seated before his grand piano. He looked downright dangerous, with his eyes shining with venomous intensity.

Even as Dunlap watched, Bloom and the pianist exchanged a furtive glance. Dunlap couldn't see what passed between them, but he didn't like it one bit.

"What d'ya do with the last bunch?" he asked Bloom.

The maestro blinked and shrugged. "What did I do with *what* bunch?"

"Your last orchestra," Dunlap said with a frown. "You got new musicians."

Bloom nodded gravely. "That's right. I sent them away. Traded them in, so to speak, for a more energetic troupe." Hands clasped behind his back, he pivoted toward the struggle, adding beneath his breath, "Although this may prove a grave mistake on my part."

Dunlap followed Bloom's line of sight and nodded. "You just might be right about that."

Chapter 4

The day began uneventfully: a gray drizzle, a color-choked sky, a beach teeming with seagulls pecking for food. Cameron started his morning with a long walk and then shut himself into his home studio to write.

His downtrodden mood made its way into his music, sad little melodies that stung the heart. This went on for most of the day. But soon the outpouring of self-pity, not to mention the countless beers, led to a midday nap that was fated to become much longer.

A noise woke him sometime later. He sat up, searching. Listening. The sun had gone down, and the feeble light of dusk pressed against the window, making silhouettes of all the furniture. He blinked, wondering what had woken him, when he heard ghostly music drifting through the walls.

What is making that sound?

He got up and went to the window. In the fading light, he was little more than a shadow. What he'd heard wasn't exactly music, really. This was a natural song, organic, comprised of falsetto voices, flowing without melody or rhythm and echoing like something born in a massive chamber. Almost like a whale song.

Fully awake now, he hurried from the bedroom, crossed the living room without turning on a single light, and then practically threw himself out the back door. The night was warm and balmy. He braced himself against the railing, panting, and looked up. The night sky was singing.

Jesus Christ, what am I hearing? He hopped off the back steps, followed the yard stones through the remnants of a fence. Beyond the sand dunes and marram grass, he dropped to his knees only yards from the incoming tide. The moon glimmered in silver brushstrokes across the ocean's roiling surface. Slowly, he raised his head and fixed his eyes on the night sky.

Music. Incredible music. The stars sprawled across space had become a choir, singing in quiet falsetto voices, and beneath their music, the glassy notes of a cosmic wind chime.

Reeling with sudden excitement, Cameron laughed to himself. *Holy shit,* he thought. *I found it. I've Attuned, just like Bloom promised.*

Waves of vibrations crashed over him, causing every atom in his body to ring like tiny bells. It was a gorgeous experience, and just as spectacular as Bloom had promised, if not at first a little frightening. Something inside him had flowered and was now taking firm hold of his mind. He was the ear in which the Symphony took place.

Hours passed. Eventually the sky blushed and then the sun broke the horizon, spilling itself across the ocean's surface. The phenomenon unleashed a chorus of angelic voices, and his entire body heard the music. This was Attuning, the act of harmonizing with the universe, and, in turn, he discovered the freedom he'd sought: freedom from years of suffering. In that moment, everything seemed in perfect balance, and he understood something of vital importance. The universe was a living symphony, and it'd been singing its song since the beginning of time. Only he'd forgotten how to listen. Everyone had.

Kneeling in the sand, while the ocean rushed and boomed before him, Cameron imagined a field of vibrations enveloping him, causing the hairs on his arms and legs to stand on end. In that moment, he became the center, immutable, eternal, limitless. He resonated with the world around him. He hardly recognized what was left of himself. But he liked it. He felt transformed; his ego stripped to the bone.

The morning air stirred. He rolled his head back, watching and listening as the cosmos sang its symphony of sullen, airy sounds.

The following morning, Cameron woke with a clear head; the music had ended. With the sun in his eyes as it shone through his windows, he made no attempt to get up, but instead chose to lie still, perfectly relaxed, and listen to the tide as it whooshed and boomed against the beach, interrupted only by the squawking of seagulls. The hallucinations had ended. The heavens had once again gone mute, a sad but necessary conclusion. How else would he have functioned in the day-to-day grind of life, when the whole world rang in cacophonic timbres?

No, this was for the best.

Still, the more he listened, the more he realized that something had changed. The noises in the room had a tinny, somewhat metallic quality to them, and he could hear very well. Little sounds became magnified. He heard beachgoers splashing in the water and roaring engines as cars drove along the highway several miles away. Something else too. Something . . . unnatural.

Tossing his sheets aside, he got out of bed and went to the window to press his fingertips to the glass. Barely audible was a faint clattering sound, light and delicate, a ghost's whisper. He frowned. Just the wind chimes. But they sounded different.

Curious, he left the bedroom, passed into the living room, and then let himself out the back door to stand in the sunshine. With his head rolled back, his arms hanging at his sides, he watched as the chimes twirled to form a vortex of tiny bones, metal, and sea shells. In turn, the chimes rang in fantastic tones, producing a strange, delicate music, as if composed of tiny bells. Stranger still, the music didn't correlate with the materials that produced it, the polished disks of seashell, the bones, and the scrap metal.

Jesus, he thought. *What the hell's going on?*

He stood listening for a long while before curiosity got hold of him and he reached a hand out to stop the moving chimes. The music ended abruptly, leaving him in a sudden hush, with only the waves booming against the beach.

Inexplicable panic shot down his spine, and he turned to look out at the beach, certain that he felt someone watching him. But on this early morning, only a few people walked the coast, and they were far away from him. Still, he felt something wrong. Before going inside, he looked again at the wind chimes, now hanging limply, and knew instinctively that they were helping him. Protecting him. He couldn't help wonder if stopping them had been a bad idea. He went inside and locked the door behind him.

Those protective little fragments of bone and shell, somehow they seemed to armor him, shield him. And he had stopped them.

A cold chill permeated him. *Bloom knows that it happened—that I Attuned. And he's coming to get me.*

Chapter 5

Nightmares began, nightmares that wouldn't go away, and Cameron became a nervous mess. He imagined he saw Bloom or his Echoes everywhere he went, from the mall, to the crowds at the Gaslamp Quarter, even in the shadows at home.

For the first time in years, he felt threatened enough to bring out his nine millimeter from its hiding place in his bedroom bookshelf, where it gathered dust behind a series of biographies. He moved it to the nightstand beside his bed.

When he left the house, he made sure to bolt the doors and set the security system. There was little else he could do. Calling the police was out of the question; Bloom hadn't done anything to warrant that. Besides, Cameron still had his doubts. Maybe his dreams were nothing more than just dreams; maybe his thoughts on the wind chimes were simply misplaced trust. He couldn't rule those out just yet.

The days came and went. By the end of the week, he'd become complacent and fell victim to routine, long walks, composing, and now, contemplating the wind chimes. In fact, he spent hours listening to that horrific construction of bones and seashells. Despite their appearance, he'd come to understand the thing as a kind of talisman; its strange clatter somehow created a powerful field of harmonics, so that whenever he sat beneath it for any duration of time, he would become at ease, still, meditative. The chimes soothed him; they made him dream. And unlike Bloom's tuning fork, the chimes took nothing from him, nor did they give him anything aside from a quiet mind and rested body.

Then again to the piano, where he submerged himself within his work. He had never prided himself on being a great pianist. In fact, during his years at Juilliard, he'd only scraped by in his piano lessons, having never exceeded the basic requirements. But now everything had changed. Attuning had blown wide his sensory perceptions, and his inner ear had become acute, unraveling the secrets of sound and rhythm. He played with the dexterity of a virtuoso, his fingers precise and agile on the keyboard.

In the past few days, he'd become caught in an endless river of music and wrote more than ever in his life, producing several symphonies and a handful of concertos and tone poems. The music flowed out of him as melodies blossomed and grew from tiny phrases to colossal giants. Mining an endless vein of inspiration, he played until his back ached and his fingernails cracked, but he refused to stop for fear of losing whatever melody had crept into his mind. All the while, the sheets of handwritten music piled up on the piano and on the floor.

It was late Halloween night when something startled Cameron awake. Drenched in sweat, he lay quietly, staring up at the ceiling. Aside from the moonlight squeezing in through the curtains, the room was dark, the shadows suffocating. Sitting up, he threw the sheets aside and looked over at the digital clock on the nightstand.

Three-fifteen a.m. He stared at the glowing red numbers, wondering what had woken him, when he heard what at first sounded like wind howling around the eaves, only that wasn't right either. The sound was too controlled, too reedy, a sustained sound that pierced the air: the sound of a musical instrument. Then he knew.

They're here. The bastards came after all.

He scrambled out of bed and went to the window, expecting to find Bloom's musicians standing outside. But the floodlights shone on a vacant lot of sand and marram grass, the whitewashed pickets of his fence. Still, the sound persisted, coming from everywhere and growing stronger until the reverberations caused the picture frames to rattle on the walls. A coffee cup fell from the nightstand and shattered.

Something thudded against his bedroom door, and Cameron spun toward the sound, expecting the door to fly open. When it didn't, he looked at the nightstand where he'd stashed his gun on the opposite side of the bed.

The doorknob spun slowly.

Cameron swooned with the blood pounding at his temples. "Who the fuck's out there?"

The door slammed open with terrific force, and Cameron braced himself, but there was no one standing in the doorframe. Something did, however, scurry near the floorboards. Then he saw them, a flood of rats, tumbling over one another and spilling across the bedroom floor like sewer water.

Disgusted, Cameron jumped onto his bed as the rodents spread toward him, creating a squealing carpet of bristly fur, glowing eyes, and lashing tails.

Bloom, you asshole, he thought, and even now heard the persisting woodwind above the squeaks and clicking claws. The Echoes were here; they'd come to kill him. Nothing else could possibly explain the rats, not overflowing sewers or mass infestation.

A shadow moved in the doorway and the musician revealed himself. Little more than a silhouette, the man was dressed in a suit and top hat, his long silver hair spilling from its brim to frame his gaunt face. Erich Lutz, Bloom's premier flutist. The Pied Piper. The man played a strange side-blown instrument, like a knobby pipe made from polished black metal.

Cameron knew it was an Archetype, no mere flute.

The instrument fired off a series of high-pitched notes.

The rats responded.

"Get out of my house!" Cameron shouted as a sudden rush of adrenaline took hold of him, transforming his fear into anger.

Still playing, the musician winked at him, a smile played at a corner of his mouth. Several rats scurried up the sides of Cameron's bed and gathered on the footboard. Claws, and then teeth, stung the tops of Cameron's feet. With a cry, he kicked a rat flying into the far wall. Another punt sent a second rat crashing into the lamp on the nightstand, which teetered. The lampshade came loose and the naked bulb washed the room in harsh light, which only served to illumine the enormity of his problem. The rats were everywhere.

The rats took to the walls, using the curtains at first, but then scaling the smooth plaster until they abandoned gravity altogether and scurried across the ceiling. Cameron risked a look overhead when a rat leaped down at his upturned face. Needle-sharp claws dug into the skin around his eyes. He shouted and grabbed the rodent and flung it away, then swatted at another that had dropped onto his head.

More rats came. They perched on the blades of his ceiling fan, crawled his walls. But then the musician withdrew from the room, and the pitch of his music lowered. The tide of rodents receded toward the door. The floorboards became visible again, and the last few rats disappeared, until nothing remained except their tiny curls of feces.

Panting, Cameron jumped off the bed, fetched his gun from his nightstand, and then rushed out into the hallway, thumbing off the safety. He charged into the living room.

The lights were on. And he wasn't alone.

There were seven of them, men and women, dressed in suits and evening gowns, sitting comfortably on his chairs and sofa, as if they'd been invited to a party. They looked at him with dark eyes within pallid complexions, like vampires. No one said a word as Cameron stood in the doorway with his gun aimed at them. Instead, they watched with quiet, expectant smiles, and this somehow scared him all the more.

"Who the hell do you think you are?" Cameron shouted, knowing full well. "This is my goddamn house!"

Christofori rose up from the sofa and stepped forward. His long black hair covered half his face, almost concealing the smile that lingered at the corner of his mouth. "Mr. Blake," he said coolly. "We were certain you'd be delighted to see us again."

Eris appeared at Christofori's side and wrapped an arm around the small of his back. Her large eyes sparkled mischievously. "Of course he is, darling," she purred to Christofori, her eyes never leaving Cameron. "We came all this way, after all."

Cameron aimed his gun at Christofori's head. "Go ahead and give me a reason to pull this trigger."

Just then Bloom made his way to the front of the group, this time in a gray suit. "Now, now, Cameron," he said, his tone thick with reproach. "That is no way to treat friends."

"Friends?" Cameron scoffed. He pointed the gun at Bloom's chest. "I want you out of my house. Right now. Or I start shooting."

"Did you really think I would just forget our agreement?" Bloom continued. "I allowed you to leave Holloway. I gave you time to compose the Dirge, to Attune." He held up the small leather journal and waved it. "That was my plan all along."

Cameron wished he'd burned the journal when he had a chance. Now Bloom had all of it: the fragments, and now the Dirge. He'd been both repulsed and shamed that something so dark and twisted could come from his mind. But he'd kept the thing as a matter of principle. "I said get out!"

Bloom smiled. "The satchel that Simon stole from you—why didn't you tell me that Simon had your *journal*? The fragments written in this book are quite powerful, even if they amount to nothing but Noise. I presume Simon had been playing excerpts from this little book the moment he claimed possession of it. Who knows the crimes he committed, the nightmares he spread to our little town." The maestro's gaze turned inward as he gave a sad shake of his head. "And now the chief has taken poor Simon into custody. Caged like an animal at Holloway City Jail. But don't worry; we will free him from that place."

At this last revelation, Cameron grinned. Dunlap had listened to him after all. At least Simon was off the streets. "That piece of shit killed my girlfriend. Simon put an end to everything we worked for. As far as I'm concerned, you're all guilty by association. Didn't you know you had a goddamn lunatic in your orchestra?"

The maestro smiled to himself and dropped his gaze to the floor. He held the little booklet clasped in both hands almost reverently. "I'm afraid you don't understand," he said calmly. "It was not Simon who killed Madison Taylor." He looked up and met Cameron's gaze. "I killed her."

Cameron blinked. For a moment the words didn't quite jell. But then his eyes grew wide as his brain made the needed connection. Rage exploded throughout his body. "No," he whispered, shaking his head in disbelief.

"It was a shame she had to die. But you left me no other choice. You needed inspiration, and so I told Simon to kill her." Bloom held up the journal again. "With the Dirge comes Attunement; now, we are one step closer to performing Armonia."

The strength drained from Cameron's arms and legs, and the gun felt very heavy in his fist. He shuffled a step to his left, braced himself against the wall. The blood rushed to his face. "She was innocent, goddamn it!"

"Madison Taylor died for our Symphony—so that we can finish what we started."

Wearily, Cameron shook his head. "It's already finished, you asshole." He barely had the strength to point his gun at Bloom's chest and pull the trigger.

One shot went wide; the second shot caught Bloom just left of his sternum. The man covered the wound with both hands, staggered back, and yelled something unintelligible.

The musicians pounced on Cameron. A fist slammed into his stomach. He bent over, gagging, and then someone shoved him, causing him to crash onto the coffee table. His head smacked the hardwood floor with a resounding thud. Something stung his arm, the prick of a needle, maybe.

When darkness came, he went willingly, picturing Madison's face before falling unconscious.

Cameron woke, lying face down while tires droned steadily beneath him. Someone had tied his wrists behind his back with coarse rope. His head swam. He felt drugged. How long had he been out? By the sharp pain of his full bladder, he imagined it had been a long time. Twisting his head to the left, he made out details of Bloom's limousine. He'd expected the Echoes to kill him after what he had done. Unless they were taking him someplace to finish the job.

Something moved to his right. Christofori studied him. "He is awake," the pianist said before disappearing from view.

"Good," said Bloom.

Cameron didn't understand. Bloom had taken a bullet to the chest.

And yet, the voice spoke again. "I want to talk to him."

Still on his stomach, Cameron craned his head back, squinting until his vision sharpened. Bloom rested comfortably on the rear seat, alert and seemingly unharmed, the bloodstained shirt beneath his suit jacket the only indicator that he'd been shot.

"What . . . ?" Cameron groaned and let his head fall. His head ached, and nothing made sense to him. The man should be dead.

Christofori crouched down beside him, grabbed a fistful of Cameron's hair, and jerked his head up. "You look at him!" he hissed. "Look at what you did. If I were him, I would gouge your eyes out with my fingers."

Gritting his teeth against the blinding pain, certain that his hair would soon rip from his scalp, Cameron opened his eyes.

"Now, now," Bloom said calmly. "There's no need for that."

Cameron shook his head in disbelief. "You–you should be dead!"

Bloom sighed and gave a woeful expression. "I suppose I should be dead. But as you can see, I am not."

"But . . . how?"

"We are Echoes," Bloom said, his tone matter of fact. "We do not suffer the death of ordinary men. Our afterlife is much, much different."

A groan escaped Cameron, his head numb with shock.

"I'll let you in on a secret," said Bloom as he leaned forward in his seat. A bitter grin lurked at the corners of his mouth. "The story I told you about our first attempt to perform Armonia was not the entire truth. You see, shortly after I took Luca Verdel from his asylum, I realized that I had made a grave error. While Verdel had indeed experienced near-death, and while he had indeed heard music during his experience, he did not, in fact, hear the voice of God. Instead of Armonia, Verdel had tapped into absolute Discord, and it was this terrible music that remained entrapped within his soul. When I discovered my error, I told my orchestra, and I let them decide our next move. The orchestra agreed that we go through with our little experiment. If Verdel could not deliver Armonia, he could at least deliver Discordia. And so, you see, what happened to us next was no accident."

Bloom sat back, his eyes gazing inward as he recalled some distant memory. "This orchestra willingly tapped into Discordia. The music recreated us, and we found great power in our new state of being. But as a result we had inadvertently severed our connection with God. At first, we were all thrilled with our new state of being. We were free, and we took great pleasure in our Discord. But it wasn't long before we began to suffer. Consider the pain of losing your parents, and multiply that pain by infinity, and you still would not know the depth of our suffering."

"But you did this to yourself," said Cameron.

"That was nearly a century ago," Bloom said, his eyes boring into Cameron. "Don't you think we've paid our penance?"

A century ago? Cameron shuddered, his mind reeling with this new information. *My God. They're hardly even human.*

"Kalek told me how he found you," said Cameron, his voice raspy, uneven. "He told me what happened at his church."

The maestro narrowed his eyes. "After the performance of our great and cursed Symphony, my enemies tried to kill me. They destroyed my body; but instead of death, I found myself in a realm of absolute Discord. I was there for a long, long time before Kalek saved me from that place. By accident, of course. I heard his music. I used it as a way back." He let his gaze fall. "So you see, after my resurrection, I learned something vital to our condition. We are unable to escape this prison of ourselves—this prison of spiritual desolation. Not even death can offer relief. So you see, the universe has left us with no choice. Our only chance for reconciliation with Armonia lies in a direct contact with it.

"So now you understand," Bloom went on. "The orchestra is sick, and it needs you. That is why you will deliver Armonia, and when the orchestra is well again, I will let you leave us. But not until then."

Cameron's gaze fell. Hadn't he known from the beginning that the orchestra was sick? Hadn't he sensed it from the moment he saw them in the Calliope? But he had ignored his gut instinct, and as a consequence, the woman he loved was dead, and he was as good as a dead man.

"What is your sickness?" Cameron asked, not expecting an answer.

Easing noticeably in his seat, Bloom said quietly, "The kind that makes life insufferable."

Chapter 6

Monday morning, Holloway woke to find flyers posted all over the town square. Slapped across shop windows, phone poles, and car windshields, they announced a free symphony for the coming Friday to be performed by the Holloway Orchestra. Citizens were cordially invited to attend at sundown; seats were available on a first-come, first-served basis.

When he arrived at his station, Chief Dunlap discovered one of the flyers tucked beneath the wiper of a patrol cruiser. He took it inside with him, and over a cup of steaming coffee, he pored over the words, hoping to decipher a clue. Why a free concert? Why now, when he had Simon locked behind bars?

"Don't you think this is strange, Bent?" Dunlap waved a hand at the flyer.

The sergeant, sitting in a chair with his feet propped on a side table, slurped his coffee before returning his attention to the far window overlooking Main Street. He nodded sleepily and offered a perfunctory, "Yup."

The chief breathed through his nose and scowled. "For Christ's sake, Bent. Are you listening to me? Bloom finds out one of his musicians is a murder suspect and all of a sudden he wants to throw a free concert. And you couldn't care less."

"I said I thought it was strange, Chief," Bentley protested. "What more do you want from me? Besides, it ain't like he's breaking the law."

"Not that we know of, anyways," Dunlap suggested.

Bentley looked at him for a quiet moment. "You went and talked to Carrie Belle's mother last night, didn't you?"

The chief nodded gravely. "I did."

"So? How'd it go?"

"How do you think it went?" Dunlap spat. "She was hysterical. Swore up and down that Bloom was behind it all."

"What'd ya tell 'er?"

"Not much. Told her Chester King was more'n likely behind her disappearance."

"Didn't say nothin' about the others?"

Dunlap's face went pallid. "Christ, no. She don't need to know about them. Not yet, anyhow."

Just yesterday they'd gotten the reports back from the Nashville forensics lab. The pair of women's underwear they'd found tucked into a hole in Simon's mattress did indeed belong to Carrie Belle. They had their man. Dunlap had known this from the moment he'd sat with Simon in the station's tiny interrogation room with its subdued green walls and its framed two-way mirror. Bald and earless, the disheveled man wore a crazed smile and giggled at inappropriate times. His handicap seemed apparent; he was an idiot, and he spoke as if he had cotton stuffed in his mouth; and yet, according to the boys in the other cells, he played the violin most weekends at the Bard Tavern.

But Dunlap had a problem; he couldn't get a coherent story out of the man. Simon had the mental capacity of a six-year-old. "Not only is he a lunatic," Dunlap said to Bentley, "but he's a goddamn retard too."

The good news was that they'd found DNA traces from Chester King, a local resident who'd spent six months at Willow Wood County Jail in 2003 for breaking and entering and assault. Chester came in on Tuesday morning for questioning. Thin and jittery, with yellowish skin and long stringy hair, Chester smoked his Marlboros to the filter as he told his story, and sure enough, he quickly shed some light on Carrie Belle Meadows's disappearance. Obviously, the man had wanted to get it off his chest for a long time. By lunchtime, he'd ratted out two of his friends, Bobbie Monroe and Martin Hale, fellow employees at Stockton Warehouse. But his story just got stranger and stranger. If Dunlap was to believe Chester—and by God, he didn't want to—it was one twisted tale.

At around ten p.m., Carrie Belle had wandered into the Bard Street Tavern, alone, wet from rain, and clearly upset. Chester, being the fine gentleman that he was, had dragged her to the dance floor, where things got more than a little rowdy.

"Simon started to play, and we started dancing," Chester explained, his eyes glazing over as he thought back. "So we start kissin' and then we go over to the stage, and she wanted it real bad, so I gave it to her." At this point, Chester shook his head, his face bent with a disgusted smile, eyes watering. He spoke in a trembling voice. "Simon done it to us. I swear to God, he did. That music of his—it made us all crazy, every one of us, even that little girl. She let me take her right there onstage, right there in front of God and everybody, and then she let the others have her too."

"How many others?" Dunlap pressed, feeling sick and saddened at the same time. He glanced over at Bentley, who stood against the wall with his arms folded, his face locked in a grimace.

"Hell, I don't know," Chester laughed, only it wasn't a laugh, but a sob. "There was a bunch of us. That's all I remember."

"So what happened then?" Dunlap said, feeling his heart race. This was it: the mystery solved. "What did you do with her?"

But then Chester got all teary-eyed and started sobbing like a ten-year-old. "We didn't do nothing," he insisted. "Nothin' that girl didn't ask for. But I swear to you, I can't remember no more. I just . . . I just don't remember."

Dunlap's next interrogation with Bobby Monroe didn't clear anything up; he, too, conveniently suffered from amnesia. He recalled even less of that night than his pal Chester.

The interrogations with the men had put Dunlap in a foul mood. He had no corpse, no more leads, something that sounded like rough but consensual sex, and then his mutant musician.

Heaving a sigh, he balled the flyer up and threw it into his wastebasket. "What a goddamn mess," he muttered. The phone rang and he snatched it off its cradle and slammed it against his ear. "Yeah?" he croaked, remembered himself, then added, "This better be good."

Cameron woke in a cold, dark place with a single sapphire light shining down on him. Someone had tied him to a chair with his hands locked behind his back. His body ached, and his memory of the cross-country car ride was a blur. The Echoes had kept him drugged and unconscious, stopping only after long periods to let him piss on a quiet roadside before shoving him back into the limo and binding his hands. He was sore and fatigued from days of hard travel.

He forced his mind back to the present. His chair was set atop a high platform. Even with the limited light, he was able to locate himself. The polished black floor, the vaulted ceiling, the dank air of a cavern—this was the Calliope's basement. And Bloom's ensemble of strange instruments formed a circle around him.

As his eyes adjusted, he made out their spindly shapes. The Archetypes still reminded him of alien insects with black exoskeletons. Surely these were the works of great artists.

But what if those artists weren't human? The thought sent a chill running down his spine.

He fought against his bindings and strained his muscles until he hurt himself. Worse, his chair nearly toppled over. Cameron forced himself to relax. Tied to a chair, a drop from this height would undoubtedly crack his skull open.

He reached out with his newly Attuned senses. The energy field of this place gave off a nasty vibration, a panicked pitch, and he quickly shut off that part of his mind, lest the sound drive him crazy. He thought about the homeless man he'd seen near the Gaslamp Quarter last week. He'd gone there with an agenda to explore his new abilities. The man had been drunk, passed out in a doorway, and his body rang with a noise like this, only on a much smaller scale. Discord.

"Bloom, goddamn it!" he shouted, sending his voice echoing throughout the chamber. He gnashed his teeth and fought at the ropes again until the coarse material bit into his wrists and his chair tottered. "Where are you?"

He eventually gave up. Panting, his head sagging, he recalled more of the limo ride back to Holloway: Bloom, somehow alive with a bullet in his heart; Christofori, holding his head up by his hair.

We are Echoes. We cannot die.

Something made a clunking sound and then a ring of lights blinked on overhead, casting the basement in an eerie blue glare that illuminated the ensemble of instruments and caused them to shimmer like black glass. Something slithered beneath the instruments, snakelike bodies that contracted and writhed. Some of the wormy creatures worked their way between the music stands; others coiled up in slimy piles.

They were not snakes. More like tapeworms, lumpy and pale, without distinguishable heads, like something Cameron had seen floating in jars of formaldehyde during science lab in his undergrad years.

Somewhere, a door yawned open, and several sets of footsteps echoed throughout the basement. These visitors stayed hidden by the dark for a few moments more before they emerged from the barrier created by the instruments.

It was Bloom, flanked by Christofori, Eris, and Lutz. From his chair perched on the dais, Cameron looked down at the four as they moved nearer. Bloom came to the bottom step and looked up. Shadows were in his eyes, and the deep blue light shimmered in his white hair.

"I hope you will forgive my lack of hospitality," said Bloom, the overhead lights giving his face a chalky-blue glow. He carried Cameron's leather journal in one hand. "I didn't mean to ignore you; however, I've been extremely busy."

"I've got nothing to say to you," Cameron spat.

"Of course you are angry with me, and I don't blame you," said Bloom, his voice annoyingly calm. "I don't know if it matters much to you, but I did not want to see that poor girl die. But I did what I had to do."

Cameron clenched his teeth. "I loved her, and you took her from me."

"That is precisely why I did it. You came to Holloway a damaged man. Your anger had corrupted your energy field so that it rang in Discord. I had hoped the Tongue would help, but your demons were deeply rooted. And so you left me no choice but to make conditions worse for you." Bloom held the journal up so that Cameron could look at it, and then said, almost pleadingly, "Madison's death propelled you into self-realization; it forced you to recognize your Discord. Now you've exorcised your Discord—you've trapped it on paper—and now you have Attuned."

"You could have tried something else, you twisted piece of shit!" Cameron struggled to free his arms. When that didn't work, he stomped his feet until his chair hopped and scraped the polished boards underneath.

"I'm sorry, but there was no other way. At least now you are ready to deliver Armonia."

Another moment of fighting his bindings left Cameron exhausted and he stopped. He let his head drop. "You're going to have to kill me, then. I will never write your goddamn Symphony."

The conductor's brow creased. "You still think you can write Armonia? Haven't you learned anything? Armonia is not something that can be isolated and captured on paper. It is continuously flowing, changing, recreating itself."

"So what the hell am I doing here?"

Bloom glanced at Christofori, who started up the steps of the dais and then disappeared behind Cameron's chair. For one terrifying moment, Cameron expected to feel a blade against his throat, but the moment never came. Christofori tipped his chair back on its hind legs and spun Cameron around until he faced the instruments at the back of the formation.

At once, his eyes went to the massive circular object that towered over the other instruments. Just as before, it was covered by a green tarp. Cameron recalled his first visit down here with Bloom and his cloaked conversation about this particular object. He'd called it a wind harp—a big one—but he hadn't said much more about it. Even early on, the thing had stirred a sense of dread in Cameron, and that feeling came back stronger than before.

"I've waited a long time to show you this," said Bloom as he walked toward the covered object. Eris and Lutz trailed quietly after him. "I would have shown you earlier, but I was too afraid you'd run away."

When the three neared the towering object, Lutz stepped forward, grabbed a fold of canvas, and gave it a forceful tug. The tarp slipped away to reveal a large black sculpture of a serpent eating its own tail. Scales were engraved into its dark sides. The entire frame was perfectly circular and about seven feet in diameter. It stood on a base that held it lofted above the other instruments.

The thing looked to Cameron like a massive wagon wheel without spokes, or maybe a circus trick—a ring of fire for tigers to jump through.

"The Ouroboros," Bloom offered, as he stepped away from it with his arms held out at his sides as if to present the thing. "The serpent eating its own tail; eternally recreating itself, the symbol of eternal regeneration."

Cameron shivered as he looked at the snake's head toward the top of the ring. Its eyes were black and vacant. "What the hell is it?"

Bloom turned around and grinned at him. "This is the Lyre—this is how you will compose Armonia."

Feeling sick to his stomach, Cameron's gaze went between Bloom and the giant black ring that seemed to float above all the other instruments. The blood pounded behind his eyes. He was absolutely terrified. "How the hell is this thing going to help me?"

"When it is time, you and the Lyre will become one; you will become a human instrument, and bonded with my orchestra, you will give us the music of your soul."

"So that's it? You're just taking it from me."

"More or less."

"Then why didn't you do it in the first place?"

There it was. That same humorless grin. "Because you weren't ready. It was necessary that you Attune first; without having done that, the Lyre would have drawn from you nothing but Discord. But now that you are ready, the machine will find the echoes of Armonia your soul has kept secret—the echoes that you've harbored since the moment your soul merged with the Overtone."

Cameron swallowed a lump in his throat. "You want me to get inside that thing?" he said in a choked whisper.

"The experience, I suspect, will be quite painful," Bloom mused. "But once the orchestra begins and we achieve communion with the Godhead, you will feel nothing but elation and awe. Doesn't that justify the means?"

"It's going to kill me, isn't it?"

"Not if you do as I say."

"So then let's get it over with," Cameron said in a low voice. "Untie these ropes and let's do it, goddamn it."

The maestro grinned dangerously. "Soon, Cameron. There are just a few loose ends to tie up. For starters, we must prepare the Calliope."

Cameron frowned. "Prepare it? How?"

The conductor looked up at the ceiling. "Don't worry, we've already begun. In just a short while, the citizens of Holloway will gather for one last concert in the hope of another life-changing experience. Only this time, we have something much more significant planned for them."

The tone of Bloom's voice sent a cold shiver down Cameron's spine. It worried him that Bloom would open his doors to the public again. "What are you doing up there?"

"Christofori has decided to perform publicly; it will be a kind of pre-show to our private concert here in the Calliope's basement."

Bewildered, Cameron turned his attention to Christofori, who was now walking up to stand at Bloom's side. The man's face looked like a piece of dried bone in the blue light.

"What's he going to play?" said Cameron, but as soon as he asked, he knew the answer.

With a glimmer in his eye, Bloom held Cameron's journal up in the air, and as if on cue, Christofori retrieved it from him.

"He's going to play the Dirge," said Bloom. "What else?"

Chapter 7

The Calliope opened its doors after sundown on the third of November. Once again, the auditorium filled every seat. An impressive, if not expected, turnout given the last extraordinary—although not completely comprehended—performance more than a month ago. The people wanted more of what they'd tasted then. No one had a clear reason why they wanted it; they just knew they did. Nor did anyone talk about it.

Bloom's staff made little accommodation for the crowd and let the people fend for themselves. As a result, tempers flared and several arguments broke out. The auditorium was filled with sobbing children and frustrated shouts. *This is ridiculous! Where is the goddamned management?* Several families turned around and hurried for the doors. But in the end, most of the guests chose to stay, even when intuition told them to leave. This was a free concert, after all, and that sort of thing didn't happen often these days.

Nonetheless, by the time the doors were closed, the Echoes had a sufficient audience for what they needed to do.

A long time passed, or at least it seemed that way to Cameron. By now, he'd given up on trying to break from his ropes. Time had become sluggish. His back and shoulders ached and his hands felt like slabs of meat with the ropes biting into his wrists. He spent the day sleeping with his chin resting on his chest. His neck ached terribly. On top of all that, he was thirsty and his stomach growled.

When he wasn't asleep, he studied the Archetypes down below him, gleaming in the sapphire light. They looked so much like living creatures that his eyes played tricks on him and reported movements from the outer rim of the formation. He wondered about them: who had made them, and for what reason. He also wondered about the worm-like things slithering around the floor just out of sight.

He'd seen the instruments do fascinating things, from spawning Christofori to the rejuvenation of the Echoes. The Archetypes manipulated sound in ways that shouldn't be possible. But that hardly answered a fundamental concern for him: what was their true purpose, and did they exist for good or evil?

Footfalls echoed throughout the chamber, and moments later a man moved into the light. He walked in stiff, staggering movements, unconcerned with the worms, and they in turn slithered out of his way.

Cameron gasped and shrank back in his chair. It was Kalek, only something terrible had happened to the old man. His face, now the clammy gray of river clay, hung loose from the bone while his eyes were lusterless. Even his rigid movements suggested atrophied muscles. Worse yet, Cameron could smell him, an odor like rotten meat.

Panicking, Cameron pulled against his ropes and shook himself until his chair nearly fell over.

"Don't worry," said Kalek, looking up at him with a grim smile. "The Viscera won't harm you. They are restricted to the ring of instruments."

But it wasn't the *Viscera* that frightened him as much as it was the old man's appearance. Kalek didn't seem to notice how bad he looked.

Cameron played along for the moment, turning his attention to the squirming creatures that churned beneath the instruments. "What are they?"

Kalek grinned coldly. "A neat trick is what they are. The Echoes have a piece of music that allows them to animate the organs of a living body; they raided a small farm just outside of Willow Wood. Turned the cows inside out. Took the innards."

It was disturbing news, but Cameron processed only bits and pieces of what he heard. What demanded his attention was the old man's face. Kalek wasn't just sick; he looked like a corpse.

"The Viscera are mindless things, of course," Kalek continued, "but all the same they are possessed with a single purpose: to find a home in the belly of a living animal and return to their natural state. They don't realize that in doing so, they will only kill the host. Sounds like a Greek tragedy, doesn't it?"

Unable to stop himself, Cameron asked in a careful voice, "What happened to you, Kalek?"

The old man touched his neck, ringed with a large purple and yellow bruise. "I tried to hang myself. I wanted to escape this evil. But I didn't get far, as you can see. Bloom found me and . . . he brought me back."

"He brought you back?"

The old man dropped his gaze, as if suddenly embarrassed. "All these years, I've been so afraid to die—afraid of God's judgment. But I was wrong. I know now that death is like going home." Then a look of disgust came over his face. His tone turned acidic. "That's why Bloom brought me back. He was jealous of me. He's jealous of everyone afforded the luxury of death. For him and his Echoes, the world after this one is something ugly and discordant. For them, there is no going home."

Something clicked then. Cameron pictured Bloom, still standing on his feet after taking a bullet to the chest; alive when he should have been dead.

"He can't die," Cameron whispered, dropping his head and turning his gaze inward. "They can't die."

Kalek scoffed at this. "No, they cannot. But they want to die. They want to end their miserable lives and return to the Overtone, the source of all things. Death has been forbidden to them for nearly a hundred years. But now they have you, and willingly or not, you are going to help them to die like ordinary men and women."

Chapter 8

*O*h, *I don't like this place. Why did I ever come here?*

It was Dory Witt's first visit to the Calliope. She'd learned about the free concert on Monday afternoon, having discovered a flyer tucked beneath her car's windshield wiper. She'd immediately thought about Charlie. She wanted so badly to see him again, to beg him to come home. *To hell with what Howard wants. My son's in trouble. He needs my help.*

So she'd come alone, leaving Howard at home after telling him a lie about visiting Susan Wymer in Willow Wood. Seemed like a good idea at the time, but now she felt uncomfortable, wedged between two strangers in a pew too close to the stage, her purse in her lap, eyes fixed on the tall red curtains draping the stage.

The place had a funny smell. Old and dusty. It made her feel unsettled. *I shouldn't have come. I shouldn't have lied to Howard.*

She'd already dismissed her hopes of finding Charlie. There were too many people here. Worse, the people were acting so strange, shouting and pushing at one another. She'd even seen a fight in the lobby, an actual fistfight. *Who's in charge here? And where is Chief Dunlap? Why did they let this thing get so out of control?*

The lights dimmed suddenly. Squeaking pulley wheels drew her attention to the stage, where the red curtains parted like the Red Sea had done for Moses. The crowd hushed as a spotlight shone down on a single man, following him as he strode across the stage toward a piano. *No, not a piano.* She leaned forward, trembling. *What is that thing?*

Time slowed. The musician moved in measured strides across the stage, each footfall sending a hollow thud echoing across the auditorium. There was something alarming about the man. He was tall and slender in his black suit. Long black hair framed his narrow white face. He walked with his shoulders rolled back and his head tipped forward, so that his eyes looked out from beneath the shelf of his brow. He moved like a vulture about to feed on a dead animal, and the illusion held, even as he slipped onto the stool and spread his hands over the keyboard.

Dory didn't like it. *His face . . . it's bone white. Bloodless. Just like Charlie's. What's wrong with these people?*

His piano was even stranger. Facing east to west, the instrument looked like something long dead, buttressed with rib-like formations, covered with a leathery skin. A shiny black skull was mounted over the keyboard.

Dory could see it too well. *Like a monster. How horrible.*

The musician began his concerto, opening with a quiet minor key, a plodding rhythm without melody, brooding base notes. The slow march of notes seemed to meander, like raindrops inching down a windowpane, falling in uncertain directions. Dory grimaced, sickened with dread. This was a gothic soundscape, interrupted at intervals with frantic fits of shrilling notes, a lunatic's laughter.

The music frightened Dory. She sat up in her seat, wringing her hands, breathless. Black dread fell over her. She wasn't alone in her panic. All around her, the audience jerked in their seats, looking at one another with dismay. A few children started to cry.

This isn't real. I'm dreaming this. Dory looked to the pianist, then covered her mouth to stifle a gasp. The man at the piano . . . he was so familiar. *Is that Charlie? Yes, I think it is!* Somehow she had failed to recognize him until now. The blame wasn't entirely hers. Charlie looked so different, so mature in that black suit, with his long flowing hair, his thinned-out face, free of acne. She felt an overwhelming pride for her son. He had become a man.

But his music. It frightened her. *Dreadful. Just dreadful. And he's scaring everyone. Doesn't he know what he's doing?* She would ask him to stop playing, undo whatever spell the town was under. And then maybe her Charlie would come back home, make amends.

She got up and made her way out of the aisle while stepping on several toes, though no one seemed to notice. Once free of the pews, she started toward the stage, her purse clenched tightly to her chest, Charlie's music causing her vision to swim. When she reached the stage, she found the steps and climbed them to the top, where she became visible to the entire audience.

She turned to look at them. Hundreds of faces watched her in a kind of stupor, with gaping mouths and sleepy eyes. A heavy man sitting close to the front stood from his seat, middle-aged and balding, wearing a sports coat and a tasteless tie. His shirt was drenched in sweat. He looked almost drunk, the way he staggered and swayed, and then he covered his ears with his hands, threw his head back, and howled. Blood so dark it was almost black gushed from between his fingers. Even from here she could see it stain the cuffs of his sleeves.

Oh no, Charlie. You're hurting him!

It didn't stop. While the piano behind her churned with sounds hardly discernible from one note to the next, several more in the audience stood and covered their ears and screamed. More blood flowed as the music reached a crescendo. When people began collapsing and flinging themselves from the balcony, Dory covered her own ears and turned around to face Charlie.

But the pianist had changed, transformed. And then panic set in as she recognized her error. *That's not Charlie.*

The back of the piano came unhinged. Its unusual design allowed its back to open in two pieces, like wooden wings, rising slowly upward and away from each other. Only they didn't open so much as peel away, like scabs from a wound. The underside of each lid dripped with viscous fluids, gristle, and muscle tissue. When she looked down into the piano's case, she found silver strings spanning across a network of bones and organs.

The piano was alive.

When the piano's double lids opened as far as they would go, Dory could see shadows swimming beneath a thin membrane being pressed by spindly fingers, stretching it like taffy. Something was trapped in there.

Suddenly the membrane ripped open. In a single bound, a black, reptilian creature lurched out from the innards of the piano and perched itself on a ridge just above the keyboard. The thing was the size of a small boy, and it crouched on the piano's music desk like a gargoyle on the peak of a cathedral. Its skin was smooth, hairless, and glistening. Its head was round, unfinished, the head of a human fetus, only much larger, and with teeth—rows and rows of needle-sharp teeth. Eyes like boiled eggs shone from within its dark features.

Another ghoul appeared, crouching next to the first.

Dory shook her head, refusing to believe her eyes. While the man who was not Charlie brought his music to a frantic tempo, she took several steps back. Both creatures raised their heads and fixed her with wide gray eyes.

Dory dropped her hands to her sides. "No! No! No!"

The music rose to a crescendo as one of the ghouls leaped over the pianist's head with the fluid grace of a cat. It was heavy, and when it landed on her and forced her down, she lay staring up at the rafters high over her head. The creature's demonic face loomed over hers, and their eyes met. As she stared into their depths, she knew it was real.

Lord help me!

The monster thrust its face closer to hers, then it yawned its mouth open wide, allowing her to see its jagged teeth, its long red tongue, the pink inner walls of its throat. It screamed, a hellish sound filled with death that ruptured Dory's ears just before it chomped down on her throat, spraying fans of blood from the corners of its maw.

Dory closed her eyes and listened—listened to the wet smacking sounds as the creature ate her flesh. With her head turned to the side, she saw more of those small creatures spilling out of the piano like rats from a sewer drain, racing across the stage on all fours, moving in their strange gait as they poured like a black wave onto the hapless audience.

Her eyes drifted to a dark area offstage where a boy wearing glasses stood in the shadows. It was Charlie. She reached a hand toward her son, but he only looked at her, his face impassive. He never moved. He never came to help her.

As darkness overcame her and she sank toward eternal sleep, Dory heard the vestiges of peaceful music, like Charlie's first days of practice, when he was just a boy and he still loved her. She closed her eyes and went to it.

As the townsfolk sat in misery at the Calliope's final showing, the Echoes came for Simon. Salvatore led the way.

Dressed in black formal attire, each carrying an Archetype, the quartet entered through the front doors of the small jail, playing their brooding music, while the Viscera slithered at their boots.

Jamie Springer at the reception desk was the first to die. She did the best she could to send out a cryptic message to any officer in the vicinity before the wormy Viscera took their stranglehold on her.

It was a short walk to the dispatch office, where the Echoes killed Denise O'Higgins and Kelley Lowell. Last, the Echoes marched to the main area, entering unannounced to find the three on-duty police officers gathered around a card table, playing Texas Hold'em. The men barely had enough time to stand and draw weapons before the attack.

Frightened eyes fell to the Viscera as those lumpy, marbled ropes of cow intestines stretched across the linoleum, moving lightning-quick. Only Sergeant Dewey managed a wild shot before the Viscera were upon the men. The creatures coiled, twisted, climbed, and when the officers screamed, the Viscera exploited this natural reaction by slipping easily into those gaping mouths, then throats, then warm bellies.

The quartet's dark music drowned out their choked screams.

Afterwards, Salvatore found the keys in Sergeant Culpepper's front pocket. Then they proceeded to the back jail cells, where they freed Simon.

And then killed the rest of the prisoners.

Something made a shuffling sound out beyond the ring of instruments, and Cameron held his breath and listened. He didn't like knowing that a walking dead man was lurking somewhere beyond his field of vision. Since their earlier conversation, Kalek had disappeared into the dark along with his Viscera. If not for the man's occasional grunts, footfalls, and sudden bone-chilling sobs, Cameron would have thought he had become lunch for the wormy things.

Even now, he could hear the slimy sounds they made as they rolled and nested. He could hardly stomach it. *Cow guts. Jesus Christ.*

Iron hinges squawked as the chamber door opened. Cameron rose up in his chair, defying the fear that suddenly gripped him. He felt fairly certain their Symphony tonight would kill him, but he refused to show weakness to Bloom. Besides, he wasn't afraid of dying; he'd caught a glimpse of it before. It felt like letting go, and he was ready to let go. But there was more than his own life to worry about.

In the darkness beyond the instruments, an orange flame combusted with a loud whoosh, and someone moved with it toward the instruments. Cameron couldn't see the torchbearer, but as the person entered the ring of instruments, the fire dropped in sweeping motions, driving away the Viscera.

Cameron waited with baited breath. He almost laughed when Hob emerged into the clearing wearing his black chinos and blue sweatshirt. "Hob, you old son of a bitch!" he shouted. "Goddamn, am I glad to see you."

With his torch held over his head, Hob moved warily toward Cameron, his eyes never leaving the floor.

"Don't worry," said Cameron. "They won't cross over into the clearing."

Hob seemed reluctant to believe him. When he finally reached Cameron's chair, he held the torch over his head and revealed tired eyes and a sallow face, the last few days of misery taking its toll. "You know what the fuck they are?"

"Never mind that," said Cameron. "We've got to get upstairs. Just get these ropes off me, okay?"

With a curt nod, Hob put his torch down—little more than some gas-soaked burlap tied around the end of a broken broomstick—and then disappeared behind Cameron's chair. Soon the ropes came away, and warm blood rushed into Cameron's hands. Groaning with relief, he stood, but his legs were tingly numb, and he nearly fell down.

"Easy there now," said Hob as he gathered up his torch and held it high. "You ought to be stiff as a board, bein' tied to a chair like that."

Rubbing his aching wrists, Cameron turned to face him, clapping a hand on his shoulder. "Thank you, pal. I owe you one. How'd you get down here, anyway?"

"It wasn't easy. I got here early this morning and hid out in the janitor's closet. I had to wait for Bloom's musicians to clear out before I could get down here. That didn't happen until just before the concert started."

A grim expression overcame Cameron's face as he looked up at the ceiling far above them.

"What do you know about that?" asked Hob.

Cameron looked at him soberly. "I think Bloom means to kill them."

Hob stiffened. "Half the town's up there!"

"That's why we've got to stop it." Cameron walked over to the boundary created by the instruments and watched the Viscera slither around the music stands. The long, flesh-colored skeins covered the floor. He squinted and looked deeper into the shadows, wondering where Kalek had gone. *Maybe he died*, he thought. It would be for the best, after all. Turning toward Hob, he gestured toward the makeshift torch. "Let me see that."

Hob handed it over, and Cameron swung its flaming head toward the floor. The Viscera shrank away from the heat.

Cameron asked, "What'd you use to make this with?"

"Gasoline," said Hob. "I got a gallon of it back there in the stairwell."

Cameron surveyed the basement, looking at all the instruments. A gallon of fuel could get a good fire started, but then they ran the risk of burning down the Calliope and taking everyone with it.

"You don't want me startin' no fires down here with all those people up there, do you?" Hob said.

"No, I guess not," said Cameron. He started farther into the band of instruments, swinging his torch as he went. "Let's get out of here. I've got a show to stop."

Chapter 9

Disheveled and barefooted, Cameron charged up the dark stairs while Hob hurried after him. When they reached the ground floor and the maze of corridors beyond, the going proved tedious. Fearing that someone would see them, they inched around every corner and took only indirect routes toward the auditorium. But they didn't get far. Peeking around a corner, they saw the end of the passageway. It was crowded with Echoes.

"Looks like you gonna have to go another way," Hob whispered. "You never gonna make it to the stage that way. Come on."

With Hob now in the lead, the two men hurried into darker passageways. They moved quickly but cautiously, and soon they followed a corridor that ran along the length of the auditorium. When they reached the swinging doors at the end, Hob stopped him with an outstretched hand.

"The lobby's on the other side of those doors," Hob warned. "If Bloom's men are posted there, we're fucked."

"We're out of choices," said Cameron as he moved past him and pressed the doors open.

The lobby was empty. Across the way, the glass exit doors acted as mirrors, and Cameron winced at his own reflection, hardly recognizable in his bloodstained clothes, and his pale, unshaven face. He wanted more than ever to simply walk away from the agony of Holloway.

Warily, he turned toward the recessed auditorium doors glowing beneath warm lights. He walked over and pressed his ear to the wood. He could hear muffled screams and strange music from the other side.

"We're too late," he moaned.

When he looked over his shoulder, he found Hob watching him with wide eyes.

"What do you mean by that?" Hob wanted to know.

Cameron pointed toward the exit doors. "Listen to me, Hob. In just a few minutes, a lot of people are going to blow through here. We need to make sure they can get out. So I need you to get those doors open. I got a feeling they're locked, so you might have to shatter them."

Hob nodded and started across the lobby.

Cameron turned his attention back to the auditorium doors. He gripped both handles, braced himself, and pulled. But the doors wouldn't give. Just as he'd suspected, the orchestra had trapped the crowd inside.

Hob ran into a similar problem. "Goddamn it," he hissed. "Locked tight."

"Find something to break them!" Cameron shouted over his shoulder. If he didn't get these auditorium doors open soon, then every person inside would die. And by *his* music. Drawing a deep breath, he threw himself against the doors. His shoulder hit hard, but the lock held.

He retreated several steps to get a running start when glass exploded behind him. Cameron turned to find Hob standing with a metal stanchion post. One of the lobby doors was shattered and glass littered the floor. Hob quickly went to work on the rest of the glass.

One problem solved. Now it was up to Cameron.

Crouching like a football linebacker, he drew a few harsh breaths, preparing to throw himself against the auditorium doors, when they exploded open all by themselves. Suddenly an endless stampede of people came charging into the foyer.

Cameron had just enough time to jump out of the way as crazed people tore past him. In moments, the place echoed with screams as the victims escaped through the shattered lobby doors.

Cameron had no choice but to wait for the first surge of people to diminish. When a woman carrying a small girl in her arms rushed past him, he decided to try. He started forward when a hand clapped on his shoulder. He turned to find Hob, huffing for breath.

"Man, you didn't think I'd let you do this all by y'self, did you?" said Hob.

"You can't help me, Hob," Cameron returned. "If you go in there, that music will kill you."

"Fine then," said Hob amid the chaos. "But what about you? Won't it mess you up too?"

Cameron shook his head. "I don't think so."

"Why the hell not?"

Hesitating, Cameron turned to look at him. "Because I wrote it."

"You wrote it?" Hob shook his head, confounded. "What the hell do you mean by that?"

Cameron sighed. Hob looked scared. His eyes were dark with suspicion. There was no time to explain.

"I'll tell you later," Cameron promised. "You'll just have to trust me for now. Can you do that?"

"I want to help," Hob insisted.

"You can help by getting these people outside." Cameron glanced across the lobby at the stream of people pressing toward the exit doors. There were trampled bodies on the floor. A few people were crawling on their hands and knees, and some had made it to the far wall, where they sat with their hands against their ears. "They need you more than I do."

Hob turned and surveyed the lobby.

"Hob?" Cameron said with a weak smile, grasping the man's shoulder as he turned. "Thanks. For everything."

"You got it, man," Hob said. "Now get in there and stop this shit."

The great open space of the auditorium reverberated with screams of desperation. Gazing out across the dark seating area, Cameron glimpsed a riot of mass confusion. The pews were filled with bodies, slumped forward, either dead or unconscious. The narrow spaces between rows were heaped with more victims. Those who were still conscious fought to get out by climbing over one another to escape the tight rows. Some were trampled to death, and the aisles were littered with broken bodies. Strangely, there was a handful of people who had no desire to leave. They stood with their hands clapped over their ears, watching the stage. Up above, people hung from the balconies, dangling by one arm until falling to their death.

Cameron looked to the stage, where amid the soft light, Christofori played his music, seemingly unaware or unconcerned with all the death that surrounded him. His instrument had undergone some sort of transformation so that its back had opened in two sections, like giant bat wings. Cameron had seen this before on the night Charlie Witt had brought Christofori through.

They've done it again. They've brought something else through. Only this time, something worse.

Just then the piano shrieked. He quickly recognized the sepulchral music, and his arms puckered with gooseflesh. When his vision darkened, he grabbed the end of a pew to keep himself from falling.

Oh, my God. Help me.

Christofori was playing Cameron's Dirge, and hearing it was like hearing his own personal nightmares come to life. The song echoed some dark and savage part of him, an aspect of anger and hurt, like something that had festered for decades. The black music sang of Cameron's darkest secrets, his greatest fears and worries. This was his own auditory nightmare, and it rang with the depth of his desperation and discord. The Dirge was his song—his personal anguish—and never in the history of time had there existed an art so completely personal. So absolutely honest. It horrified him to hear it, to share it with all these people.

My misery. My pain. And it's killing them. Oh, God. It's killing them.

Shoving his way through, Cameron forced his way down the aisle. This was surely worse than he'd imagined. He'd never truly believed that Bloom would actually go through with this—that he would kill so senselessly—but here was the proof, and now this moment would go down in the history of tragedies. It would put Holloway on the map.

Something caught his eye. Several shadowy forms, human-shaped, hardly discernible in this dim lighting, crawled over the pews, jumping from one to the next with catlike suppleness, scouring the bodies, eating when they could. White eyes gleamed wetly in the dark.

Only a few feet away, one of the creatures perched itself on a woman's chest, craned its head forward, then tore into her throat. Cameron groaned and the creature whipped its head around, glowering with silver eyes. It hissed and flashed its teeth before returning to its meal.

Cameron knew what they were. He'd seen them during the Tongue's sound-induced nightmares, and Madison had seen them too. Kalek had called them Oppari, demons birthed from a realm of Discord, born from the piano. And they were everywhere.

Sickened, he hurried on, working his way down the last few yards of the aisle, stumbling over dead bodies strewn across his path. When he reached the stage, he climbed the steps in a few leaps. He kept low in hopes of surprising Christofori. So far the stage lighting worked in his favor; while it bathed the musician and his piano in harsh light, it left the rest of the stage cloaked in shadow. After moving a few feet, a glint of chrome caught his eye. It was a lone microphone stand, set near the stage's edge. Cameron picked it up and hefted its weight. Its long tube was made from light metal, but its base was heavy enough to crack a skull. With it resting over his shoulder, he started forward again, but paused to marvel at the ferocity of Christofori's playing. Hunkered over the keyboard like a famished animal guarding its kill, the pianist attacked the keys with hands that ripped up and down the keyboard with mind-blowing precision. Cameron had never seen such an impressive performance. The guy was a genius. *And I'm going to break his fucking hands. I'll cripple the son of a bitch.*

A hiss broke the air, and glancing up, Cameron looked into wild and yet somehow familiar eyes of an Oppari. The demon had a decidedly human face, and not just any face, but his face. The image wasn't perfect; a visage molded from paraffin wax, with silver slugs for eyes, and a mouth crowded with sharp teeth. But its features bore an uncanny resemblance to his own.

The creature snarled, and Cameron fell backwards as it launched at him. Teeth snapped, lunging for his throat. Cameron held the stand across his chest and the Oppari bit down on the chrome, wailing when it couldn't bite through. Drool spilled from its maw, its pointed tongue curling around the metal as its eyes rolled with fury.

Cameron stared in horror, then shoved the creature hard enough to send it skidding across the stage. Its claws scraped the floorboards as it flailed and rolled over, then turned to pounce again. Cameron had already found his feet and swung the microphone stand. The base connected with the creature's head, shattering its skull. The face—a mockery of his own—was nearly stripped from the bone. With a scream, the Oppari went skidding over the edge of the stage and disappeared.

Panting, Cameron moved into position behind Christofori, who went on playing, oblivious to all that had just happened. Taking a wide stance, Cameron swung the microphone stand. Its heavy base slammed into the side of Christofori's head with a satisfying crunch. The musician was flung off the bench and the music ended.

Take that, mother-fucker. Standing over Christofori, he watched as the great pianist rolled on the stage floor with his arms wrapped about his head. Cameron tossed aside the stand and wiped the sweat from his mouth. He was so pleased with himself that he forgot about the other Echoes until it was too late. He heard a rush of air and then something smashed into the back of his head, scattering stars across his vision. He dropped to his knees as his ears rang like fire alarms.

An inky blur spread across his vision. *At least I stopped it. At least it's over.*

"I'll kill him!" someone shouted far away, drawing Cameron from his dark sleep. "I'll rip the fucker apart!"

Cameron's eyes fluttered open and the world swam into focus. Several of Bloom's Echoes were standing over him; just as he'd suspected, they'd been hiding behind somewhere backstage, appearing the moment he'd attacked Christofori. With a sigh, Cameron's gaze went beyond them to the dark ceiling, where runners of stage lights hung like rows of mounted coffee cans. For the second time since coming to Holloway, he was on his back on the Calliope's stage, suffering from a pounding headache.

Polished black shoes moved to his right, then Bloom crouched down beside him, appearing calm, except for the twitching corners of his mouth and the violence in his eyes. "That was not very kind of you to interrupt Christofori's concerto," he said with a patronizing smile. "And he was just getting to the good part."

Before Cameron had a chance to speak, a growl drew his attention to the piano where Christofori had gathered himself up on hands and knees. Thick red ribbons of blood ran from his face. He sensed Cameron watching him and turned. The base of the microphone stand had peeled a layer of skin from his brow and his right eye was a soupy mess.

"I'm going to rip his tongue out and feed it to him," Christofori said in a low voice.

"Bring it on," Cameron said and closed his eyes, allowing his head to rest against the floorboards of the stage. He was too tired and in too much pain to care about what happened from this point on. Maybe he'd just take a quick nap while Bloom figured out what to do with him.

Bloom snapped his fingers, and several men grabbed Cameron's arms and lifted him to his feet. The world spun around him, and he gripped his pounding head as he looked out at the seating area where crowds of people were still squeezing out through the exit doors. Fortunately, the auditorium had cleared out for the most part, but there were still countless victims in the pews and heaped in the aisles, all of them dead or dying.

"They were innocent," Cameron whispered. Following a flash of anger, he jerked his arms, but two men held him fast and didn't give an inch. "How could you do this?"

The maestro folded his arms over his chest as he shared a long look at the massacre spread out before them. "The Calliope is now sanctified. We are ready to perform Armonia. These people will not have died in vain."

Just then the auditorium doors slammed open and Charlie came sprinting down the center aisle.

"Maestro Bloom!" the boy shouted as he maneuvered the corpse-strewn aisle, clearly in a panic. He looked sick, with his black hair framing a face so white that it looked anemic. "The cops—they're here!"

Feeling hopeful, Cameron managed a wan smile. Dunlap must've gotten a clue. Once the police realized what had happened here, they'd have Homeland Security rappelling out of helicopters and bomb squads busting through the front doors. They'd put an end to this insanity.

But if Bloom felt any fear at all, his face didn't show it. He appeared as calm and calculating as ever. "Everyone, listen to me!" he called as he turned to face the twenty or so Echoes who were on stage. "We don't have much time. We must prepare down below." He pointed toward his personal Pied Piper. "Lutz, you and Oppenheim will take Mr. Blake down and have him ready; bind his hands and keep him close. The rest of you will transport Christofori's piano to the other instruments." Bloom's gaze traveled over each of his musicians. "Everyone else will wait below for my return. I want this orchestra ready the moment I get back."

The blood seemed to rush from Cameron's head and he swayed on his feet. Lutz grabbed his arm to steady him.

Bloom turned and met his eyes. "You look weary, my friend," he said quietly. "But this will all be over soon, and you will have plenty of time to rest."

With that, the maestro turned and charged down the stage steps with two musicians hurrying behind him. The group marched up the main aisle and stepped over the corpses in their way.

They walked like soldiers, preparing to battle their enemy.

Chapter 10

There had been a moment shortly after Cameron disappeared into the auditorium when Hob considered going in after his friend, even as hundreds of terrified victims tried to escape the concert hall. But Cameron's warning held him back. Something awful had happened beyond those doors. People were bleeding from their ears, frightened out of their minds. No, he didn't need to go in there. His work was here with the people. They needed him.

He did his best to help the people get outside. He started with the children, especially those separated from their parents, sobbing as they tried to make sense of what was happening. Next, he helped the women and the elderly. Fortunately, the first wave of survivors didn't need him as much; for the most part, they made the dash across the foyer without his help. But as time passed, the survivors became progressively worse for wear, with blood-soaked faces and ruined ears. Many collapsed and were trampled by the stampede. The last wave of victims could hardly walk.

So many people needed him, and thankfully, Hob didn't have to work alone for very long. Not fifteen minutes after he'd begun escorting people outside, several survivors had joined in with Hob's rescue efforts. After just a short while, his newfound helpers had established a system that enabled a steady flow of traffic from the foyer to the plaza outside, where more helpers waited.

In the meantime, Hob became so preoccupied with his work that he nearly forgot about Cameron. He worked until his back ached. Once outside with the survivors, he got a better look at the place. Down below, the plaza was crowded with people, some helping, others hurt or unconscious.

And where were the police? What was taking them so long? Warily, Hob moved down the entrance and sat on the bottom step, where he buried his face in his hands. His back ached, and his muscles trembled. How much longer could he do this? And just where was Chief Dunlap? Didn't he know that his town was under attack? Heaving a sob, Hob looked out across the plaza, where hundreds of Holloway citizens—his friends and neighbors—were tending to each other's wounds, their cries filling the air.

Cameron, I sure as hell hope you stopped those sons of bitches. He heard sirens, faint at first, but growing steadily louder, until a police cruiser came barreling over the hill and into the plaza. With a tired smile, Hob closed his eyes and whispered a quiet prayer.

Dunlap's cruiser tore along Bard Street with the force of a bullet firing. He'd gotten a call from longtime acquaintance Julia Wyatt, who had called him from outside the Calliope. Sobbing hysterically, she'd demanded that he come to the music hall. Something terrible had happened.

He knew he should have expected it—as soon as those horrid flyers had announced anything to do with those strange musicians, Dunlap knew he should have enlisted more backup for the night.

Dunlap cleared the hilltop, the tires of his cruiser leaving the ground for a few seconds before slamming back down again, causing the undercarriage to belch out sparks and Bentley to nearly bite his tongue beside him. Upon entering the Calliope's plaza, the chief got his first view of what they were in for.

Hundreds of people had gathered outside the auditorium. Panicked and traumatized, they leaned against each other on the steps or wandered the plaza, and others lay sprawled on the grass. Everywhere Dunlap looked, he saw weeping faces, hands covering ears, and clothing soaked in blood. It looked like the aftermath of a brutal battle.

"Chief," Bentley said in a quivering voice. "What the hell happened here?"

"I don't know," Dunlap admitted. He continued to nose the cruiser across the plaza until he reached the Calliope's front steps. The plaza echoed with screams and wailing sobs. "But Bloom's behind this. I bet my life on it."

Stuff like this happened in big cities like New York and Washington, DC. It didn't happen here in Holloway.

"I need you to get on the radio," Dunlap said. "You tell Kelley we need immediate backup." He shook his head. How had he let it fall apart like this? This was his town, under his protection. "I want the whole unit out here. Bert, Beaumont, Dewey—I mean everyone. Then I want you to call up to Willow Wood County and then Nashville. Tell 'em we've got a potential terrorist attack. That should get their attention."

Bentley gave him an astonished look. "A terrorist attack? Jeez, Chief. You don't really believe that, do you?"

"Well, what else would you call this?" Dunlap leaned forward and looked over the steering wheel. He recognized half the people out there. "Well, go on, Bent. What the hell you waiting for?"

The moment Bentley began calling into his radio, someone rapped on Dunlap's window, startling him. Clenching his teeth, Dunlap looked to find a brown-skinned face pressed against the glass, eyes wide.

"Hob?" Dunlap rolled down the window and looked at the man. Hob looked old and tired, and sweat dripped down the sides of his face. Dunlap was glad to see him. "What happened in there?"

Hob shook his head, panting heavily. His shirt was stained with blood, but he didn't look injured. "A lot of people are dead in there, Chief. I done what I could. Pulled a few out from the lobby—the ones who were still conscious. But I didn't go in the auditorium. That's where it started."

"Where what started?"

"It was Bloom. Bloom and his musicians. They did this—their music did this. Don't know how and don't know why. But it happened." Hob shook his head, and then a sad, wistful look overcame him. "It's awful, Chief. I ain't never seen somethin' so awful."

Frowning, Dunlap shook his head slowly, not believing a word of it. Music—no matter how loud or how awful—didn't leave people crippled and bleeding. There had to be a better explanation. But none of that mattered now; he had to get the situation under control. That meant taking down Bloom and his musicians until they could sort this all out.

"Hob, I need you to keep helping out," said Dunlap. "We're gonna need all the help we can get until my backup gets here."

With a whistle, Hob just shook his head. "It's like the end of the world in there."

"Just do what you can."

Nodding, Hob backed away from the cruiser, and Dunlap sat back in his seat with a heavy sigh. Nothing made a bit of sense anymore. *Did this with music, my ass,* thought Dunlap. The old janitor was just confused. But then, hadn't his prisoners said something similar about the night the men and Carrie Belle had lost control? That no-eared man . . . hadn't each of his prisoners accused Simon of something similar?

Bentley yelled into his radio and threw it on the dashboard with a disgusted throaty sound. "Something's wrong, Chief. I can't get dispatch to pick up. So I called Beaumont. He tried to tell me he's off-duty tonight. You believe that asshole?"

Dunlap grimaced. He hated the thought of going inside that musical madhouse without any backup, but they couldn't just sit here and wait. "Let's go. You get Bert and Fiskell and the boys from Willow Wood here, no excuses. We're going in."

Once outside, Dunlap and Bentley moved around to the front of the cruiser and stood in the beams of the headlights. Dunlap could see the bodies of wounded people on the grass better now, the headlights washing out all but red and black on the grisly scene. Sirens wailed in the distance.

"Chief," said Bentley. "Take a look at that."

Dunlap followed Bentley's pointed finger to the Calliope's front doors. Bloom stood at the top step with his arms folded over his chest, his eyes black and gleaming as he stared down at the officers.

"Chief Dunlap, you're just in time," Bloom called, his handsome smile contradicting the carnage before him. "The show has only just begun."

The backstage doors slammed open and a man wheeled a flatbed cart out onto the stage. A group of men quickly began loading the piano. It took at least six of them to do it. Meanwhile, Lutz and Oppenheim wrapped Cameron's wrists in coarse rope and then shoved him toward the backstage door. Soon the Dragon, hoisted onto the cart, went rolling past them, and Lutz shoved Cameron to hurry him along. Cameron's knees were weak, and he would have gone sprawling onto his face had Christofori not caught him by his shirt collar.

"Dear, dear, is our Tone Poet too weak to walk?" asked the pianist, his eyes flashing with anger. He clapped one hand on the nape of Cameron's neck and pulled him forward so that their foreheads nearly touched. "It seems unjust, doesn't it, that the universe should bestow such hardships on us?" His voice dripped in patronizing humor. "But we will get ours, won't we? We will teach the universe a lesson, and just think, you can take all the blame." He leaned even closer and whispered, "If you survive tonight's Symphony, I will kill you for what you did to me. Mark my words."

He drove his fist into Cameron's gut, and Cameron dropped to his knees, air rushing from his lungs. His ears rang as he struggled to catch his breath. Above him, Oppenheim stepped forward to shove Christofori away.

"For Christ's sake, Christofori!" Oppenheim shouted. "Maestro Bloom said to take care of him. He's not to be touched. You know this!"

Scowling, Christofori took one last look at Cameron and spat into his face before turning away and following the piano through the backstage doors.

"On your feet now," said Oppenheim as he grabbed one of Cameron's arms.

Chortling, Lutz came over and offered a hand. Soon Cameron was on his feet.

"You shouldn't piss him off like that," Lutz said, laughing quietly. "Christofori's a goddamn lunatic. I've seen him do horrible things to people—things you wouldn't believe."

"Enough talk," Oppenheim hissed. "We've got to get this son of a bitch downstairs before Maestro Bloom comes back."

"You mean if he comes back," Lutz said under his breath.

"Oh, he'll be back," Oppenheim said without a hint of uncertainty. "It would take more than Holloway's policemen to keep the maestro from playing his Symphony."

As the two men talked, they shoved Cameron along, forcing him to follow the piano as it was rolled through the backstage door. Cameron listened with only half an ear as he looked back over one shoulder at the auditorium and all those lifeless bodies, faces frozen in terror, seeming to stare at him from every direction. He felt sick with grief and knew that he would never forget this moment for as long as he lived; but then, he had a feeling that his life was approaching its end. Maybe that wasn't such a bad thing.

Once through the doors and into the corridors, Cameron was carried along by the entourage of musicians. As they moved deeper into the Calliope, their numbers grew as more and more Echoes came out from wherever they'd been hiding. By the time they reached the elevator at the end of the main corridor, the narrow passageway was crowded with musicians. This made getting the piano into the elevator a difficult chore. Several shouts went out, insisting that the musicians take the stairs, and soon the crowd began to thin out.

After the piano was loaded, Cameron's captors forced him into the elevator and then pulled the gate shut. Strangely, he didn't feel much of anything as the elevator shivered and whirred in its descent. With his head aching and his mind numb from shock, all Cameron really wanted was for this to end, even if that meant death. After all, so many people had died because of him, including Madison, and he had nothing left to live for. He couldn't help but think that Christofori was right. The universe had dealt him a cruel hand.

"But we will get ours, won't we?" Christofori had said. "We will teach the universe a lesson."

Cameron didn't know what to think about this. Kalek had warned him of divine trespass.

When the elevator stopped, Lutz threw the gate open and ushered Cameron out into the basement, where a crowd of musicians waited for them. They were now moving quietly across the chamber toward the strange instruments that shimmered beneath the blue lights. When Cameron heard squeaking wheels, he moved out of the way just in time to avoid being crushed by the piano as it rolled past on its flatbed cart.

With so many people about, no one seemed too concerned about Cameron escaping. He had a brief moment to himself in which he stared up at the ceiling, praying that something would go wrong up there. He doubted the Holloway PD had more than a few handfuls of men, but they had guns, and Bloom—as far as he knew—didn't. Still, he'd seen Bloom conjure real magic, and something told him that he hadn't seen the half of it.

Sighing tiredly, Cameron looked over to the ring of instruments, where many of the musicians had already taken their seats. *There's still a chance*, he thought. *Maybe they'll stop him, and then I won't have to do this.*

At this point, he had a strong sense that if they did perform Armonia, they'd end up pissing off the whole universe.

Chapter 11

Standing on the Calliope's top step, Maestro Bloom looked grim, an arbiter of death, his face like chiseled white marble, eyes dark with shadows.

Dunlap drew a shaky breath. He'd never feared the man in the past, but tonight Bloom struck him as something unnatural. Something cold.

Someone moved to his left. Dunlap risked a quick glance to find Hob nearby, rising up from a crouch, his eyes wide with fear.

"You be careful with him," said Hob. "He ain't normal. He can do things."

Do things? Dunlap frowned, his stomach aching. *What the hell was that supposed to mean?* "Bent?" he called over the cruiser's rooftop.

Bent looked at him, shrugged. Then everything changed.

A sudden skirl filled the air as a squad of police cruisers rushed into the plaza, sirens blaring, lights painting the Calliope's facade. A fire engine and an ambulance followed in their wake. In moments, two patrol cars stamped with Willow Wood PD swung into position to the left and right of Dunlap's cruiser. Bentley threw a fist in the air, shouting triumphantly, and Dunlap grinned. *It's about goddamn time.* He dropped his hand to his holster, unsnapped the leather strap, and drew his gun.

"Hold it right there, Bloom!" He raised his revolver and pinned Bloom in his sights. "If I don't see your hands in the next five seconds, I'm putting a bullet between your eyes!"

A grin touched the corners of Bloom's mouth. "As you wish, Chief."

The maestro held his hands out, palms turned upwards, like Christ showing his wounds. His hands rose above his head, a gesture natural for a conductor. In response to this motion, the sirens atop Dunlap's cruiser gave a wild, electronic shriek, impossibly loud. The chief spun, covering his ears. His eyes went from the cruiser's light bar, flashing with unnatural intensity, to Washington Hob, who looked at him with eyes that said *I told you so.* With a final pivot, Dunlap found Bentley on the opposite side of the cruiser, eyes wide, hands clamped to the sides of his head.

Something's wrong here, Dunlap thought. *Those sirens aren't supposed to make a noise like that.*

His cruiser's malfunction spread to the neighboring vehicles, causing their sirens to blare unmercifully. The noise became louder as more emergency vehicles spilled into the plaza. Dunlap clenched his teeth against the assault on his ears. The noise scrambled his vision, blurred his thoughts, shook his bowels. He turned in a circle, watching the people he'd come to help hurry away, silhouetted forms hunkering against the unbearable sound.

Bloom was now standing with his arms raised in a V, hands upturned, quivering. His fingers curled, as if summoning sound from the Calliope's long history of sound. Dunlap shook with sudden anger. His ears ached with a sharp pain. *Lord help me. He's doing this. Somehow he's gained control of the sirens.*

The Calliope seemed to magnify the mighty howl of noise.

The chief pulled the trigger. His gun recoiled, belched smoke. No blast. The bullet struck the conductor in the chest, spinning him back toward the Calliope's front doors, arms flailing. Dunlap held his breath, watching. Then he shrank back as Bloom drew himself up, face drawn in a mask of angry surprise. He glowered down at Dunlap with bald hatred, his teeth bared in an animal snarl.

He's not human, Dunlap thought.

The sirens continued wailing. Dunlap considered shooting Bloom again, but his ears were ringing, hurting terribly, and he didn't think the maestro would go down, not even with two bullets in him. Thankfully he never had to take the second shot. After a final warning glance, the maestro flexed his shoulders back, tugged at the lapels of his suit jacket, then turned away to disappear into the auditorium's doors.

The sirens died and a muffled silence fell over the plaza.

The strength went out of Dunlap's legs. He dropped to his knees, swayed. His ear drums rang like fire alarms. He looked to his left and right, finding people rolling on the ground, hands clenched to their ears. Near the front bumper he found Bentley on all fours, the sides of his face doused in blood.

"Bentley?" Dunlap made a sour face. He couldn't hear his voice over the clattering bells in his ears. Bentley didn't even look up at him. *He can't hear me either. Oh, Jesus, I think we're hurt bad.*

Light-headed, Dunlap sat on the bumper of his cruiser. He surveyed the plaza, taking note of the scattered victims, their frightened faces. Had he still had his hearing, he suspected he would have heard a chorus of miserable sobs. His gaze settled on a little girl in a white dress, standing all by herself, sobbing. Dunlap looked away. *Christ help us.* He touched his ears and brought his fingers in front of his eyes; they were covered in blood.

The car rocked as Bentley sat on the hood beside him. The two men looked at each other, neither trying to speak. Dunlap's gaze went to the Calliope's bottom step, where Hob sat with his elbows on his knees, looking dazedly at the ground. He had been closer to the Calliope, and the tonal assault had hurt him deeply, both physically and on a spiritual level.

Dunlap swallowed his confusion. *What is happening to my town?*

He turned his gaze beyond his cruiser, where patrol cars and emergency vehicles all sat with their sirens flashing quietly, their doors open, left abandoned, while most of the officers and paramedics sat on the ground with their hands gripping their ears. When his eyes returned to Bentley, he found the young man close to tears.

I know, Bent. I know, he agreed silently. Those sirens had done something terrible. He suspected the damage was permanent. It broke his heart to think he'd never hear his wife laugh again, or listen to his favorite Hank Williams song on the radio. Bloom had crippled him and probably everyone else out here in the plaza.

But this was not the time for a pity party. The town needed him. And someone had to stop Bloom.

Moments later, Dunlap and Bentley entered the foyer, where bodies were strewn across the floor. Dunlap looked at the auditorium doors across the way and thought, *My God, how many more on the other side of that door?* His knees trembled at the thought of what he might find in there. These were his people—people he'd sworn to protect and serve. He'd failed them all, and for the life of him, he didn't think he had the courage to see the massacre that awaited him.

With his revolver now gripped in two fists, he started across the foyer with Bentley at his side, both wary. They crossed the lobby, careful not to step on the corpses that littered their path. Dunlap avoided looking at their faces, afraid he might recognize someone he knew. He couldn't handle that right now. It was best to keep his distance from the truth, that his friends and family were here among the dead.

They paused when they reached the auditorium doors, and Dunlap looked his sergeant in the eye. Talking at this point was out of the question as neither of them could hear much past the ringing. But this didn't matter much; the odor of death and doom was all around them, like they'd been sealed up in a morgue.

He could read Bentley's eyes just as well as Bent could read his, and Dunlap had only two things to convey; he did that with a mere look, one that said, *It's been good serving with you, buddy. Now let's get in there and kill this son of a bitch.*

Then Dunlap kicked open one of the swinging doors and stepped inside, and Bentley followed close at his heels.

"They're coming!" shouted Lutz as the elevator's mechanisms made their whirring hum. Moments later, the car arrived with a clang. Oppenheim rushed over and opened the gates.

With his hands tied behind his back and Lutz holding him by the elbow, Cameron could only watch as the last of the musicians stepped out of the lift. Maestro Bloom led the way. Following him were Eris and Christofori. When Simon hobbled out of the lift, wearing a dirty suit and a dim expression, Cameron went rigid with anger.

"I want those doors barred!" Bloom shouted, his voice echoing throughout the chamber. "We won't have long. There can be no interruptions." Then, just before Bloom marched away toward his instruments, he gave Cameron an appraising look and said, "It's time, Cameron. The stage is set, and we have a Symphony to perform."

Before Cameron could fire back, Lutz and Oppenheim grabbed his arms and carried him forward, hefting his weight so that only his toes touched the ground. They soon passed through the belt of instruments and then into the clearing at the formation's center. Bloom waited for them and then led the way to the massive circular Lyre standing on the opposite side of the clearing. The machine was awash in azure light and seemed to hover ten feet in the air.

Panic clawed at Cameron's chest as he looked at the Lyre. To his reeling mind, it seemed alive; did the light shimmer on its scales with a sudden contraction? Did its snakehead choke down more of its own tail? But as they carried him closer, Cameron saw that it was only a machine, designed to accommodate a man to stand inside it. There were narrow stairs that curled up and around its base and even handholds set within the upper inside walls of its frame.

"The Lyre will transform you into a living composition," Bloom said calmly as the men brought Cameron closer. "Surely, a man who has composed all his life must find this extraordinary."

"Don't do this to me!" Cameron pleaded. It all became very clear to him now. His lifelong quest to capture Astral Music had been inherently destructive. What he'd wanted did not belong to him. "This is a mistake! Don't you see that?"

"This is fate," Bloom replied. "Can't *you* see *that*?"

Metal glinted as Bloom raised a hand to show a tuning fork pinched between thumb and forefinger. Cameron went rigid with sudden understanding: Bloom meant to entrance him. Still, he could do nothing as Bloom tapped a small rod against the prongs of the Tongue, and when it rang its delirious high-pitched squeal, Cameron cried out as the dark noise infiltrated his ears.

Nightmare visions flashed across his mind's eye. He saw Madison's face, her skin like hardened wax, her lips a bruised color in death. He saw the bodies that scattered along the upstairs auditorium floor, and the Oppari feeding on them. It went on and on, random images of blood and gore and destruction, and somewhere far away, he felt hands ripping away his clothes.

When he blinked his eyes open, he found himself standing high above the chamber floor. Overcome with sudden vertigo, he swayed and nearly fell, but someone standing just below him grabbed his lower leg and helped him find his balance.

"Careful now," came Lutz's recognizably German voice. "You're in the Lyre, and unless you want to fall and hurt yourself, you'd best take it slow and easy."

He was indeed standing inside the Lyre; its massive black frame formed a perfect ring around him. He stood on a plate mounted to its base, and from this height he had a panoramic view of the Calliope's vast basement and the orchestra, seated in their ring formation, spread out before him. Somehow the Echoes had gotten him up here while he'd been unconscious. They'd even stripped him down to his boxer shorts, and now the chilly air made his skin bristle.

Directly below him, Bloom stood alone, watching him quietly with his hands folded behind him.

"Look above you," said Lutz, and this time Cameron located the man just below and to the left of him, standing on the Lyre's steps. "There are handholds up there. Grab them before you fall and hurt yourself."

When Cameron hesitated, Bloom called up to him. "Listen to the man, Cameron. A fall from that height could break your neck. And you're going to do this for me whether your spine is broken or not."

With a heavy sigh, Cameron made a quick survey of the Lyre's inner frame. Leather straps were bolted at the ten and two o'clock positions and there were footholds at five and seven o'clock. Obviously, if someone wanted to use the Lyre, he'd have to splay himself spread-eagled within the circle, like da Vinci's Vitruvian Man. What happened after that point was anyone's guess; the prospect terrified him. But it was pointless to resist Bloom; Cameron barely had the strength to stand, much less attempt an escape.

Something about his doom being inescapable sent a calm over him. He felt his prickly flesh smoothen, his knees stop shaking. Even his heartbeat stopped jack-hammering. He couldn't control his immediate—and brief—future, but it was still his future.

He took a ragged breath and let the oxygen fortify him, fill him with direction. He did as he was told and reached out and grabbed the first strap, then hopped a little so that he could reach the second strap. For a breathless moment, he dangled within the Lyre's frame like a gymnast hanging from still rings as he searched his feet for the footholds. When he finally found his footing, he kept himself in place by stretching every muscle so that his entire body formed a kind of X, like a man in a giant wheel, preparing to go rolling down a hillside with it.

Cold bands of panic squeezed his stomach as he adjusted his grip on the leather handholds and waited. Panting, he looked down and found Bloom staring up at him.

"What do I do now?" he called out.

"Be still," said Bloom quietly. "You will know what to do."

Spread-eagled inside the machine, Cameron's skin crawled when the Lyre began humming as if by some inner motor. The hairs on his body stood erect as the air all around him became an electrically charged field. Then came a sudden snap, followed by an airy hiss, as silver wires sprung from the Lyre's inner frame and pierced his sides. He cried out as his torso erupted in white-hot fire. His legs buckled, and he would have fallen if not for his death grip on the overhead handgrips. Gaping, he looked down to find himself the hub of a few hundred silver threads. The Lyre had strung him through like a human instrument.

"Christ!" Cameron shouted as dark blossoms spread across his vision. His head lolled as a dreadful moan escaped him. He dropped his gaze to find Bloom, standing below him and appraising him like a work of art. Gasping for air, Cameron blinked the sweat from his eyes and said, "What did you do to me?"

"I'm afraid there's nothing to be done about the pain," Bloom called up. "The Lyre must pierce the flesh before it can pierce the soul."

Indeed, the pain came in flashes, transcending the boundaries of his nervous system. Cameron gnashed his teeth against it and somehow managed to stay conscious.

Releasing one of the handgrips, he reached down and gently touched one of the wires. This in turn caused a muted vibration to travel deep into his side. How far had the wires penetrated him? He didn't know, but one thing was certain: he was as caught as a fly in a spiderweb. "It hurts, goddamn it!"

"I apologize for that," Bloom said. "But I assure you, in just a few moments, you won't feel a thing."

The conductor turned his back on Cameron and headed to his platform some twenty feet away. When he reached the platform, he climbed the tiers to the top plane, where he pivoted in a slow circle to assess his musicians. He stopped when he faced Cameron.

"This orchestra has suffered long enough," Bloom said in an expansive voice that echoed throughout the large basement. "God has turned a deaf ear to our misery. But tonight we will be heard. Tonight our suffering ends!"

Rapt applause rose from the orchestra, and Bloom raised his hands to encourage it. The ovation lasted several moments before he ended it with a curt motion of his hand. A grin flashed across the maestro's face, and his eyes glowed like twin moons as he regarded Cameron.

"It is time to realize your full potential, Cameron," said Bloom.

"Go to hell!" Cameron called back.

"On the contrary," Bloom returned. "After tonight, we will never know Hell again. Tonight we free ourselves from it."

The maestro snapped into a position of attention, with his heels together and his arms at his sides; the surrounding musicians readied their instruments. When Bloom slowly raised his hands toward the ceiling with his palms turned upward, several disparate notes ripped free of their respective instruments and went bounding off into space. At the same time, a warm rush of air stirred, causing the maestro's jacket to ruffle and flap about him as if he stood in the path of an oncoming tornado.

The concert was beginning.

Cameron felt it too. The Lyre was responding. Its strings resonated as if individually plucked, sending little vibrations throughout his body. A low buzzing noise filled his head, causing his teeth to chatter. Curiously, he felt himself expanding, and the sensation was not at all unpleasant; in a way, it numbed his pain and cleared his mind, leaving him feeling at once satiated and fit to burst.

But his exhilaration lasted only a moment before he felt the abhorrent intrusion of another mind. Bloom had somehow gotten inside his head and was plowing his way through Cameron's memories like a man forging a path through a cluttered garage. Fortunately, it didn't take Bloom long before he found what he needed. Just as Cameron guessed, the conductor had set his search on a specific memory, and once he found it, he forced it to the forefront of Cameron's consciousness.

Suddenly, Cameron found himself in a familiar dreamscape. It was the morning of the twenty-second day of July 1984.

Awakened by the sound of tires spinning beneath him, Cameron sat up in his seat, puzzled. Hours ago, he'd gone to sleep in his own bed, only to wake up in the backseat of his dad's car. It was so early that the sun hadn't even come up yet. Up front, the radio glowed green, and a quiet song drifted from the speakers. His mother, lying back in the passenger seat, noticed him and put a hand on his knee.

"It's going to be okay, Cameron," she said. "You just wait and see. God has something special planned for you."

He closely scrutinized his mother's face, paying careful attention to the creases that framed her mouth and eyes, and the freckles that dotted her cheeks, the way her hair fell gently about her brow. It was just a memory, he knew, but his memory had never been clearer, and for one moment, he had his mother again, and the knowledge of her loss broke his heart. He reached out to touch her face when time slowed down. The windows exploded inward, showering them all with popcorn-sized chunks of glass. Tires shrieked and the car spun in dizzying circles. Through it all, his mother's eyes never once left his, and her voice, only a whisper now, echoed in his mind.

"God has something special planned for you."

The car rolled, and Cameron felt the blinding pain of several snapping bones as his tiny body slammed against metal and hard plastic. One particular collision dislodged his mind from his own body, and for a moment he free-floated high above the accident, where the Toyota lay on its roof in a ditch. Cameron didn't linger. He shot upward into the pastel colors of the morning sky, heading toward the stars. But before he reached them, the sky peeled open, and he flew into a sea of white light.

And music flooded over him.

Somewhere far away, a conscious thought surfaced: after a lifetime of waiting, here was again the sound of the universe. Cameron had it in his awareness, grasped in clear thought. Only this time, his reception was unhindered by the confusion of a dream. And he took it in greedily. Armonia was everything that he remembered; it had a visceral and deeply personal quality about it. Like a whale song, born out of glassy vibrations and wind chimes caught in an ethereal breeze, the music flowed with the freedom of running water. While melodies blossomed from time to time, they just as quickly disappeared. It was certainly the most beautiful arrangement of sounds Cameron had ever heard, and it moved him so deeply that he half laughed, half sobbed.

This music was somehow his music, his personal interpretation of the audible life stream of the universe, his individual riff on the Divine Symphony. To another set of ears, another mind, the music would have been entirely different. But this . . . this was *his* music.

Something jerked him from his thoughts. He blinked his eyes open to find the orchestra in full swing and the music from his dream echoing throughout the Calliope's basement. Formed by a hodgepodge of disparate sounds, the music was nearly incomprehensible. But here and there, snatches of music emerged, and they sounded so familiar that it filled Cameron with growing certainty that the orchestra was actually doing it. They were giving sound to a music that had existed, until now, as something secret. Something silent.

Bloom continued to conduct from his raised platform while the musicians worked without written notation. The trick of the Symphony quickly became obvious to Cameron: the Lyre allowed for a peculiar exchange to take place between him and the conductor. Not only did the machine tap Cameron's memory of Armonia, but it also projected the memory to the conductor, who then disseminated the music, note-by-note, to those surrounding musicians.

The process had a peculiar effect on Bloom. His hands and face glowed like white-hot phosphorus, a result of having gorged himself on whatever vital force he'd taken from Cameron. Then there followed a violent whoosh as ropes of light shot out from Bloom in all directions, connecting him with each man and woman in his orchestra. From Cameron's point of view, the conjoined orchestra looked like a giant wheel with its spokes meeting at Bloom, who stood at its hub.

The music shook the walls as it swelled with the weight of a tidal wave. But just before the crescendo, the musicians drew back, and what emerged was a quiet melody, like a child's lullaby, so familiar to Cameron that it drew tears from his eyes. He knew this song. It was his song, the resonance of his own heart. Hadn't his mother sung this melody to him when he was just a baby in her arms?

This final turn of events calmed him, and rather than resist, he gave himself to it. The feeling was liberating, and he felt himself slipping. When he opened his mouth to inhale, his lungs refused the air. He could feel his life force rushing out of him along the strings of the Lyre like electrical impulses along a telephone wire. Death was near.

Across the way, maybe twenty feet above Bloom's upraised hands, a sphere of light blossomed. It looked like a hole, as if they'd punctured the very fabric of reality, and it sputtered like a flame. With his arms spread open, Bloom looked up, allowing the light to flicker down on his face, and then he hurried down from the platform.

He was just in time. The moment he walked away, the Symphony reached its crescendo, and the point of light exploded with fierce intensity.

Shuddering in the Lyre's strings, Cameron cried out. Distantly, he noticed that the Symphony had stopped. For a long while, he was afraid to open his eyes, sensing that his surroundings had dramatically altered. But there was no hiding from the present moment, and he eventually forced himself to look.

What he saw broke his heart.

The coppery, visceral smell of blood was overpowering in the open expanse of the auditorium. It was dark in here, and what faint light expanded beyond the stage revealed more than Dunlap wanted to see. Hundreds had failed to escape Bloom's massacre. There were bodies in the pews and more heaped in the aisles. There were few survivors amid the carnage, but he detected movement here and there. Hands reached for him from mountains of flesh; blood spilled from the balcony.

It was worse than Dunlap had imagined. Shaking his head, he gazed at the stage. The musicians had cleaned up after themselves, taking with them any instruments they might have had. *Bloom's orchestra must have given the people one hell of a show.*

Something caught his eye. Bentley, just a silhouette, had gone on ahead and was now climbing the stage steps.

Dunlap trudged angrily down the aisle, trying not to step on the bodies strewn in his path. He finally reached the stage and looked toward the back curtains just as they parted and a young man stepped out. Dunlap almost didn't recognize Charlie Witt. The boy had aged at least ten years since the last time they'd talked. *Jesus Christ, what's happened to him?*

To his surprise, Charlie answered.

"Isn't it obvious? I found God." A cool, nasty grin spread wide across Charlie's face.

His voice rang so clearly that the chief thought he'd regained his hearing. But no, this was just a trick. Charlie somehow projected his thoughts; the boy's voice existed exclusively in Dunlap's head.

Charlie spread his hands. "Maestro Bloom has shown me wonderful things, Chief."

Just then, long tentacles slithered out from beneath the hem of the stage curtain. Colorless and oozing, they moved with fluid ease across the floor until gathering at Charlie's dirty sneakers, where they twisted, writhed, and curled about each other. Soon they covered a large portion of the stage floor.

Nearly paralyzed with horror, Dunlap grabbed Bentley by the arm and spun him around to face Charlie. Bentley jumped about a foot before taking aim at the boy. Dunlap did the same, but then hesitated. Those writhing, looping worms of Charlie's were tumbling across the stage, moving closer to the two officers.

Dunlap gagged. They reminded him of cow guts, of which he'd seen plenty when his daddy had owned half a dozen cattle. These worms looked similar, except cow guts didn't writhe and flail about like severed power lines. Bill Atwater and his slaughtered and gutted cows sprang to mind.

The fleshy worms were almost at their feet when Bentley opened fire. Splinters burst from the stage, and Dunlap felt rather than heard the shots. A few of the wounded creatures curled into constricted knots, but the others came without hesitation and soon blanketed the stage floor. Dunlap followed Bentley's lead and fired into them.

Something caused Bentley to jump suddenly and then hop on one foot while shaking the other boot. One of the worms had coiled itself about Bentley's ankle. Its tail whipped and lashed at the air as Bentley tried to shake it free. The worm disappeared up the sergeant's pant leg. A look of sheer horror twisted Bentley's face before he dropped to his knees.

Lightning quick, the worms curled around his arms and throat. One of the tentacles even lunged into the young man's gaping mouth. It disappeared down his throat.

Shaking with horror, Dunlap felt something cold and sticky slip beneath the cuff of his pant leg and tighten around his ankle. He hopped frantically on one foot as the wormy body made its way up his leg. He looked to Charlie for help.

The boy only watched with his arms folded over his chest and a crooked grin slashed across his face.

A great surge of anger ripped through Dunlap's mind. The kid was controlling the worms. Something bit into Dunlap's leg. He gritted his teeth, pointed his gun at Charlie's chest, and pulled the trigger.

He felt the recoil of his pistol and heard its muffled pop deep inside his head. Charlie staggered, blank-faced, as he gripped his chest over a rose-colored stain.

Charlie looked at him, dumbfounded, then dropped to the floor.

Dunlap felt a stab of guilt, but then the air was pushed from his lungs.

A hellish pain twisted down his spine as a worm slipped silently around his neck and squeezed tight. He gasped in pain, and the moment he opened his mouth to shout, a worm forced itself down his throat. The thing was cold and clammy and smelled rotten. It tasted like salt, like blood.

Frightened, Dunlap jerked at the creature with both hands, but its slippery length made it impossible for him to get a good grip. The worm seemed never-ending as it slipped rapidly through his hands, between his teeth, and down the length of his throat. The worst part was that he could feel it gathering in his belly.

It's inside of me! Oh Christ, it's inside of me!

The last of the tentacle slipped through his grip and disappeared down his throat. The feeling in his gut was overwhelming. He jerked his shirt up and looked down at his belly, swollen like a balloon, the flesh rolling as things pressed against it from the other side. The worm was alive, moving inside of him.

Dunlap flailed for his gun, and when he touched the cold barrel, he scooped it up and cocked the hammer.

God forgive me, he thought. He shoved the barrel of his gun into his mouth and pulled the trigger.

Chapter 12

Following a silent belch of light, the room vanished around Cameron. The walls, ceiling, and floor dissolved into a bright white light, leaving the orchestra afloat in a field of milky iridescence. But this was only a minor detail. What drew Cameron's attention—what absolutely enthralled him— was the massive shaft of light rising up through the center of the orchestra where Bloom had stood only moments earlier.

From his fixed position within the Lyre, he watched all this in wide-eyed understanding. His mouth quivered and tears ran down his face. The horrors of the past few days dissolved, and for the first time since his childhood, his heart ached with utter fascination.

I knew it. I've always known.

Without a floor or ceiling to limit his view, Cameron could trace the beam for miles and miles in either direction, as if stretching unendingly along the vertical axis of infinity. The thing was alive, moving with currents, humming a silvery whir, like some unfathomable glass harmonica. This was Armonia, the harmonic center of all things, and within that great stretch of vertical light was the mind of God.

It's real, he thought. *We found it. We found God. And He knows we're here.*

Bewildered, he turned his attention to the musicians. Most of them were still seated in their chairs and floated adrift without breaking formation, like a wheel revolving about an axle. Without a floor to sustain them, the formation should have collapsed, releasing each musician to the whim of oblivion. And yet the orchestra held; the musicians kept their places with quiet assurance. Even those who stood kept their footing, though they had nothing to stand on. Was it all an illusion then? Was the material world closer than it appeared?

Yes, thought Cameron. *Of course it is.*

Beyond all reason, the orchestra had thrown aside the veil of the physical universe, and as a result, they'd been transported to an in-between place that straddled the Calliope's basement and a realm of immateriality. The floor—even the ceiling and walls—were all here, only they had become transparent.

Again Cameron looked at the Light. Being this close to Armonia caused his spirit to hum in sympathy like a reed in the wind. Even in the midst of all the horror, with the Lyre's strings piercing his sides, he felt a kind of transcendental bliss, a feeling of connectedness to the Light. It was not an entirely unfamiliar feeling. He'd caught glimpses of it throughout his life, during moments of deep calm, or discovering some new melody on his piano, or falling in love. He'd even caught glimpses of it while suffering the loss of his family.

But those had been fleeting moments of enlightenment. This was much more potent, and his soul gave the equivalent of a great, heaving sigh of relief.

I've been lost all my life, he thought, *and this . . . this feels like coming home.*

For a brief time, as he basked in Armonia's harmonic pulses, he forgot all about the orchestra, or Bloom, or the dead that littered the Calliope's auditorium, or the consequences that would surely follow. Only Armonia mattered, and as he resonated with it, the thing yielded revelation after revelation. He knew things about it: its gentle nature, its purity and innocence, its fragility and vulnerability, its overwhelming love and perfection. Moreover, he understood his own relationship with it. Somehow, he was part of Armonia, just as it was part of him.

"All this time You were right here," he whispered, and then an age-old pang clutched his chest, stirring up feelings of anger and despair. "Why didn't You save them? Why did You take my family from me? How could You do that to me?"

Far below him, a shadow moved closer, and he looked down to find Maestro Bloom walking as if on thin air as he made his way to the Lyre.

"Beautiful, isn't it, Cameron?" said Bloom, his voice traveling with ease, somehow unhindered by the glassy whir that rose all around them. He stopped ten feet from the base of the Lyre and looked up. The two men quietly regarded each other for a moment before the maestro turned around and stared at the Light. "The harmonic center of all things. Mankind has sought a connection with Armonia from the moment of our creation."

"We shouldn't be here," Cameron said.

"Why not? Look at what we've achieved. We've done what man has always dreamed of doing. We've found God; we've bridged the gap between man and his Creator—between the physical expression and that which expresses itself. You should be proud of this, Cameron. We are among only a few who have entered the gates of Heaven in this form of flesh and blood. And you helped us get here."

"We're trespassing on sacred ground," Cameron said, incapable of drawing his eyes away from the naked column of Light and sound, even when he knew he should. "Just by standing here we're tainting it. We'll spoil everything."

As if he hadn't heard a word from Cameron, Bloom turned to look up at him. "Do you feel that? The Overtone resonates in the heart of all living things. It is something that all men sense, whether conscious of it or not."

Cameron nodded slowly. He felt it. He'd always felt it.

"The ones who truly suffer are those who can't hear it anymore," Bloom went on, "but even they are only deluded. All souls resonate in some capacity with the eternal vibrations. That is, of course, unless they themselves sever the connection. It is a rare act, indeed, but it is possible, as this orchestra has proven. And you can imagine the depth of suffering that accompanies this disconnection."

"You did it to yourselves," Cameron reminded him.

Bloom offered a sad smile. "I won't refute that. What we did was wrong. But are we to suffer our crimes for an eternity? Are we to live in this perpetual hell without even death to set us free?" The man shook his head and his eyes became black holes. "We are tired of the dark. We want light again. We want to rejoin the Divine Symphony." He dropped his gaze and added in a low voice, "So you will understand why we have to do this."

"Have to do what?" Cameron said.

But Bloom turned his back on him, and at that moment the circle of musicians rose from their chairs, cast aside their instruments, and started toward the column of Light.

Cameron shook his head with sudden understanding. They meant to merge themselves with it, with the Godhead. But Armonia was the pure and unblemished heart of all things, and this intrusion would have an effect akin to injecting battery acid into the arm of a newborn child. Suddenly, the stakes had skyrocketed; the orchestra's trespass had greater consequences than he had ever imagined.

"Wait a minute!" Cameron shouted as Bloom walked away from him to join the others. "You're wrong about this! It won't work!"

Bloom walked on ahead. He barked commands at his musicians, reminding them to wait for him before they made their next move.

"It's not meant to be touched by human hands!" Cameron shouted and inadvertently jerked his body, causing the wires to tug at his sides and send razor-sharp pains into his torso. Fresh bouts of blood spilled from the points where the wires pierced him. "You'll poison it! You'll poison the wellspring! Don't you understand that?"

This earned him an impatient backwards glance from Bloom, who didn't even stop to answer him. "Armonia will Attune our souls. Our suffering ends here tonight."

"But you'll kill it!"

This stopped Bloom in mid-stride. He swung around to look at Cameron and then spread his arms out in an expansive shrug. "Then we die together!" he called back. "What do we have to lose?"

What transpired appeared to be a carefully rehearsed ceremony. Rather than walk directly into Armonia, as Cameron had feared, the Echoes instead formed a ring by holding hands around the column of Light, like pagans about a ceremonial pyre, while Bloom strode unhurriedly toward them. The conductor had obviously laid the groundwork ahead of time: he, the conductor, would enter first into the Light, and the Echoes would then follow. But if this had been the plan, it certainly didn't work out that way. Before

Bloom reached the group, one of the musicians—it was Simon, Cameron noted with dread—broke free of the circle, reached his hands out, and thrust his hands into the Light.

The Light bellowed like a foghorn blast.

Cameron shouted in anticipation, but he'd not been prepared for what happened next: the Lyre's strings thrummed all around him, and then he experienced a kind of atonal backwash as the wires transmitted an awful noise into his body. He could actually feel Simon's black and cancerous filth penetrate him like a physical corruption. He wished the earless man had rotted in jail, that he had brained him to death at Bloom's dining table that day.

Instead, visions now flitted across his mind's eye of maggots and rotting flesh. The smell of decay invaded his senses. *This was what they are on the inside*, thought Cameron as, in that terrible moment, the condition of the Echoes became known to him. Their sickness was absolute; they were beyond redemption.

And now corruption was spreading into Armonia like a virus.

"You're making it sick!" Cameron said hoarsely, clenching his teeth. His body was wracked with convulsions, and he shook on the wires.

Down below, all the musicians watched Simon with wild fascination stamped across their faces. Some of them had begun rolling up their sleeves, preparing to follow Simon's lead by thrusting their own hands into the Light. But then Bloom was there and shoving several of them out of his way.

"Remember what we discussed?" cried the conductor. "No one goes before me. Do you understand? No one!"

At that moment Christofori and Lutz grabbed Simon by his arms, hauled him back, and threw him down. Simon wailed as he gathered himself up, but Bloom appeared over him and placed a calming hand on the man's shoulder. Simon gave a pathetic moan and looked up into the conductor's eyes.

"Hush now, Simon," Bloom said in a surprisingly gentle tone that immediately placated the idiot. "No more tears. It is almost time."

When Simon fell quiet, Bloom straightened, squared his shoulders, and turned, then began a slow and stately march toward the shaft of Light, an emperor approaching his rightful throne.

Cameron went cold as the wasted form of Maestro Bloom rolled up his sleeves and proceeded toward the Light of God.

As if warming his palms against a fire, Bloom held his hands out toward Armonia, and while he felt his body change, he paid little attention to it. What captivated him was the silvery music that buzzed in his head and caused his teeth to rattle and his eyes to water.

"You abandoned me," Bloom said quietly, his hands moving closer to the Light. "You turned your back on this orchestra, and we have suffered for an impossible duration."

Gentle whispers touched his ears. *Leonin . . . it's not too late . . . don't hurt me . . . I love you . . . don't do this . . . don't do this . . .*

Bloom drew his lips back from his gnashed teeth. His eyes darkened while at the same time burned like embers. "I have hated You for so long," he whispered back. "Those people upstairs—I killed them as an homage to my anger. I did it to hurt You. Did You not think that I would find a way to avenge myself?" Then, more angrily, he said, "I want You to fix me. I want You to save me."

Leonin . . . please, don't do this . . . Leonin please . . .

Closing his eyes, ignoring the pleading voice that echoed in his mind, Bloom thrust his hands into the Light.

A powerful belch of sound exploded in Bloom's head. There was a moment when energy flooded his body, and it should have cracked him open, but he felt only elation. For the first time in eighty years, his soul resonated with the Overtone—the divine vibration that permeated all things—and hearing it now calmed his soul like the voice of a mother to the ears of a long-lost child.

Chapter 13

"Cameron?"

Cameron opened his eyes, finding himself knee-deep in a shallow pond surrounded by thick woods. He tilted his face toward the warm sun. Ahead, a roaring waterfall, several stories high. The light here seemed brighter. He knew this place. Madison's place. The Shawnee Falls State Park. *Now how did I get here?*

"There you are," said a playful voice.

He spun around to face Madison Taylor, standing with him in the water. She wore a white gown, clinging wetly to her body. "I found you."

"Was I lost?"

Moving close, she kissed his mouth, then withdrew. He went for more, but she stopped him. "Hold your horses. We need to talk."

His smile faltered as horrible images flitted across his mind's eye: flames belching from the windows of her shop, flashing red lights, Madison strapped to a gurney. *You died in a fire. This is a dream.* "Madison," he moaned. "I'm sorry."

She nodded. "It's okay. It's almost over."

"I messed up," he said, his voice strained. "I gave Bloom the Symphony, and now he's . . . I'm afraid of what he wants to do."

"Nothing happens by chance," she said simply. "You were chosen for this—to protect the most precious thing in the universe."

"But why me?" he said.

"Because that is what you also chose to do," she said. "It has always been you. You've known this your entire life. Now it's time to fulfill your promise."

The thought terrified him. He remembered making a promise. But it seemed so vague, like a forgotten melody. *Promise me, I promise you, I love you, I promise . . .* "I don't understand."

"You don't have to. You just have to stop them." Madison's expression turned grim. "If you don't, they will take away all the love from this world; diminish everything that is good, pure, and innocent."

"They're sick. They want to be healed."

She offered a sad smile. "They can't heal this way. They can't become Attuned any more than dark can become light."

Thunder rumbled in the distance. He shivered against a chill, folded his arms over his chest. "So what am I supposed to do about it?"

"You know the answer to that question, Cameron. You know what to do."

The roaring of the waterfall drew his attention. A sudden epiphany struck him. *It's just another disguise. It's here now, listening.* He took a step past Madison. She clutched his arm, but he gently shrugged her aside.

"Cameron?" she called after him. "What are you doing?"

He splashed across the pond. The stones were smooth under his feet. Moments later he stood a few yards from the falls. Billowing mist engulfed him.

"Why won't You stop playing games with me?" he shouted, tracing his gaze to the waterfall's zenith, where frothy waters plunged over a shelf of limestone. "I can't stop them. Don't You get it? I failed You!"

The sky darkened as thunderheads gathered. The pond turned icy cold. He wrapped his arms about himself, shivering. The waterfall darkened, becoming a blackish red that spread outwards across the pond's surface.

That's blood. The water's turned to blood. And I'm standing up to my knees in it.

~⋘

What right does he have? Deceiver. Murderer. And yet Simon is the first to touch the face of God. Reverend Kalek trembled in horror with his hands clamped over the dome of his head. He stood beyond the ring of musicians, an invisible floor underneath him. From here he'd witnessed the unveiling, the stripping away of matter. The trespass had begun; an unforgivable sin. And Simon had already touched the Light, tainting it with his filth.

I knew it would come to this, Kalek thought. *Bloom and his Echoes mean to force their way into the bosom of God, all the while knowing the consequences will be catastrophic.*

Something gleamed near his foot, a piece of glowing metal. A tuning fork. Crouching, he fetched the small instrument, felt its weight, then held it before him. The Tongue shone with its own inner effulgence. He was more than familiar with this instrument of Discord. By its dark resonations, he'd given himself numerous times to nightmare trances, the inspiration for blasphemous art.

But I was never the one, he knew now. *Bloom knew that from the start. I was never suited for Attuning.*

Pinched between thumb and finger, the Tongue vibrated in sympathy with the smooth purr of Armonia. This surprised Kalek. Never before had the Tongue rung with anything but Discord. *The Tongue—it's healed.*

Shouts echoed in the distance. He looked up to find Leonin Bloom standing with his arms buried elbow-deep in the Light of God.

Defiler. Blasphemer. Kalek bared his teeth, enraged. He straightened, clenching his jaw. He knew what he had to do; his purpose became clear.

He crossed into the ring of instruments undetected. No one paid him attention, not even as he shoved his way into the huddle of musicians. They gave him passage, one of their trusted officials, allowing him to move into position behind the maestro.

The fork resonated in Kalek's hand. He raised the instrument over his head and brought it down, ramming the stem's spike deep into the nape of the conductor's neck, snapping muscles and bone.

A howl of pain. A spray of blood. Then Bloom swung on him, eyes filled with demonic outrage.

Kalek staggered, hands covering his face, then fell to his knees, bracing himself on the transparent floor. He looked up just as Bloom pounced on him, clawing at his face. The reverend saw a flash of teeth, a snarl, and then there was only pain.

Cameron woke from a vision, from dreamy scenes of Madison and gardens, waterfalls and burbling streams, of perhaps one possible afterlife. Maybe it was just a release from watching Bloom defile everything righteous and good and pure.

He awoke from his weary, pain-induced stupor just in time to witness an attack. Two dark shadows were at each other, both dead and undead.

Bloom was standing over Kalek and pummeling the old man with his fists. Kalek threw his arms over his face to protect himself, but his meager attempts to ward off the blows failed, and Bloom fell over him and drove his thumbs into the man's eyes. Blood sprayed and pooled across the luminous floor, making a striking contrast of red on white. Kalek howled in pain until a final blow crushed his skull and he fell silent.

Once again, the Lyre's strings resonated with Discord, and Cameron became the recipient of all that black noise, erasing the pleasant visions of Madison. The tone was death as it invaded every cell of his body. He felt the corruption of the Echoes and the dissonance of murder; even more upsetting, he felt how all these things affected Armonia and made it sick. And Cameron shared its sickness. His body went cold, and his soul blackened. The Discord scoured his heart with a heartache deeper than any he'd ever experienced; the death of his family paled in comparison.

But it was this pain that brought on a sudden epiphany: not only had he served as the vehicle that transported the Echoes, but he was also the hub, the connecting point of this entire conjoining. He was holding this whole thing together.

Did that also mean he had the power to end it?

All he had to do was rip himself free; but the wires were deep, and he knew the result would be deadly.

"Please don't ask this of me," Cameron whispered, even when he knew there was no other way to end this, when he knew what was required of him. He moaned and fixed his eyes on the God Light, ignoring the silhouetted musicians circled about its girth; he wanted to clear his mind. And be still. And know. After all, the universe—God—needed him, and there was enormous comfort in that. All his life, he'd struggled to find his life's purpose, only to find it here at the end, and at a much greater capacity than he'd ever imagined.

Okay then, he thought. *All right.*

He gave a battle cry and began tearing himself free of the Lyre.

The pain was unbearable. He twisted left and then right, and the silver strings tore from his flesh with a muffled ripping sound. He felt the wires moving deep inside him; felt them shift and tear his organs. The assault to his body left little hope for survival. He kept his eyes fixed on the orchestra as the column of Light became a flash of violet; the atmosphere of milky luminescence convulsed.

A metallic squeal erupted like the sound of a colossal train wreck. The connection was broken. The light went out abruptly, leaving the musicians in the darkness of the Calliope's basement. The show was over.

Screams of agony rang out.

Cameron blinked until his eyes focused. It was not all dark; the overhead lamps cast a dull blue light on the basement, its slate gray walls, its high ceiling, and black floor strewn with musical instruments, abandoned chairs, and music stands still aligned in an untidy ring formation. And there at the center of the clearing were the Echoes, only now they were walking corpses; bent and brittle things in bedraggled suits and evening dresses. Rather than faces, they bore skull-like grins and lidless eyes.

The disruption of the Symphony had had a grim effect on the Echoes, draining the orchestra of whatever life forces it had stolen over the past ten years.

Bloom—or what was left of him, with his face withered away and his thick white hair reduced to a few mere tufts—stood at the center of his fallen musicians. He looked out over his dying orchestra, and then to Cameron, and roared, "What have you done?"

Cameron swooned and toppled forward. He would have fallen from the Lyre's frame had it not been for a handful of wires still attached to his sides, keeping him hanging halfway out of the machine, slouched and twisted like a marionette tangled up in its own strings. He felt the sting of hooks in his sides, felt his skin stretch like taffy. Desperate for relief, he grabbed an overhead handgrip and hefted himself up. Only then did he dare inspect himself. His sides were split from armpit to thigh, giving him a glimpse at his own ribs. His legs didn't look any better. Blood ran hot as piss from his opened wounds. He closed his eyes. *Oh, God,* he thought. *Help me.*

Again, Bloom's voice: "What have you done?"

Cameron had hoped only to disrupt the Echoes' connection with Armonia, but this . . . this was more than he'd bargained for. *I've hurt the bastards—really hurt them—so badly that even now they're collapsing in clouds of dust.* Those still alive were little more than skeletons.

I did it, he thought. *I stopped the fuckers.* It suddenly made sense. Nothing had happened by accident. From his hearing Armonia, to his involvement with the orchestra—these things had been preordained. Cameron had been chosen to bring the Echoes to Armonia because in the world of forms, the Echoes were immortal. But at the Harmonic Core, they'd been vulnerable.

Nothing happens by chance.

Cameron blinked his eyes open to find Bloom, still standing amidst a pile of his dying musicians, watching him with strained desperation.

"It wasn't supposed to be like this!" the maestro groaned in a grating voice. All around him his Echoes moaned in agony. The basement echoed with their anguished sobs and enraged shouts. "All that we worked for . . ." Bloom balled his fists and bellowed at the ceiling. "Ruined!"

Still hanging by a few strings, Cameron managed a rueful smile. He wanted to say something clever; it seemed a good moment for wit. But his thoughts were sluggish, and dark spots gathered in the peripherals of his vision. This time, when he lost his grip on his handhold, the last few wires holding him snapped free, and he dropped.

He hardly remembered the fall; the landing, however, was much more memorable. Pain exploded throughout his body. Bones snapped and several of his limbs seemed bent at wrong angles. He rolled and lay gasping on his back with the cool floor beneath him.

Following the clacking of footsteps, Bloom appeared over Cameron; the man's snarling face hovered too close for comfort. Bloom looked worse than old—he looked like a victim of overexposure, with lesions and massy tumors covering his forehead and jowls. His eyes were filled with blood, and yellow fluids oozed from his ears and nose.

"We were so close!" Bloom groaned in an inhuman voice. "Why didn't you let us finish it?"

Numb with shock, Cameron grinned despite the sound of his own blood spilling from his body. Oddly enough, he felt surprisingly relaxed for a man about to die. "You're wrong, Bloom," he said, and coughed. He swallowed and wished for water. "It wouldn't have worked. Besides, I think you guys are royally fucked, no matter what."

Teetering, Bloom dropped to his knees. In quiet despair, he looked at his gnarled, mummified hands, then held them out for Cameron to see his fingers, now brittle disjointed sticks. Somewhere behind him came screams of panic; the other Echoes were meeting a similar fate.

"This punishment—it isn't fair," the maestro said with a choke. Most of his face had turned to ash and he looked like a grinning skeleton. "And this . . . this was our only chance to Attune—to harmonize with God. To die!"

Cameron licked his lips. "I'm sorry."

"We'll come back," Bloom went on. "Surely you know this. Long after you are dead . . . we will Echo again . . . until we get what we want . . ."

The words had only just left Bloom's mouth when his jawbone broke free with a quiet snick. His forehead collapsed like a rotted rooftop. His chest caved in with the force of a sinkhole. His body imploded, and there was nothing left of him but a cloud of dust and a heap of clothes.

We'll Echo again . . .

Empty threats. Nothing more. Cameron didn't care. His part in all this was over.

He felt his spirit leaving his body. Suddenly, the ceiling lights receded, rearing back until they became brilliant blue stars, twinkling light years away, and he was lying on the beach with an arm folded behind his head while the waves smacked the surf.

"Maybe I'll come back too," he said to the night sky, only his voice was distant and hardly his at all. "Maybe we're all just echoes of something else."

He never saw Hob enter the basement, or felt the man's old hands cradle his damaged body, or heard the soft sobs and clumsy, anguished words the now-deaf man spoke.

And Cameron didn't hear the whoosh of gasoline-fueled fire that engulfed the instruments, or feel the ground slip beneath him as Hob dragged his dying body from the basement.

Cameron's dream-self got up from his sandy respite and trotted up a small hill, shaggy with sea grass and riddled with angled slats from an old picket fence. A stone path led him to his back porch where the wind chimes hung from the rafters and clicked and clattered as its bone fragments and scraps of metal and sea shell made their strange music. The words of the gaunt-faced peddler echoed in his ears: *Don't ya see ya'self in them strings? These are your bones, my friend. Your bones.*

A distant ringing in his ears became a chorus of angels, and the music was so peaceful that it swelled inside him, and this time, when he went to it, the song absorbed him, and he became a part of it.

Epilogue

It was August of the following year, and the afternoon sun kept an angry thumb on Washington Hob as he walked along an Arkansas road wearing a faded pair of blue jeans and a gray t-shirt. He also carried a guitar, sheathed in a gig bag, strapped over his back like a deer rifle, which made the hike even tougher. His muscles ached and his boots rubbed blisters into his feet. It had been a long walk from Piney Point, some ten miles away; not bad for a man his age. But if he didn't get a ride soon, he'd have to sleep underneath a tree somewhere off the main road, and his old body just couldn't take that kind of abuse.

The events of Piney Point still resonated with him. What had happened at that little bar had been beyond his understanding. He'd played them one of his songs and something special had happened, just as it always did; only this time, his performance had taken the audience even further. Maybe his music was getting . . . more potent. Or maybe he was getting better. Why not? After nearly a year on the road and performing at every backwater dive he could find, his talent was bound to improve. Who knew how far he could take this thing?

He was still exploring this train of thought when a gray Ford truck came bouncing over the hill. Just before it passed, Hob stuck out his thumb. The truck traveled another thirty yards before drifting to a stop on the side of the road. Hob's ticker did a double thump as he trotted over to the driver's side, where an old black man with silver hair eyed him suspiciously from his opened window. When the man started to speak, Hob cut him off with a friendly wave of his hand and then handed him a crumpled note.

My name is Washington Hob, the note read. *I am deaf but I can read lips a little. I'm heading to Memphis and I would appreciate a ride from you. Can you help me get there?*

After reading the note, the driver glanced at the guitar strapped to Hob's back, obviously wondering why the heck a deaf guy needed one of those, and then shrugged.

"I'm heading that way m'self," the driver said and handed back the note.

Hob watched the man's lips, understanding them.

The man hooked a thumb toward the back of the truck. "Hop on in back."

Grinning, Hob shook hands with the driver and then climbed into the back of the truck, careful not to bang his guitar against the side of the bed. Once settled with his back against the cab, he rapped his knuckles against the back window to signal that he was ready. The truck jerked and rocked its way back onto the road, and soon Hob felt the rush of warm air as low hills and open farmlands went speeding away from either side of him. Leaning his head back, a grin settled on his face, and he closed his eyes. Despite the inevitable backache, he liked traveling out in the open like this. There was a certain freedom about it, like riding bareback on the currents of time itself. As the wheels hummed beneath him, he drifted some and let his mind wander.

His thoughts turned naturally to the horrors of the Holloway massacre. Not a day passed without his thinking about it. Of course, the television, radio, and papers never let him forget. In the aftermath of the massacre, the media had gone overboard. For the next three months, Hob couldn't turn on the television without seeing the Calliope with its plaza jammed full of emergency vehicles and flashing lights, or the EMTs carting out bodies on gurneys, or the victims lying in the grass, most of them wearing bandages like bloodied headbands. These would become iconic images, sewn forever into the weave of America's history.

Without a doubt, that night had been the longest night of Hob's life. After dragging Cameron's body to the service elevator, where he'd tried and failed to resuscitate him, the police had found Hob trying to escape the blazing halls of the Calliope. He'd been taken out in handcuffs and given a personal escort to Willow Wood Medical. Once the doctors diagnosed his ears as ruined for good, the cops drove him back to Nashville for questioning. It'd been nearly four in the morning before a reliable witness—a woman whom he'd carried from the Calliope's foyer earlier, he later found out—had come to his defense by telling everyone that he was a hero rather than a terrorist. By the time the police let him go, they'd been all apologetic smiles and handshakes; two detectives even treated Hob to breakfast before driving him back to Holloway.

They never pinned him for starting the fire in the Calliope's basement.

Burn it down, Sugar. Burn the whole thing down.

And he'd done just that.

By the following morning, all the major networks had broken the story, and by noon, Holloway was on every channel. The world was shocked by the news as the death toll exceeded three hundred, with nearly that same number seriously injured. Such a staggering act of violence was beyond comprehension. Americans wanted someone to pay for it, and that someone was the Holloway Orchestra.

But in the end there was no one left to hang. It became public knowledge that, following their brutal concert, the musicians of Bloom's orchestra had retired to the Calliope's basement, where they doused themselves with gasoline to finish their night of terror with a mass suicide. By the time the police had discovered the basement, it was burning like an oven, and the only thing salvaged from the aftermath was bone and charred musical instruments.

Obviously, investigators wanted to know more about the orchestra. Who were they and where had they come from? This was not an easy question to answer. After scouring the estate known as Orpheum Manor, federal agents had nothing to go by, not a single driver's license or even a green card. It seemed Bloom and his troupe of musicians had just appeared from thin air, which of course, made them all the more mysterious. Adding fuel to that fire was the literature discovered in Bloom's library: more than a thousand books with themes of music-based mysticism. Soon after this discovery, speculations began to circulate, leading the media to portray the Holloway Orchestra as a secret cult led by its charismatic conductor, Maestro Leonin

Bloom. This led to the grim conclusion that the Holloway Massacre was, in essence, a bizarre, ritualistic mass killing.

When the survivors' stories began to surface, recounting nightmare music, mass hallucinations, and strange creatures—some of them humanoid, some of them snakelike—the story moved into the realm of the fantastic. The fact that so many came forward with similar sightings lent credibility to the whole affair; fact or fantasy, hundreds of witnesses had seen the same thing. Even stranger were the autopsy reports, citing the main cause of death as brain hemorrhages and grand mal seizures. No one knew what to make of the abnormal bites on many of the victims.

In the following weeks, the events of Holloway were linked to a separate massacre near Vienna nearly twenty years earlier. A museum destroyed and looted; its board members murdered. Until now, Vienna authorities had assumed those deaths had been purely accidental. But when authorities traced the origins of several musical artifacts found at Bloom's estate to the museum, the mystery was finally solved. Clearly, Maestro Bloom had destroyed the museum, murdered its board members, and stolen its artifacts in order to sell to private investors. Sure enough, once investigators began tracing the threads of Bloom's fortune, they discovered more than one hundred million dollars linked to the selling of precious artifacts on the black market.

Still, many questions went unanswered. For starters, no one could explain how the orchestra had pulled off their mass murder. No weapons had been found at the scene of the crime; there was nothing to explain what had happened inside the auditorium or outside in the plaza. Then there was the matter of Cameron Blake, the famous composer, whose mangled body had been discovered in the Calliope's service elevator, apparently dragged there by someone. What had Blake been doing there, and how had he died? Moreover, had the famous composer served as an accomplice to the massacre, or had he died trying to stop it? Unfortunately, anyone who could answer that question had died in the fire.

Hob's eyes blinked open. Something burned hot against his leg. He sat up, finding the world racing past him. He'd dozed off in the back of the stranger's truck. He had no idea how long he'd been on this ride, and with only thick woods and a few farm houses on either side of the highway, he couldn't locate himself. Were they out of Arkansas yet? Unlikely.

The warmth against his thigh became a sting. Sitting up, he dug the tuning fork from his pocket, then drew his knees close to his chest while holding the instrument cupped in both hands. No doubt, this tuning fork with snakes coiled around its prongs was a strange piece of work. It was made of gold and probably worth a fortune too. The fork hummed softly in his hands, and its vibrations traveled along his arms and into his chest. How many times had the fork called to him like this? Fifty? A hundred, maybe?

Hob glanced furtively over his shoulder and into the truck's back window to find the old driver scrunched over the steering wheel, daydreaming as he cruised along the straight stretch of road. The guy wasn't paying Hob any attention, and it was unlikely that he'd hear the fork if Hob gave it a little tap on the side of the truck.

Satisfied, Hob settled back against the cab wall and tapped the fork against the side of the truck bed to his right. The fork's immediate ringing filled his head, like magic to his crippled ears. The invasive silvery tones warped his mind like a drug, causing the open countryside to somehow expand all around him, while the colors grew brighter, the treetops became glowing green embers, and the sun became an open fire that sizzled overhead. Even when he closed his eyes, a lightshow of bursting colors played itself out behind his closed eyelids.

But it was the silvery tone that swallowed him up. The sound resonated in his bones, and his spirits soared. Never had he felt so incredibly free. So harmonic. In that moment, he believed in the soul—he knew he had one—because he could feel it, and it resonated with the universe all around him. He was connected to it all.

The inspiration came like a physical force. By this same internal fire, he'd written a hundred songs at least, but not this time. For now, he felt satisfied enough to just keep all that inspiration inside, to let it simmer for a while, rather than setting it free by scribbling out a few notes.

Hob closed his eyes and grinned. The instrument made him almost giddy. Thank God he'd found the thing down in the Calliope's basement; thank God he hadn't thrown it into the fire. He'd spent many nights contemplating the tuning fork, and he'd arrived at several conclusions. First, the fork had come from the same collection of instruments that he'd set fire to in the Calliope's basement. Second, the fork had been changed by that underground Symphony. Whatever the orchestra had played that night continued to resonate with this fork.

And there was one last thing, wasn't there? Somehow, for whatever reason, he—Washington Hob—had been meant to find the fork. The fork had transformed him into an artist . . . and, miraculously, a deaf one, at that. The fork gave him inspiration to write music that transcended any genre. And through his music, he would change the world. One day at a time. Just like Clara had wanted to do all along.

Later that night in a small barroom just outside Memphis, Hob took to the stage and sat down on a wooden stool. Warm lights shone down on him as he situated his guitar in his lap, while maybe thirty indifferent faces watched him from their tables, and Hob watched them back. He let the silence of anticipation resonate for a moment, but someone soon interrupted with a shout, and then a few people laughed, but of course, it was all just silence to him. Oddly enough, he didn't miss his hearing much these days. He'd spent plenty of his life bogged down by noise. Being deaf to all that garbage did have its advantages, he supposed.

He took one last look at the bar, at the people down there, and felt their Discord.

Clearly, for whatever reasons, they suffered, and when he looked at their hollow faces, he felt sorry for them. Most of them were lonely, or confused, or disconnected from each other. Sometimes he wondered if all of mankind lived in perpetual Discord with the world, with each other, and with God.

Here in this seedy bar the Discord seemed particularly bad. He sensed their unhappiness as clearly as a bad smell in the air. And that made his being here all the better.

I'm doin' the Good Work, thought Hob as he curled his fingers around the neck of his guitar. *That's why I'm doin' this. That's what Clara would have wanted . . . to touch the world. To make a difference. To heal it.*

And he could. His music could. He'd already seen it work countless times.

Closing his eyes, Hob strummed the strings of his guitar, and he could hear the notes clearly in his head, as if his ears worked just fine. He moved into his healing song—a song he'd written under the influence of his tuning fork—and felt his heart yearn with the melody, and he felt the goodness as if it were a living presence. The goodness wanted to come here; it wanted to heal these people.

As always during his little shows, the barroom became active, for lack of a better word.

First, the overhead lights glowed brighter and brighter, like stars going supernova. Then came the warm rush of air that flapped at the women's dresses. At this point his audience noticed the activity, just as they always did. Some of them hopped out of their chairs, and some of them turned in circles, looking for pranksters hiding in shadows. By the time the room lost gravity and empty chairs and tables started floating in the air, and the ghostly whispers rose as loud as the music itself, some of his audience had scattered. They always did.

But many stayed.

In fact, those who stayed ended up moving closer to the stage, watching with dazed expressions, while their arms dangled at their sides, their mouths hung open, and their eyes streamed with tears. They looked enchanted, as if reclaiming something lost and yet profoundly important.

All the while, Hob went on playing his easy song, recognizing the way their tears caught the light, and he had to grin. *That's all right, come closer,* he thought. *Don't be afraid now. You jus' listen and let the music heal you. That's why I came here. I came to remind you. This music—it's been playin' in the background all along. And you been ignorin' it, ain'tcha? You forgot how to hear it.*

But not tonight. Tonight you hear it just fine. Just like you heard it a long time ago. Welcome back . . . welcome back to the Light.